THIS
IMPOSSIBLE
BRIGHTNESS

THIS IMPOSSIBLE BRIGHTNESS

A NOVEL

JESSICA BRYANT KLAGMANN

Published by Lake Union Publishing, Seattle

www.apub.com

Amazon, the Amazon logo, and Lake Union Publishing are trademarks of Amazon.com, Inc., or its affiliates.

ISBN-13: 9781662513121 (hardcover)
ISBN-13: 9781662513114 (paperback)
ISBN-13: 9781662513138 (digital)

Cover design by Faceout Studio, Molly von Borstel
Cover image: © GeorgePeters / Getty; © Nerthuz, © greoli, © Varunyuuu, © Paladin12 / Shutterstock

Design elements used throughout: © Simple Line, © LivDeco, © Modern Visual Agency / Shutterstock

Printed in the United States of America
First edition

To Jamison, for the coldest days

There's always something left, said the bear, his voice sounding like the roll of distant thunder long after a storm, though deeper somehow, as though with that distance there came a present sadness equal to her own.
—Andrew Krivak, *The Bear*

Prologue

1940

Esmée Taylor was making a sandwich when the teakettle told her the ship was going down. Moments later, she was tying her boots, and it was still talking to her from the stove top, broadcasting a distress call that no one else from town would hear. They were all dancing anyway.

She pulled on her father's wool coat, the metallic voice beginning to fade as she ran out the door. Her dog, Atlas, bounded full force behind her.

From the porch, Esmée could hear the music from the dance, and she paused just long enough to calculate. She balanced how much time she would lose running to get more help against the reality of doing all the work herself, and then she turned away from town and ran.

The wind whipped her hair across her face as she unhitched the boat and began rowing northeast into rough waves, toward the location the voice in the broadcast had cited. The ocean fought against her, but the rain hadn't started yet. Esmée was sixteen years old, an aspiring engineer. She'd been sailing all her life. Atlas was a 150-pound Newfoundland, sitting at the bow, square nose pointed into the wind with determination.

The sinking ship had been heading from France to Canada with eighty-nine World War II evacuees. It was already partially underwater as she approached, many of the passengers attempting to slide down ropes to lifeboats. There certainly wasn't enough room for all of them.

Esmée ferried the passengers, ten at a time, twelve when there were smaller children clinging to their mothers. She made seven trips back and forth, her shoulder muscles cramping as she continued to row with a ferocity she'd never felt before.

One of the children fell overboard when a wave collided sideways with the skiff. Atlas dove in, and the child rode on his back as he swam to shore. The rain began, and Esmée kept rowing, the passengers huddled and frozen together with terrified eyes.

Eventually, her little brother came running to the dock, and Esmée sent him scrambling right back up the hill to get help. Her throat was raw from yelling over the wind, so all she was able to say was, "Bring blankets!" By the time others from town arrived, Esmée was on her last trip back from the ship.

An older man, blinking at her through the rain, said there'd been a fire on board, and sure enough, when Esmée finally looked back, she saw the last of the flames doused by a tall wave.

The shipwreck came a few months after the radio tower had been installed at the top of the mountain. By then, many people had experienced the unexplained broadcasts. They came from various rooms in the house, from appliances, and sometimes even directly through the walls.

Her mother's favorite living room lamp gave Esmée updates about the war in French every evening at six. In the mornings, she heard her favorite songs coming through the toaster. "Parlez-moi d'amour" and "Rendez-vous sous la pluie" and "I'm Nobody's Baby." She would never admit it, but sometimes she was afraid to go into the basement because the voices traveled up the stairs in muffled, transitory fragments.

She never felt alone in the house.

When everyone was safely on land, Esmée watched as the rescued families were escorted down the path toward town, toward the drifting music and soft lights of the dance hall. Some of the men began gathering the belongings that had already washed up on shore. Perhaps some of them could be salvaged.

But Esmée and Atlas returned to the cottage. She pulled off her boots and wet clothes and relit the fire in the woodstove to dry them. She retrieved the half-made sandwich from the kitchen—cranberry jam slathered onto two thick pieces of molasses bread. Her body, too tired for anything else, collapsed into the rocking chair by the window, while the sounds of the rescued passengers being welcomed into the dance hall floated with the breeze through the curtains.

Atlas curled into a large ball in front of the fire. Esmée closed her eyes as the lamp began to flicker, and a stern, steady voice came through, broadcasting its nightly messages: the clashing of ships, the invasions of foreign countries. All the dark, unfathomable distance between one human and the next—and the possibilities that existed in that space.

PART 1
THE WAVES

2026

1

Alma used to keep the two-way radio with her at all times because she thought he might still be alive out there. Even though it was ridiculous. Even though it was impossible that he'd be able to reach her with it if he had somehow survived. The truth was, that sort of hope didn't last long, and she'd stopped expecting his voice to crackle through on the other end, calling out to her. She knew Alex was gone. Alma still kept the batteries charged and the power on—often catching fragments of a stranger's shaky transmission—but the radio was there, tucked snugly into the pocket of her jeans, simply out of habit now.

An hour before, she had watched the state of Maine disappear from the back of the ferry, her dog, Jupiter, by her side. The buildings shrank downward like they were being pulled into the sea, then disappeared. The populated world was enveloped by thick fog, and seagulls became the only signs of life for a while.

They'd told her when she bought the ferry ticket that there might be storms. Not those little squalls you sometimes saw. No, these were unpredictable and raging, and they couldn't make any guarantees that she would reach her destination. Alma wondered if, previously, they had ever made such assurances.

The North Atlantic coast was being swallowed. It was 2026, and though this consuming of the coastline had been happening for years, more recently they'd been talking about it not as a preventable situation but as an irreversible certainty. The sea level had risen above the projected average, houses sliding into the water, ocean-view decks crumbling, roofs collapsing into siding and then into sand. The communities that lived on islands and along the eastern coast of Atlantic Canada had first tried to bolster themselves against this inevitable fate. They'd built levees and seawalls. They'd constructed barriers. They'd tried to alter the landscape in ways that would improve its chances of helping itself, turning parts of the coastline into a living habitat. When these measures didn't do enough, those who could move inland did so. Some resisted at first, but eventually, little by little, whole towns had been forced to leave.

Even farther northeast than these newly abandoned places, Violette—the quiet island town toward which Alma was headed—had been spared so far. Its elevation, and its position nestled into the side of a mountain on the eastern coast of Île des Rêves, had granted it the gift of time.

Stupid and *stubborn* and *irresponsible* were some of the terms used to describe the residents who chose to stay. But those residents, they called it determined. They called it love. Alma's aunt and two cousins lived there, along with 271 others who refused to abandon their homes despite the grim future they knew would come eventually. The only thing crazier than *staying* in a place like that was to *move* there, and most of Alma's family and friends had told her she was just that.

Besides Violette, the only other inhabited town on Île des Rêves was on the western side of the island. They called it The City, and it was considered a city only because it was at least three times bigger than Violette and still had a department store. Alma's ferry from New England would dock there, and she would take "the bus to Nowhere Field." The bus traveled once a month along the southern coast—the road winding through marshes that were frequently underwater—and stopped at what had once been a baseball field. People still rode the bus, mainly as a tourist attraction: to photograph the sinking world on the way there, get out to stretch their legs at the field, and then board again for the return trip. There was no point actually going any farther. To get to Violette, Alma needed to take another boat, but there were no longer any public ferries or charters that sailed past Nowhere Field.

She'd begged for and secured her only option: her cousin Theo, who had agreed to take his own boat from Violette to meet her and bring her to the almost-farthest-east edge of the island, where Violette was tucked into the mountain like a folded piece of paper on which she would begin writing a new life.

When she'd spoken to Theo on the phone a month before, discussing her plans, he'd offered a warning. *There's nothing here anymore,* he'd told her through the static. Boring was an understatement. The phone reception was iffy. The electricity was inconsistent. Once every couple of months, he took the boat to The City for supplies because when they'd decided to stay put, they'd decided to take care of themselves. That was the deal.

You're not going bowling here, you know that, right? You're not going to get a pint of Ben and Jerry's anytime you feel like it.

Can I get a beer if I feel like it?

Well, yeah. You can always get a beer. But otherwise, there's nothing.

He'd meant all of this to caution her, maybe even to change her mind, but they hadn't seen each other in so long. Alma thought he must have forgotten who she was. *Nothing* was exactly what she was looking for, and she had no intention of ever going back.

～～

Over the course of the previous year, Alma's distancing had been measured. She'd inched closer toward the New England coast, a bit more toward solitude, again farther east, a nudge in the direction of hiding, until she'd found a place where she might be able to root down again. And this new place, she knew, would have to work, because after it, there was nothing left. There was nowhere else to go.

Everyone—Alma's mother, her extended family, the people she worked with—they all assumed she was running away from grief. It seemed like a natural response to losing someone that you love—avoidance, denial, running. The running part was accurate enough, but the truth that was impossible to explain was that she was running *toward* her grief and away from everyone else.

And she might have been able to stay a little longer, if Jupiter, too, weren't dying. The constant questions made her terrified daily, and the voices caused too much interference with the two things she needed most in life: Alex's memory and Jupiter's last days.

It didn't matter that her heart had been streaked with every shade of heartache. Memories of Alex that stood up happy, then very quickly tripped over themselves in sadness and then stumbled into a pool of anger. It didn't matter because as painful as it was, it had a name and it was real and it was her own. It was a hard thing to do at times, striding headlong into memories that caused her heart to implode. But it was far easier than letting go.

Jupiter had been sick for a couple of months, though Alma had yet to tell anyone about it, knowing that as soon as she spoke the words out loud, it would all become real. He'd slowed down quickly, and at first, Alma had thought he was just showing signs of age, perhaps a touch of arthritis. No one actually knew how old he was. Then they'd found the cancer in his blood.

It seemed cruel for him to be leaving her now, so quickly. He was as good at cuddling as he was at navigating. More than two feet tall and 120 pounds. He had been able, at one time, to follow the scent and trail of an animal over long distances, across many types of terrain. Back in Maine, he'd alerted Alma twice to a moose nearby, and he'd once tracked down a woman's missing cat five miles from home. It was thought by the veterinarian that before Alma had found him—or, rather, before they found each other—he'd been a search and rescue dog, because that was one of the many talents a Swiss mountain dog possessed. That, and therapy, the combination of the two making him exactly the kind of best friend she needed at exactly the right time. It had been a year since she'd lost Alex, and Jupiter had been there for all of that, but now he, too, was going to leave her, and that was too many losses to suffer in the company of others.

The vet told her that Jupiter would, at some point soon, stop wanting to move. It would probably happen suddenly. He told her—the vet's brow furrowed as he clicked a pen with his thumb—that if she opted to do *that thing*, no one would consider it cruel.

Alma had chosen not to do *that thing* that she hardly had words to describe. To be in a room with other people when Jupiter slipped away from her was something outside her capabilities. What might have been the best thing for the dog, Alma simply couldn't do. And she would not have corrected anyone who suggested this was selfish.

She had boarded the ferry with everything she needed in the world. The luggage was in a small room below the deck. She'd asked her brother to sell the car she left behind. She didn't want the money and told him to keep whatever he could get for it. He winked and said he'd hold on to the cash, save it for her so she could buy herself a return trip when she came to her senses, and she'd only smiled as she hugged him because she knew what an impossibility that was.

She had quit her job as a writer for *Movement*, a magazine devoted to stories about people and places making a difference. They'd offered to let her stay on tentatively, assuming she could keep up with articles from a distance, but she knew that, too, was impossible.

~~~

Again and again, Alma was reminded of the noise, the static, and this moment—standing on the ferry with Jupiter, traveling toward her remote destination—was no exception.

Despite her attempts at solitude, she was aware of a stranger's presence before she saw him because an unexplained agitation rose in her. The waves below turned red-orange and seemed to flood up, swiftly sending a pulse of anger through her. Her chest burned with it. She wanted to scream but stopped herself, fists gripping the cold railing, because she knew this fury was not her own but the stranger's.

She took deep breaths and forced her mind to override this one emotion. Then she rationalized. There was no reason for her to be angry. Alma had anticipated feeling a number of emotions on this boat—sadness, loneliness, trepidation, outright fear—but this was not one of them.

Scanning up and down the deck, Alma saw no one, yet trusted she was right. Then, behind her, he was there. The man stood under the half roof of the deck, stabbing at a cell phone with his index finger. He held the phone aloft, risking it in the rain and then pulling it back under the roof, searching for a signal Alma knew would not be found. He was obviously upset about more than just bad reception. He was mad about something that, she guessed, a successful phone call might help solve.

Alma released her grip on the railing but held tightly to Jupiter's leash. His enormous brown-black body slouched closer to her thigh. They moved to the other side of the boat, leaving the frustrated man to fight with a technology that existed less and less the farther the ferry got from New England.

Jupiter watched brown-and-white gannets circle for fish over the water, his head following their broad strokes through the sky. Behind the mist, Alma could make out the shoreline passing, green hills and rocky beaches, occasional lighthouses, but fewer and fewer homes. And then all open water as far as she could see.

The ocean was rough, smacking against the boat. Two meters high was what she'd heard one of the ferry crew members say. There were a dozen other travelers—far fewer than there would have been in years past—and none of them were willing to be outside, exposed to the rain. None of them, despite going by choice toward a part of the world that was sinking, wanted to experience the reality of that world as it passed by. But being alone was, Alma knew, the only way she could manage a trip like this, and so she was more than happy to let the other passengers gather in the dining room and the little movie theater on board, or play slots in the one-room casino. She was more than happy to be cold and wet and windswept, so long as there was quiet and space.

It was a good place to be sad, and sadness was what she'd expected. She settled in, let it roll into her like ocean waves into an empty shell, soaking her heart in salt water that burned and soothed all at once.

~~~

When the narrow heads of fin whales broke the surface of the water— such a rare thing to see—Alma caught herself on tiptoes, leaning forward over the railing almost too much, as if reaching. As if their sleek bodies might take her faster to where she wanted to go. For the first time since she'd left home—maybe even for the first time since Alex had died—she allowed herself to fully anticipate what was coming next. One brief, bright moment.

Then she planted her heels firmly once again on the deck, lingering until the whales became smaller and smaller, disappearing beneath the waves. And she retreated, finally, to the lounge below only when the sky turned stone gray and a fog settled over the water and the dampness seeped into her bones.

Jupiter squeezed next to her on the narrow couch, and Alma closed her eyes, thinking about what it might look like in Violette. Not the landscape or the sky—these were outside her control—but her life there. She imagined days going by when she didn't see another human being. Days she would spend occupied with the things Alex had left behind—a carefully packed box that amounted to half of what she'd brought with her. Nights when she could meet him again in dreams. Those dreams were painful to wake up from, but she always wanted them to return because when they were happening, there was no one there to tell her that it wasn't real.

~~~

If there were any storms, she slept through them. Alma woke as the ferry was entering The City's harbor. Through a round window, she could see the sky had cleared and the setting sun lit orange sparks on the rows of white boats tied up along the docks. She zipped a heavy vest over the hoodie she was wearing and tucked her auburn hair under a wool hat before climbing up to the windy deck. The cold stung the corners of her eyes.

The small group of other passengers deboarded and dispersed down darkening streets. Only a few lingered for the bus. The two-hour ride was quiet—the three other travelers sitting up front. Alma leaned her head against a back window and closed her eyes, Jupiter's head resting in her lap, hints of intermittent streetlights blinking ever so slightly through her eyelids. When she was younger, she sometimes took a bus to Boston for the day, then rode it home again in the dark. Driving the highway at night, they'd pass streetlights every two or three seconds, the flashes coming in bursts. Here, there were whole minutes between them.

The old baseball field was overgrown with long weeds, but the worn paths between bases were still visible. Around the perimeter, the dark shapes of trees gave the impression that there was nothing beyond them, and Alma thought, at least here, it may be true. Two of the passengers climbed the bleachers, the hollow sound of the metal ringing in the open space. They opened beers and a can of peanuts, then leaned back, putting their feet up on the seats in front of them. The third, the angry man with the cell phone, marched across the pitcher's mound and through center field beneath the dim stadium lights. His shape faded, lost in the forest.

Theo was waiting next to the boarded-up concession stand, wearing a brown canvas jacket and rubber boots, holding a sign that said *Hughes*. Alma grabbed his joking sign and reached up to hug him with one arm. His muscular arms enveloped her small frame, reminding her of his father, her uncle Hubert, whom she and her brother used to call Hu-Bear in secret because of the French pronunciation of his name.

"Welcome to Nowhere," Theo said.

"Or Everywhere," Alma said, immediately feeling silly.

They left the field and walked to the docks, and she helped him load supplies—cases of fruit and every type of battery and the beer Alma had been promised—onto his boat in the dark. They slept bobbing in the harbor, backs pressed against opposite sides of the cabin, and in the morning, Theo used his sleeve to wipe condensation from the windows, and they sailed for Violette.

Alma watched the coastline pass, noting concrete barriers that had been half pulled into the sea, and she began the work of constructing her own wall—the one that would keep her old life in the past where it belonged. Soon, she would build something new, something more authentic, on the other side.

An hour later, Alma opened the cabin door to a view of the Violette lighthouse. Painted white except for the black railing encircling the gallery deck and the roof of its octagonal lantern room, the tower stood close to forty feet tall, one narrow rectangular window two-thirds of the way up. Huddled in the shadow of the stone tower was the modest keeper's house, painted a matching stark white with a black roof. No one lived there or kept the light running anymore—especially since there were so few boats coming and going. Wiry evergreen bushes and wild roses grew close to the buildings, but otherwise the point was made up of a wide expanse of bulging granite. Leading away from the two lonely buildings, a narrow dirt path carved back toward town.

At one time, Theo told her, the lighthouse had given way to fifty yards of dense, low-growing juniper and crowberry before dropping off into the ocean below, but the cliff wall had been gouged away by the higher waves and eroded by the increased rain, its edge creeping back. It was only a matter of time before the lighthouse, and eventually the keeper's house, too, succumbed to the sea. It probably wouldn't happen for many years, but it *would* happen.

Passing the lighthouse, they rounded a bend and traveled into the inlet, curved like the arc of a great crescent moon. Violette was nestled in there, above the cliffs and below the rocky face of Onde Mountain, which rose up behind.

Alma's eyes followed the pointed tops of spruce trees to the rocky summit. At the top of the mountain, the thin frame of the abandoned radio tower extended toward the sky, though most of it was lost, wrapped in clouds.

A river skirted the mountain, flowing through town between the buildings, then beneath a stone bridge, until it finally became a thin waterfall that spilled over the cliffs. There, the river water mixed with the salty ocean waves that washed out and back in again, lapping against algae-slick rocks. There was a beach on the eastern side of the waterfall, reached by a set of wooden stairs wedged into the bluffs.

The roads that had once run in and out of Violette still existed but were no longer passable. This was a more recent development, the result of the last few years of rain and flooding, washing out the roads and leaving vehicles stranded in driveways and along ruptured sidewalks. Tourism had ceased, and so the only inn—which conveniently sat at the highest elevation—had been repurposed as a storm shelter.

Theo pointed to the uncomplicated row of buildings. Violette's main street, each structure painted a different color, looked like bold patchwork. He identified them quickly, by name and then color. A veterinarian's office (canary yellow), a bakery (olive green), a tattoo parlor (periwinkle blue), a sewing-supply shop (ballet slipper pink), a pub (apricot orange), a closed newspaper office (cinnamon brown), and a bookstore (ladybug red). "On the door of the bookstore," he said, "there's a wooden sign that says 'Fais de Beaux Rêves.' When you're standing there, looking for your next book, all you can hear is that damn sign battering against the door because of the winds blowing in off the ocean."

Alma felt that wrench of wanting to belong, of almost belonging, of being kept at a distance by a simple gap in language. Theo pretended not to notice her pleading look for a moment, then said, "It just means 'sweet dreams.'"

~~~

Seeing the seawalls that had been built along the shore and the rows of rock and timber barriers, Alma remembered being thirteen years old, watching the news reports of the sea level rise that could no longer be stopped, no matter what anyone did. No matter how many people changed their ways with reusable bags or bicycles or solar panels.

She'd been lying on the couch under a heavy crocheted blanket, playing sick to avoid going to a friend's sleepover. Her mother knew it was an act but still made a show of getting Alma settled comfortably on the couch, bringing her soup and crackers and ginger ale, and dimming the lights in the room.

Alma sat up when she saw the story come on. By then, she'd been writing postcards and letters to Alex for three years, upholding whatever their long-distance friendship was at that point, usually making more of it than she figured she should, and so the map that showed Nova Scotia—where he lived—slowly sinking pulled her upward by the chest. The man on the television was wearing rubber boots and a yellow rain-coat, gripping an umbrella. He motioned behind him at the gusts of wind whipping across the parking lot of a Bulk Barn. Rain swept side-ways, and a shopping cart went careening across the puddled pavement.

Along the eastern coast of Canada, floodwalls were being built to keep back the water. They'd already attempted plant stabilization measures—introducing more aquatic vegetation to minimize wave energy and respond naturally to the rising seas. When they projected that wouldn't be enough, tide barriers were begun, though work on these was abandoned. The effort was too great, and the likelihood of success too slim.

The man on the television talked about storms that surged more frequently and less predictably, water rushing up into the businesses and houses closest to the water. Waves crashed violently into buildings, sometimes even on a perfectly sunny day. The harsh rains brought more flooding from the other side, the runoff causing the beaches and dunes to erode, the sand pulled out to sea.

It's too late! the man had shouted over the wind, trying to control his unruly umbrella. *We can't take it back, you know. There's just nothing we can do anymore.*

One day it would be Boston and New York City. For the time being, the towns east of Halifax were expected to have to relocate sooner rather than later. Alma pictured that distant, slipping world—she could barely wrap her mind around it.

There's geology at work here, the man went on. He spoke about the middle of Canada, how it was previously sunken and locked down by ice under the earth's surface. But as that frozen center started melting, it rose up, pushing the coastline down instead—in essence, sinking it.

Alma thought of the space between her and Alex, rising and expanding, becoming an impossible, unscalable mountain. It felt like science fiction, but she knew which side she wanted to be on when that happened.

She was drawn to the unpredictability. To the chaos she saw in the man's flapping umbrella. To the strange excitement of both being scared for the people she loved, and also wishing she could disappear into that fierce storm, Alex's hand in hers.

It wasn't logical. It followed no science.

Love rarely does.

~~~

Alma pointed at the concrete breakwater jutting out, perpendicular to the shore, and asked Theo, "So, does all of that work?"

"Most of the time," he said. "We built it all ourselves, and it's hard to keep up with it. Once or twice every year we have a bad enough storm that we think we're done for."

"And how long has it been since the last one?"

He scrunched his forehead and shrugged. "Nine months, maybe. Do you know how to make a siphon in a pinch?" Alma thought she saw him wink, but perhaps it was the sun glinting off the water.

"Yeah, sure," she said. Tucked in a purposefully packed bag was the wilderness survival book Alex had given her. There had to be a section in there about it. Alma crouched and wrapped one arm around Jupiter. She squinted at a tiny yellow kayak skimming past the beach. "Well, we're here now, aren't we?"

As they docked the boat, Alma noticed a statue positioned near the waterfall, overlooking the cliffs. She blinked and leaned forward over the railing to see better. It was a girl and a dog frozen in the act of forward movement. They looked bright and alive despite their being chiseled from granite.

"What's with the statue?" she asked, trying to sound casually curious.

"Oh, that," Theo began, pausing with an armful of paper bags, "is one of our best stories. So in 1940, a French ship wrecked just off the coast. A sixteen-year-old girl, Esmée Taylor, and her giant Newfoundland, Atlas, transported the passengers in a twelve-foot skiff in rough seas and thick fog to the shore of Violette. The passengers pulled themselves ashore and were sent up to the communal hall, where the town was having a dance and dinner party for absolutely no reason at all. That's just what we do. Of course, the rescued folks could have boarded a new boat and continued on as planned. But instead, they decided to stay. Can you blame them?"

Alma could tell he'd told the story before. But besides always loving a good story, the people of Violette were quiet and kind. And now, it seemed, they were the last 274 people for nearly a hundred miles.

Make that 275.

"It's not any old place, Alma." Theo's voice had grown deeper, softer, drawing her closer. "You should know that. There are other things I haven't told you yet."

Theo hinted at these things with his gentle tone of warning, perhaps to instill in her just the right level of fear. But Alma wasn't afraid at all. She thought she knew exactly what she was headed toward and exactly why.

2

"Honestly," Theo said after days of knocking on Alma's door, "you add a whole new level to the word *hermit*, and that's *our* word. *We* defined that term, right here."

She'd just finished laying Alex's belongings on the kitchen table for the sixth or seventh time in the span of a week. The metal box she'd brought with her had been curated carefully, like a tidy, private museum. Alma arranged it all on the table: letters and postcards he'd sent over the course of their childhood, along with a few of the ones she'd sent to him; photos; identification books for plants and wildlife; his Zippo with Ursa Major etched onto it; his pocketknife; his compass; the QSL card he'd sent when they first spoke on the radio; and a faded piece of yellow paper on which they had written a series of numbers. It was called a one-time pad, something Alex had devised from a distance when they were twelve, which used false addition and false subtraction to produce a mathematically unbreakable code. It was more of a game than anything, a way to make being apart more fun, but once they were finally together, they realized they didn't need to invent clever ways to communicate.

She'd attempted to use the code only once. He had mailed it to her along with a Morse code transmitter made of army-green plastic—clearly a toy, but she'd spent an entire afternoon in the backyard, hunched in a canoe her uncle Hubert had made, sending out signals until she heard the strands of long and short beeping in her sleep at night.

Alma flattened the paper on the varnished wood table and touched the corner where they'd written their made-up call signs, remembering how furious she'd been when her brother had borrowed the transmitter without asking and lost it. It had seemed wrong to replace it, and despite her now being an adult capable of forgiveness, it stung to have lost even one irreplaceable thing.

But there were two irreplaceable things, actually.

Next to everything, Alma placed the two-way radio she'd been carrying in her pocket since the day Alex had disappeared. The scene was notably incomplete with Alex's radio missing, but it had been with him at the time he was lost.

She turned the knob on the radio to find a clear channel and held the button down and took a breath but wasn't able to say it. After setting the radio back down, she slouched in her chair, glanced at Jupiter, and said, "Come in, Jupiter, this is Alma. What exactly are we doing again?"

Jupiter blinked up at her and let out a long sigh, and they stared at each other like that, on pause for a few moments, before Theo's knock jolted her from her radio daze. When Alma opened the door, Theo peered past her into the cottage. "Are you done yet?" he asked. "What could you possibly still have to do?"

"I'm getting really close, I promise," she said, stepping aside so he could see whatever he'd like of the small living space in which she'd been slowly and methodically moving in, pausing frequently to sit on the floor or at the kitchen table with Alex's postcards between her fingers and Jupiter's heavy weight on her lap.

"Hey, you can hide away as long as you're happy. I'm not going to force you to come out. But no matter how happy you think you are, I promise you'd be much happier with two things: Bea's rappie pie and a Breakwater Blanche."

With so few things to move into it, she'd drawn out her time arranging and rearranging furniture inside the little cottage with its bold turquoise walls. Rain dripped in through the white tin roof, spattering onto the woodstove, but since she wasn't using the stove anyway, she parked a metal pot there to catch the water. That way, too, she could use fixing the roof as a reason to stay home. The backyard was fenced in by boxwood and rosebushes and had enough space for two raised garden beds and one lawn chair. Its size didn't stop her from making long, systematic work of weeding and trimming branches.

Plants were placed in the windows, a dozen books organized on the shelf first in alphabetical order by author, then alphabetical order by title, then by height, then by how many times she'd read them.

Her mother had sent her off with a new phone—a bendable thing the size of a credit card, made from recycled plastic—and all she had to do was tap it twice to turn it on. But she'd left the phone sitting on the table untouched for a week, then remembered Theo telling her reception was spotty, and anyone who did still make calls in town had, at best, an old flip phone the size of their palm. Alma tossed the phone into the hall closet, trusting that a nagging guilt would remind her to call home as soon as she was brave enough.

Aunt Bea had invited her over for pie right away—making very clear this was a standing, open invitation and she was willing to drop everything to engage in the elaborate making of rappie pie—but still Alma had not been anywhere but the general store for a box of nails and some lavender tea. Bea, Theo, and Emerson were possibly the only three people in the world who might truly understand her need for solitude, for overt reclusiveness at times. They'd had their share of sorrow just as she had, and were well versed in the unpredictable way grief operated inside a soul. That shared melancholy wavered slippery as kelp beneath the surface. Perhaps that was how Alma knew she would belong.

"What's a Breakwater Blanche?" she asked, squinting at Theo suspiciously.

"Good lord. It's a beer, Alma."

~~~

A few days later, she found herself standing at the base of Onde Mountain, her heart rattling, her hands damp and cold. She gripped the straps of her backpack, staring at the beginning of the wooded trail as she waited for her cousins. Jupiter nudged her thigh, and her fingertips reached and found his ear. She said, "This is fine."

Theo and Emerson had convinced her to meet them for this hike by claiming it was a kind of rite of passage to climb the mountain, and by reminding her that she was required to be on the beach later that evening anyway for the town bonfire. There was no getting around it, so she might as well warm up—and maybe even get a little buzz—beforehand.

She couldn't argue with that.

As far as what they were going to do, and why this particular activity was a rite of passage, they'd said only that it was a surprise.

"Oh my god, it's actually true," Emerson said as he came up behind her and wrapped his arms around her shoulders. "She's really here! And she doesn't even look that old!"

The last time she'd seen her cousins was nearly twenty years before, when all three of them were so young. Still so naive and unaware of what tragedy felt like. A lot had happened since then.

Theo and Emerson were twins, four years older than Alma, yet they couldn't have been more different from one another. Theo was a bear, with thick black hair and a disorderly beard. He was shaped like Bea and had the same gentle voice. Emerson—with his thin frame and already-graying hair—was a prairie dog like his father had been. He was, Alma could tell, hungry. For life, for experience, for whatever was on the menu.

Alma hadn't been on a proper hike since she'd lost Alex. Her ability to feel at home in nature had withered, and her legs felt unsteady and resistant as she began the climb. Her cousins—having spent their whole lives on this mountain—took off ahead, looking back once in a while to make sure she was still with them. It was hard not to grumble about it, but she couldn't deny that she'd avoided hikes and anything that involved being in nature for much of the previous year. Her body seemed to oppose the very idea of the wild.

Which was not to say that she didn't *want* to connect to the land. It hadn't always been this way. She used to spend every weekend with her father wandering the woods, cross-country skiing, finding the next mountain to climb. She remembered once when she was eleven or twelve, on a bird-watching field trip with her class, the whole group of sixth graders marched up a trail by the local Audubon. Every so often, one of the boys in her class paused just long enough to kick over a bright-white mushroom clinging gently to the soil on the side of the path. It had infuriated her, the harming of delicate wild things that could do nothing to defend themselves. It made her insides rage, and she'd felt a desperate desire to protect the land, but her voice felt trapped somewhere.

The trail was well worn but dense with pines. Beneath the canopy, it was colder, though sweat dampened her clothes within minutes. It was hard to talk, too, as she reached for tree trunks to pull herself up. Farther on, hardy bushes and stunted oaks crowded in. Moss crawled over the bark of every fallen tree. Fog obscured the view of the peak above.

"Ma's still asking when you're coming by so she can make a big Sunday dinner," Theo said. He took three hop-steps up and over a boulder to catch up to Emerson.

"You mean *you're* wondering," Emerson said, pulling back a branch and letting it snap into Theo's face.

"Oh, shut up," Theo said. "You know you're waiting for it too. Any excuse for Ma's dinner, right?"

Emerson shrugged. "When he's right, he's right."

The two of them rambled on as they hiked. About Theo's fishing and supply trips, about Emerson's filming endeavors. Once in a while, Emerson turned to gaze somewhere off the mountain, somewhere in the distance, with a look of expectation. Alma guessed that whatever he was looking for, it wasn't there. It was somewhere else, across an ocean perhaps, and he was ready to run for it. They talked more about their mother's cooking, and old memories of meeting in Nova Scotia when they were kids. Despite the fatigue in her legs and her breathlessness, Alma felt almost comfortable here. Almost at home in this place, and she wasn't sure if it was the town or the people or the possibility that she might find her place in the wild parts of the world again.

Her eyes watered as she almost recognized an old self returning, one that was able to just be there and smile. One that could breathe.

Perhaps it was their bluntness that put her at ease, as if they dealt with the world on very simple terms, taking out the guesswork and complications. "Life is shit sometimes," one of them said. And they didn't ask her how she was feeling at all, or if there was something they could do to help, or if she wanted the phone number for their therapist.

Jupiter plodded along behind her, and she knew this would not be something he could do for much longer. But he seemed happy now, as if he, too, was returning to an old self. Alma saw a hint of feathery color—purple, blue—off the trail, but it was too hidden in the bushes to make it out, and she was barely keeping up with her cousins as it was. She made a mental note to come back and identify it with one of Alex's books.

The hike took almost an hour, and as they neared the top, the trees became more stunted, and lichen-covered rock cut through the soil. The radio tower stood before them, immense in comparison to what Alma had envisioned from the beginning of the climb. The base of it was ten feet across, and it rose like a giant's arm into the sky. Next to it, dwarfed by its massive height, sat a red shelter, paint peeling from the weathered boards. The plywood door had been torn off, either by wind or by kids.

Emerson said, "This is kind of the only thing worth seeing in this town, by the way. I probably should have said that before."

"There's more than one—" Theo began, but Emerson smacked his arm.

"There are plenty of great things about this place," Emerson continued. "But if you're going to live here, this is the one you're going to need to embrace."

The word *embrace* came tinged with warning, implying that it would not be an easy thing to accept. But Alma had been forced to accept—and embrace—many difficult things over the last year, and she knew that no matter what it was, this one wasn't going to compare.

She took long breaths of the damp air, turning to look back at the town below and the inlet beyond. It was all so small and distant. From there, like it was a tiny sculpted model, she could see waves crashing against the granite shelf that was creeping closer toward the lighthouse each year. Alma could see how the force of the tide, like some giant hand, had used its fingertips to scrape away the rock and dirt. The ledge jutted out, and beneath it the earth curved in, scooped out, and dropped into the dark sea. The lighthouse was still a good ten yards from the edge, but its fate seemed certain. Barriers had been built around it—stones, concrete blocks, bags of sand. But they would be no match for the water when the time came.

This high vantage point, 893 feet above sea level, felt like the safest place Alma had been in a long, long time. Emerson dropped his backpack from his shoulder as he and Theo disappeared into the red shelter. Alma took another look up at the tower before ducking inside behind them.

Jupiter lingered outside. He seemed hesitant, alarmed by something unseen. In the past, when he'd acted this way, Alma always found that there was indeed something there—a moose, a coyote—and she'd come to trust his instincts in those moments. But there was nothing she could do here.

The walls were covered in graffiti. *You Are Not Alone* was spray-painted in red cursive. Alma wasn't sure if the message was supposed to be one of hope or caution. There was a picture of a blue octopus, another of a giant yellow flower. Names were scratched into the wood. Someone had written *give a phoque*—a play on the French word for "seal"—with a black line drawing of a seal giving the finger.

Alma turned her back to it, discomfort shaking loose inside her. She tried to smile as Emerson handed her a beer. Theo winked. "One Blanche. Made right here," he said; then he opened a container of maple-oat scones that his mother had made.

They sat together in a circle. Alma felt herself melting as she took a bite. A hint of maple sweetness, an earthy aftertaste of oats. She put her hand over her heart. "Okay, tell her thank you, and I'll be there this weekend."

"You can thank her yourself. Bonfire's tonight," Theo said. "Don't forget."

Alma felt her stomach tighten because she'd forgotten already. And the thought of being around so many people, particularly strangers, made her want to burrow into a hole, but she knew that it needed to happen one way or another. *It's not going to be like it was,* she kept telling herself. *You're going to connect this time. You're going to be present.*

"So, this tower," Emerson said, leaning back to peer out through a broken window, "is called the Lynx Tower. It's a repeater that was put up during World War Two. It was set up as a link for international short-wave radio stations, and all kinds of broadcasts would come through.

"Then the station shut down, but the broadcasts didn't stop. We still hear them. They come from everywhere and nowhere at the same time. Here, watch."

Emerson placed a silver mechanical drafting pencil in the center of their circle. Alma remembered every time she'd seen Hubert, he had an aluminum pencil like that one tucked into the front pocket of his flannel shirt.

Theo and Emerson kept their eyes fixed on the thin, shining object between them. Alma's eyes blinked back and forth from one cousin to the other, unsure what they were waiting for. Emerson checked his watch, and Alma looked down at her own bare wrist, where no watch ticked back at her.

She was about to ask, when the metal pencil began vibrating against the floorboards, and a low, deep voice started speaking.

This is your news . . . but this is not *your galaxy!*

There was a loud banging of a gong, and the voice spoke again but was more distant, muffled as if talking through layers of bedsheets.

Cosmic Chronicle X, X, X . . .

Each echo of the letter *X* got a little further away. Pulled, it seemed, into the vacuum of space.

Alma's cheeks felt tight as a foreign sort of smile took shape on her mouth. She glanced around the room and then back to the talking pencil, resisting the impulse to poke at it. "Seriously? What is that?"

"Comes on every day at the same time," said Theo. "We think it's a radio show, meant to be like those old ones from the fifties. Not sure where it originates from."

The voice transmitted by the pencil began narrating, speaking as if performing the nightly news but clearly of fictional cosmic events.

"This is insane," Alma said. Unable to stop herself, she reached for the pencil. When her fingers touched the aluminum, all sound ceased. As soon as she released it back to the floor, the account of Fig Unakite, hero of the Beetleweed Galaxy, continued. "That has to be the coolest thing I've ever seen. I knew about some of the things people heard around town, but I didn't realize . . ."

"They've just sort of always been a part of this place," Emerson said. "Since we were born. Even before my earliest real memories, I have these vague impressions. They're just feelings that come back now and then, like someone was talking to me while I was lying in my crib.

"You hear them come out of appliances, mostly. Voices, songs, beeps like Morse code."

Alma thought about the two-way radio in her backpack, never far from reach, and she was glad she'd turned it off. It would be embarrassing, she realized, to have it flicker on unexpectedly, as it sometimes did. She thought about Alex's unbreakable code and their made-up call signs, which seemed silly then but terribly important now.

Outside, the wind rattled the shelter windows. It howled between the bars of the tower, and the tower groaned in response.

"When we were kids, we used to climb up there," Theo said.

"Well, the stupid kids did anyway," Emerson said.

"That's offensive," Theo shot back. "It was obviously the brave ones who did."

"I don't know." Alma laughed quietly. "I might have to agree with Emerson on this one. It doesn't seem like the brightest idea."

"Don't dare me," Theo said, but he was already out the door. Even as Emerson shouted after him that no one was even remotely thinking about daring him.

Theo grasped the metal bars and began climbing with urgency. The fact that he'd had a beer first only added to the terror that Alma felt as she watched him.

He scaled it quickly, confident as a teenager who knew no boundaries. Alma looked down at the ground. Someone had built a firepit on the barren rock, and she kicked a charred log with the tip of her boot to avoid seeing Theo go any higher.

"It's not really as scary as it looks," Emerson whispered.

Alma winced as she glanced up again. "No, I think it's exactly as scary as it looks."

"Usually, we just come up here and scream things into the void," Theo yelled as he continued up, one hand over the other. Then his voice came ringing through the wind: "Suboceanic!"

Emerson shouted back: "Penultimate!"

"Come on, yell something," Theo called down to Alma, and she immediately drew a blank on every word in her normally confident vocabulary.

"It's stupid. Come on, we need to get back!" Emerson shouted up. "Bonfire's starting in a bit!"

Flames were already burning on the distant stretch of beach. A tiny candle flickering from where they were. Alma peered into the shelter one last time, noticing a half-collapsed desk in the corner where the station had been set up. There were still exposed wires twisted, hanging from the walls. She reached inside her backpack for the two-way radio—a habit of making sure it was always within reach—but didn't take it out. She didn't want to remind her cousins of her loss, to open the door for discussion or questions.

She was zipping her bag again when Theo began descending. With his head tilted back and eyes still trained on his brother, Emerson said, "You know, Theo's the kind of guy that goes hiking in the middle of nowhere with nothing, assuming someone else will have bear spray, you know?"

Alma began to say, "What does that even—" when Theo's foot slipped.

He let out a frightened, jarring scream that sent a current of dread through Alma's whole helpless body. She started to run toward him but froze as she watched Theo's body drop in what seemed like slow motion through the space in the center of the tower. One bar, then two, his hand finally catching the third. The beer in his jacket pocket fell to the ground, brown glass shattering, strewn across the rocks.

"Jesus, Theo," Emerson said, grabbing his brother by the arm as he reached the ground safely. "You really are a shithead. How you made it to thirty-six, I'll never know."

Theo used his jacket to brush what he could of the glass into a pile. Then he shook his hands out and shrugged his shoulders a few times, like he was ridding himself of some unwanted weight. "Oh, you think that's the first time that's happened? That kind of shit sticks with you. It's better than being boring, though, eh?"

But Theo's eyes kept darting up to the tower, as the three of them crouched to pile bits of glass into a paper bag in silence. Alma let go of the breath she was holding, released her tightly curled fists, and waited for the block of ice in her chest to thaw.

<center>~~~</center>

She could smell the smoke from the bonfire before they reached the beach. The flames grew as she and her cousins returned from the mountain, a little tired and shaken by Theo's almost-fall. The people of Violette gathered on the sand. It was a tradition in Violette to honor the story, year after year, of the ship that wrecked off their coast and brought an unexpected change of course to their history. Of the brave girl who chose to act and saved them all.

Blankets and coolers were pulled out, and people began cooking. They hauled giant pots of stew down the stairs, serving it in wooden bowls on top of mashed potatoes. They brought platters of beer-battered fish and an enormous number of croissants. Theo's girlfriend, Lucie, owned the bakery, and they'd laid a table with shortbread and jam cookies, piled next to whiskey apple cakes and bread pudding and scones.

Bea sat cross-legged on a checkered blanket. She held a mug with both hands in her lap. Theo walked over and wrapped an arm around Lucie, who stood in a circle with three others. She had her sweatshirt sleeves rolled up to her elbows, flour smeared across the front. Emerson had run home to get his camera, and soon he would be setting up somewhere, trying to find the perfect angle to take videos of the festivities.

Most of the town's residents were on the beach, and though Alma would normally have done all she could to avoid such a crowd, no matter how much she liked everyone in it, she knew without asking that this event wasn't optional.

Alma put a blanket down near Bea, and Jupiter lay on one corner of it. "I've been waiting for this big beautiful creature," Bea said, leaning forward to run her hand over Jupiter's back. "So lovely to see you, too, sweetheart. Oh, he reminds me of this big retriever we used to have, Clementine. My gosh, did she know how to comfort a troubled soul. She'd come in from the backyard if I was crying. Like somehow, she just knew. When Hubert died, she didn't leave my side for weeks." Bea grabbed hold of Jupiter's ear affectionately and said, as if talking to a baby, "I bet you're there for her now, aren't you? You were sent down from the stars, I'm sure."

Alma felt her chest cave at the way Bea could acknowledge her sadness without directly asking her about it. "Oh, you have no idea," she said, not wanting to admit out loud yet that she would soon have to face losing Jupiter too. It was too hard to talk about any of it. She took a sip of her drink, gin with muddled blueberries, the intense sweetness washing down the ache that had lodged in her throat, and said, "I don't know if I should thank you or apologize for my being here. I know you like solitude as much as I do."

Alma hadn't seen Bea in many years, but her aunt hadn't changed much. She still wore oversize, thickly knit sweaters with collared shirts beneath them—sleeves pushed up to her elbows—and long skirts. She still braided, then twisted, her hair into a bun at the very top of her head. It was whiter now than it had been years ago, but otherwise exactly as Alma remembered. Bea's eyes looked tired despite her speaking with liveliness and gesturing with her hands to make her points.

"This isn't the most popular place to be right now," Bea said with a wave that encompassed the entirety of the town and the beach and the ocean. "So don't worry. You were always more like us than anyone else.

Hubert said that all the time, when we'd travel all those miles to see the family. It was always great for a time—all the excitement of being with family. But then, you know, you go back home and find that things are quiet again."

They were silent for a little while, Alma sipping her gin until her legs began to tingle and she was able to think of something to say. It felt late, as usual, like the moment had passed, but she said it anyway. "Whenever the family would get together, I always secretly wanted to run away with you and Uncle Hubert. Is that horrible?"

"That's just your nature. So what, you're quiet and sensitive. It doesn't mean there's something wrong with you. It doesn't make you a bad person. Hell, it doesn't even make you all *that* unique."

"It's so quiet here. Not that there isn't noise. It's just different. I don't know, the atmosphere." Being told she was too sensitive since she was a child had certainly left the impression that something was wrong with her, that she was extremely different. "I always wonder, Isn't being a good listener worth anything? Can't you do something good for the world without standing in a crowd or shouting from a podium?"

"Do you know who invented the foghorn?" Bea asked.

Alma shook her head.

"No, not many people do." Bea leaned forward to pull her long skirt over her ankles. "His name was Robert Foulis, and he never patented the foghorn or made any profit from it. Ships were colliding because of the fog, and there wasn't anything—bells, alarms, what have you—loud enough. He realized it was a simple matter of physics. The lower the frequency of a note, the farther the sound carries. He got nothing out of this discovery, of course, but it was lifesaving."

"Well, it's not exactly the quietest invention. Anyway, I hear you."

"You'll find it one of these days," Bea said. "It's probably not going to be that grand-scale-amazing kind of thing that most of the people out there notice right away." She motioned to the dark sea and whatever was out there beyond it. "You're not going to be famous for it. But it will matter, to someone, somewhere. Either in this lifetime or another. There's a place for quiet people in this world. This seems like a pretty good one, even if it is slipping away."

"Does anyone ever talk about leaving?"

"Oh, sure. And they will, someday. Once the water gets too high or the storms cause too much destruction. But we're a community of endurance here. We're all tied to this place somehow, whether it's the land or the history. The radio waves, they're like the moisture in the air. They seep into your clothing and hair, and they stick. They hold on to you. Have you had the dreams yet?"

"I . . . no," Alma said, because she had dreams, lots of them, but not the kind Bea was talking about. Not the kind stitched together by radio waves and the voices of past broadcasts.

"You will. Here," Bea said, pulling her sweater down over her shoulder to reveal a cursive sentence tattooed on her arm. "I don't show this to everyone. But have a look." In the flickering orange light of the fire, Alma read the words: *Rien n'est éternel*. Bea traced her finger over the tattoo and said, "It means 'nothing lasts forever.' The night that Hubert didn't come home, I dreamed about it. It was repeating over and over, and when I woke up, the words faded, but I could still hear them, like someone was whispering them to me from heck knows where."

Hubert was Alma's father's brother, a quiet giant of a man who built canoes for a living. Alma's chest hurt with the pain that Bea must have felt when she lost him, knowing that same pain too well herself. For a moment, her throat choked with an almost-cry, but she managed to stop it, then tried to find the words to say that Hubert was the best guy she'd known, even though she hadn't spent much time with him. Still, more than enough of her childhood days had been passed lying on her back in the canoe he'd built for her parents, daydreaming about Alex.

"See that guy over there?" Bea pointed across the beach to a man sitting alone near the waterfall. A raven hopped in the sand in front of him. They were both silhouettes against a cornflower sky. "That's Oren

Ainsley," she said. "It's his work. His father was a pretty well-known painter, lived up the coast a ways. Oren's done tattoos for more than half the people in town at this point, all something that came in their dreams. This place's history goes beyond the fate of one ship—my own grandmother was on that boat, you know. But there's so much more. Like I said, it's in our skin and our bones. That has everything to do with why we've decided to stay."

Alma opened her mouth to say what would surely have come out bland or cliché, but she was saved by Emerson, who stepped carefully across the rocks with his video camera. "Hey, Ma!" He tossed them each a shortbread cookie with his free hand.

"Oh, the nerve!" Bea shrieked when she missed hers and it landed in her lap. She covered her shoulder again, smiled for the camera, then lifted her cup for Alma to toast. "To the opposite of forever," she said. Alma clinked her ceramic cup against Bea's and quickly took a bite of the cookie so she wouldn't have to think of the right words or say any words at all.

The bonfire's flames grasped for the rising moon. The fire was fueled by old planks from boats that couldn't be salvaged, scraps from building projects, brush from people's yards, and a few carved sea creatures made by kids for the occasion.

There was music. As the land crumbled little by little into the sea, there was still music. Fiddles and accordions. Traditional folk songs and old French tunes. The music was a kind of narrative of the town and its history. The sounds of the instruments mimicked the sounds of nature around them and brought the land to life. A cello like the sighing of a whale. A bow against fiddle strings like a cawing seabird. The steady beat of a drum like the flapping of wings or the thumping of fish tails in a bucket.

A man with a white beard, wearing a thick cable-knit sweater, was sitting on a pile of lobster traps. He seemed intertwined with the rest of the group, yet confidently alone. The dogs trotting around the beach kept stopping by him. Each time one came, the man covertly reached into his sweater pocket to draw out a treat.

Bea caught Alma watching him and said, "That's the writer Hayden MacKenna. He's written a bunch of books, even one about this place. Oh, you're a writer. Should I introduce—"

"No, that's okay," Alma said quickly, standing up and brushing sand from her jeans. "I was just going to take Jupiter to the water."

Overlooking the beach was the silhouetted statue of Esmée Taylor and her dog. Alma had never felt as confident or strong as Esmée must have when she heard the broadcast and knew, somehow, that it was more urgent than anything she'd heard before.

Kneeling in the cold waves with Jupiter, she wrapped her arms around his neck, thinking if she closed her eyes, everything else besides the two of them might disappear. Instead, thunder cracked over the water, reverberating off the mountain and shaking the earth.

A swift gust of wind rushed straight through Alma's jacket, followed by the first slapping of heavy raindrops on the sand and a bolt of lightning that lit the sea. People gathered their blankets quickly and without discussion, piling food and drinks into coolers and hauling them up the wooden steps that climbed from the beach to the top of the cliffs.

"All right then," Bea said, drinking what was left in her glass, "you're stuck with us now."

Emerson folded his tripod and used his jacket to shield it as he crossed the beach. He helped Bea up, and they all shuffled quickly to the stairs. Theo and Lucie, both with duffel bags slung over their shoulders and hoods cinched tight around their faces, were waiting when they reached the top.

Fear came in a vague sort of way, Alma not knowing what to expect but feeling a childlike clinging to her aunt and cousins, who had been through this many times. She followed them up the dirt path to the hotel turned shelter and entered an open, brightly lit room, where others had already begun to gather to wait out the harsh wind and rain.

Small groups congregated on the floor and played rummy or cribbage. They busied themselves with games and stories and food. Everything from the bonfire was simply transferred from one location to the other, spread out on card tables inside—rolls and pies and doughnuts. Folks filled their mouths when they weren't speaking, just something else to distract them from the shaking windowpanes. Alma watched their faces. They seemed so casual, as if waiting for a light drizzle to pass before resuming their evening chores—but there was a hint of worry behind it all. A concern for the future. That inevitable future, in which the waves didn't recede and buried the town for good.

Alma sat on the floor, Jupiter's soft, warm chin resting in her lap, leaning back against a brick wall that vibrated with every roar of thunder. She felt the rolling sea inside her chest, great swells rising and subsiding with crushing force. When she closed her eyes, she was beneath those waves, in some dark depth of the ocean, rocking with the tides.

Yes was what she said when Theo asked if she was okay. But she was somewhere else. In some distant future. The time would come when Violette, and its people, were overtaken by storms—either driven away or swallowed by them. It would all be lost.

But this would not be that time.

3

The first dream came that night, after the storm, after Alma had walked home in a daze at three in the morning, wrapped in one of Bea's wool blankets. She collapsed on the floor with Jupiter and slept there, because that is what you do when someone you love is dying, and because she didn't want to sleep alone either.

In the dream, she was standing in the almost-dark, viewing the town from a distance. She didn't know where she was, but she was cold and wet, and the voice—like a man speaking into an old, crackling microphone—was saying something about waves. Then the horizon lit up, a blinding flash merging both sky and sea into one radiant beam. Alma felt her heart exploding and, at the same time, her stomach rising to her throat like she was falling a hundred feet into nothingness. There was a pain in her chest and her neck. Her lungs filled with water, as if she was drowning. A sense of calm surrender and then dizziness took over, and she gulped for air, thinking she might collapse. A moment later, darkness returned.

Alma was still there on the floor, with Bea's blanket pulled tightly up to her chin, when she woke to the moth's wings on her skin. One arm was bent beneath her ribs, the other resting heavily on Jupiter's side. Her cheek pressed against the smooth wood floor. When she opened her eyes, she was breathless, not sure where she was for a moment.

Her heart was beating into the floor, so hard that she thought its pounding was someone trudging in boots down the hallway.

Beneath her T-shirt, Alma felt the wings fluttering. Her hand reached to her stomach, where she trapped the frantic insect, closed it inside her fist, and tossed it to the floor. The movement was quick and fluid.

Then she saw the moth upside down, legs pedaling the air and wriggling in an attempt to right itself. The feeling from the dream slowly seeped into her conscious mind, the memory of something she hadn't actually experienced but that also seemed too real to let go. The pain, the free fall, the surrender. When they hadn't found Alex, one assumption had been that he'd fallen from a cliff's edge near the trail he'd been on. Alma had tried too many times to keep herself from imagining it, but it always crept in somehow, and she'd dreamed about it often.

This, however, was something different. The voice she'd heard in the dream was still right there, just out of reach. If she heard the man talking again, she knew she'd recognize it in an instant, telling her to listen, that the waves were coming for her.

Everything in the cottage was damp—the morning fog let itself in through the barely open windows. It did not feel like a normal day, this day that had dawned after more violent rain and wind than she'd ever seen, and after this dream she was sure had something to do with the dreams everyone in town had. But Alma still resolved to do normal things. To get up and make coffee, eat breakfast, and feed Jupiter. Wave to Theo and Lucie as they walked to the bakery. Tell Emerson—when he came by as he did every morning—that she'd meet him for coffee later, after she got some chores done. Attempt to fix the bicycle she'd bought used from a kid down the street.

And do the one thing she'd been putting off since she'd arrived in Violette.

Paint bubbled up and peeled from the closet door, the moisture in the air having worked its way beneath multiple coats of gray. Alma turned the brass knob, opened the narrow hall closet, and reached for the metal box on the top shelf.

She had promised to call her parents when she arrived in Violette, but after almost two weeks, she hadn't even turned on the phone. It remained inside the dark box, inside the dark closet, while Alma pondered how to explain once again the circumstances of where she was living and why.

How to explain the chaos of the storm that had happened the night before. How people had filtered, bleary eyed and still a little drunk, one by one out of the shelter toward their homes to assess the damage, and how Alma felt somehow lucky to be there with them. The water hadn't reached the old inn, but it was ankle deep in the houses and shops closer to the shore. Nothing to be done in those predawn hours; they waited for the sun, for the water to recede, before doing what they could to dry their homes and scrub the walls.

How to explain that, despite the tragedy of it, she had found it strangely enticing, had almost wished the rain and thunder had gone on longer. These were not things she could say out loud, and it was never good enough for most people in her life to have her reasons and keep them to herself.

There always had to be a *why*.

She unlatched the box and retrieved the phone, tapping the thin plastic twice and waiting. When nothing happened, she dug farther for the magnetic charging pad, then set both on the floor at the end of the hallway. After a moment, a spiral twirled on the screen, and Alma sat back against the wall, knees to her chest. She looked at the box sitting there, looked at Jupiter lying on the rug next to her. Only his eyes moved, flickering up to hers and then down again.

"We don't have time now," she said, even though all she wanted was to reread one of the postcards or hold Alex's compass in her palm, feeling its magnetism. "We have other things to accomplish." The dog stretched out on the rug as if to assure her he had all the time in the world to wait for her to complete these imaginary things. Alma drummed her fingers on the floor, then on her own thighs. She let her gaze wander left toward the kitchen and wondered if she should make more coffee. Then her eyes rolled over to the right, where a stack of books sat on a brown armchair. She could have chosen any number of distractions from sitting in a hallway and waiting for technology to pipe up.

But she was always going to choose this.

"Fine, if you insist," she told Jupiter, reaching for the first thing her hand touched in the box. It was the postcard in which Alex had proposed, permanently splattered with rain, mud, and blood. He'd made the postcard himself, using a photo from one of their first dates. They were at the summit of Mount Katahdin, side by side, his cheek against hers. He faced the camera, but his eyes were directed sidelong at her. Beneath a wool beanie, her long red hair spilled over her shoulder. One of her eyes was closed against the bright sun, her nose scrunched in the kind of smile that was so big it came only with pure, joyful abandon. The photo was awkward and imperfect, and it was Alex's favorite.

For a moment, she felt the wind of the mountain peak brushing the back of her neck, heard the screaming of a hawk overhead, saw out of the corner of her eye the freckle on Alex's cheek just an inch away from hers.

She closed her eyes and saw treetops spinning, felt the earth drop from beneath her.

Then the phone blinked to life, the vibration startling her, and by that point, Alma was ready to turn it off again. She forced herself to begin the call before she had the chance to stop herself.

Alma had told her parents before she left Maine that she'd try to come back once or twice a year, but that was a lie. Had it been true, she would have felt panic at the thought of cars loading onto ferries, highways of speeding traffic, busy gas stations, crowded grocery stores. She would have imagined the probing questions coming from family members she hadn't seen in years: *What have you been doing, why haven't you been back, how have you been holding up since . . . you know?* She would have been sweating just imagining herself trying and failing to answer these questions.

Instead, she breathed deeply, an ocean between her and that kind of anxiety, with the certainty that she would never have to do any of it again. Alma stood at the counter, spinning a coffee mug with her fingertips.

Her parents had her on speakerphone.

"It can't be that hard, can it?" her father asked, his voice distant like he was talking from another room, when Alma told him how difficult it would be to come back. He assumed Alma's hesitation had more to do with her aversion to traveling and crowded places, something many people in her life misunderstood as mere preference—as a simple decision she'd made to be reclusive.

"I don't know what you were thinking, going to a place like that," her mother continued. "It's a little too . . . adventurous for someone who fell out of a tree at summer camp because you couldn't climb down." Her mother laughed, as if the joke were a light one, made of things too long past to hit any nerves.

But Alma flinched at the number of reasons those words pained her to hear. She'd let her family continue believing this embarrassing lie of a childhood story, telling it over and over like it was some kind of hilarious inside joke, and she'd never told anyone but Alex the truth. That she hadn't fallen at all. That she'd jumped, praying for exactly what had happened—a broken arm—because she'd wanted to be sent home from summer camp. That she hadn't been able to manage the multiple anxieties, sadnesses, swirling desires and frustrations she'd been absorbing from the other kids since she got there.

That she'd had to get away somehow.

Dark flames began to flicker in the corners of her vision, and she tried to blink them away. In the past, when she was upset enough, Alma blacked out, taken over by it. She'd learned to calm herself, though, to push back against the emotion.

But the reminder didn't just make her angry. It also hurt because there was a hint of truth in it. She desperately wanted to be adventurous, to know the natural world that Alex had known so well, but lately there always seemed to be some distance between her and the wild. When she looked at trees now, she didn't find solace. She found memories of disturbing moments, endless trails to be lost on, and the assurance that whether she was there or not didn't matter. They would just keep swaying, and the world would go on without her.

She turned to the refrigerator, holding on to the door handle for a moment to shake off the anger, the hurt, the troubling visions. As she opened the refrigerator and reached in for the milk, a melodic voice spoke through the cold air: "The fairies turn the people into trees, across a green expanse the bees . . ." The rest of the poem trailed off.

Her parents didn't seem to hear. Alma sucked a slow stream of air into her chest and said, simply, on the outbreath, "There's more here than it sounds like. Bea and Theo and Emerson are taking good care of me too. So, I'm fine."

"Do you remember that trip we took to that woman's home? She was a writer—what was her name—and she lived on an island too. We had to take a boat. Where was that, I'm drawing a blank on all of the names."

"Isles of Shoals!" her father called from wherever he was.

Alma smiled, remembering the day trip with her family, hopping off the small charter boat and wandering the dirt trails of Appledore Island, the historic home of the writer Celia Thaxter. The old hotel, the cemetery, the garden bursting with red poppies and purple foxglove.

It was the kind of day she liked to recall, that reminded her she'd had a childhood to be nostalgic about. It wasn't that she didn't. It wasn't that her home wasn't full of love. She'd just gotten lost somewhere along the way, left behind, it seemed, by a fast, loud world.

"Do you know that's the only time I've ever been on any island at all?" her mother said. "And just an hour offshore. I can't even imagine where you are right now. It feels so . . . far."

Alma had known for a long time that their brief trip to Appledore Island had planted the seeds of her wanting to be a writer. But it wasn't until just then that she realized it had also planted the seeds of her being in the place she was now.

Breaking away from one life for another did not leave a clean edge—not on either side. She could have a nice childhood and a loving family and still need to leave it behind. Both things could be true. And escape was not without its regrets.

She thought she'd tell her parents this. That she missed them.

Just then, a moth darted into her hair, and her hand shot up to swat at it, knocking her coffee onto the floor, the mug shattering.

"You sure you're okay over there?" her father asked.

As she knelt, collecting the mug's broken pieces, a shard of ceramic cut her hand. Alma winced and said, "Just these moths. I—yes, I'm fine. Really. I have to go. Sorry."

She held her breath, waiting for someone to say goodbye. Another moth fell from the ceiling fan and flapped its delicate wings in the puddle. She turned the phone off and picked up the insect, holding it gently in her palm.

~~~

Alma tossed the phone back into the closet, pausing briefly when she saw the postcard Alex had sent following the "accident" her mother had mentioned, when she'd jumped from the tree at camp. Before she'd told Alex that it wasn't an accident and he still thought she'd fallen, the book *99 Survival Skills* had arrived in the mail. Alma smiled through tears, remembering the brown paper he'd wrapped it in, an old grocery shopping bag, addressed to *Alma Hughes, failed camper*.

On the first page of the book, he'd written, *In case you ever find yourself in such a pickle again. You got one thing right: don't shout for help unless you're dying. Hope your arm is feeling better.*

It was signed simply: *A.*

The PS: *Page 60, "Animals are creatures of habit. They follow the same paths repeatedly. Use this to your advantage. Make their paths your path."*

Alma opened Alex's *Guide to Plants of the Northeast*, the scribbly drawing of a pine tree on the cover. Alex had always been able to spend hours absorbing the information in such books, then even more hours wandering and naming what he saw, while Alma flipped through the pages of the same books quickly, impatient to just get outside and find solitude. Once she was out there, though, she realized the imbalance. She didn't feel quite at home there, not knowing which plants or trees or birds she was with. And then, since losing Alex, she hadn't wanted to be in the wild at all, which presented her with a peculiar problem. She couldn't be around people, but she couldn't be in remote places either. It wedged her into a special kind of isolation—a kind that, she realized now, was the wrong kind.

Between pages 24 and 25 was a pressed flower. Blue-purple, so old and dry it seemed a miracle it hadn't turned to dust at the mere touch of her fingers. Alma thought of the flower she'd seen on her way up the mountain the day before, and immediately the rest of her day seemed clearly laid out. The mountain would be a big undertaking for someone merely attempting to breathe in the wild again, but suddenly she needed to prove something. To herself, to her parents, to the memory of Alex, she wasn't sure. She held on to the book, squeezing it until her fingertips were white.

When she reached the front door, she noticed the number of moths had increased. They were everywhere. Climbing the curtains and vine-like plants and scaling the window frames. Squeezing in through the cracks in the boards and gathering on the ceiling—a beating gray congregation. She'd never seen so many insects in one place.

Emerson was waiting on the front porch, about to knock.

"What's going on?" Alma asked as she stepped outside, a flurry of wings fluttering past her into the house. She shielded her face with her hands and ducked, feeling silly for reacting so dramatically.

But Emerson shivered, too, and said, "I don't know what's going on, but I swear, if one more moth dives into my coffee or attacks me in the bathroom while I'm brushing my teeth . . ."

"It's so weird. Has this happened before?"

"Never," he said.

"It's like little eclipses everywhere."

"Little what?"

"It's just . . . that's what a group of moths . . . never mind." Then she asked if he was up for coffee later, the way she did every day, whether they ended up having it or not.

"Where you headed?"

"Um . . . just to Bea's. To return her blanket. Then, I don't know yet."

He looked at her a moment—seeing, she supposed, no blanket—then patted her on the shoulder and said, "Later. You got it, kid." And he was off down the street, touching the tops of each fence post as he passed, a spring in his step that never seemed to leave him. Alma dropped the plant book into her backpack and ran back into the house to grab Bea's blanket.

〰

The world could be categorized.

This was what Alma thought as she walked, hugging the wool blanket to her chest. With the right tools, all things could be identified, inventoried, and categorized. Then all situations would have responses, and all problems would have solutions.

Alex had believed this. There was a strange sense of comfort that came from having his plant book with her, as if the simple indexing of the natural world could make it more manageable, less threatening.

Alma passed Lucie, Theo's girlfriend, on the road. She was dragging her kayak down to the water, forehead cinched in determination. Alma waved, and Lucie smiled momentarily, shaking her blonde hair from her eyes; then the look returned, and she continued marching by. "Every other damn month," Lucie said. "Hey, Alma."

Lucie stomped down the path toward the ocean, grunting each time she heaved the kayak along. When Alma entered her aunt's cottage, Bea was standing on a stool in the corner of her living room, one hand gripping a handheld vacuum cleaner.

"A few years ago it was ladybugs," Bea said, holding her long white hair back and sucking a moth from the ceiling. "They were crawling over the light fixtures and the picture frames. I have to admit, I preferred them."

"Where are they coming from?"

"Oh, sometimes creatures just get swept here," Bea said.

"I saw Lucie outside," Alma said. "She seemed—"

"She's not mad. Just worried in her own way. Theo's getting ready to go for another supply run in a day or two. She's never been a fan of that." Alma noticed the look on Bea's face—a kind of worry that could not be mistaken for anything else—as she stepped down from the ladder. The worry of a woman who has already lost someone at sea.

Alma and Bea shared the particular kind of grief that was tinged with the mystery of what happened to their lovers. They would walk through life with a lingering sorrow that transformed into worry for every moment to come after, for every person they held dear. *When?* they would always be asking. When would the time come that they would lose someone else?

Bea turned her eyes to the window and shrugged something off and said, "What was it you came for? Oh, the blanket. Could you drop it in the workshop and I'll wash it later? I'm going to let these guys outside. Even though they'll probably just end up coming right back in." She opened the back door, and the screen crashed closed as she disappeared.

In her uncle Hubert's workshop, nothing seemed to have been moved since he died. There was a half-built canoe in the middle of the shop, propped on concrete blocks. Alma touched the rough side of the vessel, wondering if her aunt ever did the same, then remembered Theo saying Bea rarely went into the workshop.

Rolls of birch bark lined one wall of the workshop, and buckets filled with tea-colored water held old strips of the bark—the never-to-be-used lashing that would have finished off the canoe. Alma assumed they were unusable now, having soaked in this water for years.

Alma found, placed randomly on shelves, hand-carved wooden figurines—a puffin, a seal, a turtle. She pictured Hubert years ago, sitting at the kitchen table while Bea made her big dinners, whittling away, wood shavings falling to the floor.

She set the folded blanket on a bench—careful not to disturb any of the other bones in the workshop—and left quietly, offering a silent wave to Bea as she passed the backyard, grateful that Bea was not the kind to ask about plans.

The roads that traveled from Violette to the surrounding towns had been washed out from runoff, the pavement collapsed and crumbling. Large sections of asphalt lay strewn like puzzle pieces across the ground. Muddy streams ran through the gaps now, and swamp grasses sprouted up in between. Alma walked these wild, broken roads in the direction of the trailhead, Jupiter lumbering behind her slowly, as the vibrant houses and shop buildings shrank and the phone in her cottage closet became just a tiny, fading bit of plastic memory. Until she was able to leave it all behind and focus again.

~~~

How different Alex's understanding of the world had been, knowing the names of things. Knowing which things were to be feared and which offered healing. She wondered if it was possible to befriend the wilderness again. People—they had always been hard for her, but in a way that remained unapproachable. Nature had been hard for her, too, but at least it didn't discriminate. It was hard for everyone. And it *was* possible to know and understand it. If she acquainted herself with it, perhaps she could move through it the way Alex had, with a sense of ease. Perhaps she could move forward and find her place.

Her eyes searched between the trees on either side of the mountain trail as they began the hike up. It was lush green from all the rain. "All right . . . where were you?" she asked no one, still clutching Alex's book. Jupiter was sniffing beneath a berry bush, his nose covered in wet soil when he looked up at her. Usually, she was talking to him. "It was close to here, right?" she said, slapping three mosquitoes at once on her forearm. "God, these bugs. This can't be normal."

They were nearly a third of the way up when she found it. As she parted branches and ducked under boughs, the violet flower stood out like a stray brushstroke against the deep green. A few feet farther in there was another, then another. As she followed the painted trail, Alma checked the book, finding that the dried flower and the one she was looking at were indeed a match, reading the word *hepatica* over and over until it no longer resembled a word at all but became a pure vessel that held all of what she'd lost inside it.

Alma knelt, breathing the world in.

The sky darkened, and there was the unmistakable calm in the air, the way it felt before a storm. Another storm, right on the tail of the last one, seemed unlikely. But so far nothing about this place was predictable. An owl startled her, flying so close she felt the brush of its wings on her forehead. It landed on a branch with the body of a red squirrel clutched in its talons. The frantic silhouettes of brown bats flitted through the trees, snapping up the abundant mosquitoes.

It all seemed out of place, somehow backward.

Alma turned to Jupiter, and a dizziness washed over her, a kind of magnified déjà vu. She knew she'd been here before, and she tried to remember. But before she could process any of it, Jupiter began breathing unsteadily. He collapsed on the trail and began shaking. He weighed so much that even with her whole body draped over him, Alma couldn't hold him still. She squeezed her eyes shut and kept her hands wrapped around his front legs.

No, no, no. Not yet, she thought.

When he stopped shaking and his breathing was less violent, his inhalations came long and slow, followed by short bursts on the exhalation. And then she felt the absence of it. No rushed vibration of recycled air or heaving expansion of lungs. No frantic heartbeat. She looked up and noticed the bats again, congregating now in a tree beside the road. The air was suddenly still and silent.

Jupiter was gone. This was not something she could allow herself to believe, and yet she knew it to be true. She watched his still body, waiting to see that she was mistaken. Waiting for him to breathe again, to twitch, anything.

It was then that the flash of light occurred.

The whole sky lit up—the world lit up. The illumination was duplicated, sky and ocean together becoming one pulse of light. Alma was blinded, everything disappearing behind an intense brightness.

She blinked, her entire body shuddering, before the brightness was sucked back up in an instant, as if into a vacuum. She was still on the ground, rain splattering her cheeks, her teeth chattering. Her walkie-talkie had fallen into the mud and was screaming at her, though she hadn't even turned it on. The voices coming through were incredibly loud and urgent, broken by intermittent static and a high-pitched whine. It was impossible to decipher the words.

Light does not need a medium, as it moves 300 million meters per second through space. Sound, on the other hand, is much slower, traveling through air at roughly only 340 meters per second. And so, the deafening crack that followed the light arrived as Alma was pulling herself to her feet, a deep shock vibrating through the earth. The mountain seemed to shift beneath her. Though her vision was still blurred, Alma saw the bats fall from the tree all at once, their tiny bodies dropping into the mud. The owl was still there, but its eyes were closed, and it had released its prey.

The sound of breaking glass—windows and streetlamps—exploded from town. She dove to shelter Jupiter purely out of instinct. She covered his still body with her body, and watched as a giant ocean wave swelled up over the distant town. Twice as high as any of the houses, it crashed down on the main street, enveloping buildings in white spray for a moment before sliding back out again, taking with it fences and picnic tables. Roofs dripped with the residual foam.

As the wave was drawn back out to sea, Alma was struck by how much it simply became one again with the ocean. As if it had changed form for one brief, hostile visit to Violette, but then disguised itself once more in an alarming stillness. The storm that had been so threatening seemed to have vanished as quickly as the light.

And when it was over and there was a return to some semblance of calm, Alma felt Jupiter move beneath her. It was quick, a breath of air, a rising of his body. Alma realized she'd been holding her own breath, something she did unknowingly when concentrating or scared. She'd been biting her lip and tasted blood. Her gaze swept her surroundings as she began to notice concrete things again. The shaking, silvery evergreens. The kaleidoscope of houses at the bottom of the mountain. The solitary point of the lighthouse in the distance.

And, somehow, Jupiter's animated form.

He was leaping back and forth over the trail and nearly pushed her over. Alma thought she must have been mistaken. Not that Jupiter was alive now—that was clear enough—but about him dying in the first place. She reasoned that his breathing had been so slow that she'd wrongly felt it stop altogether. That was all it could be. With the blinding light and the deafening bang and the bats dropping like deadweights around them, she just hadn't been paying close enough attention.

Having been tricked into knowing what it would feel like to truly lose him, knowing that she still may—no, *would*—lose him at some point in the future, Alma reached to grasp Jupiter around the neck. She was both thankful he was still there and infuriated that she would have to go through his death twice. She gripped his fur between her fingers and he yelped and she remembered that he was still a sick dog, that she couldn't treat him like a puppy. She couldn't take his warm fur, his blood and bones for granted.

Alma let Jupiter go and stood up, the wind plastering her wet hair to her neck. The air seemed colder than before, and it was still far too dark for morning. Spots floated in front of her eyes. An uneasiness—she couldn't quite place it—hovered.

She needed to get back. "Let's go." Alma patted her knee for Jupiter to come to her, but he was jumping through the bushes. She hadn't called him like that in over a month, with the intent to move quickly and for him to follow. She rubbed her wet, cold hands together, cupped them and blew into them. "Let's go home," she said, louder and with more excitement, and she began running. And Jupiter didn't just follow—he ran ahead.

As she reached town, a policeman on a bicycle darted past, blue and red lights blinking from his handlebars. The town's nurses and doctor, along with the veterinarian, wove through the streets on foot, searching for anyone in need of medical care. People argued, screaming excitedly as if they couldn't hear their own voices. There was shattered glass glittering on the pavement. A woman sat in the grass, dabbing at a scraped shin with a tissue, another man kneeling in front of her, holding her hand. A man walked up the beach stairs, dripping wet, shaking his head. Another ran down the street, tripping over untied shoelaces, frantically looking for somebody. A trickle of blood rolled down his temple, and he was trying to call out a name, but no sound came from his mouth.

Whenever someone passed, she felt a wave of anxiety run through her body. Everyone Alma saw seemed disoriented, in a state of shock. She heard a woman describing a ball of fire in the sky over the mountain. Three boys on bicycles, their front tires touching, leaned in close, waving their arms above their heads, reenacting the event. Several people said they'd initially thought a bomb had gone off and were afraid to come outside. Someone said meteorite. Someone said aliens, and Alma couldn't tell if they were joking.

Glass crunched beneath her boots. It was scattered so completely across the ground it was impossible to step anywhere else. Somehow Jupiter seemed to find spaces between the shards—he walked lightly, not making a sound. That's when Alma realized what it was, the strangeness. It was quiet. Not entirely silent, but muffled. There was a ringing in her ears. Her senses were dulled. Everything seemed to be muted and moving more slowly, even the ocean waves.

She began humming to herself, the vibration calming her, and pulled Jupiter close. No one seemed focused on anyone or anything other than themselves. They all seemed lost in their own chaotic worlds, each looking for an explanation for what had happened, what they'd seen.

But there was nothing to explain it.

Then a moment came when everyone on the street paused and looked around, as if noticing one another's presence for the first time and grasping that they were not alone in this. There seemed to be an invisible question hovering: *What do we do now?* Was someone supposed to give the okay to go back indoors? Once they got back inside, what then?

When she reached her own house, Alma found her windows broken just like everyone else's. The shards had gone into the cottage, and the light bulb above the front door had shattered as well, leaving glass on the porch steps. The bodies of dead moths were everywhere, strewn across the ground, the porch railing, the windowsills. A blanket of fragile, dusty wings.

Alma looked down at Jupiter and finally fully absorbed that he had led the way back to town, bounding down the hill like a bear, unencumbered. He looked young again. Not on the outside—the fur around his eyes and ears was still soft white, and he still had the same lean build that came with his illness. But there was a youthfulness in his steps and a brightness in his eyes. She pressed a hand to his chest to find that his breathing had returned to normal, evenly paced ins and outs. A steady heartbeat.

Emerson ran down the sidewalk to her door, reaching to hug her. "Are you okay?" he asked. "Why are you soaked?"

"What? Oh, don't worry about it. I'm fine. You guys?"

"We're fine too. Ma was in the garden at the time. She said when the light flashed, the closed flower buds all opened at once. She came inside in a kind of daze but couldn't stop talking about how beautiful it was to see them all open up like that in fast-forward. I was just reading the paper, but Theo was walking home. He's the only one who seems really out of it. Like he can't remember things. He's probably just disoriented. That seems to be the popular reaction."

"Well, it's over," Alma said. "Whatever it was." She paused. "What was it?"

Her cousin shrugged, and turned to look down the street toward the beach, the tide still higher than Alma had seen since arriving. "I don't know," he said. "I've heard meteorite, military training operation, and contact from outer space. You?"

"Same." She laughed. "I have no idea. I need to take it all in. And *this* . . ." She gestured to Jupiter, who was rubbing his shoulder against the side of the house. His fur was still wet and muddy.

"What?" Emerson asked. He stepped aside and peered past her.

"That," she said. "Jupiter."

"Jupiter?" he asked. "Like the planet?"

"What? No. Jupiter. My dog, Jupiter, he's right . . ." Alma pushed down frustration, knowing the whole event had been intense for everyone. But she had seen her dog die, and then come back, and he was right in front of Emerson. She paused long enough to see that Emerson wasn't playing a game with her. Besides not seeing the dog, he also seemed genuinely confused about who or what Alma was talking about.

Her mind ran through every possible reason that her dying dog—who she had been so sure had *actually* died—was now more energetic than ever. Perhaps something had happened to Emerson when the flash occurred. Or something had happened to her. Was Jupiter really there, or was she so in shock at his death that her mind had brought him back? Or—she swallowed hard at what seemed too insane a thought—had she invented him in the first place?

No. He *had* been there. He was there now.

Thankfully, Emerson changed direction in those moments of confused pause, while she tried to wrap her mind around what was happening. As Emerson stepped down from the porch, he said, "I should probably be filming this, right? If I was a real filmmaker, I'd be out here with my camera, but damn, I was just so thrown off guard I didn't think."

"Is it crazy—" she began. "It seemed like it came from the mountain."

Emerson glanced at the peak behind them and said, "Crazy is what we do here."

"I'm getting that sense," Alma said, trying to sound casual and not panicked, hugging him again. "Come by tomorrow?"

"As always. Coffee later. Go dry off and get warm."

Alma nodded as he left, grabbing a broom, anxiously sweeping the moth carcasses and tiny bits of glass into a pile. She shook away thoughts of Jupiter's almost-death, his future death, and her own questionable sanity.

She gathered blankets and the pillows from her bed and laid them on the floor beneath the window where Jupiter usually slept, and where she'd been sleeping too. She sat on the floor with her knees drawn up to her chest, Jupiter's warm back pressed against her, unsure of what else to do, waiting for something even though she didn't know what.

Alma closed her eyes, the sparks of light still burning there, and listened. The two-way radio was on the floor next to her. She thought she heard the rhythmic sound of someone speaking, but it was just the waves outside.

In and out, in and out. Always present, yet never the voice she was hoping to hear.

PART 2
FIELD DISTURBANCE

2026

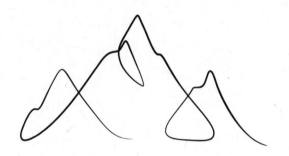

4

Lucie St. Pierre, in the water

Lucie St. Pierre didn't see what tipped her kayak, if something had tipped it at all. She'd stopped paddling for a little while and was letting the boat and her mind drift. She felt alive, for the first time in a long time. She thought, for the first time in a long time, about leaving.

If Theo was always going to stay, there was nothing she could do about that. He had some weird sense of duty, and she admitted to herself that the very thing that frustrated her about him was also what she loved. It didn't mean she had to follow him, though.

Baking was what she would have turned to at one time, but the truth was, she didn't feel like baking much anymore. It was always pinned to her, as if that was who she was. In happy times, in sad ones. In frustrated ones, lonely ones, painful ones. Lucie was the one an entire community counted on to bring comfort in the form of food.

They had become exhausting, both the love and the kitchen alchemy. And this place. She had never chosen to come to Violette. It was a decision made for her, and as with most decisions she did not make herself, the question inevitably arose—if she had chosen, would this have been it? And as with most questions Lucie was reluctant to answer, once it came up, it refused to go away. The island had been good to her, and she'd been happy. There was no question about that.

But she watched it slipping away, each year a higher tide and a more violent flood. Each year, fewer seabirds and seals to keep her company on the water.

She'd hauled her kayak to the beach that morning, then paddled against the waves until her arms felt like they might fall off. Until fatigue overtook her doubts. Then she'd turned the kayak around and let it float back in with the tide. She told herself that by the time she got to the beach again, she'd have made up her mind—either she'd find a way to love this place again, or she'd say goodbye.

She was almost back to the beach when the sky darkened, the clouds turning a gray tinted with green. The kayak drifted past a few cottages along the shore. Some people were outside on their decks with binoculars, tracking a rare seabird. A few kids ran on the path. A man was riding a bike.

Someone on the dock pointed to the sky behind her and yelled something about the clouds. Maybe another storm. Was he talking to her?

Then she was in the water.

For a few moments, she pumped her arms and legs, though somewhat wildly—her body unsure of which direction it was headed. Lucie wished she'd taken a larger breath before being capsized, although she would have, she figured, had she known it was going to happen. She looked up and saw the sky through the water, light fractured into a shade of blue-green she had never seen before.

Then everything lit up. It was all white. The sky above the water, the water around and below her. It was whiter than white—she was surrounded by an iridescent, impossible brightness. She was shaken by a pulse that reverberated through the water just after the light, and taken toward shore by the rush of an enormous wave, and that was all she could remember. After that, she was pulling herself out, dripping wet, and collapsing onto the sand. For some reason, her body felt like it didn't belong anymore. Like it should have stayed in the sea for good.

The next thing Lucie knew, she was sitting on the wet sand, the storm retreating as if it had simply changed its mind. Water dripped from her clothing and hair, and though she knew she should be shivering, she did not feel cold.

She blinked water from her eyes and tried to replay what had happened. Her kayak had tipped—though why, she had no idea—and though she was a good swimmer, she'd found herself flailing in the water, attempting to find her way up.

People around her seemed upset, and somehow also trying to reconcile their recent experiences. "Excuse me," she called to a man standing nearby. The man did not respond, only bent down next to her and picked up a brown button. He held it close to one of the buttons on his own plaid shirtsleeve, judging whether it was a match, and when Lucie asked again, "Excuse me, what's going on?" the man simply continued without any recognition of having been asked a question.

She climbed up from the beach, wondering why people seemed so lost, though not quite as lost as she felt, and she was about to ask someone else if they knew what had happened, when she noticed the moths. Earlier that morning, they'd been crawling over everything. Now, their dead bodies were spread across every inch of the sidewalk.

Lucie walked toward a young boy who kicked his way through the piles of dead moths, looking around as if in shock. "Do you need help?" she asked. But the boy didn't turn. It seemed he, too, had chosen to ignore her. She touched his shoulder, but he just shivered and brushed off his sleeve, then stared out across the ocean, scanning left to right, left to right, as if whoever he was looking for might be out there somewhere on the horizon. She touched the boy's shoulder again, making solid contact, but he simply shoved both hands into the front pocket of his hoodie, looked at his feet, and began to walk away.

It seemed too impossible to even think. But even as this passed through her mind, Lucie thought, *Sometimes the impossible still happens to be the thing that makes the most sense.*

If it *was* what she was too afraid to even think about, then she wished she had someone to talk to. At least one other person with whom she could debate and argue and say, "No, that couldn't be true." She touched things: tree trunks, fence posts, a deck chair that had fallen over. She walked over the bridge, running her hand along the railing, and then nudged a woman's bag that was lying on the ground. Lucie moved to stand directly in front of the woman, blocking her line of sight to the water.

The woman gazed straight through to the waves, and Lucie knew she was alone.

The sky was still darker than it should have been, and greener, and everything was wet the way it was when a big storm hit. But the storm she'd thought was coming was nowhere to be found now.

When Lucie reached her cottage door, she hesitated. She already knew she couldn't simply move through walls. Her hand had rested firmly on the tree and on the railing, and she'd been able to move the woman's bag. It seemed she was not a ghost—at least not the typical kind. Lucie pushed both hands against the side of her cottage, pressing harder and harder still. She was really there. Part of—and somehow not part of—the world.

Lucie's roommate, Odette, opened the door and stood there, half in and half out, leaning with her hand on the doorknob, looking for something or someone. Lucie slipped inside. The cottage was dark, candles lit in the kitchen and living room and, strangely, Lucie's room. She stood in the hallway and watched Odette come back in and walk slow circles on the spiral rug in the living room.

Odette seemed confused, stopping to pick things up and look at them as if she had no recollection of where they'd come from or why they were there. She touched Lucie's purple scarf hanging from the corner of a mirror. She used her foot to turn over a leather boot on the floor. She picked up a photograph. In it, Odette and Lucie were standing together behind the counter in Lucie's bakery.

Odette picked up her phone and punched in a number, holding the photo an arm's length away. She glared at it while she waited. "Come on," she said. She tried three more times before the call went through and someone answered. Odette used the voice she always did when she was trying to pretend something wasn't wrong—higher pitched and a little shaky. "Hey, Mom. What? No, I'm fine. We had a strange storm here. It was quick and rough, and the tower on the mountain was struck by lightning maybe? There was a flash of light. I'm fine, but I feel like something happened to me, or to my memory. I'm sitting here with a photo that was in my house, and I don't have any idea where it came from. I'm in this photo, but I don't know the other person. I don't even know whose room it came from. There are so many things in my house right now that aren't mine, but I don't know who they belong to. I think I'm losing my mind."

Lucie stood up, crossing the room so she could hear better. She stood in front of Odette, while Odette continued telling her mother about this mysterious person and her mysterious belongings. None of it made sense. Odette's mother knew that they lived together. They'd met before. If something happened to Odette's memory, at least her mother should have reminded her. But perhaps it was all worse than she thought.

Perhaps she was not just dead, but forgotten too.

It seemed the only explanation. Lucie did not cry, although she didn't know why, because that is what she would have expected to do. Instead, she sat next to Odette on the couch. Just a few days ago they were sitting right there together, watching an old movie. They'd talked and told stories. Stories that only they could tell. And now, all those moments were gone, Lucie's story seemingly forgotten along with her. It was, if anything could be, worse than being dead.

When she hung up the phone, Odette seemed no less confused than when she'd first called her mother, and she began crying. She put her hands against her face, pressing her palms into her closed eyelids and swearing to herself. "Fuck, fuck, fuck," she whispered.

It was then that Lucie wondered why she'd chosen to go home, rather than to find Theo, who may very well have been responding the same way Odette was. Or to check on her own mother, who was lying in a dark hospital room on the other side of town. Her mother didn't remember her before the flash of light, so what difference would this make? It was selfish, Lucie knew, but some kind of gravity had lifted inside her when she realized she was no longer needed.

The streets were eerily empty as she walked to the bakery. Lucie felt her senses heightened. She could hear the ocean waves like they were crashing inside her skull, and somehow every bird that used to blend together into one noisy background was suddenly calling out to her individually. The dampness in the cold, salty air was giving her goose bumps, but she couldn't feel them.

The bakery was open, despite the windows being shattered. It seemed the need for normalcy prevailed, and there was no more important place for this than the place that provided coffee and pie. Lucie walked in behind an elderly couple and sat at a high bistro table in the corner.

Life seemed to be carrying on. Lucie pressed her lips together and tried not to think too hard about what she no longer had. Sure, she had been thinking of leaving, but now it was taken from her. She looked around and saw Hayden MacKenna, the writer she chatted with just about every morning after handing him a double latte. He was at a table across the room, lifting up a pen and setting it down again. He did this a few times in a curious, experimental way. Lucie's eyes narrowed then, because as she looked directly at him, he glanced over his shoulder, then down at his chest; made eye contact; and smiled.

Lucie lifted a hesitant hand, a questioning wave. And he waved back.

5

Hayden MacKenna, at the bookstore

Hayden MacKenna had never minded being hot, but this was something different. He couldn't explain the chills that ran up and down his spine, the crawling skin, all while sweat formed on his brow and he thought he might pass out from overheating. His body seemed to radiate pure fever.

The street was as crowded as it ever got on a regular weekday morning. Since the storm the night before, there was plenty to do, and another storm also seemed to be advancing. This time of year, though, at least lately, they were always advancing.

Suddenly dizzy, Hayden leaned against the wall of the bookstore, focusing his eyes on the horizon, trying to catch his breath. He wondered if he'd have to go inside and bother someone to help him home. They knew him well there and would surely be happy to help. If they didn't like him all that much, they at least appreciated his writing. Over the years, he'd secured only two kinds of acquaintances in Violette: fans of his writing and enemies. There was no one in between anymore.

He wondered if this was it, the final moment, as his chest began to knit itself together and close up, tighter and tighter. Though his seventy-fifth birthday was just two weeks away, he had given little thought to his affairs—who should be notified, who should get his money, who should be the one to rummage through his messy office drawers for potential posthumous publications after he was gone. As a writer of stories, however, he *had* given thought to who and what he would be thinking of when death arrived. It seemed a particularly important aspect of one's own story, and he wasn't about to let it pass without heavy plotting.

But this wasn't going to be that moment—he was sure of it—and so he did not think of Alphie Roy just then. He thought, instead, of the mountain and its cloud-hidden, windbeaten tower. They stood as a reminder to him that there were things in this world that were steady, that lasted, even if they had broken down in the process.

He'd written four novels, two collections of short stories, and even one experimental and surprisingly well-received book of poetry. Aside from these, he'd also written a nonfiction book—unpublished—about the radio tower. The book had been a culmination of theories, ideas about sound waves and echoes, about reverberations that came and went continually throughout time. But despite the truth that everyone in Violette had heard the mysterious broadcasts, from light bulbs overhead and forks at the dinner table, and even infusing their dreams, his publisher had deemed the book far too inaccessible.

This library of work had cost him significant loss of sanity, sleep, and relationships; enormous amounts of whiskey, coffee, and cigarettes; and every ounce of true joy he'd ever had. Hayden had spent a lifetime earning his immortality.

But that did not mean he would let go easily. With one hand on the wall beside him, and both eyes focused on the peak of Onde Mountain, Hayden MacKenna arched his back and attempted to stand tall.

It was there, with his feet on the bookstore doormat, on which the words GO AWAY, I'M READING were printed, that Hayden MacKenna realized he did not get to choose, and that gripping to one's own existence is only a recipe for disappointment. He fell to the concrete and died there, eyes shifting to the sky that had grown unusually dark, just as a flash of light illuminated everything around him.

When Hayden opened his eyes again, he was no longer sweating. Chills had stopped tickling his skin, and his breath flowed in and out of his chest easily. Hayden had always enjoyed this time of morning. Despite the people moving around on the street, they were usually doing so with such purpose and order that it seemed inaudible.

Now, however, what he saw was chaos. It was as if he'd blinked and the world had gone from soundlessly tidy into momentary darkness and then out again to complete disarray. He was still lying on his back on the concrete, but he could tell that something was wrong. There was a sense of confusion as people ran around him, all attempting to gather information from one another.

For a moment, Hayden thought they might have been talking about him falling to the ground, having what he assumed was a heart attack. But, as he sat up, wondering why no one was stopping to help him, he saw that this had nothing at all to do with him. It was much bigger. A fire, an explosion, the Big Wave? He tried to guess. But all he saw was broken glass and shouting people. He stood up and reached for a woman passing by, but she didn't stop. He called out to a man standing in the bookstore doorway, but the man did not seem to hear him. Hayden walked over and stood in front of the man, but the man appeared to be looking straight through him.

"I've just had a heart attack," Hayden said. "But I think I'm okay."

The man still did not respond. He took a piece of gum from his pocket, shoved it into his mouth, and walked away.

Hayden entered the bookstore. He was the only one there, the aisles dark and vacant. He touched the shelves, let his fingers bump along the spine of each book as he passed. When he reached the shelf of his own books, he found only an empty space where they should have been. It seemed odd, and then he saw them all—fifteen or so—in a pile on the floor, like someone had just pushed them off the shelf from behind.

A dim light flickered at the back of the shop above a small wooden table. A lone bulb that hadn't broken. Hayden sat in a chair too small for him and unbuttoned the top button of his shirt. He felt strangely good for someone who had just had a heart attack. He was sure that was what it had been. Is this how people recovered from them, if they were lucky enough to survive? Better than they'd been before? With his arms stretched above his head, he took a deep breath. His lungs hadn't felt this open in years.

There were footsteps, and the bookstore owner, Emile, came around the corner. Emile walked right past Hayden, brushing shoulders, but didn't seem to notice. He knelt beside the pile of Hayden's books, picking one up and turning it over to look at the back. He seemed confused, not as much by the pile of books on the floor as by the existence of the books themselves. He picked up others, glancing at the covers, the descriptions on the back, the author photo inside, random pages throughout. Emile was perhaps Hayden's sincerest fan. There was no reason for him to wonder where these books had come from.

When it appeared that he had seen enough, even if not quite enough to explain the books, Emile stacked Hayden's novels neatly on the floor in front of the shelf. Why he didn't pick them all up and put them back on the shelf where they belonged, Hayden didn't know, but he could only watch.

"Just put them back, Emile!" Hayden shouted.

Emile stood and continued walking down the dark aisles, straightening the other rows of books that had shifted, then disappearing once again.

With no customers and so little light, it occurred to Hayden what a sad place a bookstore must be at night. Night after night, the lights turned off, each of the books left deserted on the shelves like tombstones, even the ones by living authors. The whole place with its musty paper smell suddenly seemed like a hall of ghosts.

And he was not supposed to be one of those ghosts.

Outside on the street, people were still sitting on the sidewalk examining injuries, still shouting at one another in clusters as if they couldn't hear their own voices. And as he walked back to his apartment above the newspaper office—trying and failing and trying and failing to get the attention of the people he passed—the pieces of the story began to come together, and he was sure that he was right about having had a heart attack, but wrong about having survived it.

Hayden climbed the stairs with a strange mix of renewed vigor and internal resistance, as if he wanted his old achy body returned to him. Inside, he made himself a drink, because *what the hell*, and tossed it back quickly, then pulled a knife from the silverware drawer and pressed the blade to his fingertip. Nothing. No sensation, good or bad, and this amused him for exactly twenty-five seconds, after which he had no idea what to do with himself. Should he go to bed and hopefully wake up from this dream? Keep drinking until, perhaps, he felt something? Should he go back outside and see if he could figure out what he'd missed that caused such turmoil? He didn't want to do any of these things, though he could think of no other options.

After sweeping up the glass from the broken window, and turning his potted plants right-side up again, he decided to do the only thing he knew to do. He poured himself a second drink and sat at his computer and began writing. Who knew what was going on. But it wasn't his place, he decided, to ask those kinds of questions. His mind—now that he was dead and able to reflect with at least a little distance—continued to drift toward Alphie. So, he wrote about and for and to Alphie. Apology after apology.

He typed all morning, pausing only to reenact his lunchtime ritual, which was to go to the bakery, order a double cinnamon latte, and write a little more by the window. He sat on a high stool, no use for the coffee he couldn't order anyway, and intending to finish the story he'd begun the night before.

The fact that he was dead and somehow still there and that no one could see him anymore didn't bother him as much as the fact that he'd been struck by inspiration, finally, after many years of waiting for words to come back to him, but now no one would ever read what he imagined could be his best work yet. Suddenly, the old advice he'd given to many students along the way came rushing back to him. *Write for yourself, not for someone else, not for an audience. If you truly love to write, if you have to write, you'll do it even if no one else ever sees it.* The idea stung now that he was sitting there with no hope of an audience ever again. How had he, back in his teaching days, not had an ounce of empathy for those with so little certainty of their futures, with no guarantees of success?

He wondered where Lucie was, since an afternoon never passed that he didn't see her smile. It would be the first time he'd see her without any possibility of her knowing he was watching, and this curiosity felt voyeuristic, but also a bit like a father watching his daughter from the kitchen window as she played outside. He would never reveal it to her, but he freely admitted to himself that despite having no children himself, he'd come to look at her with a fatherly kind of adoration.

When she walked into the bakery—*her* bakery—Hayden was suddenly unsure of himself. He realized he had to be doing something, and so he picked up his pen, although he couldn't formulate words anymore and pretending to write for appearance seemed stupid when no one could see him anyway. He set the pen down. He wondered if Lucie knew yet that he was dead. Had someone found his body, assuming his body was still there to find? This seemed like the kind of thing he should have been concerned with earlier, when instead he was typing away like a college writing student with his first big idea.

But what happened was utterly unexpected. Lucie came into the bakery, looked around as if not trying to find anyone in particular, but rather taking in the whole scene in the same way he was. Lucie's eyes followed a few of the patrons, traveling the perimeter of the room, until eventually they landed on Hayden.

Hayden looked behind him, then at the front of his shirt, and then back at Lucie. Had she . . . seen him? She waved. He waved back. As she crossed the room, Hayden felt both excited that she was there—wherever *there* was—with him, and also saddened by the fact that she was *there* with him because it meant that she, too, must have suffered a similar fate.

"Mr. MacKenna," she said.

"Lucie."

"I don't . . . How did you . . . Have we . . . ?"

"I don't know, my dear." He took her hand. "But I'm so happy to see you."

"What happened to you?"

"It seems I had a heart attack on the doorstep of the bookshop. Fitting, I realize now."

"I think that I drowned. But we're still here."

"Well, something like here, anyway. Although I'm not sure why. This can't be what happens when people die." Hayden paused to consider something. "Did you die before or after the storm?"

"During, I believe."

"It was unusual, even for here."

"The tower. Odette said it was struck by lightning and there was a flash of light. That was about when it happened. Could that maybe . . . I don't know. Is that stupid?"

"Huh. No, that could have done it."

"Could have done what?"

"Could have been the thing that turned us into whatever this is. Ghosts, or apparitions, or spirits. There's a name for it, I'm sure. It all makes sense now."

"Nothing about this makes any sense, Hayden. Literally nothing."

Occasionally he'd rambled on about his theories to Lucie when she served him coffee, testing the waters, curious just how crazy things would sound when he said them out loud. But this development was beyond anything he'd even considered back when he was writing his apparently too cryptic book about the tower.

Hayden held his hand up in front of his face, turning it and examining the way the light glowed more around his fingertips than before. He scribbled this detail into his notebook. "Well, I, for one, don't have a problem with it. So far, it doesn't seem so bad. We're still here, but invisible and able to observe everything without being observed ourselves."

"But we're not just invisible," Lucie said. She looked around the room at the people sipping coffees and eating pastries. "We've been forgotten. By everyone. Odette had no idea whose stuff was in her house. My stuff. Photos of me."

Hayden closed his notebook. He sat back in his chair and clasped his hands on the table. "Oh," he said. "Well then, that's different, and far less desirable. It explains my books too." Lucie looked confused, but he'd suddenly lost the thread of what he was saying. "Well, I'm going to make a quick visit. There's someone I need to see."

After Lucie begged him to stay with her, to stick together and devise some kind of plan for getting out of their situation, he agreed, with the caveat that he took care of one item of business first. She seemed genuinely afraid to separate, and so he promised to meet her at the bench by the bridge, the one closest to the statue of Esmée Taylor, in an hour.

The two of them left the bakery together, Lucie muttering something about guilt and Theo and her mother as she wandered back toward town, her head tilted to the sky.

Hayden climbed the hill to the wildlife refuge not nearly as out of breath as he would have been if he'd been alive. He wondered, actually, if the heavy breathing he *was* doing was just a habitual act, something he thought he ought to do more than needed to.

The barn was gray and weathered, its perch on the edge of the cliffs ensuring a good beating from the salty wind that swept off the ocean. On the bald rocks below the building, seabirds gathered as if they knew this was a safe place. And there was something about it that would make Hayden feel this way, too, if the man he was there to see didn't despise him and if Hayden hadn't been so horrible to him in the past.

Crossing the grassy field, a black fox with yellow eyes and a white-tipped tail paused as if it could sense Hayden there; then it slipped inside the barn, out of sight. As Hayden entered the dark barn, birds flew overhead. There were cages lined along one wall, a puffin walking around in one, wings ruffled and sticking out at awkward angles. Inside another, a marten with a bandage on its paw stretched lazily, and in yet another, a squirrel stood frozen with a nut between its paws.

The black fox jumped across some bales of hay and then climbed a ladder to a loft where a man was sitting with his legs dangling over the edge.

Alphie Roy.

Alphie held a sandwich in one hand and a beer in the other. The fox, when it reached Alphie, sat and waited patiently for Alphie to break off a small piece of bread. A baseball hat partially covered a bandage on Alphie's temple, but otherwise he looked as if he was trying to simply maintain some sense of routine, just as everyone had. He finished his food and petted the fox on the head before descending the ladder, and Hayden was struck briefly with fear that he might be seen.

He was not.

After Alphie passed, Hayden climbed up to the loft to get a better look around. From there he could see the whole of the operation. Alphie walked past each enclosure, sipping his beer every few moments and letting his hand graze the bars so the animals inside could touch their noses to his fingertips.

In the middle of the floor, a sea otter pup swam circles inside a plastic children's pool. The pup batted a ball and chased it when it floated away. Alphie knelt and began feeding the otter with a baby bottle.

Hayden noticed a desk in the corner and recognized a familiar cover even from high above. It was *The Light on the Way Down*, the first book Hayden had published and the one that caused all the heartache that followed. Had Alphie forgiven him? That seemed too much to ask. Was it a reminder of where he had come from, all he had overcome? Or was it simply a paperweight, perhaps for other, more important documents beneath?

At one time, they'd been lovers. At one time, they'd both been writers. Living together in a small apartment in Montreal, they'd had desks on opposite sides of the same room. With their backs to one another, they'd spend all morning writing, then take walks along the canal while they talked and tried to sort out some problem of plot or character or pacing.

Alphie had started the wildlife rehab in his family's barn not long after he and Hayden stopped speaking. He'd decided to leave people behind and throw himself into taking care of the animals. Alphie had always been a nice person, but Hayden found this new path borderline saintly. He couldn't believe how many animals suddenly popped up needing help.

They'd both gotten so old, but Alphie had grown into himself quite well, despite being disappointed by life, and was as beautiful as he had always been. Hayden had not fared as well, made clear by his current circumstances, but at the very least, he finally didn't need to duck behind a building or slip into a shop to avoid running into Alphie. He really couldn't decide if he was happy or sad that it was only possible for him to be there now because he was dead. Because his friend could not see him, could not remember him. Could not shout for him to get the hell out of his barn.

So many sounds surrounded them. Birds' wings beating in the air, the scratching of claws through dirt and hay, the wind smacking against the side of the barn and the ocean waves crashing against the cliffs outside. Hayden watched Alphie, the black fox following him like an obedient puppy. This was all he'd wanted to do for decades—to sit in the same room as this man again. No talking about the past. No talking about anything. Just listening to all the sounds.

Hayden admitted to himself, quite reluctantly, that it was only then, when there was no apparent risk involved, he had finally found the courage. He could have stayed—he wanted to stay—but he'd promised Lucie he'd meet her, and he was the only one she had now.

He looked down at his dangling feet and considered the loft ladder, but thought, *Well, here's to no risk.* He hesitated briefly before pushing off the ledge and dropping to the floor, landing on his feet in the straw—still dead, but otherwise unharmed. Then he left the barn and all the wounded creatures that dwelled inside, and made his way down the hill toward the bridge where he'd planned to meet Lucie. It seemed there were more people out on the streets than there ever were before, as if they suddenly had a new appreciation for the world. Kids rode bikes, groups of people practiced yoga on the grass by the river, a woman painted an overly large canvas with an image of the cliffs and the ocean.

When Hayden reached the bench by the bridge, he saw Lucie talking with another woman. He'd seen the woman before, he thought, at the bonfire. New people tended to stand out lately. She had shoulder-length mahogany hair and a radio sticking out of her back pocket. A dog the size of a small bear was running impatient circles around her feet.

6

Oren Ainsley, on the roof

Oren Ainsley was sitting, knees drawn up to his chest, on the roof of his house. The rain had stopped, and he was enjoying the way the rising sun touched the tips of the trees, lighting them ablaze. He'd recently decided to make a point of choosing one thing each day to be grateful for. For much of the last decade, it had been harder to find things to put on that list. But now, back in town, there was a woman who had loved him once, and a ten-year-old girl who he hoped loved him still. It seemed, even with only this, that the list had lengthened significantly.

Fey, the raven, was in the sprawling evergreen bushes fifty feet away, where Oren's lawn ended and a long path down to his tiny beach began. She stretched her legs out in long strides from one craggy horizontal branch to the next.

On the roof shingles next to him, Oren had a notebook and a thin black marker. Off and on, he'd been picking it up and sketching. After years in Violette, his tattoos now walked all over town, the images reflecting people's dreams, the town becoming a kind of living text, giving a second tier of life to the landscape.

Below him, the garden was dying. Even though he hadn't watered it in weeks, the sky had overdone it. The rain had been too much. Mosquitoes harassed him constantly, and suddenly there were masses of moths as well, but the sun was coming up and would—if he was lucky—chase these annoyances away.

He could have chosen to stay there on the roof all day. Chosen to wait for the sun to be directly above, for his shadow to disappear and then return again as the sun began its arc downward. He could have chosen to lie on his back and watch seagulls careening overhead.

There was nowhere else he needed to be.

And, if he had done this, it's likely that his foot would not have been caught on the broken shingle, and he would not have fallen from the roof to his death in the garden below.

In the moment before he fell, he caught a glimpse of Fey taking flight. It was that specific kind of flight that birds do when there is a disturbance in the air. In the movies, someone shoots a gun and the birds all spring off the branches at once. She flew, black wings against the bruised sky like an eel in a clouded ocean. Oren might have thought that she knew what was coming. He might have thought that she had some say in the matter. Her knowledge of the world and its circumstances seemed to probe further into the future than his, as if she pieced together the components of the present with such speed that she could foretell the most obvious of outcomes.

Her dependence on the world was so minuscule—even her love for Oren and his love for her—that whatever she saw was neither good nor bad, desired nor undesired, welcome nor unwelcome. She would not miss him when he was gone. Things simply were what they were, and she observed them, as passively as a rock observes the wave that laps over it.

Well, he might have thought about these things. But—as he used the wooden fence post to pull himself up from the ground and parted the choking tomato plants to walk away from the place where he had fallen—he couldn't remember what he'd been thinking on the roof before he died.

Oren lived in an old whitewashed cottage that his father had left him. The rooms were cramped and musty, the smooth wood floors sloped and the ceilings low. In the back room, his father's paintings took up nearly every inch of wall space. His father hadn't hung them there, Oren had, and though he rarely went into the room, the paintings— quiet because they were pieces of canvas smeared with oils—were constantly shouting at him anyway. They'd been a reminder of the kind of artist Oren was not, and maybe for this reason—regret or desire—they were the first thing he thought of after the fall.

Fey sat at the end of the garden path, waiting for him, beak pointed upward. Oren's eyes followed the beak and saw a darkened sky. Something had happened, he knew this much. All the windows in his cottage had broken, and there was no accounting for the way the plum tree—which had defied all odds in growing there in the first place—had dropped all its shriveled plums to the ground while he was unconscious. There was no logic to the hundreds of dusty moth carcasses scattered across the lawn, while Fey flew to his feet as alive as ever.

He'd seen this iteration of death many times in his dreams. It always happened the same way, although he could never tell if he was the one dying in the dream or if he was just seeing a vision of someone else's death. But it had visited him so many times that now he was sure this must have been *it*. Although the rest of it—the part that came after, where he was still standing there in his own garden—was unexpected. Did the dead always walk as ghosts through the same world they'd only recently left?

Oren looked back at the spot where he'd landed, thinking if he was dead, his spirit would have exited his body. Thinking he would see himself there, lying twisted on the ground, and wondering what it would look like to someone, whoever that was, when they did find him. When he'd fallen, he was sure he'd broken his neck and maybe even his arm. But it seemed the only body he had was the one he was still in, as there was nothing in the garden but the weeds and failing tomatoes.

Perhaps, then, it was not the fall that was destined to kill him.

With Fey perched on his shoulder, he hiked into town, following the coastline along the cliff edge and then down the hill, reaching the edge of Violette in an eerie daytime darkness. Glass glittered on the pavement like stars that had lost their way. He tried to ask someone what had happened but didn't try again when he found that the person clearly hadn't heard—or even seen—him.

He passed a man standing by the river, one leg propped up on the bridge railing. The man ran his hand over his calf multiple times, and Oren thought he might be hurt, but as he got closer, he recognized the man as someone he had tattooed once upon a time, and what the man was looking at was not a wound but a cursive phrase that Oren himself had put there in ink. The man seemed confused by its presence on his skin.

It wasn't five minutes later that Oren came across a couple with matching moon tattoos. He overheard them talking about not remembering them at all—not having chosen the design, not having sat in a chair with their arms under a vibrating needle. He remembered the dream that had inspired the tattoos—they'd both heard someone reading lines from a story about a man who was in love with the moon, who climbed a ladder to reach her, who then looked down with longing at his abandoned planet.

But they compared their skin and shook their heads, and didn't seem to notice him.

When he reached his shop, he climbed through the broken window and brushed glass from the counter. The people he'd seen on the street hadn't remembered their tattoos, but the shop was still there, his leather stool still pushed against the wall, the lamps and instruments organized exactly as he had left them the night before. But, strangely, his book of drawings and photos of all the tattoos he'd done in the past was missing.

Outside, people were closing and locking the doors to their shops and pubs, even though the shattered windows left gaping holes that anyone could use to enter. He walked closely to people, sneaking looks at as many of his tattoos as he could, while no one could see him. He followed just behind them on the boardwalk and sat next to them in the park. No one seemed to remember these strange images or where they'd come from. What Oren saw and heard again and again with each encounter was that the ink was still there, but the artist—and even the dream that had inspired the art—had been forgotten.

Oren made his way down the long path to the lighthouse, and as he reached the tall white tower, Fey flew from his shoulder to the gallery deck railing, cawing out to no one.

They visited the lighthouse often, but rarely during the day. Always at night, when the chances that he'd run into other people along the way were much slimmer and he could watch the waves move beneath the cliff wall, slow and repeating. It was where he came to think, to sort out the world. Beneath the tower, he climbed the giant granite boulders that spilled toward the sea. Waves pummeled them as they always had, white spray just barely reaching the place where he sat.

Usually, in the dark, he made a game of trying to follow Fey's wings—black, with only the subtlest of movements against a black sky.—Usually, he imagined fish dreaming with their eyes open, seabirds asleep in their cliffside burrows. It was different in the daylight. Seeing things in the light, from this new perspective, somehow seemed fitting on this particular day, when his circumstances had changed so much.

He took his sketchbook out of his back pocket, and with a fine black marker, he divided the page into four angular boxes and began laying out his thoughts in comic book style. In the first box, he sketched the rooftop and the cartoon figure of a man sitting on it. In the second, he drew the figure falling to the ground. The third box he left blank, and in the fourth, he drew himself walking away toward the raven—the only creature who knew what had actually happened. Fey could not fill in the third box for him, so he'd have to unravel the story on his own.

He stretched his arms. The swirls and characters and symbols that decorated every inch of them had meaning. They told stories: they held within them a moment of who Oren had been at the time they were put there. They had a purpose, and he'd hoped to give that kind of purpose to others as well. But what did it all really mean anyway, and where was it all going in the end?

What mark had he left on the world? Some scratches on bodies that would also one day die and decompose. When people came into his tattoo shop, they often had fears about the permanence of putting ink on their bodies. Whatever they chose would be there forever, they said, and even though he'd reassured them that nothing was truly permanent, he'd never thought much about how silly this idea was until now. What would endure, he realized, were his father's paintings, which Oren had gone and brought from Ireland himself. They'd been kept in the dark basement of a museum, and Oren had taken them back, unable to leave such beauty in darkness no matter how much he and his father had disagreed.

Oren realized then that one thing was true: his father's passion had remained a passion until the day he died, while Oren's love for tattooing had faded considerably into a general interest and then even further into a dull obligation. For all the times they'd argued about what was true art and what wasn't, at the very least his father had done what he loved.

Just before he died, Oren had been cataloging gratitude. Recently, he'd learned there was a chance his daughter may have come back into his life. In fact, he'd spoken to her mother and written their address down the previous morning—a conversation he'd considered a great victory. But he would be forced now to make his peace with the impossibility of their tentative plans to meet, and he did make his peace with it, for now, because he knew how quickly things could change—the good and the bad in equal measure.

Nothing, nothing, nothing in this world was actually permanent—he finally understood this truth—not even, when it all came down to it, the granite beneath him. Perhaps not even death. The thought spun his mind in too many directions.

Life should be much simpler than all that.

As simple as fish and crabs and sea otters. As simple as clams tumbling across the seafloor and giant whales rocking to sleep on vast black tides. This was the only solace he ever had—that it would all go on with or without him.

When the sea returned to its normal smoky blue, the sun no longer obscured by clouds, Oren was still sitting on the edge of the cliff, Fey beside him. A fierce wind was moving in off the ocean, Oren's clothes flapping against his chest and Fey's feathers ruffling up. The lighthouse stood steady, silent through its battering by the wind and waves.

Oren returned to town.

He continued taking in as much of the world as possible before this—whatever *this* was—ended. Fey flew ahead, and they followed the boardwalk toward the bridge. The writer, Hayden MacKenna, was sitting on a bench on the other side of the river, talking with two women. One was the owner of the bakery across the street from his tattoo shop. The other, the one with the black-and-tan mountain dog, he didn't know, but he could see, even from a distance, that she was special.

They all seemed to be talking about something important, which he took as an opportunity to learn more about the morning's event. Since he had no need to worry about his safety, and the shortest distance between two places was a straight line, he jumped into the river and swam across rather than taking the bridge.

He crashed into the water, then trudged up toward the bank, and as he pulled himself out onto the grass, his long hair dripping and his shirt clinging to his skin, he realized the group had turned to watch him.

Fey flew down and landed on the redheaded woman's shoulder as Oren said, with as little shock in his voice as he could manage, "Well, I guess you're all dead, too, then, eh?"

7

They'd watched Oren Ainsley step out of the water, a look of astonishment on his face when he realized he was not invisible to them, a moment they had all experienced, but by then Alma was no longer surprised. Not when she heard the word *ghost* for the fifteenth time. Not even when the raven flew to her shoulder without hesitation, as if they'd been friends in some other time or universe.

She'd stumbled into Lucie after she'd finally had the courage to get up off the cottage floor. When she'd looked at Jupiter and said *walk*, his head jolted up as it had when she'd first found him. They'd gone toward the beach, stopping at the bridge to assess the state of the town after the flash of light, where Lucie was talking to the writer Alma had seen at the bonfire. Alma waved, and Lucie's reaction was so dramatic that Alma stood startled, looking behind her to see who Lucie was actually waving to. "She seems excited to see us," she told Jupiter.

"Oh no, are you?" Lucie asked as they approached. "My god, Alma, I'm sorry."

"For what?" Alma said.

Lucie stepped closer and whispered, "Well, if you can see me, you must have . . . you know. Died."

"What? No," Alma said. "What are you talking about?"

"That's just, well, the only thing we can think of to explain what happened to us. We seem to be ghosts. Me and Hayden. And I guess you, too, then."

"Oh," Alma said, drawing the word out as she began to absorb that whatever Lucie was describing about herself was the same thing she'd experienced after the flash of light, but with Emerson, and about Jupiter. "No, I'm not, but Jupiter . . . and you . . . oh."

"I don't understand this," Lucie said. "I feel like I'm dreaming some horrible dream."

It was clear right away that Alma was not one of them because she was still seen and heard by the other people around them, but she was also the only one who could see and hear the presumed dead. She had known Lucie before and remembered her now, which was far more than they could say for Lucie's own roommate. And though she'd never actually met them, she remembered the writer and the tattooist from the beach the night before.

There was no obvious explanation for why Alma was the only one, but she was there with them now, so she was immediately careful not to *look* like she was talking to no one. And she was somehow tied to them, too, because though she had not died, Jupiter had, she was sure of it now.

"Should we be looking for other . . . ghosts?" Lucie asked.

"I walked all over town, many times," Oren said. "I didn't see anyone else like us until I saw you."

"If they're out there, we'll find them," Hayden said. "There are only so many people in this town. And if what happened to us was coincidental—the lightning and our deaths—three already seems like a lot."

"Four," Alma said, pointing to Jupiter.

"Of course," Hayden said. "I'm sorry. Is the bird a part of this too?"

Oren opened his mouth but changed his mind and leaned against the bench, then simply said, "She's something else altogether."

"Well, either way, we need to call this something. Give it a name," Hayden said.

"Does that really matter?" Lucie asked. "At this moment, there are four people, one dog, and one bird here who know about whatever *this* is. And I'm just hoping it will be over before too long."

"Doesn't matter to me," Oren said. "And I'm with the baker, for what it's worth."

"Lucie," she said. "I'm Lucie."

"Well, it should matter," Hayden said, suddenly irritated. "Names are important. They give things significance. How do we talk about something without the damn words for it?" The group looked at Hayden in silence, until finally he threw up his hands and said, "You can leave it to me, if nobody cares. I'll think of something."

The four humans—three dead and one living—plus one dead dog and one possibly mythical bird, who had yet to name their circumstances, decided to split up to look for others and to see what it was like to move through the world now that they were not quite so alone. The group planned to meet later at the lighthouse, because it was lonely and quiet there, and if there was ever a place for creatures who had left-and-yet-not-left the earth, that was it.

Before departing, Lucie grabbed Alma's hand.

"Theo probably doesn't remember me," she said, "if what happened with Odette means anything for the rest of the people here."

Alma was surprised that, though the look on Lucie's face was one of confusion and desperation, Alma felt nothing when they touched. Nothing good, nothing bad. Just . . . nothing. And nothing, well, nothing was good in her mind.

"I can try to—"

"No, don't," Lucie said quickly. "If you could, don't tell him anything about this, please. If he doesn't remember me, maybe that's for the best."

"Why would that be . . . ," Alma began. "I don't know if I can keep something like this from him. Emerson said he's already acting confused."

"I don't know what was going to happen between us," Lucie interrupted, "but maybe this is the way it should be. For now, anyway. If he doesn't remember me, he can't suffer for losing me."

Alma could understand this. She looked at the others, wondering if they, too, would allow her to feel the same sense of calm she'd felt when Lucie reached for her. "Don't worry," she said. "It can be between us, for now."

~~~

Hayden looked like all the fishermen Alma had seen in movies as a child. Thick white beard streaked with gray, heavy wool sweaters. She pictured him sitting in the dark corner of a pub after a long trip out on the water, cradling a pipe, eyes hiding beneath a newsboy cap. But Hayden had never wanted to be a fisherman. In fact, he'd intentionally steered as far away from it as possible and despised being on boats.

This was what he told Alma a week after the lightning flash when they met again by the lighthouse. She'd been walking alone—well, walking with Jupiter, which to anyone else would have looked like walking alone. It was still too unreal, this middle ground she was treading between the dead and the living. And it was still hard to accept the idea that Jupiter had died, when he was still right there in front of her.

It was impossible not to feel crazy and intertwined with it all. She'd been staring out at the water. Then Hayden had come up behind her and whispered her name and she'd jumped so much she'd nearly tumbled into the sea.

They sat on the rocky face that overlooked the inlet, brown kelp rolling in the waves below. Though she'd really only just met them— aside from Lucie, whom she'd known only a few weeks anyway—Alma had felt a sense of responsibility for this small group. And then, on top of that, for the first time in her life, she didn't feel an overwhelming number of emotions when they were around. She found that when she was sitting next to Hayden, for example, there was a very simple line drawn between what she was feeling and what he was—if he was feeling anything at all.

At that moment, with her dog lying beside her on one side, and the aged writer sitting on the other, the waves below were just waves and the clouds above were just clouds.

"We're stuck," Hayden said. "I know exactly what this is."

Oren and Lucie had spent the previous few days wandering around town, looking for others like them and trying to understand what had happened. They'd almost been caught a number of times. At her bakery, Lucie saw a teacup left on a table by a customer and couldn't resist picking it up. The woman at the neighboring table began rubbing her eyes, and Lucie quickly dropped the cup. Oren returned to his tattoo shop to look one more time for his book of photos. He shuffled through drawers for nearly two minutes before he noticed the woman who had walked in. She stood, staring, until Oren looked up and realized she was likely watching papers flutter out of the drawer of their own accord.

But Hayden had spent most of his time at the lighthouse, watching the sea, because he didn't need to be told. He knew. Hayden placed a manuscript in Alma's lap. The paper was old and water stained, and there was a simple sketch of a mountain on the front page. *Their* mountain, which Alma recognized right away. The book was titled *Tower of Echoes*.

"Well, I know you haven't read this one," he said, then paused, as if waiting for her to tell him which of his books she *had* read. "Anyway," he went on, "the radio tower is the key to all of this, I'm sure of it. I wrote about the tower here, a long time ago. No one was willing to actually publish it—too weird, they said. Too quote unquote experimental. Even I thought I was crazy for a while."

"So, what does it say?" Alma asked.

"Well," Hayden said. "We've all heard the broadcasts that come through our houses from the tower on Onde Mountain. People just assume that someone's out there, talking into a microphone, maybe on the other side of the world, but actually *there*, currently speaking."

"And you disagree?"

"That certainly happens, of course. But I think it's more than that. I think some of the broadcasts are coming from somewhere else, from another time. Definitely the past, but also maybe the future. Like the tower holds a collection of echoes. Have you heard the stories, the dreams?"

"Not many, no," Alma said. "I haven't been here that long, and I don't . . . get out much. How did you come up with this theory?"

"Let's just say I've experienced things that have led to the conclusion."

"What does all of this have to do with you and Oren and Lucie? And Jupiter?" Alma buried her hand into Jupiter's fur, her feet dangling over the edge of the cliff. Sometimes, she couldn't stop herself from thinking about what it would feel like to fall, always brought back to the most likely cause of Alex's death. Still, she frequently found herself close to these places—ones where enough space and gravity existed and she was in control of whether she decided to use them.

"We're like those broadcasts, those echoes. Like any other sound wave that the tower has collected. When it was struck by lightning—as we all seem to agree that it was—it's like instead of going wherever we were supposed to go, we got trapped instead."

"Did you have any ideas about the rest of it? A way to make the echoes go away?" It wasn't even close to what she'd meant to ask. It sounded harsh. She bit her lip, wishing the right words came to her more easily.

But Hayden just laughed. He clasped his fingers in his lap and looked into his palms. "Ha! Honestly, I never even thought about that.

But *Echoes*—that's a good word for us. Thank you. I absolutely despise the term *ghosts*. But also, I do think, somehow, this book was meant for you. I wrote it for this fictional person, this character that was an amalgamation of experiences I heard over the years through the tower, all pieced together. Maybe the character isn't all you, but it's like I knew the idea of you was out there even before I knew the real you existed. And that somehow you'd be able to make sense of my theories."

"What can *I* do?" Alma asked.

"I don't know. Maybe you should read the book. At the very least, I'd like for someone that I loved very much not to have forgotten me. If there's a way for you to help me do that, I'd appreciate it."

It wasn't an answer. Not really. She wished he would elaborate more on these pieced-together experiences, these things he'd heard. But what he gave her was enough of a reason to think about it. As Alma left, Lucie was walking around the lighthouse tower, looking the sides of the structure up and down. She whispered something to herself, which, when Alma passed, sounded like a list of ingredients. "I'm afraid I might forget," she said. Oren was standing farther down the shoreline, as close as possible to the cliff edge without falling off, his toes sticking out into the air. He rocked back and forth as if the very idea of consequence did not exist.

‿‿‿

Two days later, Hayden was standing on Alma's doorstep as she was about to leave for Bea's. "Why are you here?" he asked, his arms crossed over his chest.

Alma considered telling him the truth—that she'd lost her fiancé and had run away from everyone because she had a particular problem with not being able to separate her own feelings from those of others and this had seemed like a good place to become lost in one's own world—but instead she just said, "I have family."

Hayden squinted at her. "Well," he said, "this isn't a place people just *come* to, is it? Not now anyway. But it doesn't matter. I already know why you're here."

"And why's that?"

"Because you can't be anywhere else. Can I come in?"

"I really don't know how I can help you. And why do you think I can't be anywhere else?" Alma attempted to stretch herself across the doorway, but her elbow missed the doorframe and she lost her balance. She caught herself and stood up straight, blocking the space more confidently the second time.

"It's the same reason we're all still here. Except the rest of us were here already and chose to stay. You're the only one who, when it made the least sense, decided to come. The question is why."

"I'm not very good with people," she said.

"That's obvious enough."

"I talk to my dog a lot. It was weird before, when he was alive. It's even weirder now. I don't do well with most of the people I do know, let alone strangers."

"What's the story with the dog, anyway?"

Alma flinched. "There's no story. He's just my dog. What was it you wanted me to do again?"

"Alphie Roy," Hayden said. "He runs a wildlife refuge north of town. I want you to go and apologize to him for me, and remind him that I existed. I can't do that on my own."

Alma considered this. She tried to imagine herself strolling up to a stranger's home, apologizing on behalf of someone that the man didn't remember anyway, attempting to explain who this person had been, the fact that he'd died.

"I'd sound crazy," she said.

"I considered that. But you know, I have an idea. I used to run the local newspaper. It's been sitting there, just a dark office, for over a decade. You can use the office and write my story there—it's practically already written. Then you can print it, let people in town read it, and make sure Alphie sees it. Who knows, maybe the other Echoes will have stories they want to tell, too, and it could be a way to remind people of who we were."

She opened the door wider to let Hayden inside, leaning against the counter where she'd been reading one of Alex's letters. She folded it up behind her back and slipped it into the envelope.

"You left this, by the way," Hayden said as he passed her, handing her the printed copy of his book, then sitting at the kitchen table. He examined a jade plant in the center of the table that had dropped nearly all its leaves. "All I know is I need you. We need you. And you seem like you could use an occupation."

Alma laughed. "I've always hated that idea. That people have to have a job to do. What if I'm happy?"

"You're not. Don't think so hard. It'll be good for you. See? Now we need each other."

After he left, Alma sat at the kitchen table with his manuscript. She brushed aside the fallen jade leaves and turned to the first page. It began like a series of rambling fragments, glimpses into thoughts or memory. But whose thoughts, whose memory, she wasn't sure.

> Sound is a mechanical wave that requires a medium to travel from one place to another. These are things you learned in elementary school, when Mrs. Murphy drew a picture on the board of an arcing line with the wavelength measured horizontally and the amplitude vertically. Distance was drawn as a long flat stroke through the middle.
>
> Then she divided the class into pairs, and each pair got a piece of yarn, a spoon, and a ruler. You tied the yarn around the spoon, then wrapped the other end of it around your fingertips, pressing

them against your ears. You leaned forward a little. The spoon hung like a pendulum at your waist.

When your partner tapped the spoon with the ruler, you heard the sound of a bell.

The impact of the ruler created a vibration, a wave of sound. The yarn acted like a conductor. You alone—because you were the one with the conductor pressed against your ears—heard the sound.

You watched your partner's eyes widen when it was his turn.

When you tried a larger spoon, the sound was less like a bell, more like a gong.

For a long time, you dwelled on the idea that whoever was holding the string was the only one who could hear the sound. As if that wave was created for your ears alone. A broadcast that no one else could hear but you.

Echoes occur when a sound wave reaches a barrier, the end of its medium, and reflects back. An echo can occur only if the barrier is at least seventeen meters away from where the sound originated. The reflected sound must return to the ear at least 0.1 seconds after the original was created.

Later, you did another experiment, this time with your father. You stood next to him, one hundred meters away from a wall, a stopwatch in his hand, two wooden blocks in yours. He counted to three, and in unison, you clapped the blocks together and he started the timer. He stopped the timer when you heard the echo of the clap. The speed of sound equals distance divided by time. It seemed like an easy equation.

But, as you crouched to do the math, your notebook folded open on your knee, he stopped you. "How can we be sure the number is correct?" he asked.

You shrugged, looked down, and continued to scribble. "Even if it's not, it couldn't be that far off, right?" you said, and he told you that human reaction time can account for errors, which means you have to employ more than one method for certainty.

So, you tried something else. Your father started the timer when you clapped the blocks, just as he had before. But this time, when you heard the first echo, you clapped the blocks again. You did this over and over until you were in sync with the echoes. Ten times.

You sat on the pavement and wrote the same equation, this time with the distance multiplied by ten. You compared the second equation's results to the first. They were almost the same, and this seemed satisfying. But then you looked at your father again, and he told you that if you remembered one thing, it was that the very small details in life matter a great deal.

~~~

Later that evening, Alma found Bea in the backyard painting a weather vane, humming to herself. "I swear I'm only doing this because I can't bring myself to do anything else," Bea said. "Life is just too wild for words sometimes, so then you're left with paintbrushes."

They talked about the flash of light. The gaps in people's memories. The forgotten dreams. Despite the group that had hiked up the mountain to confirm that, yes, the tower had been struck—two antennas near the top had burned and collapsed into one another—there was still no answer to the strange way people were responding to the event. Bea and Emerson had managed to keep some perspective, assuming whatever it was, it would sort itself out, but Theo—he was the one Bea was worried about.

"He just seems lost," she said. "Like he's missing something important, but he doesn't know what it is. Nobody does."

"Where is he now?" Alma asked.

"On the boat, again. He'd just gone out when the storm rolled in. He thinks if he goes back on the water, maybe he'll remember or figure something out."

Alma had decided on the way over that she couldn't tell anyone else the specifics of the situation until she had a better grasp on it herself. But it was hard not to mention Lucie, the answer to Bea's questions and Theo's mounting confusion. Saying anything would likely only create more distress. Alma was a little relieved to think of Theo out on the water, where she wouldn't have to lie to him about knowing exactly why he was feeling unsettled. About knowing exactly what—or who—he was missing.

"I'm sorry you were alone for all that," Bea said, and Alma found herself frantic for a moment, looking for Jupiter, but he was just there, on the other side of the fence, sniffing around beneath Bea's lilac bushes, and she realized Bea was not referring to his death.

"Oh, the light," Alma said. "It's okay. I don't mind being alone."

"You didn't come by just to check on me, did you?" Bea asked. "Because you know I'm always okay being alone."

Alma almost reached out to touch Bea's arm. But she felt Bea's uneasiness moving through her right away and pulled her hand back.

"No, no. I just thought I'd run something by you. I'm thinking of taking a job."

"Why do you need a job?" Bea asked, and Alma smiled.

"It's less of a job, more of a project."

"Sounds like a decent idea. So, what's wrong with it?"

"I don't know. I guess I'm just curious if you think it's worthwhile. The town newspaper hasn't been running for years, and the office is just sitting there empty. I was thinking of opening it up, writing some stories. Maybe stories about people here. Would anyone want to read that?"

"Shoot, I didn't even remember that we *had* a newspaper." Bea squinted and bit her lip as she dabbed a tiny white dot gently onto the fox's eye. Suddenly, the fox was looking at Alma.

Bea put down her paintbrush and said, "When it comes down to it, we're all just a culmination of experiences. And when we lose those, what do we have? I think people here could use a little hope right now, something to remind them what living here is all about."

"It is, honestly, a little outside my comfort zone. Although it *is* something I can do."

"It's not easy, you know, living with Theo going off the way he does all the time. Every time he leaves to get us supplies, I see a replay, over and over, of what I imagine Hubert's accident was like." On cue, the wind picked up and rushed through the lilacs, and Bea held tight to the weather vane to stop it from flapping back and forth.

"So why don't you say something?" Alma asked. "Why not ask him not to go? Someone else could go."

"No," said Bea. "That's the thing. Someone else can't go. He's the best person for the job. We need him."

Alma thought about Hayden saying he needed her—that *they* needed her—and about her being the only one that could remind people about him and Lucie and Oren. She considered his ideas about the radio tower and pictured his manuscript sitting on her kitchen table.

There were three people who had been forgotten by everyone, except for her. Lucie's own fiancé had forgotten her. Jupiter was standing right next to Alma, and yet Bea couldn't see him and didn't know that he'd ever existed. If she tried to talk about any of these people, or of her own dog, she would sound insane.

She searched for a way to ask for Bea's advice without actually revealing anything. The best she could come up with was, "Do you believe in an afterlife?"

"I believe in monuments," she said. "Monuments to who we were, something left behind. Maybe it's a canoe floating on the water. Maybe it's as simple as that."

Alma considered this. She had a box full of Alex's things, and they were all precious to her, but she'd never thought of them as monuments before. She had his story, full of sorrow as it was, permanently intertwined with her own. That was a monument.

All Hayden had asked for was a story.

Clouds gathered over the ocean, dark and rolling in toward shore. Bea began picking up her paintbrushes—red and orange and yellow smearing the front of her dress. "Bury me in this, will you?" she said, and she slipped into the house, the hem catching in the door for a moment.

"Come on, bud," Alma called to Jupiter, covering her mouth with her hand as soon as the words escaped. Bea turned to pull her dress free, the door clanging shut, and Alma thought she caught a smile through the screen before she vanished.

PART 3
DREAMING IN FREQUENCIES

2026–2036

8

Contact, 2004

When she was ten, her family drove two hours from their home in Sebec, Maine, to Bar Harbor, where they boarded a four-hour ferry to Yarmouth, Nova Scotia. A meteor shower was expected the day after they arrived, although they hadn't needed to go so far to see it—its occurrence coincided with a vacation that was already planned. One-half of Alma's very large extended family on her father's side—which had remained close as Alma and her many cousins grew up—traveled with them to visit the rest of the family that lived on the coast a half hour north of Yarmouth.

The boat docked, and they drove up the coast to a row of rental cottages along the rocky western shore, where Alma's father and his brothers had each rented an A-frame cabin for their respective families. Alma and her brother, René, their noses used to the smell of the ocean, spilled out of the car like fish from a bucket, their legs cramped and itching to run to the water. Her cousins swarmed the tennis courts and horseshoe pits, but Alma and René went looking for snails. They crawled down the black ridges barefoot toward the tide pools, fished around with their fingers until they came up with limpets and periwinkles and tiny green crabs.

The family gathered in a big hall in the evening to eat and drink. They were a family who liked to celebrate almost as much as they liked to compete. Alma's uncles had organized Olympic-style games for the kids, though Alma avoided joining in at all costs. They let her duck out because they knew she was the quiet one, and they liked her for that, but also because there were so many little ones running around that they couldn't keep track of who was doing what. She watched from a seat in the back of the room while René and her younger cousins played a magnetic fishing game.

One uncle walked around with a clipboard. They were all expected to sign up for a group skit to entertain everyone while they ate. Alma's heart pounded until she found out it was only for the adults. They were drunk and having too much fun. They laughed until they cried watching one another act out their favorite movie scenes. Someone walked around with a video camera.

Uncle Hubert and Aunt Bea arrived from Violette then, late into dinner, with the twins, Theo and Emerson, trailing behind like lifeboats bobbing on waves. They had just turned fourteen, and Alma always watched their family's calm composure with envy. Although Hubert was born in Maine with Alma's father, he'd moved away to the island when he met Bea. He built canoes, and Bea painted canvases and weather vanes, and the rest of the Hughes family talked quietly when they weren't around about how they must not care about family anymore and how they didn't put as much effort into these gatherings as the rest of them. How weird they were. There was always a little awkwardness when they arrived at a family function, but it was soon forgotten when the food and the scotch came out.

The following evening, the whole group lay on blankets on the beach with their eyes upward, waiting for streaks of light to fall from above. In the dark, one of her cousins got up and began to run around as if possessed. He charged into the water, splashing and shouting at the sky. He pulled seaweed up from the muddy bottom of the ocean and smacked it around. Then he scaled the dunes on all fours like a gorilla and ran across the grassy field in the dark, until eventually he slammed into a tree and broke his nose.

Alma had heard that eclipses could make people do irrational things, but she'd never heard that about meteor showers. Perhaps all celestial activity had the potential for penetrating the minds of humans and finding their instability, their volatility.

The meteorites darted across the sky in all directions, with varying degrees of brightness. Alma tried to follow them from where they originated to where they disappeared, but she found it too frustrating. It was easier to focus on one static constellation and trust her peripheral vision would be strong enough to catch the shooting stars as they dropped through the atmosphere. She chose Cassiopeia.

Each time she saw one, seemingly born of the darkness, a tail of light stretching and fading in its wake, her breath stopped in her throat and she reminded herself to exhale.

Later that night, while the parents played cribbage and the cousins played dominoes, Alma heard a voice from outside. It sounded like a dulled radio transmission, carried by the wind. She swore it was saying something about a man in the water. She sneaked out of the cabin, walked past the tennis and croquet courts and picnic tables, and found herself alone on the beach beneath the stars. The pebbles stretched in either direction until it was too dark to see anymore, and the water glittered with the reflections of stars. She tried to find Perseus in the sky, or Andromeda, the part of the sky where the meteorites had been earlier, but instead she saw a pulsing light on the horizon. A beacon, far off in the distance.

She was surprised to find that she wasn't the only one who saw it. A man materialized in the darkness and climbed down the rocks. He took his shoes and socks off and left them on the sand. He rolled his pant legs up to his knees and began wading into the water, not stopping when the waves reached his clothing. When he was in up to his waist, he dove and swam, heading farther and farther out. The light continued to beat there, and Alma wondered if it was possible to see a lighthouse from that far across the bay.

After a minute, the man was out of sight, and Alma heard her parents calling from the cabin. Assuming the man knew how to swim and that it was just too dark to see him, she ran up the path and back inside, saying nothing about what she'd seen. The kids drank hot chocolate and invented games, hiding behind the twin beds and using their dominoes as ammunition for their pretend war. She and one of her cousins had brought radios—big boxy things with knobs that had to be turned exactly right to find a clear station—and they extended the antennas to make swords.

When they'd all gone back to their own cabins and should have been sleeping, Alma lay in bed with a quilt pulled up to her chin. She hoped the man had turned around and swum back to shore. With her radio resting on her chest, she turned the knobs, curious about what stations she might pick up there, so far from home. Through the crackling of an AM station, she heard a man's muffled voice repeating over and over: *Man in the water, man in the water.* It was the same voice she'd heard earlier. Alma turned the radio off quickly and closed her eyes, the way she would if one of her parents had just peeked into the room to make sure she was sleeping.

The voice on the radio could not have been talking about the same man she'd seen on the beach. She tried to sleep but kept thinking about the broadcast. Somehow it seemed meant for her ears.

In the morning, Alma thought she saw the man again, standing in the tall grass behind the beach. But that was impossible, because a moment later, the rumbling of a helicopter vibrated overhead, and a crowd of people accumulated on the shore, and the man's body was being dragged from the sea. A frantic woman appeared on the beach, crying, saying the man must have been drunk. He must have drowned.

Alma heard the broadcast come through again, this time on one of the radios attached to a rescuer's belt: *Man in the water, man in the water.* It was the same call, the same voice. They'd only found the man just then, so how could she have heard it the previous night? How could she have heard it before the man had even started swimming, and again when she was lying in bed just a short time after?

Sitting apart from the crowd was a boy about Alma's age. His black hair was shaved in the back but long over his forehead. He'd climbed on top of a boulder to see better but crouched and hugged his knees, as if he wasn't sure he really wanted the view after all. His eyes kept shifting from the choppy waves to the woman crying on the beach.

As more people gathered, Alma sneaked away and climbed onto the rock to join the boy.

"Do you know what happened?" she asked.

"Not really," the boy said, shivering even though it was a warm summer day. "Some guy drowned, I guess. People were just acting weird, all confused, and then eventually they found him out there, in the water."

Alma thought of the night before, the pulsing light, the man swimming beneath the stars, and how she'd left just after losing sight of him. There was no way anyone would ever know this, but if someone asked her, she wouldn't be able to lie. She wasn't sure if she was responsible for what happened. She wasn't sure how to open her mouth and speak the words.

"Did you know him?" she asked. Alma turned her head away, pretending to follow a seagull overhead. Her heart had begun beating fast as the agitation of everyone around began to seep in.

"No," the boy said, shifting to sit cross-legged, looking down into his lap. "I just don't like being in crowds. Especially when people are . . . upset."

"I . . ." Alma tried to think of anything to say to help him, but she had the same problem and didn't know how to help herself. She wanted to ask why he didn't just leave but was afraid of pressing too much. She reached into the back pocket of her jean shorts and pulled out a cassette tape. "Here," she said, handing him an album by The Tragically Hip that she'd taken from her father's car. "Do you have a player?"

The boy shrugged but didn't answer. He took the tape and pressed his thumb against the crack in the plastic case. The sun glinted, a tiny spark of rainbow light.

"Have you heard it?" she asked.

The boy shook his head, eyes still focused on the chaos below. The helicopter lifted up higher into the sky and flew off, leaving the beach in a stunned quiet.

"It's *In Violet Light*," Alma said. "Well, you can read. I mean, I'm assuming you can. It's my dad's, but he probably won't ask for it back for a while, and I'm sure I can figure out a way to explain it. Just listen to it. It always makes me feel better. I'll give you my address. You can send it back to me when you're done with it."

"Why doesn't your dad listen to CDs?"

"He has this really old car, it's like an '88, and he won't put a CD player in it, so he just keeps listening to tapes. But that one just came out. I mean, it's not old."

She'd never heard so many words come out of her own mouth at once. Her breath was tight in her throat. It wasn't until after she'd walked away that she realized she hadn't told him her name, or asked for his, or given him the address like she'd said she would.

The following morning, she saw him on the porch of the cabin where he and his mom were staying. His mom was bringing suitcases to the car. Alma quickly wrote the address on a piece of paper and told herself to keep her mouth shut as she strode up and held it out.

"I'm sorry if I was being annoying yesterday," she said.

He was wearing a sweatshirt with the hood pulled over his head, and when he looked up, Alma saw he had headphones on and was holding a cassette player in his lap.

She hid her smile by looking at her frayed shoelaces.

He reached for the piece of paper, and Alma backed away because she didn't want to say any more stupid things whether he heard them or not.

A few months after she returned home to Maine, the first letter arrived. There was a photo with it—a color photo taken of another black-and-white photo. It was one of those educational signs with information about a place's historical significance. In the picture, a farmhouse was surrounded by four wooden radio towers. The house was at the edge of a cliff, white-capped waves below. There were hundreds of antenna cables connecting the towers. The burgundy cursive writing at the bottom corner of the sign said, "Glace Bay, Nova Scotia, 1910."

The letter was addressed to *Miss Hughes*, with the return address written in the top left corner of the envelope: *Alexandre Laurent. Weymouth, Nova Scotia.* The handwriting was remarkably good.

The text:

> *Dear Alma,*
> *We went to the Marconi National Historic Site, but it doesn't look anything like this picture now. It's where the first transatlantic wireless signal was sent by Guglielmo Marconi. I'm writing a letter because this place reminded me of you, and we're always having make-believe conversations in my head. Like I'm sending you signals. Signal back if you want.*
> *Alex L.*
> *PS: Do you know Morse code? You should.*

The Tragically Hip tape wasn't returned, but Alma hadn't expected it to be. She hadn't actually expected to hear from him ever again. And she *really* hadn't expected a letter in which he asked her to respond.

She swallowed her lemonade and laid the letter and photo on the grass. The fact that there were hundreds of miles between them made no difference. She laid herself in the grass, too, and wondered what kind of imaginary conversations he was talking about and if the library had a book about Morse code.

9

Alma took Hayden's offer to use the old newspaper office and inherited, in this way, all she would need to design and print whatever she'd like. She hadn't actually written anything since leaving the magazine job, and the idea was intimidating, but for the moment, all she had to do was wait for Hayden.

The newspaper office was in the basement of a brick building, beneath Hayden's apartment. He'd warned her it was perpetually flooded, water always seeping in even on dry days, so everything had been raised up somehow—on shelves or hangers or blocks—to avoid it getting wet, and when Alma asked why he didn't just move the office somewhere else, he said, "It's the quietest place in Violette aside from the lighthouse. No one ever thinks to come find you there." And that was all she needed to hear.

When she'd gone inside for the first time, she stood in the doorway in tall rubber boots and glanced around at the boxes of old copies of the *Violette Chronicle* and unused newsprint, dozens of crates of office supplies, the antiquated printing equipment—an offset machine propped on concrete blocks to avoid the puddle below. Alma tried to remember where she'd been less than a week before, when she'd been so sure that all she needed was to categorize the world, to identify and name everything, put everything in its right place. But then all those plans had been so quickly upended. Rather than walk long hours in the woods with books about plants and wildlife, she'd been thrown these new, quite unknowable circumstances.

Lucie and Oren continued looking for other Echoes, just in case, but they spent most of their time at the lighthouse, where Lucie could watch Theo's boat pass in and out of the inlet, and Oren could test his boundaries. He had tried dying again a number of times, jumping from the cliffs, jumping from the lighthouse. Swimming out to sea farther and farther, each time returning more disappointed by the lack of fatigue. But they hadn't found any other Echoes or anyone else who could see them. And they still hadn't gained a better understanding of why they were there and for how long.

Oren asked Alma to go into his tattoo shop, to check the little pad of paper sitting by the cash register, and bring him the address he'd written down the day before he died.

"It's important that I get it before someone goes in there and tears the place apart," he said. "Not that anyone will, but just in case. I don't know what I'll do with it at this point, but I need to have it."

He could have gone on his own, slipped unseen into the shop and retrieved the address. But the newspaper office sat just a few doors down, and Alma had been going there almost every day.

As she stepped out of Turas Tattoo—a scrap of paper clutched in her fist with the name *Lille* written at the top—she caught Theo waving to her from across the street. He'd just returned from gathering some supplies and carried a large box to the back of the bakery. Alma crossed the street, a light rain tapping gently on the hood of her raincoat. Theo came out of the bakery just as she reached it, and she noticed his eyes looked tired, less vibrant than usual.

"You okay?" she asked.

Theo looked back over his shoulder and shrugged. "Sure, I guess. Do you know the woman that runs this place?"

"Odette, yes."

"She's just always giving me these weird looks. And she's kind of standoffish. I don't think she used to be that way. I remember coming to the bakery with supplies and feeling super excited. Now I dread it. I think I'm just really tired, imagining things."

Alma glanced back to see Odette standing in the window, watching Theo leave. She did look angry, or at least unhappy. Alma hooked her arm with Theo's as they walked back toward the dock, even though the agitation he felt passed through her immediately. Sometimes it was worth pushing back. And if she couldn't tell him the truth, she at least owed him this much.

"You know," she said, "that's something that happens to me all the time. I'm always thinking people are mad at me, or have some problem with me. When I really think about it, though, it usually turns out I'm just picking up on something else they're going through."

"It's more than that," he said as they crossed the bridge. He peered over the side at the muddy river flooding the banks beneath it. "I probably shouldn't admit this. I feel horrible about it. But when I see her, I keep thinking she doesn't belong there. Just her presence makes me kind of angry."

"Maybe Odette's just having a hard time with something, and when you're near her, you feel it too. I'm sure it'll be okay."

"I wish there was some kind of reference book or something. Humans can be so damn confusing. So, what do you do, when you're picking up on other people's moods? What's the answer?"

Alma spared him the complicated equation she often used herself, in which energy equaled distance between herself and other humans added to the time between interactions, minus interruptions and life's social obligations, and multiplied by the volume of fresh air per day.

"Space," she said. "And time. Just don't take anything personally. I promise you, it doesn't do anyone any good."

"Maybe I'll hike up the mountain."

"When I said distance, I didn't mean the top of a radio tower."

Theo laughed. "Don't worry. That nonsense, I think, is finally behind me." He looked out at the sea, his eyes not resting on any place in particular. "I got back just in time. Weather." He said it flatly, as if the idea of danger and destruction no longer interested him.

Alma returned to the newspaper office, not entirely sure she'd succeeded in helping Theo, knowing there was little she could do to explain what he was going through. Pressed with a kind of guilt, too, not just for Theo but also for Odette, who probably went through something similar each time Theo came to the bakery.

As Alma tore open boxes and scrubbed the walls and cleaned spiderwebs and moth carcasses from the windowsills, peeled off sheets of paper that had been plastered to the sides of cabinets, she could hear Hayden in the apartment above, his feet shuffling across the floor as he paced back and forth and muttered about the nuances of character development.

Still looking for some order, somewhere, she often found herself holding stacks of newspapers from years ago, scanning for the stories that Hayden had printed about the radio tower. There were reports of things people had heard in their living rooms, their kitchens, their dreams. She tried to connect dots, draw a line between one experience and another.

One article, printed in a 1992 edition of the paper, was about three teenagers who'd discovered they were all having a similar dream in which they heard voices talking about their deaths as if in a news report.

Mayra Bell said, "It's only that we were making a game out of it that we compared stories and realized we were all hearing the same kind of broadcast. The voice said I would die frozen on a vast expanse of ice."

Davona Perreault said, "I was at the bottom of a lake. I had no eyes anymore by the time I was pulled up by a fishing net. Just gaping sockets."

Aiden Simonet reported what he'd heard in the third person, exactly as it was broadcast to him: "Mr. Simonet was old, so much older than anyone ever imagined he'd be, rocking in a wooden chair, muttering nonsense to himself. One day, his heart just stopped."

The dreams had occurred in 1945, but the newspaper story was written forty-seven years later, after two of the three had died. Hayden had written the article because Mayra had indeed frozen to death after getting lost on an expedition in Alaska. Davona had actually drowned, just as the voice in the dream told her she would. And Aiden, well, at the time of the article, was sitting by a window in the hospital, old and no longer able to communicate.

These kinds of stories weren't enough to make sense of the Echoes. They didn't reveal anything new about why they were there. In fact, an account of three people who had heard something about their futures being passed over radio waves only complicated things. Alma put the newspapers back in the box and opened to the next chapter of Hayden's *Tower of Echoes*.

> With the advancement of so much technology, you've always found this fact surprising: that the science of acoustics is still not well understood. Many people consider acoustics an art—in addition to a science—for this reason. What makes music enjoyable is due in large part to the way the sounds bounce off walls, ceilings, floors, other surfaces in a room. And yet this is still too complex to fully predict and manipulate.
>
> A sound is a simple thing: a vibration in the air, a pressure wave in which molecules bounce off one another. Sound waves move away from their sources like three-dimensional ripples outward.
>
> In a concert hall, only a small part of the original sound reaches our ears, and the rest is either absorbed or reflected off other surfaces and heard

as echoes or reverberations. Every time a sound wave bounces off a surface, a new sound wave is created. If the reflected sounds reach our ears less than 0.08 seconds after the original sound was made, we hear them as the same sound, which can make music sound fuller and richer. Surfaces closer to the original sound reflect sooner than the ones that are more distant. If the reflected sound comes back later, it can be perceived as an echo instead, which interferes with new waves and makes everything sound muddy or blurry.

Someone sitting close to a stage may hear mostly direct sounds and very little reflected sounds. This is actually considered a less desirable experience than the one felt by those sitting, say, in the cheap seats.

Ultimately it comes down to trial and error. The exact combination of sounds, the size and shape of the room, the materials with which the room is made, and where the listener is positioned all play into how enjoyable the sounds will be. These variables are often impossible to guess at, and so a sound may linger for a brief time or a long one, and this—the amount of time it takes for a single, fleeting sound to fade—is known as reverberation time.

It is also sometimes called decay time.

How many times did you sit in a room and try and fail to understand yourself? A hundred? A thousand? You felt your own energy, your thoughts and emotions, all bouncing around, seemingly disconnected vibrations, and you could never quite pin them down or predict what they would do next. You could never tell when they would begin, or from which direction they would come, or when they would fade, or if they would simply cease abruptly, without warning.

～～～

His story was not practically already written.

Hayden mulled over one version and then another, wanting it to be exactly right because it was, in his eyes, his only chance at presenting himself sufficiently to Alphie. And who didn't want to rewrite their own history, at least a little? At least the parts they regretted? He'd start down one road, convinced it would lead him to some currently hidden truth about the whole ordeal, about how and why he'd betrayed the man he loved, only to lose that path completely. He'd shout, "Oh, forget it," and storm off toward the lighthouse. There he would sit watching the sea, and it would be weeks before he even tried again. "I've never had so little faith in my writing abilities," he said. "It's unbelievable, but I guess it's because it suddenly means, literally, everything."

He said he wasn't coming down until he was satisfied, and then one afternoon, after three months of writing, Hayden yelled down from the apartment window—Alma was sitting on top of the desk cross-legged, sorting pushpins into piles by color—that he'd done it. He'd found the heart of his story, and while he could easily write it himself, he'd always liked the idea of a biographer. And this was even better, because he could simply hand her the pieces of the story and watch from the sidelines as they were compiled.

Alma found that, after a long break from writing, words did not flow so easily. Even when she knew what she was going to say. She struggled at first to type out sentences that did not feel awkward and forced together.

She'd expected to be a little rusty. But Alma also suspected there was another reason for the extra effort it took for her to pull together Hayden's story in a way that captured its true heartache. It was a story she'd listened to in one sitting, in its entirety, with her eyes closed. She had the strange experience as she listened, too, of not feeling Hayden's sadness. Of not absorbing his regret. It seemed her previous writing ability had relied heavily on the fact that she *felt* so much. For the first time since the Echoes had died, she found herself almost wishing she could just switch on that part of herself.

But eventually, little by little, she, too, became satisfied with the telling, and Alma published Hayden's story as a chapbook, something small that could be passed around town—thicker than a flyer but leaner than a book. She'd dusted off the old printing press and found it didn't work anymore anyway, so in the end, she designed the book on some old desktop computer software and printed it in black and white. She bound the fifty miniature books herself with black thread, which kept her busy enough that her mind couldn't dwell on how far she was straying from her original plan of simply being with her memories of Alex. She still had Jupiter after all—a fact she hadn't fully accepted yet, despite counting herself lucky. He sat at the window of the office, barking occasionally when people passed on the street. Alma gave up shushing him when she remembered no one could hear him anyway.

In between sewing books, when her fingers had cramped, she read more of *Tower of Echoes*.

> The sound returned seconds later, although it was never supposed to take so long. There was no explanation for why the voice you heard, your own voice, was just as loud, just as strong as when you spoke into the microphone.
>
> It takes a radio wave 0.14 seconds to travel around Earth—moving at the speed of light—which

means that is how long a radio transmission echo would normally take. The amplitude should decrease after multiple trips around the planet, and yet you said your name, and the echo returned three full seconds later at full strength. It was like a ghost speaking through the airwaves.

A ghost of you.

The Norwegian Jørgen Hals first heard this phenomenon in 1927, after picking up signals from a Dutch shortwave transmitting station. Years of investigating, and these long-delayed echoes are still a mystery.

There are theories. A radio wave reflected off the moon or another planet. Signals bounced off Earth's upper ionosphere and sent back along the same path, rather than continuing full circle around. Even the possibility that the most efficient means of alien communication would be to transmit our own signals back to us.

Ultimately, these strange echoes have not been studied enough, despite the fact that current resources and technology could likely solve the mystery with ease. The truth is, the problem isn't important enough. It doesn't affect human communication enough to be worth anyone's time.

You write and you tell stories and nothing changes. You wonder what makes something worth the attention—how much of a disruption one would have to create to be of interest to science. To be of interest to the world. To be enough.

On the day the story was printed, Alma found Hayden at the top of the lighthouse. He stood hinged forward with his elbows resting on the railing. "This is just where I realized that I was in love with a man," he said when Alma reached him. The wind whipped her hair across her eyes, and she pulled her hood over her head. "Except," Hayden continued, "that he was up here and I was down there."

A group of albatross rode the wind down toward the cliffs. "It takes a really strong heart to lose love like that," she said. "It takes an even stronger one to admit that it could have been different, if only you were braver." Her words felt jumbled, like she wasn't making any sense, but she figured Hayden needed to hear something reassuring, no matter how inarticulate.

Hayden said, "If the world doesn't remember us, at least there's something out there. Even if Alphie doesn't fully remember me, maybe he'll know that there was someone that loved him, who would do anything to go back and do it all again. Or it'll drive him mad."

"I'll take it to him today, if that's still what you want."

"Thank you. I don't know if I want to see his reaction, so I think I'll keep my distance." Hayden opened a box by his feet and brought up a stack of notebooks. "You know, as a writer, I never thought my biographer would get it right. I'm an asshole, I know this. But you captured it perfectly. We have to remember not to keep things too precious, okay?"

He looked over the railing, down to where the edge of the cliffs threatened to pull the lighthouse into the sea, and dropped the notebooks over. The books flapped and fluttered on the way down—the pages like the wings of strange seabirds—then were lost in the waves.

~~~

That afternoon, Alma and Jupiter hiked to where Alphie Roy's barn sat bravely facing the wind and salt spray on the northern shore. She held the thin book tightly in her hand. The black fox with yellow eyes

117

that Hayden had described came trotting out of the great barn door immediately, as if he'd expected her arrival. He paused halfway down the path and waited for her to follow.

Alma didn't see Alphie until after she reached the barn. Before entering the wide door, movement caught her eye, and she passed along the outside wall of the building to find Alphie throwing buckets of silver fish onto the rocks below. Seabirds came scuttling up the beach to peck at them and drag them off. Before he even turned, Alma felt a sadness sweep toward her.

"You scared me," he said, placing his hand on his chest.

"Sorry," she said. "I brought this for you. I know you don't know me, but I wrote a story, and I promised someone I'd make sure you got it."

Alphie looked confused, but he took the book and tucked it under his arm, walking toward the barn. When he said nothing, Alma caught up and asked, "What is it that you do here?" She was already well aware of his sanctuary operations, but in moments like those, when she had to think quickly of something to say, she frequently ended up asking a mundane question she already knew the answer to.

"Oh, it's an essential thing, really. Wildlife rehab." Alphie spoke like his words were tripping over themselves to get out, but then he pulled back, self-conscious. "Although it seems there are more and more birds every day. Most seabirds are resilient against these harsh waves and strong winds. They ride them and travel great distances every day to find food. But a lot of the time—more and more lately—they get exhausted and stranded here. They get blown inland. For some reason, it happens a lot in this particular cove."

"Maybe they've learned that it's a safe place," Alma said, her hand instinctively reaching down for Jupiter. He kept in step with her, her fingertips brushing the fur on his back. The black fox, equally in step with Alphie, kept looking back, as if he sensed another creature was with them but couldn't reconcile the fact that none was present.

"Well, I hope so!" Alphie said. "That's so nice of you to say. I've spent a lot of my life trying to make sure that if no other place in this world is safe, at least this one is. Forgive my excitement. I'm alone so often, I forget to control the volume of my voice."

Alma realized that despite the brief sadness she'd absorbed, she'd also forgotten to be self-conscious. She wondered if it was because Alphie had no memory of what may have been the saddest moments of his life. She wondered if, when Alphie read Hayden's story, he would remember their love and that contentment would leave him, the deeper sadness returning.

"I'm more than happy to read your piece," Alphie said. "Who did you say wanted me to see it?"

"A friend," Alma said. "I'm not sure if you will remember him, but it would be better if you just read it to find out."

"Yes, of course. I should be better with visitors. Here, let me show you around before you go."

Alma followed him into the barn, but Jupiter stayed outside. As she passed a pen in which a dappled seabird tapped at the dirt with its black foot, she realized the fox had stayed behind as well and was walking in slow circles by the door as if still sensing that presence.

"That's one of the last black-legged kittiwakes," Alphie said. "She's kind of a miracle, really." He reached his hand into a grassy enclosure, and a spotted green frog with one back leg hopped awkwardly onto it. "I rescued this guy from a raccoon—I try not to intervene too much in the workings of nature, but these guys are losing their wetlands, and I couldn't help it."

"Have you always done this?" Alma asked. Again, the answer already within the pages of Hayden's story. She realized Alphie might be the person most like her in Violette and, though he was incredibly kind, he probably just wanted to be left alone.

"Oh no," he said. "I wanted to be a writer. Or a musician. Or some-thing. But I didn't have the stamina for it, or a thick enough skin. This isn't exactly a job, but I'm much more at home with these creatures than anywhere else I've been. That might sound crazy, but I've been feeling a whole lot crazier than that these days."

"It's not crazy at all," she said. "Anyway, that's my hope with writing, you know? Making people feel less alone, a little less crazy. Maybe it will help somewhat."

"I'll be sure to read it," he said. "I'd love to feel less crazy. But I'm certainly not alone." And with that, he led her to the middle of the barn, where, on the floor, an otter pup was lying on its back with a foam ball clutched between its paws. As Alma knelt and reached her hand out to the pup, she glanced over at Alphie's desk and noticed a book wedged beneath a lamp so the bulb pointed upward.

The book was *The Light on the Way Down*, by Hayden MacKenna.

10

Hayden MacKenna, printed, hand sewn, 2027

I'm here to tell you that Hayden MacKenna existed because I believe I'm the only one who can.

He asked me to open like this: His life began in 1951. He was born at home in a small cottage in Violette. Perhaps your parents knew his parents. Perhaps your mother bought a quilt from his, or your father fished on his father's boat. Perhaps you remember that he was a child who was always sick. That, he will tell you, is something he never regretted. And he regretted many things.

He regretted, for instance, not trusting Alphie Roy that day, on the walk they almost took in the snow.

But this is getting ahead.

For two weeks during his eighteenth year, Hayden had no voice. He'd come down with a common cold after a day on his father's boat, and when the cough didn't go away for over a week, it turned into full-blown bronchitis. The bronchitis stuck around for another week, until one morning he found himself leaning over the bathroom sink, coughing blood onto the porcelain, his chest feeling as if it were being pressed upon from all directions. He looked up at himself in the mirror and saw his own teenage face, cheeks drawn down and eyes glassy. Not that he knew a thing about age at the time, but to him, he felt—and looked—like someone ten years older.

One more heave and he passed out. When he woke up, he was in a hospital bed, staring at the white ceiling, an IV in his forearm, the tube connected to a bag of clear fluid. There was a humming sound that at first Hayden thought was some hospital machinery but turned out to be human. The humming was coming from the bed on the other side of the room. Hayden lifted his head off the crisp pillow and strained to see. All that was visible were the bottoms of two feet, one of them bandaged, the other tapping along to whatever song the human was humming.

"I've been in this room for forty-eight hours and I don't know if I'm going to make it another second," his roommate said that evening while they sat facing one another, their dinners in their laps. Something about his hairstyle—long and parted on the side—suggested he was younger than Hayden. But in truth, Alphie Roy and Hayden MacKenna were the same age, and yet, in such a small town, Hayden had never seen him before. Alphie spoke a little more, some sentences that Hayden didn't catch. Hayden nodded and gestured to his throat, indicating that he couldn't speak.

"Ah," Alphie said. "That's no matter. I can talk enough for the both of us. Especially if I'm stuck here much longer. I feel like I'm going to go mad."

Hayden wanted to ask him why he didn't read a book or take up drawing or do something to pass the time. But since he couldn't ask, he shrugged and offered Alphie the cookie that had come with his meal. Just the thought of eating something crunchy and sweet made his throat ache.

Alphie hobbled over to Hayden's bed, taking his dessert and nodding a thank-you. "I was in an accident," he said. "Bicycle. Went straight over the cliff and probably should have been a lot worse off than this. But my mother's always telling me I'm lucky—what am I saying? She's always telling me I'm blessed, with angels watching over me and all that.

Either way, here I am, with a good couple of weeks of therapy left." He crossed the room, his bandaged left foot tap-tapping the tiles. When he reached the window, he turned and said, "At least I have you now."

It wasn't until later that Hayden found out Alphie had only just moved to the island a few weeks before his accident. At that time, they were both about to graduate—Hayden from the high school and Alphie from homeschool with his mother. Hayden had always been interested in literature and science, rather than more physical activities. His father had wanted him to become a fisherman, but Hayden had always complained that the damp sea air bothered his lungs. His father thought this was weak and lazy, but now that Hayden found himself bedridden with bronchial inflammation, it seemed he was vindicated.

Hayden lay in bed, coughing and heaving, but mostly sleeping, while he recovered from what he hoped would not turn into pneumonia.

The cough had rendered Hayden's vocal cords unusable, so he spent his time looking around the room from the white ceiling to the white walls to the off-putting slightly less white tiles of the floor. The one reprieve he had from the hideous brightness of the room was the window next to his bed, through which he could see the branches of a tree growing close to the building, and beyond that a blurry blue etching that was the sea. Had it not been raining for days on end, dark clouds hanging low over the ocean, Hayden might have recovered sooner.

He was always glad he didn't, though, because it was there in that bare room with only one window to the stormy sea that he discovered two things. The first was that he wanted to become a writer. He'd always known he wouldn't be a fisherman, and had known that more practical jobs were not for him—not because they were practical and he was impractical, or because there was something wrong with practicality, but because when he thought about these other occupations, something felt trapped in his stomach. And with no voice and very few visits from his father and all the time in the world to invent stories in his head, he decided that was all he needed to do.

That language was of such importance to him was confirmed one evening after visiting hours were over and the doctors had gone home and there was only one nurse left at the dim-lit check-in desk. In the dark of their room, Hayden read beneath a small lamp that hung from the wall. He almost didn't notice Alphie's awkward hobbling across the room, into the hallway, and out of sight.

When he came back, Alphie was carrying a small bucket of paint in one hand, a paintbrush balanced on top of it. With the other hand, he used a step stool as a kind of walking cane. Hayden couldn't imagine how Alphie had gone down the hall and taken these things unseen, but he continued reading his book, glancing over its pages frequently to catch Alphie perched on the stool, his arm swooping and curling in wide arcs over his head.

It wasn't until the morning that Hayden opened his eyes to see the words, painted in green across the ceiling: "All great ideas are dangerous." That was when Hayden discovered the second thing: he needed more unpredictability in his life, and Alphie Roy—having clearly lost his mind—was the embodiment of that.

"Thought we could use a little spice in this place," Alphie said, pointing upward. "That's Wilde, by the way."

Hayden found that his voice was beginning to return in a slow rasp. "I know," he whispered, and his eyes barely left the words on the ceiling until the day he walked out of the hospital.

It took Hayden a few weeks to find Alphie again, which was a considerable amount of time in a town of two hundred people. During that time, Hayden had started writing, despite his father's disapproval. He'd tried to avoid the docks as much as possible so that he didn't bump into his father, or one of his father's friends, or God forbid, his father's girlfriend. He missed being there, because even though he did not want to be a fisherman, he did love the ocean and the experience of acquiring stories from men and women as they left the boats. In the hospital, he'd taken the stories they'd told him and woven new threads into them in his mind. After he'd recovered from his illness, he started writing them down, turning them into full stories that he dreamed of one day publishing.

It happened only by chance that Hayden saw Alphie one afternoon, pedaling his bike on the boardwalk. Hayden followed him, hoping Alphie would turn around at some point and see him, so that he wouldn't have to walk so far to catch up and risk being seen by his father. But Alphie seemed determined to be somewhere, and he rode quickly and with purpose, the wind whipping his hair back.

When he reached the fork in the path, Hayden was relieved to see that he did not turn toward the docks but instead toward the lighthouse. He followed and watched as Alphie entered the stone structure and disappeared into the darkness. Then Hayden traveled the perimeter of the lighthouse a couple of times, his eyes on the ground, while he waited for Alphie to come back out. He stood beneath the deck that surrounded the light and looked up, just as his old hospital roommate—it seemed they'd been stuck in that room for ages, and then the time it took to find him again even longer—emerged and looked down.

Alphie took a step back when he saw Hayden, as if Hayden were some kind of déjà vu in human form. A ghost perhaps. He shook his head and rubbed his eyes.

"You gave me a heart attack," Alphie said. "Where did you come from?"

"I saw you on your bike," Hayden said. "Can't even tell you were in the accident. You look totally normal."

Alphie laughed at this. "Well," he said. "I *am* totally normal. Except—and you wouldn't be able to see—that my left foot is about a half size smaller than my right now. Isn't that crazy? They said that can happen with casts, but seriously, it was only a couple of weeks."

Hayden wanted to ask somehow, without seeming intrusive, if Alphie had thought of him since they'd left the hospital. He pointed to

Alphie, then himself, and said, "Did you . . . ," then stopped. He tried again, "What have you . . . ," and again stopped. "I'm just wondering—"

"Oh, I think about you all the time. This morning, though, I heard something through the sink—a voice that wasn't yours, but was talking about you. Actually, talking about us. That's why you scared me so much." Alphie glanced back over his shoulder at the mountain, where the tower stood guard over the town.

"Oh," Hayden said. "What could anyone have to say about us?" He remembered the only time they'd been together before this, the dreariness of the hospital room and the mist through the window and how Alphie had been the only bright thing there. "Maybe it was some broadcast from the hospital?"

"No," Alphie said. "It was definitely about us, but it had nothing to do with our past. I think it was from the future."

Hayden gasped.

By 1970, they had moved to Montreal, into an apartment that looked out over the canal. More often than not, they were inside, sitting at their desks on opposite sides of the room, typewriter keys clicking until long after dark.

Hayden was always trying to weave some large, intertwined story that had its roots on the docks of their hometown, while Alphie wrote in great detail about only one thing in particular: his bike accident. He relived and reinvented it over and over.

Sometimes, in the winter, they wore ice skates and held hands and spun swift circles around the other skaters. Often, they noticed people looking at them with eyes that lingered many moments too long. Hayden would shyly pull his hand away, startled by the fierceness with which Alphie took it back.

In the summer, they rode kayaks side by side, Alphie blowing him unabashed kisses and shouting adoring phrases across the rippled surface. Hayden always returned these gestures with awkward waves or nervous giggles.

Every afternoon, the two would-be writers walked down the street to get a bagel and a coffee, and on their way back, they stopped—at Alphie's insistence—by the canal to toss pieces of their bread to the geese.

It was there that they found Ivy. She was lying in the grass beneath a tree, her light-brown fur matted with what they thought was water but later determined to be dog saliva. Hayden had been ready to walk away, but Alphie couldn't leave the creature behind like that, especially once he'd touched her tiny squirrel chest with his fingers and felt her weak squirrel heartbeat.

They took her home and washed her while she was still unconscious, and when Ivy woke up, she was still wet, her wide black eyes blinking up at them from beneath the folds of a towel.

"Aren't you a little miracle," Alphie said, and Hayden laughed a little too loud. He was more of the mind to let nature decide the creature's fate. When he thought about it now, those first few moments with Ivy were the first moments he would have gone back and changed if he could.

But the truth was, it irked him to see Alphie lying on the couch with the little furball curled up on his chest, when before the furball's arrival, it would have been Hayden's head there. The chattering rodent noises quickly replaced the clicking of Alphie's typewriter.

Rejection letters from magazines came in—*Cosmic Horror, Galactic International, Astral Fiction Review*—and as they did, Hayden realized more and more they were addressed only to him. Alphie didn't seem to be receiving any, although his work wasn't getting accepted either. Hayden finally pieced together the reason for this: Alphie had stopped sending work out.

"I need a break," Alphie said. "This constant trying-to-be-a-writer thing is too much sometimes. Don't you ever wonder why you're doing it at all? What's the point of it, and where is it going?"

Hayden stumbled to answer. "Of course I do. That's what 'being a writer' is all about. It's uncertainty and all that starving-artist bullshit. This is the life. If you don't trust that it's going somewhere, then it never will."

Ivy was eating peanuts from Alphie's palm, which was resting open on the arm of the couch. "I don't have it in me right now," he said. "The words aren't coming like they used to, and I just need to rest my mind a little."

"What you need," Hayden said much more harshly than he'd intended, "is to bring that rodent back to the park, stop dwelling on that stupid bicycle accident that happened years ago, and find some new material."

He knew it was a mistake. And it was only made worse later by the fact that he was so utterly wrong about the quality of Alphie's writing and choice of subject matter.

Hayden was never proud of what he'd done, and he'd never meant for it to happen the way it did. Yet somehow, he found himself there one afternoon while Alphie was out for a walk, shuffling through a stack of papers left on his desk next to the typewriter.

He read the openings of a dozen stories, all about the accident. None of them was particularly good or interesting. One described the broken leg Alphie had sustained. One delved deeply into the reasons Alphie was on the bike in the first place—apparently, he'd just had an argument with his mother. None said anything that hadn't been said before.

And then, nearing the end of the stack, Hayden began reading a particular opening that made his chest burn. He took the page over to the window while he read so he could keep an eye out in case Alphie came home. His eyes scanned the same paragraph over and over, and by the time he'd read it ten times, he already knew that he was going to steal it, even if *steal* wasn't quite the word he would have used for it at the time. Alphie hadn't been working much, and from what Hayden had seen, he hadn't touched that pile of papers in at least a month. He was planning on giving up anyway.

Hayden slid the single sheet into his own folder and put the rest of the stack back on the desk where he'd found them, ensuring that they looked as disheveled as before. He watched Alphie walk down the street toward their building, a small bag slung over his shoulder like a purse, from which the plume of a rescued squirrel's tail curled out.

Hayden could see this, and the top of Alphie's baseball hat, and he could tell that Alphie had his eyes on the ground. A few moments later, he was opening the door to the apartment building and Hayden could picture the way he had taken the stairs, driving his heels into each step and pushing off hard, like he intended to launch himself into the air.

As soon as Alphie walked through the door that afternoon and looked around the room like he suspected Hayden had done exactly what he had done, everything seemed different. Hayden considered putting back the writing he'd taken from the desk, but he couldn't bring himself to do it. At times, he was convinced that Alphie knew, because there was no other explanation for why, on that very afternoon, things had changed so much between them.

Over the next few months, Alphie drifted away. It seemed the longer Hayden held on to the page, the further they grew apart, and yet also the more convinced Hayden was that he could have written it himself. Eventually he convinced himself that he had.

It was called "The Falling One."

A matter of perspective, **Alphie had written**. *Plummeting through the air, the soaring body looks no different to a spectator whether the Falling One tripped and fell or chose to jump. It is all the same. The Falling One alone possesses this secret knowledge of intent. So, can one change his or her mind on the way down? Can one who has accidentally fallen turn the act into an intentional* *one? As you somersaulted toward the earth, you caught sight of the ocean lit by the rising sun. It was such an impossible brightness that you thought you were glimpsing heaven. It was then that you changed course and decided you hadn't fallen at all—you had leapt.*

Hayden imagined Alphie sailing through the air on his bicycle, then the inevitable plummet that had followed. One day, when the house was quiet yet again, he sat down at his desk and began writing a middle and then an end to Alphie's beginning.

From that moment, any writer's block that Hayden had was gone, which made it all seem worth it. He wrote consistently every day, for long stretches. He sometimes got the impression that Alphie knew his words had been stolen, but other times it seemed as if Alphie was simply walking on a cloud, his head somewhere else entirely. He certainly didn't seem to have much motivation to be writing himself.

Hayden joined a writer's group and began spending his nights out. They met at any of Montreal's local pubs, drinking and talking about their work, the work of the Greats, and what it meant to be an artist in Canada in the seventies. When Alphie asked to go with him, Hayden lied and told him it wasn't a social event. It was only for people in the group—*writers*—and Alphie had given up on that. Later, Hayden admitted to himself that two things were true—he had felt abandoned by Alphie at the same time that he was ashamed to be seen with him in the world.

They began to fight constantly. As Hayden refused to let Alphie into this other part of his life, eventually Alphie no longer cared. Perhaps it was what hurt the most, when Alphie finally snapped: "I don't want to be a writer anymore, dammit! Go off with your friends, I don't care. I love you, but I'm just not like you."

Hayden had been so sure at one time that they'd been exactly the same.

Hadn't they?

It was one of those solo nights at the bar that Hayden met Mathilde. She was taller than he was, had wide hips and a touch of a lisp. Her hair was long, wavy, fell down past her waist and often into her eyes. He had never felt such admiration for someone other than Alphie. Had never seen such free-spiritedness. Alphie had turned away from him, and Hayden barely took a breath before all too easily diving straight into that mess of hair for refuge.

He spent nights at Mathilde's small apartment near the bars, claiming that he'd been too drunk to walk home. Once, when he'd been bleary eyed and very tired, Hayden watched Mathilde pull a cigarette from her bra and light it. He wasn't as attracted to this act as another man might have been, but there was something about the way she did it—as if she felt comfortable only because she knew he wasn't interested. Somehow that made it all the more attractive, though he figured— though it couldn't be helped—there was something categorically wrong about this knowing deception.

Still, he reached out and touched her black lace bra.

Alphie slipped further away. When he did sit at his desk, it was to read, and he simply stared at his book and then out the window. Back and forth like this for hours, a squirrel perched on his shoulder. He took in other animals. A pigeon. A stray cat. They slept in the kitchen cabinets. The only communication that happened in their apartment was between bird and feline, or rodent and reptile.

A few days after Hayden finished a draft of his first novel, Alphie announced that he wanted to move back to Violette. He needed the ocean air again. He wanted to open an animal sanctuary. At the time, Hayden was standing there, the only printed copy of his book held with both hands. He gripped it tighter.

"I was going to ask you to read this. You can't read it if you're in Violette."

"I can read anywhere. But I'm not happy here anymore," Alphie said. "I haven't been for a long time. I think that's obvious. And you don't seem happy either."

"You'd be happier if you participated in life once in a while. If you came out, met people, *wrote something*."

"I can't write anything. I've been trying, and I'm just not inspired. I don't even remember what it felt like to be inspired."

"Because you need to *get out*, Alphie. Have some experiences that don't involve wounded animals. Then maybe you'll remember what it felt like to *live* and you'll have something to write about."

"But you don't want me to go out with you. I'm not good enough for your little club, and when we do take a walk, you act like we're just friends."

"That's not true. I'm not embarrassed about being with you. I was just . . . trying to encourage you to write again. I know it was harsh, but I thought it would push you in the right direction."

"Well, it didn't. It's only pushed us apart."

Alphie might have looked hurt, but if he did, Hayden didn't see it. Hayden didn't know what expression was on Alphie's face at that moment because he was walking to the open window with 352 typed pages in his hands. He held them over the edge of the sill, the wind swirling the white curtains.

"I'll do it," Hayden said. "You'll be responsible for the destruction of my first novel and any hope that I had for a writing career."

Alphie sighed. "Honestly," he said. "Don't be so dramatic. Get away from there. Jesus, sit down and read me the first page. We can talk about me moving back later."

Hayden crossed the room and sat on the mustard-yellow love seat. The opening of his novel had hardly changed at all since he'd started. He began reading, his voice shaking at first and then gaining confidence. He'd read the passage so many times then that he'd completely lost any sense of its origins. The words truly felt like his own.

When he finished, he looked up to see Alphie squinting at him. "Really?" Alphie said. "Is that a joke?"

"What?"

"You didn't write that. That's mine."

If you understand nothing else, understand this: that Hayden MacKenna really did believe it. It doesn't make it right. It probably doesn't even make sense. But it's true.

"I . . . uh . . . ," Hayden began, searching for the words. "I don't know what you're talking about. This is my writing, my book." And to him, at least at that moment, he really believed it.

Perhaps, given enough time, Alphie could have convinced Hayden to embrace who he had become, and who they were together. It's possible. But Alphie had run out of energy. "You know what? I don't care enough and I'm done anyway. It's yours now."

He returned to Violette, Ivy in a little pouch slung across his chest. Hayden watched him push his suitcase into a taxi, watched him climb in and slide across the seat to the side of the cab farthest from the apartment window. When the car drove away, there was no hand on the glass. No leaning over to peer through for one last glance.

It felt like no goodbye at all.

It was three years later that Hayden, too, left Montreal and returned to Violette. He, too, pushed a lone suitcase into a taxi, leaving behind a furnished apartment, among other belongings. He brought with him only his typewriter, the manuscript for his second book, and his wife, Mathilde.

Alphie did not come to meet his boat as it docked, but the rest of the town did. Hayden had made them all proud when his first novel, *The Light on the Way Down*, had come out, and they stood with hardback covers open, pens in their hands for an autograph.

Hayden and Mathilde moved into a cottage that sat on the hill near the river. The house—which was the biggest and undeniably most desirable in town, with the best view of the inlet—had been empty for years. Mathilde had taken up painting, and so the front room with the largest windows was hers. Hayden set up his writing desk in the back, pretending not to care that there was only one small window and telling himself once more that a writer should have to suffer in order to create.

Three months after arriving, Hayden finally got up the courage to talk to Alphie. "Not at all," Mathilde said, when he asked if she minded him going for a walk with his ex-lover. Reluctantly, Alphie had agreed.

The first snow of the year had fallen. They walked the path they used to walk back when they'd first met, up the hillside. The river was covered white. At one time, they'd have been able to find their path through the snow easily. The way seemed so obvious. But this time, Alphie grabbed Hayden's arm as they stepped off the boardwalk.

"You're going the wrong way," he said. "The trail is over here."

"What? No, that's ridiculous. It's this way."

Alphie crossed his arms and shook his head. He'd grown thinner, his frame bent. "You don't think I know the way? I've been here three years on my own, without you."

"We always went this way. The trail is here." He pointed to some footprints in the snow, despite the fact that they seemed, admittedly, to be uncertain, meandering tracks. "Look, someone else has been here. I'm sure this is right."

"You think you can rely on someone else to tell you where your own trail is? Is that what you're telling me?"

"I . . ." But Hayden had nothing to say.

They stood side by side, both with arms crossed over their chests, neither prepared to accept that the other was right.

Hayden never got to say what he'd come to say. Never got to ask for forgiveness. Suddenly, Alphie's stubbornness made him defiant against the very idea of apologies.

It may have been better for them to have argued. If they had, truths may have come out, apologies may have flowed, and forgiveness may have been granted. They may have been able to move forward. Instead, they said nothing, and their walk ended before it began.

That was the last time Hayden MacKenna spoke to Alphie Roy.

Hayden had considered, many times since that day, Alphie's words—which he had gone on to publish as his own—about the secret knowledge one possesses of intent, and he decided to change course.

If he could have gone back in time, he would have done better than just admit he was wrong at that moment. He would have simply followed Alphie's lead in the first place. He would have never argued that Alphie had a much firmer sense of direction than he could ever hope for.

He would have never hesitated at all.

11

Alma found Lucie on her hands and knees by the lighthouse, peering over the cliff edge into the rough, iron-gray waves.

"Where's Hayden?"

"Don't know," Lucie said. "With you, we were hoping."

"He didn't come with me. Did he go for a walk?"

"That's what we thought at first," Oren said. "But he didn't say anything to anyone, and it's been hours. We thought maybe he'd fallen into the sea or something. But we haven't found him there either."

By nightfall, Hayden still hadn't returned, and Alma and the others wondered if he'd been so worried about Alphie's response to the story that he'd wandered off to the woods and gotten lost.

In the morning, they got their answer. The body of Hayden MacKenna, renowned writer and local curmudgeon, had been found on the sidewalk, just steps away from the bookstore. The shop owner, Emile, had been the one to find him on his way to open the store in the morning. It appeared Hayden had died of a heart attack. What was strangest was that everyone who'd known Hayden MacKenna not only remembered who he was, but they remembered *forgetting* him as well.

There wasn't a clear reason for why this happened, but only one thing about this particular day was different from any that had passed in the previous months. Alma had written Hayden's story, and at least one person had read it.

"That was it, wasn't it?" Lucie said when they'd gathered again. She was standing in the darkened doorway of the keeper's house as Alma approached. Lucie leaned against the doorframe, a copy of Hayden's story in her hands. "It's absurdly simple. The story is what it took for him to leave us."

Alma thought of the word *resolved*. His Echo had been resolved.

Lucie disappeared inside the keeper's house, and Alma looked to Oren for some direction. He crouched to pick a few juniper berries, piling them into his palm.

Alma said, "Are you two going to want to write your stories now and move on?"

Fey perched on his shoulder, shaking out her wings. He passed her one berry, then another. "I imagine that the idea of leaving this in-between place will become increasingly appealing. I can't say when. What I *can* say, though, is that I'm not ready yet. I have too much I still want to learn."

～～

Hayden's funeral was held a few days later. Many people from town were there, since most had read at least one or two of his books, and if they hadn't, they at least kept a copy of *The Light on the Way Down* tucked away somewhere on a shelf. The Violette cemetery lay on a slope between the church and the beach. The headstones—thin and white—had begun sinking and leaning. Alma stood with Bea and her cousins, their backs to the ocean. A fog drifted up from the water and lingered that morning, layered over the sprinkling of dandelions. Long, flattened strands of grass reached back toward the earth.

Because Mathilde had died years before, and nobody else knew what kind of funeral Hayden had wanted, the pastor of the church read from Corinthians: "For this perishable body must put on the imperishable, and this mortal body must put on immortality. When the perishable puts on the imperishable, and the mortal puts on immortality, then shall come to pass the saying that is written: 'Death is swallowed up in victory.'"

It was terribly unoriginal, Alma thought. Hayden would have hated it, and she smiled to herself just thinking about the rant he might have had afterward—a rant he would have thoroughly enjoyed. She remembered part of Hayden's story, something he told her but chose to leave out of the final piece. The actual last thing that Alphie Roy had said to him, as they parted ways at a fork in their not-trail: "It is agonizing, the disposition of the human mind to construct obstacles in one's own path, when the world itself has given us none. Life is so much easier than you think, Hayden MacKenna."

As far as the town knew, other than Mathilde, no one had *really* loved Hayden MacKenna. They'd all known about his brief relationship with Alphie, but Alphie himself had written Hayden off, and so when the story was printed, there was some vague, unsatisfying chatter about it, like a sort of gossip the town had circulated long before and which was not nearly as titillating as it had been the first time.

But Alma saw Alphie Roy leaning against a tree, his arms crossed over his chest. Perhaps he'd been crying, but the fog made it hard to tell. She wished that Hayden could have been there to see that he'd come and that he'd mourned. That he had *remembered*.

"We are rarely given the opportunity to finish everything we'd like to," the pastor said, as if completing Alma's thought. "But Hayden left behind a good number of reminders of his worth on this planet—all of his novels and stories, and even some of the poems."

At the top of the hill, the church stood, yellow with cherry-red trim. Lucie and Oren walked along the ridge, dark shapes in the mist, and Alma wanted to slide into step with them, but she hadn't been to any kind of town gathering since before the tower was struck, and she knew that it would look odd if she wandered off alone so suddenly.

"And why did we all forget?" the pastor went on. "It seems impossible, and yet impossible things happen all the time. Hayden—he was a believer in the impossible. I'm sure there's a reason. We'll just have to wait for that reason to be revealed. Although if anyone does know, please do enlighten me."

Bea whispered, "I always had a little bit of a crush on him. Back when we were younger. It might have been the idea of the struggling artist. I read the story. I do like a good love story. But I have to ask, Was it fiction?"

Alma nodded in the direction of Alphie, who had slumped down into a squat, his hands reaching to pick something from the grass. He laid them carefully in his open hand. Jupiter had wandered over to sit next to him, though Alphie didn't know it. Still, Alma liked to think that Jupiter's presence could be a calming, soothing one all the same.

"It was something left behind," Alma said. "I thought, since I inherited the newspaper office, I could do something worthwhile with it."

When everyone who wanted to say something had done so, Alphie offered a reserved wave as he walked toward Alma. "This is going to sound crazy," he said, "but I've had this hole in me. I didn't know what it was until you came and brought me that story. After I read it, I remembered. Before, I had tried not to think about Hayden for so long." Alphie pressed one hand against his stomach like he was about to be sick. He closed his eyes and shook his head. "This is so much worse," he said.

"I'm sorry," Alma said. She saw pieces of a jay's egg in his other hand.

"It's okay," he said, exhaling a short, halfhearted laugh. "I didn't mean to make you feel bad. I'm glad for it. I can't explain the gap in my memory, why I forgot about him and then was suddenly reminded by you, but I wouldn't have wanted to forget forever."

"I know," Alma said, searching for better words when she saw the questioning look in Alphie's eyes. "I mean, I wouldn't have wanted to forget either."

"Have you read his book?" Alphie asked. "Not the one that everyone's read. You've been working in the newspaper office, right? Have you found the *other* one, the one he didn't publish?"

"How did you—"

Alphie smiled shyly. "Oh, I became friends with Mathilde. She brought me birds that had flown into their cottage window, an injured salamander once. Hayden didn't know. But she told me about the manuscript. The one about the tower."

Alma began to nod, then felt suddenly nauseated by Alphie's sadness. The sky was clearing, and tufts of white clouds seemed to be rushing overhead in fast-forward. She nearly fell over but caught herself and said, "I don't know what to make of it yet. It's really . . ."

"Experimental?"

"It's definitely different. Not so much experimental as, I don't know. Science fiction?"

Alphie looked up at the tower on the mountain, hidden still by low clouds. "My thinking," he said, "is that the thing Hayden couldn't get published was probably the one thing we all should have read. Everything in it is true."

After the funeral, Alma returned to her cottage, plucking from her door the latest addition to a collage of sticky notes. It read, "What to do when later never comes . . . to be continued." All the notes were from Emerson, who'd still been coming by each morning while she was away at the office and the lighthouse. She turned on her phone to find seven messages from her parents, asking whether she was coming back for her high school friend's wedding, or another cousin's baby shower, or the family Christmas gathering.

She turned the phone off without even attempting a return call and sat on the edge of her bed, exhausted. Thinking of Alphie's words about Hayden, she opened *Tower of Echoes* to where she'd left off, two-thirds of the way through, conscious of the fact that she still hadn't made sense of who Hayden was talking about and how it had anything to do with her or the Echoes.

It was the 1960s when scientists in Peru recorded a strange phenomenon. They found that radar signals sent into space were echoing back from somewhere around ninety miles above Earth.

The sound they received came every morning, grew stronger until the sun was directly overhead, then faded again. During a solar eclipse, the echoes vanished. Yet during a solar flare, the echoes increased and became more powerful.

There was no explanation for decades. Since the first recording, none of the rockets or satellites sent into Earth's upper atmosphere provided any insight into the nature of these echoes.

It was discovered many years later that the echoes recorded in Peru were caused by the sun. Ultraviolet light strips oxygen and nitrogen molecules in the upper atmosphere of their electrons, then sends those energized electrons careening off at very high speeds. When the energized particles interact with other particles, it causes these ions to vibrate in patterns, which forms waves strong enough to reflect radar beams back and create what is essentially an echo.

The next time you flew after reading this study, you looked out the plane window, the clouds nestled softly below the aircraft. Above, there was only blue sky, but you squinted anyway, knowing that there were hundreds of miles more between you and the thermosphere. You'd barely scratched the surface.

Up there, hidden, the northern lights rolled in waves. But you'd seen them once, in a dark, remote part of the Canadian wilderness. Now, at that height, it was hotter than you could imagine. Thousands of degrees hot, and yet the air was so thin it would feel freezing to humans.

Through the plane window, you tried to send thoughts up there, messages, beams from your eyes, anything. Anything at all that might reflect back and tell you that there was, in fact, something else out there.

Alma leaned back and let her weight drop. Her feet still planted on the floor, she closed her eyes.

When someone knocked on the door, she felt too tired to sit up. She half opened her eyes and saw the fuzzy outline of Emerson standing over her.

"Where've you been?" he asked. "You hardly come by anymore, and then you run off as soon as the writer's funeral is over. What's up?" He sat down at the round kitchen table, his legs too long to fit beneath. He crossed one ankle over the other, leaned back, and sipped from a thermos. "I mean, you've always been quiet, but this is . . . you've been particularly absent."

Alma shrugged. "I've just been busy," she said. "I'm taking over the town paper. Maybe you heard that." As hard as she tried to avoid it, the sentence still ended with the tone of a question, as if even she didn't quite believe it. But now she had been spending time with three humans and one dog who existed only in some space between life and death, and conversation proved more difficult than she expected.

"Sure," he said. "But you haven't been *here*."

"I've been doing a lot of writing. I feel more inspired when I'm outside, walking around."

"Hmm." Emerson turned toward the living room, where Jupiter's bed was still nestled into the corner, a rubber chew toy and a fleece blanket strewn across the floor. "And what's all that?"

Alma rubbed the back of her neck. "What time is it?"

Emerson squinted at her. "It's four in the afternoon. All right then, don't answer my questions. Come on, let's go." He held out his hand.

"Go where?" she asked, her body heavy. According to the clock, she'd been lying there for hours, but she still felt just as tired.

"Stop being so dramatic and pull yourself together, kid. I need your help with something. You're a journalist, right?"

She groaned as he heaved her deadweight upright. "Something like that," she mumbled. "All right, all right."

"Come on," he said again, already halfway out the front door.

Alma whistled for Jupiter, which prompted Emerson to throw back a questioning look. "I . . . ," she began, then simply said, "Never mind."

They walked toward the docks together, the sun reflecting a shimmering orange light on the smooth water. Emerson fumbled with his camera equipment while he walked, dropping something onto the dirt path and cursing. He bent to pick it up, dropped something else, cursed again.

"Can I help you? Here, give me that," Alma said, taking one of his bags. "Are you going to tell me what we're doing?"

Emerson sighed, sitting on a rock wall. "Thanks," he said. "I'm working on a short film. Sort of a documentary about this place and the people. The whole idea of staying here is something we've committed to as a town. Sort of. We knew eventually some people would want to leave, it was just a matter of time. So, I want to know why."

"Why what?" she asked.

"Why Victor, that man down there, has suddenly decided to go." He pointed to the docks with two fingers, closing one eye as if aiming.

Theo was there, too, hauling jugs of water onto his boat. A man—she assumed Victor—was sitting nearby on a duffel bag. "He convinced Theo to take him on his supply run and leave him behind in The City. It's been years since someone actually left for good. I'll do the filming. There are questions for you here, but feel free to improvise."

Alma took a crumpled piece of paper from his hand. While she did have experience interviewing, she felt like she'd reached her capacity for talking to people at the funeral earlier. The sleep hadn't helped. Jupiter sat invisibly at their feet, and all Alma could think about was veering off the path, finding Lucie and Oren.

Emerson fiddled with his lenses, finding the one he wanted and stuffing the rest into his bag. "Do you remember when we were kids and the whole family would meet at the beach in Nova Scotia?" he asked.

"Of course," she said. "Those were some of my favorite times growing up."

"But you never talked to anyone!" he said, incredulous. "You were always hiding away like some weird cave creature."

Alma rolled her eyes. "You're remembering wrong," she said.

"No, no. I specifically recall you lurking under a table at one point while the rest of us were putting on a play."

"I don't like being in crowds." She shrugged. "Even when it's people I love. You already know this. It's why I'm here."

"I thought you were here because . . . never mind. Sorry."

"Because what?" she asked.

"Nothing. To run away, I guess."

"Well, yeah," she said. "Kind of. More like running *toward*, but that probably only makes sense to me." She elbowed him. "What's going on with you?"

"I don't know," he said. "I guess I'm just having my own kind of crisis. I've thought about leaving too. Maybe not right away, but it's been on my mind."

"But if you go . . ."

"I probably won't come back. I just want to make sure everyone's going to be okay, you included."

"Don't worry about me," Alma said. "Worry about Bea. Worry about Theo. But the fewer people here, the better. Sorry, that came out totally wrong. You see why I hide under tables."

"You do kind of suck at conversation," he said. "But please, stop hanging out by yourself so much. I know you think you're better off, but at least come by once in a while, okay? For me. You can't just be alone all the time."

Alma stopped herself from saying that she wasn't alone. That she'd never felt better, never had such clarity in her life, than when she was with Lucie and Oren and Jupiter. But she just smiled, pretending to swing her feet gently so she could reach Jupiter with them.

"All right," she mumbled.

"All right," Emerson said. "Let's go talk to Victor."

Alma examined Emerson's interview questions. They would have been simple and easy enough to ask if she didn't feel like crawling back into bed, but as it was, she resolved to pep herself up and do this one favor for her cousin. It was the least she could do.

They approached Victor, who was hunched over in a heavy coat and a brown wool beanie, nervously tugging on a length of fishing net in his lap. "Excuse me," Alma said quietly, kneeling on the planks in front of him. Theo passed by, a coil of rope over his shoulder and an amused look on his face. She raised her voice a little, pointing over her shoulder at Emerson. "Do you mind if I ask you some questions?"

"Sure," Victor said, but his eyes were searching somewhere beyond Alma, out on the water. "I've still got half an hour. Why not?"

She tried to focus, despite his distraction. "I'm helping my cousin here with a story. I'm just wondering why you've decided to leave so suddenly."

Victor laughed, then grew defensive. "Who wants to know?" he said. "It's my decision, my life. I don't hold it against anyone who's decided to stay in this sinking town, but it's not for me."

Alma swallowed hard. She'd thought she was tired before she followed Emerson down here, but Victor was suddenly consuming all her energy.

"Sorry," she said, sending Emerson a look of alarm. He shrugged and gestured for her to keep going. "I'm just . . . I'm nobody. We're just trying to document things, you know, for the future. No one's judging."

"I don't really want to be on camera," Victor said.

"I know the feeling," she mumbled, looking up at Emerson, who reluctantly stopped filming and dropped the camera to his side. "Is it really because of the sinking?" Alma asked.

Victor sighed, pulling at a segment of the tangled fishnet with his fingers. "No," he said. "All right, I'll tell you a story, if that's what you want. It's not easy to explain. I got a letter, about a year ago, from an old friend. Who am I kidding? She was the love of my life. We grew up just outside of Boston, went to college together. We both loved reading, had the same favorite collection of poems. We lost touch when I moved away, out here, and I've regretted it ever since. Then this letter came from her, and it had some lines of poetry written in it. It was cryptic. It was confusing, but with a sense of determination, if that makes sense. I couldn't figure it out for the longest time, but then, after the writer died, I remembered. The lines were from one of his poems, about a place we used to talk about traveling to one day. But before MacKenna died, I'd just forgotten everything about it. Ah, dammit."

He began tugging the net more aggressively, tapping his feet, looking up every few seconds to see where Theo was. His eyes flickered with urgency.

"Hayden," Alma said, taking the tangled net from his hands. "He was the thing you'd forgotten."

Victor nodded.

"So why now?" Alma asked. "What made you decide to leave now, after all this time?"

"For months, I thought I'd lost my mind. Sometimes I just looked at the letter and wanted to tear it up because I knew I *should* have remembered. I just didn't. And I had no way of knowing how to get in touch with her. When MacKenna's story came out, it all came back. I'm relieved, but I also have this sense of, I don't know, time is fleeting? So, I'm going there, to see this place—real or imaginary, who cares—and see if she's still there. That's why I'm leaving. Otherwise, I'd go down with this drowning town, just like everybody else."

"What was the line from the poem?" Alma asked.

Victor took a thin book from the pocket of his oversize coat and opened to a dog-eared page and read, his voice cracking: "'Your first concern is that the lake has disappeared overnight. Your second is that it did not take you with it.' It's about a place in Patagonia where a large body of water suddenly goes missing and the people of the town go crazy. She always thought it was an alluring sort of story, even though it was only a few lines long. Is this what you wanted?"

"Yes, yes, of course," Alma said. "Thank you so much." She handed him the untangled net, then grabbed Emerson by the bag slung over his shoulder and pulled him away. She didn't know what she'd been expecting, but a story about Hayden MacKenna wasn't it. What if Hayden had never been remembered, and Victor had gone on for the rest of his life feeling lost, wondering about his lover's message? Alma thought of the remaining Echoes, how their absences might affect others in the future, in ways that neither she nor they would probably ever know.

She was walking fast, but Emerson stopped midstride. "You didn't let me film and you didn't even ask any of my actual questions."

"Sorry."

"What was all the poetry talk for? What did he mean, he *should* have remembered?"

"I don't know. But it wasn't nothing. It's definitely something. Maybe not something good." Alma continued walking ahead toward the beach, where she'd seen the familiar shape of Fey flying down to the lichen-covered rocks.

"That's cryptic," Emerson shouted. "Hey, what do you know that I don't?"

～～～

This is what joy looks like with nothing to lose: Lucie walking through town, peering through the windows of houses to watch the occupants eat baked goods from the bakery that she had built. Oren, scaling cliff walls untethered, not worrying about falling into the violent waves below.

They had no need for alcohol, but they drank anyway, and when they did, they always started by saying, "This one's for Hayden," because if not for him, they wouldn't have known that they had any control over their circumstances. The ability to let it extend onward and also to end it when they chose.

For weeks, the Echoes ate nothing but cookies from Lucie's bakery. Alma brought them to the lighthouse in boxes, saying, "You don't know the looks I get when I buy all of these." She watched them take one, then another, then another.

"You know you want one," Oren said, reaching toward Alma with a molasses cookie the size of his hand. As he leaned in her direction, the top buttons of his shirt open, she noticed for the first time the tattoo on his chest. Three lines, like rays of light, shining out from his heart. His eyes were like the tigereye stones she'd bought as a child from the Audubon nature center.

Alma could have gone back home to her cottage. Since the Echoes had no desire to get their stories into the world and move on, her presence wasn't exactly necessary. When she thought too much about it, there was guilt at the idea of others who might be suffering. The Alphies and the Theos who had lost something and couldn't place what that thing was. The Victors who'd nearly lost their minds over it.

But it was easy to not think too much about it because, for the first time in a long time, she was comfortable. She recognized a parallel freedom in her own situation. At the end of the day, she was no longer exhausted. There was still plenty of energy to talk long into the night to the Echoes, with Jupiter by her side requesting infinite belly rubs. She didn't mind when they spoke of past sadness or previous uncomfortable states of being, because when they did so, they were simply observing from a distance—curious, but not dragged down. Their feelings were mere oddities to be explored rather than something to consume them.

Alma went home only to sleep. Otherwise, she spent her days with Jupiter, at the newspaper office or at the lighthouse, where she didn't have to worry about someone seeing her talk to an imaginary dog. Jupiter, who had spent the few months before his death barely able to move, let alone play, had a renewed vigor for things as simple as playing fetch. Alma realized that she couldn't go and throw a tennis ball to a dog that no one else could see, and so she began playing with him at night. In the dark, under moonlight, she tossed sticks that were instantly lost to shadows. Jupiter ran after them, the shape of him vanishing, too, and then he'd emerge again, joyful and bouncing in a way that Alma almost couldn't even remember.

Her sense of time fell away. Whether she slept or didn't, whether she had been home to take a shower or hadn't. Occasionally she went all day before realizing she hadn't eaten breakfast. The world began to swirl around her in a delightfully yellow-orange blur.

And it was in that blur, sitting on the ground with her back against the keeper's house, facing the wide expanse of ocean, that she reached the end of Hayden's manuscript.

You're wondering where this is going. Why all this talk about sound waves and echoes and science. What, if anything, this has to do with a radio tower.

Here is the thing.

The radio tower is a place where echoes linger, and it has long been believed that echoes are entrances to other realms of existence.

For example: There is a panel of rock paintings called the Holy Ghosts in northern Utah's Horseshoe Canyon. They are shapeless, hovering figures. There, it is said, if you yell in the direction of the ghosts, the paintings of the figures speak back to you—spirits communicating from beyond the rock.

The people who painted these images had no knowledge of the way sound works. They knew nothing of sound waves, and at the time, echoes could only be explained supernaturally. Places where echoes resounded the most have been found, not so coincidentally, to be the ones that were considered the most sacred.

You were tempted to scream but couldn't bring yourself to do it. Instead, you clapped your hands self-consciously a couple of times. When you stood in this place, you were enamored with the idea that the quality of the sound you heard was almost exactly the same as what was heard by the people who had painted the walls centuries ago.

Running your hands over the rock, you tried to imagine a portal there, a way through to some other world. Maybe a world where you actually belonged. A place like that would have to exist somewhere, and why not here? You knew that, as a mere mortal human, you would find nothing, but that did not mean you could not believe the mythology.

Someone walked into the cave behind you and banged a drum, the beat vibrating off every surrounding surface. You closed your eyes and waited, always much more comfortable with ghosts than you were with the living. In that echo, some ancient goddess opened a door.

And that's when you knew. You knew they were there. They had been there before, and they were there again. They would always be there.

Alma blinked, reading the words a few times. *They had been there before, and they were there again. They would always be there.* Hayden had said that, somehow, he'd written the book for her, despite having no concept of her existence at the time. And he'd thought she could make some sense of it. He'd also said he thought most of the radio broadcasts came from another time. From the past. Maybe even the future.

The voices were out there, of everyone gone before, rippling and echoing back over those radio waves. And if Hayden, Lucie, Oren, and Jupiter had still been there, then—something sharp snagged in her chest—that meant Alex could be out there too. Maybe she could hear him. Maybe all she had to do was listen.

12

Communication, 2008

Alma was in her basement. She was fourteen and had just received the envelope that contained her results from the amateur radio test, her license, and her call sign. She'd used her saved birthday and holiday money to buy some used radio equipment she'd found listed in the newspaper. Alex had sent a letter with the frequency to use, and said he'd be there, waiting.

As she pulled the headphones over her ears and held the microphone close to her mouth, she pictured him in a garage or a basement like hers. She reached for the transceiver, dizzy to hear him, but her own voice was suddenly lost somewhere. It had been four years since the day they'd met on the beach in Nova Scotia. Four years since a man had drowned and somehow brought them together.

Mountains can stand in the way of a signal. But in their case, the mountain between them was a benefit, not a hindrance. The repeater that stood on the top of Stone Hill allowed their signals to bounce over what seemed an impossible distance.

Her hand shook as she held down the talk button and spoke her call sign into the mic. "Listening," she said. Ten minutes later, she tried it again. After an hour of repeating this, playing with all the knobs and buttons and switches on the transceiver, she left to get a glass of water, returning to a broken, robotic voice speaking through intermittent static.

"This is . . ." He stated his call sign and asked, "QSL?"

Alma forgot everything. Her mind leapt through the number of things she'd learned to earn her license, trying to recall the chart of all the Q codes, then briefly thinking this must not be real before she responded: "QSL. Yes, I hear you. This is . . ."

"Hey, Alma," he said. "Darkest One."

"Hey, Dire Wolf," she said, laughing so he wouldn't hear the nervous waver in her voice.

"What are you doing?"

"Nothing." She clasped her hands together, leaned closer. "I almost missed you. What are you doing?"

"Talking to you."

She was surprised by the deep, mellow tone that four years had brought to his voice, and she wondered if she sounded any different to him. She tried to visualize his face, his shoulders, wherever he was, but all she could conjure up was the same image of him from the beach years ago, sitting on the ground in a red hoodie, headphones on, a cassette player in his lap.

They talked for two hours. She told him about new music she was listening to, and he told her about books he was reading. Each time she let go of the talk button and let his voice flow into the room, she scribbled furiously into a notebook—all the books he mentioned, things she could talk about if the conversation started to dwindle—retracing all the letters until the pencil marks indented the paper. She doodled some hearts, some suns and moons, mountain peaks along the bottom of the page.

At one point, something fell and crashed behind her, and she turned to see her brother, crouched behind a bicycle, giggling and making kissing noises.

"Get out of here, René!" she yelled, throwing a wadded piece of paper at him. When he scurried up the stairs, she turned back. "Sorry. Repeat, please."

Alex told her about a hike he took with his family up Sgurra Bhreac on Cape Breton. "They call it the Big Rock," he said. "There was a wildfire burning south of us. My mom and stepdad got to the top and looked at the flames and smoke, and then they ate an apple. An *apple*, Alma."

Hearing him say her name again in a sentence—*an* apple, *Alma*—made the hair on her neck tingle. "What did they do after that?"

"They talked about the view like nothing was wrong and started hiking back down. I gave them a head start and stood there for a really long time."

"What did it look like? The fire?" She'd seen pictures of wildfires, but she'd never seen the actual flames or the smoke. She'd never seen trees alight.

"Seriously, like the fucking end of the world. At least how I imagine it. At the real end of the world, though, I want to be alone. Is that bad?"

After she'd recovered from the excitement of hearing him swear, and had a moment to think about what he'd said, she coughed out the words, "I, uh, no. I don't think so." She didn't want the world to end, not yet. First, she had to see him again. Alma was glad he'd said *alone*, and not *by myself*, because she knew how to be alone with other people, and she suspected he did too.

He understood her, she was sure of it. He wanted the same things—solitude, quiet—when nearly everyone else had made her feel like there was something wrong with this. She thought of school, where gym class was supposed to be the most fun, but just finding a partner to play catch with seemed hard. She thought of dances and other after-school activities, where she awkwardly walked into rooms full of people, trying and failing to attach herself to a group already engaged in conversation. She thought of how angry it made her that her grades suffered due to participation points, when she knew she was learning just as much without having to shout answers out loud or be part of big group projects or give a presentation. She liked people, but if she could be invisible, if she could be a part of things without the pressure of having to talk, she would.

She smiled at this contradiction to his wanting to be alone, choosing to see the glitch in his logic as a sign that he meant apart from everyone *except* her.

A week later, the QSL card arrived in the mail—a three-by-five-inch note card confirming receipt of a communication over radio. It was pale yellow and had the town and province printed across the top in red. In the blank spaces, Alex had handwritten his call sign and hers, the date of the transmission—the first time they'd heard each other's voices since the day they met—the band, and the power input. His name was signed at the bottom.

There was still so much distance between them, but she tacked the QSL card to her wall and let the possibility curl up inside her like a periwinkle into its shell. She let it rest there.

They could be alone together, couldn't they?

They were like mountains. No one ever asked a mountain to do anything but be there, and a mountain never asked anything of anyone. You could be scared at the top of a peak, but the mountain would still be there under your feet, strong as ever. You could smile while standing on a mountain, and you didn't have to have a reason.

13

The last box in the newspaper office that Alma hadn't opened sat stupidly on the top of a bookshelf, where it had, over the years, edged closer and closer to tipping off. Alma stood on tiptoes on a stepladder, bracing herself for the weight, not knowing if she should expect heavy or too heavy. Her fingers grasped the slippery corners.

It was too heavy. The cardboard box crashed to the concrete floor, the top bursting apart, old newspapers spilling out. As she shuffled the papers back together, throwing away the ones that had been soaked by the eternal puddles on the floor, she found she was holding one dated 2022 that had a picture of the Marconi National Historic Site on the front page. In it, there was a square building that looked no different from a house with the exception of the flags flying from its roof and a large window that spanned most of one side. On the grass in front of the building, kids were flying kites. At the very left of the photo stood a metal tower and next to it a sign, the kind describing interesting details of the site.

She'd seen this image before, from a different angle, in the photo Alex had sent her in his first letter. *I'm writing a letter because this place reminded me of you, and we're always having make-believe conversations in my head.*

One hundred twenty years before the date of the paper, Guglielmo Marconi had made wireless history, at a time when communication was extending itself in all directions, beyond what could be accomplished by simply sitting in the same room.

Everyone, reaching out. Trying ever harder to speak to one another, to as many others as possible. Just over a century didn't seem like that long ago when Alma thought about it.

And yet somehow it seemed like an eternity since Alex had been reaching out to her from that same place. Attempting to connect without knowing if his letter would ever make it to Alma's mailbox. Miraculously, it had. And, miraculously, they had found their way to each other again.

A salamander wiggled from inside the rusted desk drawer, its shiny black body scurrying across the floor and up the wall. Jupiter's eyes followed it, though he didn't lift his chin from the floor. A short burst of static sent Alma's hand to her pocket. She clutched the two-way radio with cold fingers, holding it near her ear. She'd been paying attention again, even closer than before, but everything she'd heard so far was frustratingly inconsistent.

There had been something about constellations, and Alma recognized the voice and accent of a philosopher whose name she couldn't remember but who Alex used to quote frequently. But as he spoke, another broken voice came through—a stern woman giving a speech about a new type of alert system, something about weather. Equally unclear. The voices spoke on top of one another, and then there was silence again.

She was going to listen. That was her plan. But somehow, every time she thought she'd found the right station, the right frequency, the voices escaped her. "This is a stupid plan. We're never going to hear him with this much interference. We need to be closer. We need a stronger signal." Alma flung the newspaper across the room. It flapped against the rain-splattered window and fell to the wet floor, soaking up water.

"Easy now." Lucie appeared in the office doorway. She crossed the room with slow, silent steps, her blonde hair long down her back, wavy from undone braids. She picked up the wet paper, studying the photo on the front page. "Want to tell me why you're throwing things around a wet basement?"

"I just . . . never mind," Alma said. Jupiter nudged her with his backside until she nearly fell over. She crouched down next to him, as her walkie-talkie erupted with a silvery female voice talking about an upcoming live concert by Françoise Hardy. Alma fumbled to turn the volume down, watching Lucie fold the newspaper and set it on a broken filing cabinet.

Alma wondered if, by getting closer to the source of the echoed broadcasts, and maybe by bringing an actual echo with her, she'd be able to hear more directly. She said, "I'm going for a hike tomorrow morning. Want to come?"

～～～

That night, Alma stayed at the lighthouse until dark, only because her own cottage was beginning to feel less like a refuge than being near the open space and the sea. Sometimes she found it hard to sleep in her own small bed in her own small room.

Two teenagers came by after sunset. Alma watched through the small, foggy window of the keeper's house as they crouched behind a granite boulder outside, kissing, the boy running his hand over the girl's shirt. Alma's chest hurt and her body tingled at the thought of touching someone real again. She stepped back, and her foot caught the handle of a metal bucket, knocking it over. When the teenagers heard the crash from inside, they jumped up, startled, and ran down the path back to town.

After they'd run off, Oren's voice came from above. "What's going on down there?"

Mortified, Alma stepped outside and looked up to find him sitting in one of the lantern-room windows, his legs dangling out. "Nothing," she said. "It's just too damn dark to see in there. I tripped over something. What are you doing up there?"

"It's okay," he said, his eyes two sparks of moonlight. He sighed heavily and leaned into the open air. The ocean was glittering silver, the clouds above lit from behind, radiant against the black sky. "I miss it too. I used to stare across this ocean every night, thinking about going back to Ireland. Thinking what I might have left back there. It always seemed too difficult to manage. Now it would be the easiest thing in the world, but the truth is, there isn't anywhere else I'd rather be than here."

Alma pulled her sweater tighter around her. It would have been easy enough to climb the ladder, open the hatch door, and sit on the ledge with him. But there was no chest to put her head on up there—not one that would last. There was no hand to hold on to hers or to run through her hair—not one that was currently any closer to her than Alex's. She waited a few moments, in case Oren was going to say something else, thought about saying that she didn't want to be anywhere else either, and then said, "Good night."

~~~

It was getting colder, the heavy wind bringing with it a promise of the darker, grayer days to come. At sunrise, Alma zipped a fleece up to her neck and walked to Lucie's house. She carried a backpack stuffed to near bursting with blankets, food, and water. Her plan was to spend the night at the top of the mountain in the shelter, listening for something, taking notes on what she heard and when so she could look for patterns and, hopefully, navigate her way to Alex's voice. She had no idea what she would do if she actually heard it, but that was a problem for another time. First she had to find him—find his Echo.

Lucie was waiting on the porch, and on the way to the trailhead, they passed the cemetery and church. The path wove between the graves, beneath an immense maple tree that held, cradled in its branches, the nest of some giant bird. Two headstones leaned into each other, like lovers walking down a street side by side, the names covered by lichen and impossible to read. The tilted granite stones sank into the soft earth, the last of the season's wild roses clinging to them.

At the base of the mountain, Lucie said, "Theo used to make me hike up here all the time, back when we'd just started dating. He used to scare the shit out of me, climbing the tower. I haven't been up there in I don't know how long."

"I've only been once," Alma said. "I was on my way up for the second time when the storm came, and the lightning struck the tower."

"And we died." Lucie handed her a canvas bag. Alma reached in and took out a small red radio, pretty new but designed to look old fashioned, like it had been transported straight from the fifties. Alma had remembered seeing it in the bakery, warbling Ella Fitzgerald, and had asked Lucie to borrow it. Lucie jumped at the chance to sneak into the bakery and retrieve it without being caught.

"This should work," Alma said, stuffing the radio into her backpack.

As they began to climb, Lucie said, "I know you lost someone. Theo told me that's why you came here."

Alma just nodded, words always failing her when she attempted to actually talk about Alex. Ahead of her on the path, she spotted some tracks in the mud, thinking they might be ermine, wishing she'd brought Alex's tracking book just to know if she was right.

"So why did you need to come here?" Lucie asked, her forwardness taking Alma by surprise.

"I guess I didn't. I just knew it was far away from everyone else. I'm not very good at talking about things." As they passed the place where Jupiter had died, Alma glanced into the woods, looking for the hepatica she'd seen before, but the season had passed and it was all lost in a sea of red and brown. Lucie took long strides ahead, Jupiter keeping pace with her, while Alma struggled to not fall too far behind. This was her mission, and so she searched for a well of strength and momentum and hiked faster.

"Do you think you should?" Lucie called back over her shoulder.

"Should what?"

"Talk about things?"

"Do you think I should?"

Lucie shrugged, parting branches that had grown over the trail. "I don't know." She held the branches for Alma.

Alma caught up, breathing deeply. "Everyone else seems to think I should. Like it's the only way out of grief. Like wanting to be alone is a problem. Means I'm avoiding reality and there's something wrong with me."

"Do you think there's something wrong with you?" Lucie smiled. "For what it's worth, I don't think there is."

"Thanks."

As they reached the summit, Alma noted the colder, thinner air. They were surrounded by low-growing trees and bushes, nearly bare now. The rusted metal tower looked exactly as it had the last time she was there—intimidating and yet somehow comforting—with the exception of the collapsed antennas. The shelter roof was sinking more than before, and the door, which had already been torn off, had been moved into the bushes. They sat outside around the firepit, which Alma filled with pine needles. She propped small pieces of wood into a tee-pee and then lit the kindling. It smoked for a few moments before the flames shot up.

"Shit, that's a good fire," Lucie said. "You learn that back in Maine?"

Alma sat cross-legged on the rocks and took the radio from her backpack. "Just learning things all the time," she said.

"You sound like Oren."

Lucie poured Alma coffee from a thermos, Alma positioning the radio on a rock and turning the dial. She adjusted it, the sound coming in clearer. A man was counting, the numbers seemingly random. On the next station, a woman was singing a song, the style of music something Alma had never heard before. It was metallic and smooth all at once—a continual low ringing in the background. Alma went back and forth through each station a few times, listening carefully to each one, hearing nothing of interest. She switched the radio off.

"What is it you're expecting to hear?" Lucie asked.

"In Hayden's book, he said that the broadcasts people hear are not just happening in the present. They're from the past, present, *and* future. And since I'm able to see and hear you and Oren and Jupiter now, I should be able to hear Alex too. I just have to find the right frequency . . . this is all just a theory. I know it sounds stupid."

"It doesn't sound stupid," Lucie said, twisting the ends of her hair. "If there's a chance, you have to go for it, right?"

The words finally came, along with the instinct to stop them and hold them in, but somehow Alma felt safe in a way that she hadn't ever before. "Alex was the only person I knew that was like me. Since the first moment we met, he just understood what it was like to need quiet and solitude. No one else wants to let you do that, you know? They'll just tell you that you're detached and snobby and a thousand other things. I can't tell you how many people have said they thought I was some horrible bitch before they got to know me. But he just got it. And we spent so long apart, trying to be together, and then we were finally together and he was taken away."

Alma felt herself starting to cry. Lucie put an arm around her, and it felt like a cold ocean wave enveloping her. Alma leaned into it, taking a deep breath and a long sip of coffee. She pulled the two-way radio from her pocket and laid it on the ground. "When we were kids, we used to have these walkies. It was just a game. We had no idea what we were doing. We even had these made-up call signs."

"What were they?"

Alma laughed through tears. She'd never said them out loud to anyone before. "Oh my god, it's embarrassing. I was Darkest One, and he was Dire Wolf. They were more like old instant messaging handles than radio call signs. It's a long story. They came from this album we listened to when we first met."

Lucie turned the radio back on, and tuned in to a station where someone was reading a story in French. Alma recognized some of the words from the classes she'd taken in high school. *L'oiseau. Sourire. Baleine.*

"I was thinking of leaving," Lucie said. "Not just leaving Theo, but leaving town. And not going to that sorry excuse for a city on the other side of the island. I was going to go farther."

"How much farther?"

"I hadn't decided yet."

"Did you stay because of Theo?"

"I wish I could say that I did, but no. God, he's such a sweetheart and I love the hell out of him. But we just weren't going to make it. I was staying for my mother. She's been in the Violette hospital for ages, and this is going to sound horrible, but I was waiting for her to die so I could go with a clear conscience. Then I ended up dying first, how about that?" Lucie reached into her bag, taking out a small snow globe the size of a golf ball. "Here. I don't know why, but I stole this out of my own bedroom. It reminded me of you for some reason." She squinted at a plaque on the front. "Theo made me watch a lot of *Battlestar Galactica* when we first met."

As she passed it across the fire, the outer glass reflected swirls of orange flames. Inside the globe was a long gray starship. A sticker on the front of the base had been scratched almost entirely off: B   STAR GAL TI . The bottom was stamped with the year 2004. She tipped it upside down and back again, and tiny stars lifted and fell gently around the ship.

"I met Alex in 2004," Alma said. She'd never had a close girlfriend. But Lucie could have been one, Alma realized as she turned the snow globe in her hand. So many things came close to being said—*I love this* and *No one has ever given me anything so cool or meaningful* and *You're so kind and beautiful* and *Theo loved you so much*—but Alma just held the globe to her chest and said, "Thank you."

Lucie reached out, passing her hand through the flames slowly. She did not catch fire. Her gaze concentrated on the red-and-white glow of her fingers. "I wish you'd come sooner."

Alma tipped her head back and studied the stars, Cepheus directly above them, holding his arms up in prayer. Her chest felt like the garnet star that burned in the constellation, unstable and about to supernova. "Me too," she said.

～～～

Throughout the night, the radio spoke into the darkness. They'd moved into the shelter, Alma crawling into her sleeping bag on the cold, hard floor. Jupiter's back was pressed against hers. In the middle of the night, Alma woke to voices accompanied by so much static it was impossible to make out the words. Every once in a while there was a burst of something clearer, in what she thought was Japanese.

Lucie sat over the radio, still listening, taking notes. She whispered: "I read just before I died that there are seventy-five star systems out there that we have reached with Earth's radio technology. And they could reach us too. They think there's something like thirty habitable planets in a hundred-light-year radius that could have detected our radio signals by now." Lucie turned the radio dial, jumping from one staticky voice to another. "If that's true, anything could be. It sounds like a good case for Alex's Echo being out there, don't you think?"

Alma pulled her sleeping bag tighter around her shoulders. They'd been there all day and night, and she hadn't heard anything that had brought her closer to Alex's voice, and she wondered why she'd even expected to. She didn't say so then, but Lucie's case of the many star systems out there didn't provide comfort. It only made the universe seem that much vaster. And it felt even less likely that amid all of it, Alma would find exactly what she was looking for.

"I don't even know what I'm listening for," she said.

"You'll know it when you hear it," Lucie said. "Just keep listening."

Then Alma was silent. The Echoes were silent. The airwaves were silent.

~~~

In the morning, as they hiked back down the mountain, the dark silhouette of a red-tailed hawk flew over them. It lifted off from its nest at the top of a dead jack pine and passed over Alma and Lucie and Jupiter, bringing with it a wave of cold, salty air.

Lucie held Alma's hand while they were still a good distance from town, letting go only when they'd returned to their version of the civilized world. Real people, real voices. Alma tucked her hands into her jacket pockets then, wrapping her fingers around the snow globe. It wasn't the thing she'd gone in search of. The stars inside weren't even real.

But it was still so much more than she'd gone up with.

14

Bea never would have asked. Alma knew this, but she also knew that her aunt liked her company, and she'd promised Emerson she'd visit more often. This is what Alma reminded herself as she stepped up to Bea's cottage with a five-pound bag of potatoes clutched in each fist. She used her foot to knock.

It was an elaborate mess of work to make rappie pie. When Alma walked into the kitchen, there were already another forty pounds or so of cut potatoes soaking in five-gallon buckets on the floor. Bea had pulled the juicer onto the counter and was pressing the potatoes in one by one, piling the pulp into a large pot. The house was already steaming and hot with the smell of chicken broth.

Emerson smiled from the kitchen table, where he was cutting the cooked turkey into small pieces. Bea leaned over the stove, peering into the steaming pot of broth, her white hair piled onto the top of her head, disheveled.

"Am I late?" Alma asked, watching through the window over the sink as Jupiter ran into the backyard, chasing a chipmunk.

"Not at all," Bea said, wiping her hands on a towel and taking the bags.

"I brought some brandy too," Alma said, letting a canvas bag drop from her shoulder to the table. "Apple."

"Perfect," Emerson said.

When Theo arrived, he was wet and tired, taking off his boots and collapsing onto the couch in the living room. From there, he yelled back out to the kitchen, "I thought you were going to restart the newspaper, Alma."

"I am," she said.

"Huh. But, have you written anything in the last year?"

Since cleaning out the newspaper office, she had printed Hayden's story, and otherwise, a few other small articles, mostly about animals Alphie had rescued—a snapping turtle, a raccoon. She'd even managed to track down a wildlife photographer who'd taken serendipitous photos of an eastern red-backed salamander as it slithered beneath the plastic pool in her backyard.

"I'm publishing a book," Alma said. "One that MacKenna wrote." It wasn't true until that moment. Until then she hadn't even considered it, but suddenly it seemed like a good idea. A great idea even. She had what she needed to print at least a couple of copies of *Tower of Echoes*, and nothing would have made Hayden happier than to know he'd had a posthumous publication.

Emerson stopped chopping at the table and said, "Let me know when you do. I'll read it. Also, there's talk about more people leaving The City now too. Like, a lot of people. I guess they're close to giving up."

Bea threw her towel at him. "You don't want to plant that idea in peoples' heads. We're all going to hear about it one way or another, but don't hand it to them and get people all wondering and curious about whether or not they should go too."

Alma eyed Emerson, scanning his face for some hint of their conversation the day they'd interviewed Victor. She wondered if he still thought about leaving. But he was absorbed again in his cutting, his tall frame bent over the cutting board.

"We're going to have a big meetup at the lighthouse soon," Theo shouted. "Maybe you can print up an invite. We need as many hands as possible to repair the seawalls. The cliff is eroding pretty fast, and the walls are going to get washed out one of these storms. Okay, I'm done. Someone bring me a drink?"

They poured the brandy and spent the afternoon juicing potatoes, mashing the pulp with chicken broth and boiling water, layering a large pan with the potatoes and turkey. Alma helped Bea finish assembling the pies—two large pans—and topped each one with butter.

The pies were going to cook for a couple of hours, so Bea retreated to her bedroom for a nap, as she'd taken to doing whether she'd had any brandy or not. She was slowing down, and lately Alma was more aware of her own age whenever she saw her aunt. Alma was tired a lot, her stamina for almost everything shorter. Her neck and shoulders were sore if she spent a day hunched over the computer, and also if she slept for more than six hours.

She could feel her cheeks, hot and pink. As she splashed cold water on her face, Alma caught herself in the bathroom mirror. A rare occurrence. She noticed silver strands, light streaks framing her face when she pulled back handfuls of red. There were lines around her eyes and above her top lip. Just seeing her own reflection made her tired, but she didn't want to sleep anymore. Not alone in her tiny cottage, where her only real comforts came from a dog that she was keeping on borrowed time.

Theo and Emerson were playing cribbage in the living room. The sound of the heater singing the top fifty songs from 1952 drifted throughout the house. As Alma walked in to join them, she was startled by the figure at the back of the room. Lucie sat on a bench in a darkened corner by the piano, her head tipped against the wall, her legs crossed. She held her finger to her lips.

Alma tried not to audibly gasp, sitting in a chair opposite her cousins. Once in a while she caught Theo staring at random things for unusually long periods of time—the sleeve of his shirt, a wooden sailboat his father had carved, the cat stretched out on the coiled rug.

"Do you guys remember that episode of *Battlestar Galactica*," Theo said, as Emerson began dealing cards, "where Kara is trying to kill Scar, and before that, they show the wall of all the people they'd lost?"

Lucie straightened in her seat. Alma's eyes flicked over to her, then back to Theo. "I've never seen it," she said.

"I saw a snow globe at your house the other day. I had the weirdest pang of sadness when I saw it, which I can only attribute to how much I truly loved the show. I figured you'd seen it."

Alma cleared her throat. "That was a gift," she said. "From a good friend."

Lucie tapped her feet on the floor and said, "He's talking about my favorite episode."

Alma looked away quickly, tugging on the ends of her hair as Theo went on.

"Well, they're fighting, and Kara gets distracted because she's thinking of Anders—her supposedly dead husband. Spoiler, sorry. Then Kat's the one who ends up killing Scar, but she gets all braggy later on, and Kara makes this toast about all of their fallen comrades to put her in her place. That's not the point I'm trying to make."

"What point are you trying to make?" Emerson asked, waving his cards in the air.

"I can't remember." Theo sighed. "That was such a good show."

"Hey, Starbuck," Emerson said, "this game is supposed to move quickly."

"Ten."

"Fifteen for two."

"Twenty for two."

Their hands moved in fast, mechanical motions, jumping pegs along the board. Alma could barely keep up with what cards they put down, let alone do the math. She leaned back and closed her eyes and thought about the previous day when she'd climbed the mountain again, alone, listening for signs of Alex. She'd brought Lucie's radio but this time hadn't turned it on. Instead, the sounds she heard came streaming through the antenna itself like it was a speaker, from some frequency the radio itself wouldn't even have picked up. She'd heard someone being interviewed—apparently the person had seen a ghost standing on their back porch one evening. But Alma quickly realized it wasn't anyone in Violette. Their accents were German, and it was simply a show that attempted to prove the paranormal. When the broadcast had originally taken place was unclear. After that, she'd heard a series of numbers being repeated in a monotone voice, and then something in French. She'd quickly taken her pen and written down what she could capture.

"Thirty."

"That's a go."

When her cousins had had enough cribbage, they both put their feet up on the coffee table, checking their watches frequently and engaging in lively conversations about methods of beer brewing and whether to use vodka or gin to make cranberry liqueur with the thirty pounds of cranberries Theo had foraged.

Emerson got up to light a fire, and at some point, Lucie slipped out without Alma noticing.

An hour later, Alma was filling a glass of water at the sink as Bea emerged from the bedroom. She wore an embroidered sleeveless top, her flannel shirt tied around her waist. As Bea opened the oven to check on the pies, Alma caught sight of the tattoo that Oren had put on her arm years ago. She'd forgotten all about it.

"Almost ready," Bea said, and she closed the oven door and shuffled quietly into the living room and sat in a chair by the window, put on her glasses, and opened a bird book. The evening warblers crowded her bird feeders, while the starlings gathered in massive swooping numbers in the indigo sky.

"What did you say it meant again?" Alma called to her from the kitchen.

"What does what mean, love?"

"Your tattoo."

"Oh, gosh. I don't know." Bea examined her arm. "It's been there for so long, I can't remember even getting it now. It sure hasn't aged well. What could it . . . ?" Her eyes followed the black birds through the window.

Rien n'est éternel. Nothing lasts forever.

Alma's skin tingled. She could feel the symbols etching themselves onto her, like urchins crawling over her body, and the need to have this actualized was suddenly all she could think about. They sat together at the rectangular dining room table made by Hubert from a giant piece of driftwood, and Emerson pulled the crusty edges from the pie and piled them onto Bea's plate.

"She's got dibs on the edges," Theo said. "Always has, so don't even think about it."

"I would never."

Alma tried to slow her heart so she could savor the thick, salty potatoes and turkey they'd all waited so long for, but in her mind, she was already hours ahead, biking up the coast, knocking on his door. In her mind, she was cataloging all the words and images that she'd accumulated over the years from correspondence with Alex. A whole life—past, present, future—laid out in ink.

~~~

Oren's cottage sat perched with a view of the sea in front and the forested hills behind. When she reached it, Alma passed through the garden, which was no longer a garden but a years-old tangle of dried tomato plants and squash vines. The wire fencing was curling to the ground between tilted wooden posts.

Through the window, she saw him inside, sitting in a corner at a small table with a stack of books in front of him, his feet propped up on another chair. She tapped on the window frame—he hadn't replaced the glass after the big storm—and he waved her in.

He continued flipping pages as he watched her enter the room. She stood in the doorway.

"Can you give me a tattoo?" she asked. She was embarrassed to find herself out of breath suddenly, as if saying the words had released something she'd been holding inside too long.

"Now?"

"Yeah, now. Is that something you can still do?"

"I think so. But hey, come in. Let's chat a bit first. There's no rush, right? You're my first guest in . . . a couple of years."

She glanced around the cottage. To her left there was a sitting area where, instead of a couch, there were pillows piled along the perimeter of a red-and-yellow rug, a low, round table in the middle. The walls were floor-to-ceiling bookshelves, and in the gaps between groups of books, the bones of sea animals were wedged in as bookends. To her right was a small, dimly lit kitchen. The counter was made of a massive piece of stone, and beach stones created a spiraling maze around its surface.

"Your house is . . . not what I expected," she said, picking up a piece of smoky quartz from a shelf and gripping its cold, smooth shape in her palm. Her fingers closed around it, the sharp, pointed end of it pressing into her skin.

"My father left it to me when he died," he said. "I never would have been able to afford it on my own." He closed his book and let it rest in his lap. "You can have that," he said, nodding toward her closed hand. She found she was still grasping the quartz and quickly put it down on the kitchen table. "Actually, you can have anything you'd like. I have no need for it now, and no one else to give it to."

"You have a daughter," Alma started to say, then stopped herself from going on because she liked the idea of being the closest thing Oren had to a best friend, even if it was by default.

"Ah, Lille," he said, standing up and stretching his arms above his head, his fingertips grazing the low ceiling beam. Little wire ornaments in the shapes of various animals—bear, wolf, gull—hung from the light fixtures. When Fey flew into the house, her wings grazed them and sent them swaying. She landed on his stack of books. "I'm sure she doesn't even know I exist now. And as much as I'd love to leave her everything, this is all there is. Rocks, trinkets, old books. You appreciate these things. Take it, please."

"She will," Alma said.

"She will what?"

"Know that you exist."

"Oh." Oren gazed at the speckled ceiling, then nodded. "Perhaps."

"Your father grew up in Ireland?" Alma asked as he crossed the room. She stepped aside as he passed into the kitchen, his brief touch as light as air passing over her skin, but also somehow heavy and lingering. He adjusted the smooth stones on the table, then picked up the crystal and placed it in her hand.

"I want you to take this. And yes. My father was Tadgh Ainsley, the painter. Well known over there. Not quite so much here."

"Is he why you became an artist?"

"He'd have disagreed with your use of the term *artist*. He never thought what I did was very creative, or maybe he didn't think it was hard enough or controversial enough. What I did wasn't *real* art to him."

"Do you have any of his work?" she asked.

Oren hesitated. "I have . . . ," he began; then he sighed. He rested his elbows on the counter. "I have almost all of it. Of course, it's also yours now. I'm glad you're here. I've been wanting to show it to you for a long time."

"You have?"

"Yeah."

"Why haven't you?"

"Well, why haven't you come to visit?"

She had no answer. She almost said that he hadn't invited her, but it felt too playful, borderline flirtatious, so instead she followed him into the next room, where dozens of painted canvases covered the walls.

"Can I?" Alma asked, reaching to touch the closest one.

Oren took a step back, crossing his arms over his chest, and shrugged. "Like I said, they're all yours. Do what you like."

In the first painting, a bald man with sharp features was leaning, shouting into a microphone. Behind him, protest signs were layered over one another. In the next, barefoot pilgrims climbed a mountain by way of a rocky dirt path. The point of view of the painting was from below, close to the heels of the men and women depicted, looking up toward the mountain peak.

Alma paused to take in each one. Postal service workers standing in a line. A man giving a radio interview, his mouth close to the microphone. The paint was thick and the colors neutral. There was plenty of contrast, but Tadgh Ainsley never seemed to stray too far from tones of brown and gray.

As she finished circling the room, finding herself back where she began, Alma noticed a thirty-six-inch-tall canvas on the floor, propped against the wall, backward. She hesitated, but then picked it up and turned it around. On top of a giant, churning wave, a man rode a white horse. He was massive and mythical—his body turquoise, his long hair and beard white. He held a long tree-branch spear over his head.

"This one is amazing," Alma said. "The colors. It's like another world. It's magical."

Oren moved in next to her to look, as if he'd never seen it before. "Ah yes. It's Manannán mac Lir, so it's absolutely another world," he said.

"These paintings should all be in a museum somewhere," Alma said.

"They were. Sort of."

"Why isn't this one on the wall?" she asked.

"Because," Oren said, clearing his throat. "It's mine."

"*You* painted that?"

Oren smiled. "Yeah, yeah, don't look so shocked. It was for a color theory course in school." He touched her elbow with feather-like fingers, guiding her away. "Let's head back upstairs and talk about this tattoo."

~~~

She handed Oren a folded piece of paper—a series of lines and dots. Three lines, two dots, three lines, two dots. He hadn't tattooed anything on anyone in many years, so long that he said he considered himself retired, but he'd make an exception for her, especially when her request was such a simple one. Alma sat in a chair in the narrow room, her forearm propped palm up on the armrest. Oren spent some time fiddling with equipment on a metal table, then swiveled a stool up close to her, the needle in his hand.

"What is this?" he asked.

"It's Morse code for the number eighty-eight. It means 'love and kisses.'"

He gave her a sideways glance and shrugged, but didn't ask any more questions. Perhaps he'd done this so many times he was used to strange, personal requests. His curiosity could no longer be piqued. "You've never done this before?"

She shook her head.

"Don't be nervous, it's nothing," he said.

It wasn't nothing. It was so much more than nothing. It was an elemental force she hadn't expected, a surge of air and water and fire rushing from her wrist up through her chest. Alma closed her eyes and breathed into it.

"Wow," she said as she exhaled.

"There you go," he said. "Just stay relaxed. Tell me what you've been hearing lately, on the radio." The needle moved over her skin in tiny circles, and he stopped every few moments to wipe away ink and blood with a towel.

"Not much," she said. She pressed her lips together. "There's a lot of noise, a lot of static. Sometimes I hear strings of numbers, sometimes old music. Yesterday, there was some French. I got *voix ambiguë d'un cœur* . . . but that was it. I couldn't catch the rest. I translated it—'ambiguous voice of a heart'—and it could mean something, if I knew where it was coming from."

Oren shook his head, amused. "*Voix ambiguë d'un cœur qui au zéphyr préfère les jattes de kiwis.* That's the rest. It's a French pangram. You still think it's worth your time, sitting there listening to random broadcasts?"

"I do," she said. "I know it's worth it. He's out there. I just have to be listening."

"And what if you spend all your time waiting and never hear him? What then?"

"I'll hear him."

Oren shrugged. "Whether he's out there or not, either way, it just seems there could be more for you moving forward with the living instead of reaching back to the past. Just a thought."

Alma was surprised she could feel anything anywhere other than her arm, but her chest knotted with a kind of desire to hold on desperately to something that had the potential to slip away.

"The past is where I live and I like it that way," she said flatly. "Everything that really matters to me is in the past. Alex, Jupiter, this place . . ." She paused, the stinging in her arm suddenly making her brave. "Even you."

"What were you doing there?" Alma asked the next time she saw Lucie. It had been a few days since she'd caught Lucie hiding in the corner of Bea's house, watching Theo. Alma was in the newspaper office, using the same software she'd used for Hayden's story to design an actual book from his manuscript. *Tower of Echoes* wasn't all that long, but still it was painstaking to retype it. She was nearing the end of that tedious part of the project, and getting closer to the fun part—designing a cover, printing it all out, and binding it. A cold front had blown in, and there was no heat in the office, so Alma typed wearing a thick wool coat, a hat low over her eyebrows and a scarf wrapped around her neck. Her fingers were stiff.

"I peek in once in a while to make sure he's doing okay," Lucie said. "Most of the time he seems fine. Once in a while he gets distracted, or he gets this far-off look in his eyes like he's deep in thought. I wish I knew what about."

"I'm guessing he's thinking about something he doesn't fully remember," Alma said.

"If I go," Lucie said, "he'll remember. But then his fiancée will have died. Is that better?"

"I don't know." Alma considered trying to convince her to stay a little longer. An invitation hovered in her throat, and she almost asked her to climb the mountain with her again, to sit and listen to the voices echoing.

But before she could ask, Lucie said, "I need a favor."

"Sure, of course."

"My mother. I was hoping you'd go see her for me."

"I—" Alma began, wishing she'd asked before so casually agreeing. She didn't like hospitals, for the same reasons many other people she knew didn't. But she especially didn't like the feelings she got as she walked down the hallways, the sorrow and grief of those who'd been admitted along with those who were visiting. She'd gone to see her own grandmother in the hospital in Bangor once, before she died, and Alma had had to run outside to the woods shortly after arriving. When her parents found her half-asleep in the moss under an oak tree, they were disappointed in her, but it couldn't be helped. She'd never been inside the hospital in Violette, which sat at the end of a dogwood-lined dirt road at the back edge of town. "Is it a big place?" she asked, even though she knew the answer.

"It's Violette. There's no such thing."

"Right. How long has she been there?"

"Years. I can't remember how many anymore. But going there now, she doesn't know I'm even there, and I'm getting the feeling that she doesn't have much time left. I just want someone to be in the room with her, someone with a hand she can actually feel, one more time before she's gone."

Alma knew the requirements of a task like this. It wouldn't be an easy thing for her to do, to be in a place with so many suffering people, but she was certain that Lucie would have done it for her. She also knew what this meant—that Lucie's mother was almost gone, and so Lucie was thinking of going too.

"Of course," Alma said.

The wind roared outside and plastered wet, dead leaves against the window.

"When she goes, I go," Lucie said.

~~~

Lucie's mother, Delia St. Pierre, sank into the mattress, the cushions swallowing her. Alma felt her disorientation as soon as she walked into the room, but had armed herself against it by bringing Jupiter along to counter any negative feelings. She sat next to Lucie's mother and said quietly, "Hi, Delia. I'm Alma. I'm a friend of Lucie's. Of your daughter's." There was no response from the woman, whose skin appeared to be slowly melting from her bones, so translucent her blue veins could be seen beneath her eyelids.

There was a whisper in Alma's ear, but when she turned, there was no one else in the room. She touched Delia's hand and knew something was different about her. It wasn't just her feelings that Alma was taking in, but her thoughts as well. From inside Delia's mind, Alma heard a frightened woman screaming to get out. Alma pulled her hand back and stood up, walking over to the window. From there, she could see the ocean, enveloped in mist, a frigid grayness coming toward the town.

She thought again of the time she'd gone to visit her grandmother, how the collective sorrow had flooded into her. Then she thought of Hayden and the joy he'd discovered once in this very building. Touching the top of Jupiter's head, Alma whispered, "We can handle this. It's for Lucie," then took a deep breath and sat once more with Delia St. Pierre.

"Okay," she said, "tell me what's in there. Tell me what you have to say." But when she listened, really listened, Alma heard only fragments of thoughts. Tiny bits of sentences and ideas. *Sunrise, free fall, meddle, kettle, black.* The pieces didn't make any sense, but Alma tried to retain as many of them in her memory as she could, hoping they'd be of some use to Lucie later. *Happening, bustle, trip.*

These seemed like the ramblings of someone who did not plan to stay much longer. Of the multitude of disjointed thoughts that swarmed Alma's mind, the one that kept playing in her head after she left the room was the word *watcher*, which, later, Alma thought might have been two words: *watch her.*

There were only a few rooms in the hospital, and as Alma left, she avoided looking into any of them but couldn't help herself as she passed room 6. No one was in there, so she slipped inside briefly to peek at the ceiling, the painted-over words of Alphie Roy still partially visible.

All great ideas are dangerous.

There was something warmer about that room that didn't exist in the rest of the building, and she stayed there, letting that glow trickle through her bloodstream for another moment, wrapping that feeling around her as she pulled on her coat. It was November and just beginning to snow as she stepped outside and started the quiet walk home. But, when she reached the street to her cottage, instead she turned northeast and kept going, not thinking about what she was doing until she was there, sitting in Oren's darkened living room, her arm tingling with new ink once more.

～～～

Alma told Lucie about hearing Delia's words, desperate to escape from inside her mind. She told her that her mother was still in there, wanting to get out. Lucie nodded. "That sounds about right," she said. "She's gone in and out of this before, since I was a kid. She told me that when it happened the first time, she was sitting with a friend having tea. She had a headache suddenly, and was asking her friend why everything was so loud. She complained about the pain in her head, but when her friend didn't respond, Mom realized that she wasn't speaking out loud. She was trying to but couldn't."

As she spoke, Lucie squinted. She touched the corners of her eyes and then inspected her fingers. They were dry, though she seemed confused as to why there were no tears.

"She was trapped in there. Trying to speak, but her brain couldn't make her mouth do the things she wanted it to. She was out for a few years that first time. She came back for a while, and told me that story, but then, not long after, she went inside again. It seems like torture—being stuck like that."

～～～

A few days later, Delia was gone.

"Are you sure this is what you want?" Alma asked, but Lucie had made it clear that she didn't think in terms of *want*. It was her responsibility to do the right thing. She'd seen her mother off, and she couldn't let Theo go on the way he was, distantly confused and inexplicably sad.

"All I know is something important happened when Hayden left us," Lucie said. "Being remembered had meaning, and there is something not quite right about a person's existence being extracted from the world."

Alma knew she was right. But she felt a twinge of envy at the calm confidence Lucie had always emanated, when she was alive and also after, when she was sitting there in the dark, ready to say goodbye to her life. Though Alma was, when it came down to it, a runaway, she still wondered if she'd have the ability to accept and let go with such ease when the time came.

"It's funny that I was thinking of leaving Violette when I died. This wasn't exactly what I had in mind. But hey, I guess I'm getting what I wanted one way or another." Lucie must have caught her troubled gaze because she reached a hand for Alma's and said, "You don't need any more ghosts hanging around, okay?"

Alma wanted to say that she'd take as many ghosts as she could get. "Okay."

They sat together on the desk in the newspaper office until late at night, the candles they'd lit eventually curling in on themselves, Alma writing as quickly as she could, Lucie trying to slow down as every thought seemed to spill out, one somersaulting over the other. It came easily; she'd known for so long what she was going to say.

~~~

The morning Alma placed the stapled pages of Lucie's story on a table outside the bakery, the two of them walked to the lighthouse. Oren was there waiting. The three of them faced the sea, silent. Lucie kept alternating from searching up and down the shore, to looking down at her own hands with curiosity, as if she expected at any moment for her form to simply vanish.

Eventually she said, "This is ridiculous, waiting for something to happen. I don't even know what I'm waiting for. I'm going to the water. I want to be where I died . . . when I die."

She gave Alma a tattered index card and a long hug that felt like being wrapped in a gentle tornado. Then Alma and Oren watched her descend the cliff steps to the beach where she'd put in her kayak the night of the flash.

"I didn't say goodbye to her," Oren said. "Do you think I should have?"

"I mean, yes, probably?" Alma looked at the index card—a stained, handwritten recipe for what had been Lucie's famous molasses cookies—to avoid having to look up through teary eyes.

"Nah, she seems happy," Oren said. "I'm not going to bother her with any unnecessary drama."

"I feel like all I ever do is say goodbye to people."

Hayden was gone. Lucie was gone. All she had left was Jupiter, Oren, a dark office, and a whole spectrum of frequency bands to search. It was all just out of reach and slipping away from her like kelp floating on a wave. Soon, she'd have nothing.

"What are you going to do now?" Oren asked.

Alma turned away, burying her chin into the collar of her thick scarf. "Are you next?" her muffled voice demanded. Oren pulled her to his chest, and this time it wasn't like a tornado, but like the stratosphere had fallen to envelop her shoulders. He smelled like wet moss and salt. "I don't know what to do," she said.

A short, amused laugh.

Alma glanced up at him, noticing three tattooed swallows traveling up his neck and beneath his chin. "What's so funny? All I have is you and the ghost of Jupiter. And I know Alex is out there but I haven't heard a single thing to prove that it's even possible, even though I still *believe* it's possible. So, what's so hilarious?"

"Oh, I'm just wondering why you're still waiting around for someone to find *you* on the radio when you're perfectly capable of reaching out yourself."

"Not this again."

Oren took her shoulders and spun her to face him. "All right, yes, I still think you're wasting time on this mission, but just so we're all clear, what is it you're trying to do again?"

Alma broke out of his grip and sank onto a cold rock. "I'm trying to find the voice of someone who is dead." The words were getting less difficult to say, starting to sound less crazy, she realized.

"And, did you try sending a signal?"

She thought she had, but . . .

He handed her a heavy hardcover book, and while the title—*Guide to Amateur Shortwave Radio*—made it obvious enough what he was suggesting, she wasn't done feeling sorry for herself.

"What am I supposed to do with this?" she asked, knowing it was a stupid question.

"Christ, Alma, are you really waiting for one voice in a billion voices to just speak to you, or for some signal to just come breaking through the airwaves? You walk around with a radio in your pocket twenty-four hours a day. If you want to send a signal, go and send one!"

"Shit," she said, looking back toward the mountain. Despite testing it every once in a while, she'd come to think of the two-way radio she and Alex had played with as kids as a kind of sad, foolish game. But Oren was right. She'd listened, but she hadn't tried to really send a signal, to really reach out.

"I knew you'd figure it out," Oren said. "That's from the cottage, by the way, so it's technically yours. It's been on *your* shelf for ages. Good luck."

He slapped her on the back and told her he was going to stay away from the cottage for a while to give her some space, so she could be alone, and she was shocked by how much the word *alone* stung. As he walked away, hands in his pockets, shoulders hunched, leaving her there with an almost-renewed hope, he called back, "Don't keep waiting around for us, okay?"

"I won't," she said, eyes locked with Jupiter's. Sitting on the granite, Alma flipped through the book and made a list of things she had and things she would need. She scribbled hasty, nearly unreadable notes until her fingers were stiff from the cold, but it didn't take long for the path to become clear.

Clutching the two-way radio, her index finger holding down the talk button, she said, "This is Darkest One. I repeat, this is Darkest One. Do you copy?" Alma braced herself for whatever was not going to come calling back to her, but static broke through as she released the button. Someone said, "Copy that, Darkest One," and even though it wasn't Alex, even though it was a fading woman's voice that sounded remarkably like Lucie's, Alma began laughing until her eyes were burning with tears.

She held the button down again. "We miss you," she said. Then she turned to Jupiter. "This is going to work. But we're going to need more than what we have."

〜〜

Of course, she couldn't tell Theo the real reason she needed the supplies, the reason she was planning to set up a radio station in the dark, flooded newspaper office that she'd inherited from a dead writer. But she owed him some kind of explanation, so she said, "It's a hobby."

She showed him her books about amateur radio and a list she'd made of items she needed from his next supply trip. He gave her a questioning look after reading it, but said, "You're strange, you know that? And you know you don't need all this clunky equipment anymore. There is far better technology for this. Far, far better."

Again, Alma found she couldn't explain. That it had to be this technology, this equipment—the kind that was old and clunky and familiar. The kind only two kids who dreamed of each other in frequencies, who called themselves Darkest One and Dire Wolf, would understand.

"Not for this," she said.

15

Lucie St. Pierre, printed, staple bound, 2030

Lucie's mother used to tell her there was no such thing as an accident. Lucie assumed this was her mother's attempt at an optimistic view of the world. Everyone was where they were because that was where they needed to be. Who knew why, at this point or that point. It didn't matter.

It was just another way of saying what Lucie had heard from the mouth of the priest at their church as he clasped the hands of widowers. *Everything happens for a reason.*

On the nights when Lucie lay in bed, listening through thin walls to her mother and father arguing, all that seemed like a lot of bullshit.

Here's what I can say about Lucie: her brightness couldn't be found inside her. It was all around her, which sounds all kinds of cheesy, I know, but it's true. It was visible when she created something, which she learned to do eventually, but there I go again, getting ahead.

Lucie waited in the car while her mother grabbed a few last things from the house. Delia St. Pierre wanted it to be clean, and for it to look like she was just out for some groceries. Nothing out of the ordinary. With the window cracked, the humidity seeped into the car, and Lucie pressed her cheek against the glass. She needed air. When her mother slid into the driver's seat and slammed the door, she had a smile on her face. Lucie wouldn't forget that. It was a free smile, the kind you let light you up when you have nothing left to lose.

They drove from Salem, Massachusetts, up the coast toward Portsmouth, New Hampshire. Her mother had maps sticking out of her canvas shopping bag, but she didn't look at any of them. What she did consult was a list of addresses. She held the index card pinned to the wheel as she drove.

An hour later they were turning onto a long dirt road. The empty house was at the very end, tucked behind oak trees, but by no means small. Her mother parked the car, and they both leaned forward to see through the windshield. It was two floors, the slate-blue wood siding peeling off. The porch wrapped around the front and one side, boards dipping and the railing splintered.

She had never seen a place that looked quite so abandoned. Lucie thought of her father then, and what it was they were running away from. He would feel abandoned, too, she realized. She pictured her own home deteriorating over the years, her father falling apart inside along with it. It saddened her, but that wasn't why she did what she did in the days to come.

A piano sat on the caving porch. It was the lone object that had been left behind by the previous owners. It crouched there in the darkness of the porch roof, the keys yellowed, some of the black ones missing altogether. Lucie crawled along the cracked boards on all fours and found a couple of them under the pedals.

Her mother tried the front doorknob. This was the best she was going to get, that was clear enough. So why waste any time really judging the place? She kicked the door open with her toe and stepped inside. The floorboards groaned. Lucie wondered how long it had been since someone had come to even peek inside these windows.

It was open and empty. Lucie banged on the piano keys, and the sound reverberated through the entire frame of the house. She felt it vibrating. Her mother's face appeared in the window behind the piano and startled her. Lucie had every expectation of seeing a ghost there. She just hadn't expected the familiarity.

Lucie pounded on the piano keys some more. She had taken lessons when she was younger, though she quit when she was eight, and now, seven years later, she already couldn't remember a single song besides "Heart and Soul," and even then, her fingers tripped over some of the keys.

Through the window, she saw her mother wandering aimlessly through the empty rooms. The floors were bare wood; the only things left on them were some painter's cloths and stray nails. All the walls had been slathered white. There was nothing in there that Lucie needed to see. If her mother wanted to run away from her father, and take her along, and take her *here*, she had no opinion.

As they backed the car down the long driveway, Lucie watched the house become smaller and wondered what her mother was thinking then. Were her dreams shrinking as well? Was this real, or was this going to be another fantasy that slowly slipped away for her the further she got from its reality?

The following day, Lucie's father took her to lunch. He sat across from her in the booth, and there was a sadness in his eyes that she had never seen before. He'd started wearing a baseball hat lately because his hair was going, and he scratched nervously beneath the visor.

"When I was a kid," he said, "my mother used to always buy these tissues that came in a box with the same picture on them. It was a scene of a log cabin with a waterwheel. The cabin was by a river. I used to look at it and imagine I was in the picture, pretend I lived in the cabin. It was a kind of escape for me. I don't know what I thought I needed to escape from." Lucie sipped her soda through a straw and said nothing. No one said anything for a few minutes.

"Your mother is sick," her father said finally, just as the waitress came with their plates. She wedged her hip into the table and put the food down in front of them. When she left, her father stared into a chicken-fried steak and said again, "She's sick, Lucie. She has no sense of reality. She lives in a fantasy world. Do you understand what I'm saying?"

Lucie nodded, but she didn't really understand. Both her father and mother seemed to be stuck in some strange, fictional realm, which only made her doubt her own ability to judge the world around her. She bit into her grilled cheese, pretending it wasn't too hot, so she wouldn't have to say anything in response.

A few days later, her father walked around the kitchen island, lifting stacks of bills and magazines, muttering to himself. He yelled up the stairs to Lucie's mother, "Where's the checkbook?"

Delia yelled back, "I don't know! How should I know?"

Lucie could have chosen differently. It isn't that she could have thought harder about her words before she said them. That would imply that she hadn't considered the idea of sabotaging her mother's plans. And she couldn't explain the impulse to do it. She truly didn't care one way or the other. Perhaps she just wanted to see what would happen, or to shake things a little. Perhaps it was just that she could.

Still, as soon as the words left her mouth, she knew it was one of those moments that would change the course of everything, and which she could never take back. From the kitchen table and through a mouthful of Cheerios, Lucie blurted out, "She probably dropped it at the other house."

"What *other* house?" her father whispered angrily. Lucie glanced up at the ceiling, as if she might be able to see her mother—upstairs doing who knows what—through it. She said nothing.

"Lucie," her father said, and something about the way his voice got low made Lucie trust him. Made her think for a minute that he might understand and that everything would end up being okay if she just told the truth.

After she told him, and he pounded up the stairs, and things began crashing against walls, she remembered. He never did understand, but somehow he always convinced her—and her mother—that they should try again. He was her father after all. But that morning, objects were thrown, her mother probably one of them, and Lucie began pacing around the kitchen. Covering her ears did nothing to block the sound, and so she opened a cookbook and began reciting a cookie recipe out loud. *Two cups flour, one cup sugar* . . . The act of saying the ingredients and measurements took her to another place. It was like a meditation in which her mind drifted out of her body.

What people always *thought* they knew about Lucie—that her baking was a way to reach out and connect to the world—was simply an assumption. In truth, it was a way for her to reach into herself, to block the rest of the world out. The problem with baking as meditation, though, was that after you were done, you were left with bread, cake, cookies, and any number of pastries you couldn't possibly eat alone. She always thought it a little dishonest that she got so much peace out of baking, as she gave her baked goods away and perpetuated this dishonest impression of herself.

Eventually, Lucie's mother did find a way out. She met a man whom she saw in secret for months before plotting to run away with him. This time, Delia St. Pierre didn't tell even Lucie about her plan until the very last moment.

For the rest of her life, Lucie would always remember the scene: Her mother standing in the dark by the front door with a backpack on, her hair in a ponytail that had fallen to one side. She looked frazzled, but there was more spark in her eyes than Lucie had seen there in a long time. Her mother gripped the straps of the backpack and said, "You can come or not. It's up to you. But I'm really leaving this time. And I'm going right now."

Lucie didn't have to think hard or long. She'd known what she would say if her mother ever asked this question. Lucie said, "I have to get some things," and her mother said, "Be quick."

Upstairs, Lucie was surprised to find once again that a nagging mischief—or was it darkness—had crept into her that urged her to take the world and its problems less seriously. To toy with it. This was *her* reality after all. She briefly wondered what would happen if she took too long to pack. Would her mother leave without her? Would she wait and risk getting caught? Lucie shook the idea away. At her core, she knew it was wrong to even entertain the thought, but she couldn't help it.

She opened a duffel bag and quickly filled it with clothes and books. She had notebooks for school and notebooks filled with recipes. It occurred to her that she didn't know where or if she'd be going to school when they got to wherever they were going. It occurred to her that she had no idea where she'd be sleeping that night or the next.

Her father was working late. They left the car at the state park close to the harbor, beneath a dim streetlamp. Her mother's plan was that when they found the car, the conclusion would be that they'd gone for a hike and gotten lost. They'd spend days just searching the woods before anyone would think she'd intentionally run away.

Lucie knew her father would be onto them immediately, but she followed her mother on foot in the dark, to the boat, where this new man, whoever he was, was waiting. As she stood there, Lucie found herself daydreaming that she was someone else, a character from a World War II movie she'd seen once. She was escaping certain violence, some injustice that she knew existed even if she couldn't always see it. Her mind wandered and created stories, and she wondered then who she inherited her imagination from: her father or her mother.

And whose mind did she want to have?

Lucie kept following silently, boarding the boat and shaking the man's hand. His name was Martin Pelletier. He was a large man with curly hair. He wore orange bibs and rubber boots. He smelled like the seawater that gathered in pools and housed hermit crabs and urchins.

But he put one hand on Delia's shoulder and the other on Lucie's and squeezed very gently. "It's all going to be just fine," he said, and Lucie felt a sense of trust that was foreign.

They slept to the sounds of a lapping ocean. Through the floor, Lucie heard occasional booming sounds, like a creature beneath them was bellowing their names. There was no turning back, despite imagining her father coming home and finding an empty house. Despite wondering how he would survive when he rarely made his own meals, or even coffee in the morning.

They stopped a couple of times along the way, but two days after leaving New England, Lucie and Delia and Martin Pelletier got off the boat in Violette.

∼∼∼

Delia was happy, Lucie thought, even though it seemed clear to everyone but Delia that Martin had simply done a kind thing for a person in need. He lived in his own cottage, a few doors from Lucie and her mother, and he only came by every other night to bring them fish he'd caught or pass on the kind of inconsequential gossip about the town that Delia unabashedly enjoyed.

Lucie didn't go back to school to finish her last three years of high school, and instead set up a bakery with Martin's help. The people of Violette were a stubborn group and liked what they liked, but Lucie's cookies and brownies were an undeniably required indulgence once they'd tasted them. She found that the recipes she was most nervous to try ended up being the ones the town enjoyed most. Perhaps it was her penchant for needing to experiment. Needing to test boundaries and cross borders. The darkness that was inside her was transferred to her baking, but somehow, when others ate what she'd made, that darkness turned to light.

Martin died after they'd been in Violette for only a couple of years. To Lucie, he had simply been one route to another life, but to Lucie's mother, he had been so much more. He'd been the only way out. Lucie never knew if her mother actually loved him, but none of that really mattered. He was a kind person, and he'd done a kind thing for them. He'd grown up in Violette, with his parents and his sister, Beatrice.

Once Martin was gone, however, Delia began talking about things that had happened in the past as if they were happening in the present. Sometimes she told Lucie that she'd had lunch with her husband, Lucie's father, and other times it was with Martin. Though neither of these could possibly be true, Lucie accepted that her mother's illness was going to be her responsibility. She'd taken it on when she stepped on that boat.

Eventually, Lucie had to tell her mother they were taking a trip to the flower shop one afternoon, when really they arrived at the hospital. The hospital in Violette was not equipped to manage patients like Delia, and they encouraged Lucie to take her mother to a bigger city so she could be properly cared for. But Lucie knew that wasn't an option. The only thing her mother had that was true was the knowledge that Violette had saved her. What was less true, though no one could know how much, was Delia's certainty that if she left, she would be found.

Delia spent the next few years of her life slipping into and out of her alternate conscious states, while Lucie's bakery thrived. She didn't intentionally forget her mother there, but she found herself busy trying to keep up, and she questioned her own judgment so often that each time she visited the hospital, she left wondering what was real and what wasn't. Sometimes, Lucie further imagined her father's solitary life. It probably wasn't all that solitary, but it couldn't have been as happy as it might have been if they all—all three of them—had been a little kinder to one another.

Lucie thought often of that scene: her mother standing by the door, asking her whether she was coming. It seemed to Lucie particularly kind of her mother to not say in that moment that she wasn't going to let Lucie screw things up for her again. She never did say that. For the rest of her life, Delia St. Pierre insisted she never held that against her daughter. She never blamed her because she knew it had been an accident.

That might have been the worst thing about it, because it was a lie. Lucie hadn't slipped and mentioned her mother's leaving plans to her father. It had been calculated, at some subconscious level. She'd felt sorry for her mother quite a bit more often than she did her father, but that morning at the breakfast table, she'd felt sorry only for herself. She didn't want to belong to a family split apart, the kind of family that no one belonged to.

That her words had come out accidentally was a lie that Lucie recognized, but she also wondered how much it was a lie her mother had to tell herself. Because she didn't believe in accidents. She didn't believe that things happened unnecessarily. Perhaps she couldn't bear to think of it on any other terms.

As Lucie was leaving the hospital one afternoon, a man with a bandaged hand was on his way in. He attempted to hold the door for Lucie with his bad hand and yelled, "Jesus, Mary, and Joseph!" before trying and succeeding with his good one.

He pressed his bandaged fingers to his chest and said, "Just trying to be nice, and you see? Always a lesson, though, eh? Bea, my ma, would say we're not just meeting here by accident."

And Lucie, who had been reciting a cranberry tea bread recipe in her head to avoid thinking about her mother's vacant eyes, was suddenly shaken from her trance. "Excuse me, what did you say?" Her head full of a thousand spinning stars.

16

The body of Lucie St. Pierre was found on the beach, caught in a tangle of seaweed. The woman who found her was out for a walk with her dog when she spotted Lucie's long blonde hair, which looked distinctly different in the morning light from the mustard-colored rockweed splayed out across the stones.

The woman didn't panic, as she would have expected to after finding a body, but instead knelt calmly and removed a limpet shell that was caught behind Lucie's ear. She dropped the speckled shell into the water and then stood, shaking herself out of a daze and turning to run back to town, her dog lingering behind.

The pieces of Lucie's kayak were never found, and no one could explain the way she looked like she was reaching out for someone, her body frozen in a state of transition forever. No one could even begin to grasp where she had been for the past four years, and why she looked exactly the same as the last time they remembered seeing her.

Since she no longer had any family, the funeral home held a wake for her, the casket closed and topped with an abundance of red, pink, and white roses. There was a funeral, which, again, most of the town attended, because they all knew her as the one who'd kept them sustained with comfort foods throughout long rainy days and cold winters. No easy task, and one they were more grateful for than they realized after they found that she had drowned.

Lucie's bakery, which Odette had been running without her, brought trays of food, now remembering that Lucie would have wanted that. People bit into jam cookies and berry pies. They licked chocolate from their fingers, giving one another uncomfortable smiles. Something about it felt wrong, but it could not be helped. Having finally remembered the source of those flavors they had loved so much, they all felt overwhelming relief. As if a yearslong itch had been scratched.

Alma walked to the funeral with Theo. She held on to the crook of his arm and kept looking up at his eyes to see if she could tell what he was thinking or feeling. He sighed every so often, but otherwise his expression told Alma nothing. She was used to feeling the pain of others, so it was a mystery why suddenly she didn't feel any now.

"Stop it," he said.

"What?"

"I'm fine."

"I just—"

He seemed almost too calm, whispering finally as they approached the gathering, "How did you do this? How did you remember when I didn't?"

"I don't know why me," Alma said, then, gaining the courage—"Maybe because I feel a lot, at least when I'm with people. I feel . . . energy. Are you mad I didn't tell you sooner?"

"At first, yes. But I think I *almost* understand now. And I trust you, that you had your reasons. That you did it when the time was right."

Alma realized she was holding her breath. Theo had the book she'd printed with Lucie's story rolled tightly in his hand, the staple binding already loosened from the book being opened so many times.

Oren stood apart from the rest, nodding to Alma when she glanced back. She wished she could leave the crowd and run to her uncle's workshop, where Theo had stored her supplies to build the radio station.

There was no lengthy scripture reading like there had been at Hayden's funeral. The pastor, in fact, did little more than mumble,

"Well, we don't always understand . . . things aren't always . . . she was a lovely woman, though, wasn't she?"

Then one person after another stood up to tell a story about Lucie. At least they attempted to, but as each began to speak about a cake she'd baked for their wedding, or the time they'd fallen in love while sitting in her bakery, they inevitably faltered. It was remarkably consistent, the way their eyes glassed over and they stared into space, the words trailing off and getting lost to the wind. No story was finished.

Alma heard people whispering afterward about becoming distracted by the fact that they—along with the entire town—had somehow forgotten Lucie for a full four years, only to all remember her again at exactly the same time.

And this had happened with Hayden as well. Wasn't it all too coincidental? Who else had they lost and forgotten? And who was this woman who'd written the story that reminded them—she was still a newcomer in their eyes—and why hadn't *she* forgotten?

Alma felt an even stronger urge to run. Then someone was taking hold of her wrist and Alma was dizzy, the blue sky vanishing and the space around her becoming gray for a moment. She blinked. It was Lucie's old roommate, Odette, pulling her aside.

Odette's eyes were red, her cheeks glistening. She pressed one hand against her chest while the other continued to firmly grip Alma's wrist. "I don't understand," she said. "I had all these things in my house for years. I had no idea who they belonged to. I finally threw them away. Photos and books. Clothing, pillows, a fucking *toothbrush*. How could I have forgotten for so long? And how could you have not told anyone? What's wrong with you?"

Alma tried to back away.

But if Theo could understand, it was possible Odette—and all these people—could as well. The question returned, the one Alma had considered after Hayden disappeared: How does one explain the absence of a memory, a gaping hole in life that has suddenly come back? Its impact could be felt in any number of ways, although it was becoming clear that they were mostly negative.

"There's nothing wrong with me," Alma said, scrambling for the right thing to say and finally settling on the truth: "But I can't explain it. I can only say that Lucie trusted me with her story. If you can, just try and see something good in all of it. You have her memory back."

Odette laughed a bitter, angry laugh. She let go of Alma's arm as if just realizing she was touching something revolting. "As if that's better. What does that even mean?" she said. "There *is* an explanation for these things. There *should* be an explanation for everything. You know, people say 'things happen for a reason' not because they have faith. It's because they're too lazy to figure out what that reason is. Her mother was right. There are no accidents."

A tingling of anger crept up into Alma's stomach. It burned in her chest and throat. But she wasn't the one angry or hurt, bitter or betrayed. Odette was. *None of it is real,* she thought, glancing around, feeling the eyes of everyone on her, suspicious.

"And who are you again?" Odette called, as Alma found herself sprinting toward Bea's house, thinking only of how the radio waiting there would take her back to Alex and far away from the awkwardness of reality.

〜〜〜

Bea took the recipe card from Alma, raising it to the dim light in the kitchen, squinting to read the list of ingredients for what felt like a long time, though Alma didn't want to interrupt. When Bea's eyes met Alma's again, she said, "She didn't really have a choice coming here. She was always kind of traveling with the current, easygoing, but also tough. I remember the day she stepped off my brother's boat. I thought she was going to raise some hell. But all she ever did was make people happy. Fat, but happy."

At the top of the recipe card, in pencil, Lucie had written *Hermits for a Snowy Day*. These spiced cookies had been the one recipe Lucie herself fell back on each time she felt she needed something to raise her spirits. The winters in Violette were long when Lucie had arrived as a teenager, and they seemed to grow longer and stormier every year. This year, the year that Lucie left Violette—and the world—for good, Alma tugged to untie the scarf from around her neck, wondering what she had that compared. This one three-by-five-inch card had brought light to a town full of cold, grumpy people year after year. She hadn't brought any light to the world, as far as she could tell. Her only impulse had been to hide from it.

"Grab the flour from the pantry," Bea said as she opened the cabinet over the stove and began sorting through spices. "I haven't had a hermit in years, and I just realized I'm in need of one . . . or a few." They followed the recipe to the letter, even pausing to debate the intricacies of what it meant to "roll the dough two fingers tall and cut the bars twice as thick as biscotti."

Alma pushed up her sweater sleeves and floured a wooden cutting board and rolled out the dark, fragrant dough, catching a glimpse of her tattoos each time she rolled forward. The Morse code spanning the width of her wrist, and the beginnings of tree roots. The trunk of the tree disappeared into her sleeve, the tree's branches reaching toward her elbow. She had asked Oren to come with her, a little too urgently, while they were at Lucie's funeral, arguing that no one would see him but it would make her feel better, and the way he had said *absolutely not* seemed cruel. Then the way he'd explained how rude it would be to sit in on people who didn't know he was there made her feel selfish, and she'd almost pointed out that Lucie had done it all the time, but she knew how flawed this argument was, so she stayed silent and let him disappear into the snow.

"How's the newspaper?" Bea asked.

"Oh, it's fine." Then, with no intention of actually doing this, Alma said, "I'm going to start printing more regular stories, I think. I have some ideas."

She had zero ideas beyond setting up a radio station and using the newspaper office as a sort of second home. Theo had brought her the antenna she'd asked for, and the transceiver, headset, and microphone. She was anxious to go set it up, but her arms were covered in flour and Bea had poured her some of Theo's cranberry liqueur and there was the gentle warbling of "Moon River" coming from the flickering bulbs overhead.

"Do you think this is what she meant?" Alma asked, holding two fingers horizontally next to the flattened dough. "Is it the right thickness?"

"I guess it depends on whose hand we're using." Bea laughed and dabbed at her eyes with the corner of her apron, and Alma couldn't tell if she was just laughing that hard or if she was trying not to actually cry.

Alma used a long knife to cut the dough into wide strips and laid them on the baking sheet. "Hardest part is waiting, right?"

Bea said, "She used to bring me one of these cookies every afternoon. I liked them at the end of the day, when all the flavors had melded together more and the edges had hardened a little. I don't mind waiting."

When they were done, Alma brought two cookies out to the workshop, where Theo bounced from one frosted window to another with a cloth in his hand. He swiped at the windowsills and rubbed at the dirt-stained glass. Alma stomped snow from her boots in the doorway. In the corner, there was a space heater that ticked as the fan spun, pumping a weak stream of warm air into the room.

"These are supposed to last forever, I guess. If you keep them right."

Theo paused to take a cookie, dark brown and studded with raisins. "Ugh," he said, the kind of *ugh* that was immensely complimentary.

"Whoa," Alma said, looking around the workshop, where there was now actual space to move. Hubert's old, half-finished canoe had been moved to the ground. The buckets of soaking pine strips had all been emptied and pushed against one wall, the floor swept and the tools organized on the workbench. The space was stark and empty.

"So, here's the plan," he said. "We're going to get this canoe out and clear more room, then start all over in here."

"Bea's okay with this?"

"She's getting there. There comes a time when you have to let go. It's time."

Alma picked up a long blade that had a curved handle on each side. She gripped a handle in each fist and held it out in front of her. "You sound like me. A little crazy, but I'm sure you have your reasons. So, what's the reason? After all this time, why are you suddenly cleaning out the shop?"

"I've been feeling for a while now that there's something missing, which sounds cliché, I know, but it's like I had something and then I lost it. It's so hard to explain, but the point is, I realized a few weeks ago that I'm just not happy. I go out fishing, make supply runs, always a little unsure if I'm going to make it back. I need something else in my life. Some other purpose. I think maybe I'll build canoes, like my dad, see how that works out."

"Lucie would have—" Alma stopped, but it was too late. A look passed over Theo's face, one of doubt or concern, but then he smiled.

"That's the thing. I feel lighter now. There was this kind of weight on me—of not remembering something that was just under the surface. But now that I know what it was—even though she's gone—I'm free. And this place is going to be gone one day, so I might as well do something useful while I can."

Alma lifted a box of rusted handsaws, hatchets, chisels. She wondered if she'd have felt that freedom if she'd known what happened to

Alex. If she had just let go instead of searching. "Is all of this going?" she asked.

She helped Theo carry the old canoe outside, and they looked at it lying on the snow. It had been wasted sitting in the shop, drying out, cracking. Theo stood with his hands on his hips, tapping the frame with the tip of his boot. It rocked side to side and then stopped.

"Are you sure you can't fix it?" Alma said.

"I wish I could. But no," Theo said, drawing an imaginary circle around the canoe and the pile of scrap wood. "It's time. There's a farmer out near Alphie's sanctuary. He's going to use the wood for some garden beds." When he caught Alma looking at him, speechless, he hugged her with one arm and said, "What? It's fine. Your radio equipment is over there, by the way. And that figure too. Ma wants you to take it."

The pyramid of boxes in the corner was intimidating, but she couldn't carry them out of there fast enough. She helped Theo lift the canoe once more and load it onto the trailer he had waiting, then returned inside on her own. She wrapped her fingers around the puffin that Hubert had carved, then pocketed it and lifted the boxes in a kind of fever, forgetting for a moment where she was taking them. So many places now—the office, Oren's house, even the lighthouse—felt like where she belonged. None of them her own cottage.

〰

Alma borrowed a space heater from Theo and plugged it into the corner of the office with the one outlet that didn't look like it would immediately electrocute her. The desk Hayden had left behind threatened to collapse if she tried to push it across the floor, so she set up a makeshift one close to the heater—a piece of plywood propped on two filing cabinets. She placed the two copies of Hayden's book at the center. Each had a different cover, though they were both watercolor paintings of Onde Mountain and the tower that Bea had done.

The book was a reminder of her mission. She opened the box of equipment she'd ordered, the handheld radio made of much heavier material than the one she was used to.

As a kid, she'd only gotten into amateur radio because of Alex, so they could speak across the distance. And the walkie-talkie she carried with her had always been for fun. They'd only used it while hiking, and it wasn't nearly as powerful as what she now had sitting before her. After the transceiver was set up and the antenna was mounted to the metal filing cabinet by the window, she plugged it all in and held the microphone in her palm and—despite having been given a real call sign once—spoke her made-up name onto the waves.

"This is Darkest One, monitoring."

She tuned the transceiver to find the repeater at the top of the mountain and tried again. There was only silence, broken by occasional crackling. Alma took a bite of one of Lucie's hermit cookies and leaned forward on the desk, her chin in her hand as she chewed. She attempted broadcasting her name a few more times, scanning to find other channels, letting her voice get louder and braver each time.

This more powerful transceiver, unobstructed, without interference, could reach into space. With all that distance, how could she not find him?

Aside from her name, she didn't know what else to say. Words weren't immediately available, and so she opened one of Alex's wildlife books, then another, flipping to random pages.

"'Snowshoe hares are often incorrectly called rabbits. Rabbits have young that are born blind, hairless, and helpless in underground burrows. Hares are born aboveground, already covered in fur and with their eyes open. They can run almost right away.'"

Before she could hear more of the painful nothing that was the response she knew she would receive, she kept broadcasting:

"'The jack pine is a resilient tree, surviving—even thriving—in the worst of conditions. These trees are some of the first to grow again after forest fires. The heat causes their cones to open and release their seeds. This is the way they reproduce.

"'The mark left by a leaf after it falls off the twig is called a leaf scar. It is, as a matter of fact, a point of healing.

"'Seaweeds do not have roots. Instead, they have holdfasts, which grip and cling to rocks to keep them from drifting away, even in the roughest of conditions.

"'Bamboo corals are deep-sea corals, growing on hard ocean floors. When they die, sections of their skeletons look much like the stalks of bamboo.

"'Purple sunstar. Seven to thirteen arms. Usually seen offshore. Daisy brittle star. Blood star. Moon jellyfish.'"

Alma kept speaking into the microphone, her voice trailing off at times, until she couldn't hold her head up any longer and she rested her cheek on the desk and fell asleep, her fingers heavy on the call button.

It was there, with her face still pressed against the rough wood surface and her feet cold in her boots beneath her, that she heard it. When it happened, it was real. They were real numbers spoken by a real voice. Later, though she would never admit this to anyone, she questioned whether she was dreaming. The numbers seemed random at first, strung together quickly as they floated into the dark room. But then they took on a kind of order, and Alma listened closer for the pattern. She fiddled with the knob to get a clearer transmission, the voice sounding familiar, though she couldn't place it.

8. 12. 20. 25. 8. 12. 20. 25. 8. 12. 20. 25.

The numbers repeated a few times before she recognized what she was hearing. It was a date. The month: August. The day: the twelfth. The year: 2025. The date of their last hike, which meant—it must have been—the date that Alex died.

Her hand shaking, she reached for the microphone and held the button down. The words tripped over themselves to get out of her. "Darkest One. This is Darkest One. Can you hear me?"

The voice spoke through the static, something she couldn't make out. Then the words stopped, the numbers stopped. All broadcasting stopped.

Alma slammed the microphone on the desk and pushed her stool back. Taking a deep breath, she tried again, adjusting the transceiver knobs to alleviate some of the static.

"Dire Wolf," she whispered. Then, louder and louder, until she was yelling. "Dire Wolf . . . Can you hear me? Everything is so much harder than I imagined. All of it. But I'm not going to stop. I'll be here as long as it takes."

<p style="text-align:center">~~~</p>

Alma was walking by the lighthouse the next day when Violette had its biggest storm yet. When she heard the thunder, she turned quickly back to town just as the swell surged over the cliffs. Passing the beach, she watched as the steps that led down through the rocks were crushed like bird bones and swept away. The wind whipped the rain sideways, carrying with it lobster traps and fences and roof shingles. Looking out on the churning gray waves, she saw someone's boat carried away, bobbing and helpless.

Most people fled to the shelter on the hill and waited. From the window there, the view of the ocean was entirely obscured by dense fog. Alma turned and crouched beneath it, closed her eyes, and thought of Oren, alone at his cottage.

All the homes by the water had flooded, most irreparably damaged. Siding was torn to shreds, roofs lifted and blown off. The water pooled up to their knees as people waded down the street. Fences and lawn chairs and most of the town's remaining boats had been taken by the sea.

Alma heard from a coast guard broadcast that the Isthmus of Chignecto, which had long been threatened by the rising sea level, had finally succumbed. There could no longer be any passage from Nova Scotia to New Brunswick by land.

Violette had been lucky. Other towns on nearby islands had had no choice but to evacuate, but they—so far—had been spared enough to continue making the decision themselves, though no one knew exactly why. Still, more people than ever—even the ones who had been the most determined to stay—now talked of leaving. Some would repair or rebuild, but the dialogue began to circulate through the room, with shaking, urgent voices: soon there would be nothing left to stay for.

~~~

That night, after the storm had passed, Alma rode up the coast, switching on the headlamp attached to the handlebars, Jupiter bounding behind her. It was different at night. The wind was biting, and stray flashes of lightning sparked across the sapphire sea every few moments. Her head was open and full of air.

She dropped her bike in the garden and knocked on Oren's door. The only light was in the dark corner where he read. When he opened the door, he said, "So, you got your radio."

"I've heard things," Alma said emphatically, as if he'd simply stated his disbelief in what she was doing.

"I believe you."

Alma entered to find all of Oren's father's paintings lined up against the walls. The works looked renewed—still dark, but also clean and crisp, emerging from the canvas like city streets Alma could stride onto.

"And you've been busy too."

"Always trying to learn something," he said. "I've been practicing restoration."

She moved slowly through the house. "Wow. It looks . . . it looks like you've done them all. Is this one of those last things before you're ready to . . ." She didn't want him to respond, to say he was ready to leave her.

"No, no. That's not what I'm waiting for," he said. "Honestly, if I can make it that long, I'd like to see Lille turn twenty. I don't know why, but I need to see her reach that second decade. It was an important year for me—I figured something out at that age, even if it took a while to reveal itself."

Jupiter squeezed past her and knocked over one of the paintings. Alma jumped to pick it up, thankful for a distraction from the reality that Oren's lingering had nothing to do with her, but was simply a matter of waiting for a specific moment in time—a previously determined time that she didn't have to think about right now.

"Where is your painting?" she asked. "I never asked you, are there more, or is that the only one?"

"It's not the only one I did like that. But it's the only one I kept," he said. "Come on back here."

She followed him into the small back room, where he previously kept gardening tools and bags of potting soil. The tools had been cleared out, and he'd taped to the walls dozens of a child's drawings on tiny, yellowing pages. There were rainbows and cat faces and flowers with clouds above them. Some were colorful, painted with watercolors, but most were drawn with a simple ballpoint pen.

"Are these yours too?" Alma asked. "Your first exhibit?"

"Lille's," he said. "She did these all at once, the last time I saw her, just before I died. She was ten."

"Sorry," Alma said.

"Don't be sorry." He stood back and surveyed the walls. The black ink drawings that Lille had pulled from her imagination, not something she saw in front of her. "Yep," he said, nodding as if reassuring himself. "I always enjoy finding a new way that she might be like me."

"What's this?" Alma asked, examining what looked like an antique gramophone that sat on a shelf at the back of the room. "I want to call this a gramophone, but I know it isn't one."

"I didn't tell you how I got my father's paintings," Oren said, "though I suspect we'll get to that eventually. Well, there were other things I acquired at the time. Suffice to say, this was among those acquired items. It's a phonautograph."

"And you *acquired* it?" Alma said, touching the tube at the end of the cone that turned to inscribe sound vibrations.

"Like I said, we'll get to that. The first sounds ever recorded were never meant to be played back. The idea was to create a picture of what the sounds looked like, the way we capture earthquake activity. The man who invented this realized that there was no way to prove that what he'd done was real, so he gave up. But others built on his work. It wasn't much later that Edison was recording and playing back 'Au clair de la lune.'"

"Always learning something, huh?" she said quietly.

He took her arm and turned it, tracing his fingers over the lines he'd tattooed there. The lines and dots—her code. The tree's roots, followed by the trunk and limbs, stretching from the middle of her forearm to her elbow. Above its curving branches, Oren had outlined a circle on her bicep that would become a compass.

"Are you feeling adrift, Alma Hughes?" he asked, as they sat down to finish it.

She laughed. "Always, a little, I suppose. Well, not so much anymore. Not like I was when I lost him."

"You never told me about it," he said, his eyes glancing up, though his face remained downward.

She'd never told anyone the story before. So she let herself. She told him about Alex. How they'd gone out into the wilderness and she'd woken up with no sense of where she was. She told him how long she had wandered and how she didn't know what to do with herself anymore after she'd been found, and she couldn't bring herself to talk to anyone, but no one would just let her be, except for Jupiter.

"And then you came here."

"Yes, I came here."

"I read," he said, "that often, when people get lost in the woods, they'll come to a main road and they'll just walk right across it. Or they'll turn around and go right back where they started. People who've done this have said it was because they didn't believe the road would take them in the right direction. But I tend to think it's just easier sometimes to be lost."

"Well, I'm finding my way now. Finally."

"Ah, yes. You heard something."

"Yes," she said. "Last night, I heard the date Alex was lost. It repeated a few times."

"And then?"

"And then it stopped."

"And you think this means something. I can assure you, it doesn't."

"How do you know? How can you be so *assured?*"

"Alma, how many combinations of numbers have you heard over the radio? How many years have you been listening to random strings of numbers on that little walkie you carry around, trying to force them to make some kind of sense?"

"It's not a coincidence," she said.

"That's exactly what it is. You're just hearing what you want to hear. Trying to rationalize random things. So, you heard numbers that could have been a date. What now? You're going to spend even more hours sitting in there, waiting for the airwaves to lead you further into the past? What's wrong with the people who are still here?"

"They're not him. Or Jupiter. Or you."

"We're not *real*, Alma." He set the needle down after the thin points of the compass were complete. She examined the tattoo, turning her arm so the north point faced actual north.

"It's late," Oren said. "You need to sleep."

"Every night I sleep, I wake up one day closer to everything and everyone being gone."

"The world will still be here."

"And what if it isn't?"

"I am of the mind that we should assume it will be."

Oren held her hand as she climbed into bed. He covered her and lay down behind her, propping his head on his fist and resting an arm on her hip. Alma's eyes traveled the length of a winding spiral tattoo that spanned his forearm. Lying in a bed with a man for the first time since being with Alex, she realized that she no longer felt desirable. But she no longer wished for something to happen that would prove to her, and maybe to him, that she had been, at one time, beautiful and lovable. Sexy even. She wanted this, only this thing that was happening right at that moment, to be real, and nothing more. And it seemed possibly the cruelest thing that what she was asking for was not that much, but it was still too much.

"God, I wish you all hadn't died," she whispered as she drifted off.

～～～

In the morning, before sunrise, they walked the shoreline path, where they could see the town in the distance, so much dimmer than when Alma had first arrived. The electricity was even less consistent, but there were also just fewer people, and so fewer lights.

"Here," Oren said. "Watch this. This is my latest obsession." He retrieved some smooth flat rocks from his pocket, then pulled his arm back and arced it sideways as he launched the stone out onto the water. In the predawn dark, Alma could just make out the moments when the rock grazed the surface, bouncing farther out before it disappeared into the depths. It was farther than anyone should have been able to throw.

Alma took one of the stones, hurling it as far as she could from the cliff. It cleared it but dropped into the sea without a sound. She said, "What are your other obsessions?"

"Oh, you know. Tai chi. Archery. Origami. What about you? Do you get crazy for things, besides the obvious?"

"I don't know," she said. "Right now, it seems to be tattoos and radios. I guess that's the obvious, but I never thought it would be my answer to that question."

"What did it used to be?"

"Lists."

"What kind of lists?"

"All of them. I wanted to catalog the world."

She thought of her notebooks back in the newspaper office, where she'd recorded dates, numbers, coordinates, weather forecasts, names of songs and books, quotes from interviews. Perhaps she hadn't strayed as far from that as she first thought.

Oren shook his head, and she sensed he was about to scold her again, but he just said, "I know you think you need to find him. But you should be where people can also be there for you in the end, you know?"

"You mean not here," she said. "You said that your father's cottage and everything in it was mine now. Now you're saying I should leave?"

"I mean, family. I'm saying"—Oren sighed—"that you should at least *try* to be with the *living*. When was the last time you actually called home?"

Alma said nothing, unable to explain the many ways in which she thought of Oren as family.

"It's been years," he said. "I'm all for distancing from society and being a loner. I'm a champion of that. But do it out of the power to choose, not out of weakness."

"I'm not weak."

"What exactly was so terrible about home again?"

She thought for a long moment. "When I was ten," Alma said, "I saw a man on a motorcycle get hit by a car. The car ran a stop sign; the motorcyclist hit the side of the car's hood. The guy flipped up and did circles in the air before landing on his back on the pavement. He was okay, some bruises and scrapes, but he got the wind knocked out of him in a bad way. When I saw it happen, I couldn't breathe at all. I was just standing there watching, but I felt my lungs collapse, and I blacked out. That's what it's been like my whole life. Whatever anyone else is feeling around me, I feel it too. But not like I understand what it feels like. Like it's actually happening to me."

"So, you feel things, more than most. Can't you use that to your advantage somehow? I'm happy that you're here, I really am. And the cottage *is* yours now. But did you really have to run away? I know you're stronger than that."

"You don't understand. I love them, I do, but I can only be with people for so long before it's too much. If I call, they'll just try to make me come back. And I can't do that. You don't know what it's like. I've never known whether I'm feeling my own feelings or someone else's. I never felt that way with Hayden and Lucie. I don't feel that way when I'm with you. It's easier here."

"There are people who love you here too. You have Bea and your cousins."

"Well, I go see them, but when I'm in town, people look at me differently. I was weird to them before, and I'm even weirder now that I'm the one who *remembered*, when they didn't. I like being alone, where I can be me and not have to explain myself."

"Things are so much easier than you think," he said.

Alma stopped walking. "That's what Alphie said. To Hayden."

"Well, he was right."

Oren bent down to pick up a clamshell. It was still two halves sealed together, but one half was chipped, leaving a sharp opening into the tiny, dark world inside. "What baffles me is that you've come this far in life and never realized that what you have is a gift, not a curse."

"It certainly feels like a curse," she said.

He put the shell in her palm and closed her fist over it. She looked away. She felt cracked in half, her insides raw and exposed, but at least she knew that what she was feeling was her own. She held on to it, not asking if what he really wanted was for her to leave so *he* could be alone. All this time, the idea had never occurred to her.

His hands wrapped around hers, he said, "You're magic, Alma Hughes. You have fucking superpowers. You should use them."

She resisted the urge to scratch her arm where the freshly tattooed skin was hot and throbbing. "Well, whatever the hell that means, I *am* using them. I'm using them to find Alex and to be here with you and Jupiter. You realize my so-called superpowers are probably the only reason I can see you."

Oren threw up his hands and began walking back to the cottage. Admittedly, she knew perfectly well that she wasn't doing anything like what he was suggesting. But if she had the power to reach people through some sort of exchange of energy, there was never any question who she'd be reaching for.

17

A postcard of a waterfall, and the blotchy, vague shape of a man and woman paddling a bright-red canoe beneath it. The block lettering in the upper left corner said, **ALLAGASH FALLS**. Beneath that, slightly smaller lettering, a star between each letter: **M*A*I*N*E**.

The postcard began:

> *Hey, Alma.*
> *So, I'm a wilderness guide now and I'm moving to Maine. How about that? I start in Allagash in a month. My mother isn't crazy about it, but it's time for me to do something else. It seems we're finally going to see each other again. I vote for a canoe trip.*
> *Yours,*
> *A.*
> *PS Remember your dad's old car? Did you know "88" is Morse code for "love and kisses"?*

Alma didn't know what to expect, their entire friendship blooming and growing over the span of more than a decade apart. She was all the things she thought she should be—excited, nervous, hopeful. But she also knew that his moving to Maine was mostly coincidental and had nothing to do with her.

They met at a campground near Eagle Lake, three hours north of Alma's house. As she pulled up to the campsite, gripping the steering wheel, she noticed the sleeves of her baggy hoodie, stretched out around her wrists and beginning to form holes at the seams. When she'd left the house, the sweatshirt had seemed cool and casual. Now it felt unflattering and maybe even a little messy, but she'd stupidly worn only a fitted tank top underneath, and that was suddenly too revealing.

Alma wondered if he would recognize her. A month before, she'd cut her bangs—a decision she'd regretted instantly. They curled awkwardly over her eyebrows, and she was self-conscious about the number of times she tried to adjust them.

Of course, Alex probably looked different, too, but she couldn't imagine it. She tried to picture the boy she'd seen last, and then a skinny adult who had grown into that haircut—long and black, hanging over his eyes, but shaved in the back. That was what she saw when she closed her eyes, so that was what she was looking for.

He was crouched by a firepit, poking at a stack of thinly split logs. Of course, she'd known that she wasn't driving up to meet a taller version of the little boy she'd met years ago. It was still a shock to see him—tall and broad shouldered, his black hair still falling over his ears. He had a clean beard and a leather cord wrapped around his wrist. She noticed his muscular arms—his T-shirt hung loose and thin, a rip in the collar—and she was dizzy trying to envision all that his life had contained before this moment that she was unaware of.

They'd written to each other for years, and she'd been so excited to finally sit in perfect comfort next to the person who understood her like no one else, but this man building a fire was just another stranger. What was a postcard every few months, anyway? Ultimately, she wondered, what did she really know about him? A panic rose inside her, and she almost backed away, got into her car, and drove home before he saw her, but then he stood up and turned around.

"Alma," he said. His voice was soft and deep, and it had a hesitation in it that she recognized hearing in her own voice when she tried to appear more confident than she actually was. She steadied her breathing and smiled. This was going to be okay. He reached into his back pocket, then held out some folded papers.

Alma looked at what he'd given her. It was the liner notes from the *In Violet Light* cassette tape. "Where's the tape?" she said.

"Melted. Summer of '09. Front seat of my first car. Buick. Black leather seats."

"Sounds hot," she said, then felt her ears burning. She tugged her bangs out of her eyes.

She still wasn't sure whether they were supposed to hug each other, but it seemed like the kind of move that, if not executed within the first few moments, never would be. She pressed the side of her face to his chest, wrapped her arms around his waist, the cassette notes in her fist. He fell back a step; then his hands were on her shoulders. He pulled her away a few inches and said, "It's really, really good to see you again, Darkest One."

It was embarrassing and everything to her all at once. "I—" she began, then forgot what she'd meant to say. He turned toward the firepit and began rearranging the logs into a tent.

"Who taught you to build a fire?" she asked.

He laughed. "No one," he said. "I'm a complete fraud. They had no idea when they interviewed me." He flicked a lighter open with his thumb, then held the tiny flame to the kindling.

When it didn't catch, Alma said, "Here," and thrust the liner notes at him. The weathered paper lit up quickly, and he wedged it between two pieces of wood.

After a few moments, the fire ignited, and she stared at the flames while she tried to think of how the rest of the night would play out. She held her breath, wondering where they would set up their tents, what they would talk about, how they would decide it was time to say good night and go their separate ways until morning.

When she pulled her gaze from the fire and turned around, Alex was standing there holding a beer in each hand. He said, "Red ale?" and she exhaled. They drank by the fire and wrapped potatoes in tinfoil and nestled them into the coals until they were hot and blackened. Alma leaned against his shoulder, letting her eyes close, and they didn't bother setting up her tent at all. They crawled into his, with the constellation Draco, standing watch over his garden, winding across the northern sky above.

In the morning, they hiked, and Alma didn't think anything could possibly ruin the simple joy of reuniting with him. But joy is often tinged with sorrow.

He'd been talking about tracking, and books he'd read and wilderness tracking courses he'd taken, and he showed her how to measure prints in the mud—strides and straddles and pitch. How to identify a male versus a female print. How to read an animal's emotional state by the tracks it left.

When he said this, Alma's eyes grew wide. They were following an ermine, and she reached down to touch the edges of the imprint in the mud.

"You don't sound like a fraud to me," she said.

"Here," Alex said. "This is where he had a burst of speed, because he was about to kill something. You can tell when they're stalking something, when they're irritated, when they're threatened."

They'd tracked the ermine to a marsh, and that was when they found her. Hera, the great blue heron, caught in the remains of an old fishing net, her long neck twisted, her eye black and glassy. Pale feathers floated on the water, her bones translucent.

For ten years, biologists had been tracking Hera. Over the years, she'd continued to break records in migration, once flying for sixty-eight hours straight between New Brunswick and Florida.

Now there she was, dead, and the GPS tracker strapped to her back meant that someone would find her soon enough, but Alex tried as best he could to free her anyway.

Alma remembered Alex's face, the grief that settled on his brow that softened, just barely, the anger she could see in his eyes. Or maybe it was a disappointment in himself, at already not being able to protect the wild he had committed himself to.

She was numb, frozen.

Her voice had caught in her throat as Alex pulled out a knife to cut the remaining tangles of line. She didn't know what she was trying to say, but she thought she should say something. It was one of those moments when she tried hard to think of the right thing, the thing that would somehow provide comfort, but came up blank.

It was only years later, when she wasn't trying so hard but was no longer able to tell him, that she found the words. And it turned out the right words weren't the kind that provided any comfort at all, but they were still the right words.

"We're responsible for the wild things here. Someone has to be."

If she could have, she'd have gone back and said this. Then she'd have taken out her own knife and knelt in the mud and helped him cut through the ropes.

18

On the desk, her totems stood watch. Hayden's *Tower of Echoes* manuscript and Lucie's smudged recipe card. The snow globe, swirling its artificial stars, sitting on top as a paperweight. The dark, cloudy quartz Oren had given her refracting the bright-blue moonlight through the office's front window. Hubert's carved puffin—plus a bear she'd whittled herself—observed her with black eyes. She had added some of Alex's monuments to the collection—his lighter, his compass, the piece of paper with their secret mathematical code written on it.

She was working on a story about a friend of Alphie's who was starting a hydroponic farm upriver. It was the same person who'd recycled Hubert's canoe as the base of his garden beds. She'd gone out there to see the new farm, but when the man mentioned the lost memory of a tattoo he had on his forearm, Alma had quickly handed him a notebook page full of interview questions and asked him to send them to the office.

The power was flickering on and off, so Alma wrote by hand, candles lit along the top edge of the desk. The rain came sideways at the window. She held the pen in one hand, but the other reached for the radio, turning the knobs absently as she transcribed the farmer's answers. She caught snippets of messages coming through, stopping to listen when something was clear enough to make out. Since hearing the date Alex had disappeared, nothing connected to her or to Alex had been broadcast, as far as she knew. There were numbers—always numbers, just as Oren had told her—but they were never relevant.

It was at the desk, her feet tucked beneath her in the metal chair, her head on her forearm on the desk, the radio spitting out static, that she woke to Theo banging on the window. She stood up, the chair clanging to the concrete floor.

"Are you sleeping here again?" Theo asked, though Alma could tell he wasn't there to simply check on her well-being.

"What?" she said.

"Ma's gone, Alma. Last night."

Alma swallowed hard. She thought she might fall backward, and wished suddenly that anyone—Oren, Jupiter—was there to catch her, but instead she had to catch herself. And then Theo reached out and grabbed both of her shoulders and pulled her toward him. He looked like he might crumple to the floor himself, so Alma anchored her feet to the ground and let him collapse into her.

"What happened?" she asked.

Theo began crying so hard he shook. "It's okay," he said. "People die. Fathers and mothers just like anyone else." The pulse of grief traveled into Alma's body, and she began shaking as well. A tornado spun inside her, a sharp, stinging energy gathering up piece by piece and centralizing in her chest. She thought she might burst apart. "She just went in to take a nap, and then she didn't come back out."

Alma held her breath and squeezed her eyes shut, knowing nothing she could ever think to say would suffice. She'd just seen Bea two days before. They'd made cider and sat on the back porch and talked about the changing season—how good it felt when the cold sea air was cut through with a warm gust. To be able to feel both at once was like living on the line between one existence and the other. You could open your arms wide and have one hand in winter, one in spring.

Rien n'est éternel.

The tattoos on Alma's arm tingled beneath her clothing, like smoldering coals waiting for oxygen again. What she couldn't say to Theo was that she was keeping a careful record of the monuments in her life, and that someday soon, written on her skin would be the spark of who Bea was. That she would be intertwined with it all. Another star in a growing sea of constellations.

~~~

Bea was buried in the same cemetery where Alma had seen Hayden MacKenna's and Lucie St. Pierre's coffins sink into the ground. She helped Theo and Emerson sort through their mother's belongings. Emerson wanted to keep everything, but Theo was of the mind that there could be only so many special things.

They found all her photo albums—pictures of them when they were just kids, running on beaches back when the family used to get together for reunions—her boxes of paints and brushes that she used to decorate weather vanes. They uncovered toys she'd kept from her childhood—a stuffed fox that had been hand sewn, probably by her grandmother.

In the hallway closet, Emerson pulled down a box with a VHS player and about twenty tapes. "All Ma's old movies," he said. Bea had loved black-and-white movies, mostly French, and preferred to watch them on VHS, even back when the town's access to the internet had been good enough to allow for streaming just about anything, anytime. She liked the act of pressing play and seeing the lines squiggle and adjust until the picture was clear. She liked having to rewind the tape when she reached the end, making it feel as if she'd worked for the experience to view the film. Her favorites had been Clouzot's *Les Diaboliques*, Cocteau's *Orphée*, Truffaut's *Jules and Jim*. She fancied herself an aged Jeanne Moreau.

The VHS player had been stored in the box in the closet after it had broken, along with the tapes that Bea didn't want to watch anymore if she couldn't watch them her way.

"I have something to show you guys," Emerson said. "I don't know what Ma would have thought of it—maybe she would have hated it."

They went out to the backyard, where Emerson had hung a projector screen he'd recently bought for Bea. He hadn't had a chance to set it up for her before she died, and the unopened box had still been sitting on the closet shelf next to her movies and a rolled-up poster of Méliès's *A Trip to the Moon*, the spaceship planted firmly into the drippy-faced moon's eye. A theater in Halifax had shown the film once when she was younger, and she'd convinced someone working there to pry open the glass case and let her take it. But she'd loved it too much to let it wear over time on a wall, so she'd kept it safe in the closet.

Outside, the actual moon a thin slice through the cobalt sky. Theo poured them each a mug of a beer he had brewed himself, while Emerson set up the film. "I can't believe how uncomfortable it is to sit on the ground," Theo said, as he leaned back, propped on his elbows. "When did that happen?"

"We're not kids anymore," Alma said. Though it had been only five years, suddenly it felt like a lifetime since she'd arrived, her old life in Maine an obscure dream that her memory could barely access anymore.

The ocean sent long, cool breezes to pass over them. The stars appeared, first the brightest and then little by little the more distant ones, speckling the sky above as the sun set fully. The summer triangle was easily visible, made up of three stars from different constellations: Cygnus, Aquila, and Lyra. The swan, the eagle, and the harp. Alma ran her fingers over her arm as if she could make those stars simply materialize there.

"Okay, here we go," Emerson said, as the projector light flickered to life on the screen. "This is some footage from a research project that was done a few years ago." He pressed a few buttons in the dark, and an old black-and-white silent film began playing. In it, a man and a woman were shopping at a department store. By their outfits and hair, Alma guessed it was the 1920s. A saleswoman behind the counter displayed a lacy piece of lingerie against her own chest. Her mouth moved, but there was no sound. In fact, even the music that had originally accompanied the film had been removed.

"And what exactly are we looking at?" Theo asked. He leaned over and whispered in Alma's ear, loud enough for Emerson to hear, "Do you know what's happening?"

"Shut up and keep watching," Emerson said, elbowing his brother.

A few scenes later, another man and woman were sitting at a dinner table. This time, when they spoke, a low, robotic voice filled in the previous empty silence.

"The flowers," Emerson said, putting his hand in front of the projector light, the shadow of his index finger pointed at the flowers on the table. "These researchers were able to use those tiny vibrations in the flowers here to extract the exact words being spoken and re-create their conversation. The vibrations are invisible to the eye, but the technology can pick them up and translate them into actual words."

The tuxedoed man leaned back in his chair, putting his hands up, and the mechanical voice said, *Now, now, darling. Don't you think that's a little harsh?*

"Wow," Alma said. "That's amazing. And also weird." In a book she'd found at Oren's, she'd read about the first-ever recorded sounds. One was a man saying the word *barometer* five times in a row. Another was the opening of Hamlet's soliloquy: "To be, or not to be . . ." The nursery rhyme "Mary Had a Little Lamb" was used multiple times, once even capturing someone shouting in frustration at the malfunctioning recording device. The first recorded exclamation of irritation.

Alma sat in the dark and listened to the robot-like voices, re-creations of words that had actually been uttered over a hundred years before. It seemed everyone was finding a way to keep the past in some way. Trying to revive it, all while they continued moving forward.

When Emerson's video ended, he said, "So, don't be mad at me. But I'm planning on leaving Violette."

"Wait, what?" Theo said. "You are not."

"I got a job in Boston, at a film institute. Doing things like that."

"You got a job? You applied for jobs without telling anyone? Did you tell Ma?"

"Yeah, I told her. She was happy about it."

Alma winced. In a bad movie, Theo would have accused Emerson of killing Bea with his shocking news. But it wasn't a movie at all, bad or otherwise, and so Theo just said, "You sneaky . . ." And then he held out his beer to toast his brother.

They all knew that Bea, master of harmony, would have approved. Alma smiled in the dark, nodding her congratulations to Emerson when his eyes found hers. He raised his glass. "I'll miss this place. But I need something else."

"I just don't know who I'm going to beat at cribbage now," Theo said.

"You've got Alma," Emerson said.

"What, Miss Chatterbox? Well, that's just too easy." Theo winked at Alma, half his face lit blue by the screen.

Emerson put on another film. The camera panned across a stretch of familiar beach. The scene was disorienting—for a moment, Alma forgot where and when she was. And then she recognized it. The shoreline of Violette looked so different then, the night of the bonfire just after she'd arrived. The night of her first storm. Emerson, behind the camera, called out to Alma and Bea, who were sitting on a blanket. Bea laughed and dropped the cookie Emerson had thrown to her. Alma toasted her aunt and sipped a drink.

The film was a strange mirror, a reflection of another time. Alma was surprised to see herself there, displaced, so new to the landscape that she had since come to love so much. On screen, she glanced around awkwardly and smiled shyly, as if not knowing where to put her focus or how to find words. She looked young, timid, scared.

They watched people filling plates of food, feeding the fire with more wood. In the background, Alma recognized Hayden in one of his bulky, thick-collared sweaters, standing in the shallow waves, arms crossed over his chest, sternly observing the horizon. She saw Oren sitting on a boulder with Fey skipping on the smaller rocks in front of him. Lucie stood in a circle of others, one hand twisting the braid in her hair, the other grasping Theo's.

Emerson and his camera wove through groups of people, followed the bonfire's flames as they erupted from the pile of wood and reached toward the sky. The stars were bright but obscured by smoke.

Thunder cracked, and people began picking up blankets and chairs. The camera dropped to face the sand, and the picture bounced as Emerson ran across the beach. The screen went black. That wasn't where the story ended. They all knew that.

No, Alma thought. They were not kids anymore. Life was moving forward, always. The world was not going to stop, change was inevitable, finding a way back was a struggle against the current.

〜〜〜

Emerson left a few months later. Alma had been worrying about it since he'd told her he was officially hired to work on the film project. She tried to tease him at first, asking if he wasn't a bit old to be running off on some childish adventure, but it only came out wrong and sounded mean. She knew better than to try sarcasm or jokes again, and so just before he got onto Theo's boat, she simply hugged him and said, "Send me some letters, okay? Give me something to write about besides rising tides and dead writers." The mail wouldn't come unless Theo went to get it from The City, which he'd been doing less and less as the weather had become increasingly unpredictable, but that wasn't the point.

"I will. I'll let you know how crazy the rest of the world has gone," Emerson said.

"Here," she said, handing him one of the two copies she'd printed of *Tower of Echoes*. "So you can remember the weirdness of this place."

"It'd be tough to forget," he said, kissing the top of her head.

The sky was clear, a pale blue, but they had seen things change in an instant before. The water had crept up to lap against the boardwalk at high tide, though Alma remembered when she'd first arrived and there had been space to lay out a blanket in that very spot.

She wanted to ask him to say hello to her parents and her brother, but she couldn't bring herself to. They'd stopped trying to call after realizing Alma had no intention of coming back, and Alma had been too afraid to reach out herself.

The boat began to shrink into the gilded sea, and Alma felt a hand on her shoulder, but when she turned there was no one there. She thought about going to Oren's cottage. Or to Bea's house to watch another one of her old movies. She thought about going to her own cottage and calling home. Instead, as she made her way away from the crowd and through town, the radio in her pocket began to crackle and sputter with broken transmission. She moved farther away from the group and closed her eyes, listening. What she heard didn't make sense at first, but—her feet taking her instinctually toward her basement office—she began piecing together the words: "Dar . . . est. Dar . . . est."

Darkest.

It had to be *Darkest*.

~~~

Alma pushed aside a yellow legal pad full of notes she'd taken—strings of numbers, fragments of words in multiple languages. She flipped the radio switch, and it blinked to life. Turning the knob, she scanned the channels until she found the one she'd heard before and it came in clearer.

"This is Darkest One," she said, unable to breathe.

"Hello?" the voice said. "Do you copy?"

"I copy, I copy. Dire Wolf?"

Silence. A high-pitched whine in the background.

"Hello? Alex?"

"Nope, not Alex."

"Oh. I thought you were someone else. What were you saying?"

"I was doing a test. Making sure my partner was picking up the signal on the weather station we just installed."

Alma replayed what she'd heard, frustrated by her mistake. It seemed she'd only been catching the end of the word *radar*, the end of the word *test*. His voice wasn't like Alex's at all either. It was higher pitched and more nasally and he had the twinge of an accent, though she couldn't place it.

"Are you in The City?"

"I'm in *a* city. Halifax."

"Oh. What's it like there? Is it flooded? Have you all had to move yet?"

"Don't you watch the news, or read the paper, or heck, even check your emails?"

"Not really, no. I don't hear much. I'm . . . pretty far away."

"You must be. Who's Alex?"

"My friend." She almost stopped there but added, because she would likely never talk to this man again: "He's dead."

"Huh."

"Sounds kind of crazy, I know."

"Why did you think I was him?"

"It's a long story." There was a pause, and she was afraid he might have left her. She repeated, "So, what's it like . . . the rest of the world?"

"Seems the same as it's always been to me, except that it's hotter in some places, and a lot colder in others. There's more water, and there's less water. People trying to do too many things, too fast, always wanting more. Fighting, as usual."

"Is there any good still out there?" Alma asked. Her fingertips hovered over the left side of her chest, just below her collarbone, where she'd asked Oren to put the words *rien n'est éternel* in tiny cursive.

"Well, we did make it to Mars. Does trying to find an alternative to this planet count as something good?"

Alma laughed. "I heard about that. I do hear some things. That stood out." On the wall behind the desk, she'd hung Bea's Méliès poster. The moon was always watching now, grimacing at her and Jupiter and all the other treasures she accumulated.

"Progress," he said. "We're good at that, at least. No matter the expense. But yes, to answer your question, there is still a lot of good out there. So how does this work? Why are you broadcasting to someone who's dead?"

"Also a long story. I'm listening for an echo. This place is . . . different."

"I don't believe it anymore when people say something is *different*. There are strange things everywhere. And science explains them all."

"What about miracles?"

"Don't even get me started on—" There was some static breaking up the transmission, and she missed the rest of his sentence, but she caught the word *echoes*.

"Repeat, please."

"I said, have you heard of whisper echoes?"

"No."

"There's a place in Spain, at the end of the Camino de Santiago. It's a half-circle stone bench in a park. You sit on one end, and someone else sits on the other end. You whisper something, and your voice is carried all the way around to your friend. Like you're just speaking into their ear. The curve of the bench is just right that the echo of the words carries perfectly. It's called Banco Acústico, the Bench of Whispers, and secrets have been overheard there for more than a century. It seems impossible, but it's *science*."

"The Camino de Santiago route is also called the *voie lactée*," Alma said, remembering something she'd read. "French for 'Milky Way.' When you look up at night, the galaxy is supposed to be swirling above you like it's telling you to keep going on."

"It did actually look like that. Did you know that a group of starfish is called a galaxy?"

"And a group of stingrays is a fever." She paused. "Um, hey, good luck with your weather station."

"Good luck with your dead friend. And your echoes."

Alma's finger lingered over the talk button. She almost asked for his name. She almost asked him to come back again at the same time the next day.

Later that night, as Oren tattooed the back of her neck with three speckled starfish, she was still thinking about how she'd almost begged a stranger to tell her one more story.

19

The universe on her body expanded. When she wasn't being tattooed, her body longed for the feeling of the needle pressing into her skin, the high-pitched hum. It brought a new kind of comfort to her, and so she continued asking for more. Over the course of the next few years, Oren mapped each planet of the solar system across her back. Once, while he worked on her, he said he'd seen the statue of Esmée Taylor was starting to tilt. The ground beneath it was eroding. He wondered out loud which would succumb first—the lighthouse or the statue.

"They're talking about trying to move it," Alma said. "We should climb the mountain. It's been a long time. We should go up and see what it all looks like from there."

When he was finished with the planet Jupiter, dotting the last of its faint rings, he said, "These aren't really there, you know. You can barely see them at all. They're just dust particles that the moons have pulled into orbit." He blew a long stream of air onto her back.

She pulled a sweatshirt over her newly tattooed skin, and they walked outside and watched Fey clutching and rolling a tiny skull in her talons. She used her foot to push it along through the grass. It was a mouse skull, a mouse Fey had killed and eaten, but she played with its bones with tenderness. When she nudged it up a small hill and it rolled back down toward her but off a bit to the right, she did a sideways hop to intercept it.

Oren tilted his head as he watched her. "Supposedly, consciousness is the ability to anticipate what will happen and then change one's behavior accordingly."

"So, are you coming with me?" Alma asked. "Up the mountain?"

The space between her shoulder blades felt like a smoldering fire, and it was hard to think or find words. It left her with less patience than she'd have liked.

But Oren had found something else to muse on, and Jupiter saw a chipmunk darting across the grass and bounded after it. Fey deposited the mouse skull on a bald face of rock and took off after him, and Oren bent to retrieve the skull. "Here," he said, offering it to her. "In another time, I would have taken it home and put it on the bookshelf. But, it's your home now."

"Give me that," Alma said, snatching it from his outstretched hand. "Stop talking like that. You're still here, dammit. Are you coming with me or not?"

~~

The start of the trail was covered by a stream that tumbled over rocks and down to meet the river—a new development in the terrain since the last time Alma had been there. The trail that had led up the mountain was overgrown and washed out. The woods smelled of moss and damp bark. Trees had fallen, covering the path, but Alma and Oren held hands and climbed over them together. Jupiter ran beneath the trunks, sprinting for the summit.

In several places, it looked like the trail veered off in another direction, but they were all dead ends. It seemed so different, and Alma was no stranger to the ease with which one could find themselves turned around, even when you knew where you were. She used Alex's compass to keep them on track. On her hands and knees, Alma crawled to the top, finding that the shelter had fully collapsed, the wooden desk swaying amid the debris. The tower, unyielding against the wind, still rose into the clouds—the strong, stalwart carrier of everything that had come before.

From above, shadows passed over the surrounding hills. Violette could have been just as abandoned as the shelter or any other town that had been evacuated. It looked quiet and empty, and Alma blinked, feeling like she was seeing the future.

Sure enough, the distant statue of Esmée Taylor was clearly leaning toward the beach. It had been a drier summer, and the river still rushed past the statue, but it was low, the waterfall reduced to a trickle tumbling over the cliff.

Alma and Oren sat on the rock face, leaning against the metal tower.

There was the sound of waves, and the deep sighing of a cello drifted across the ocean. He said, "My daughter loved the cello. You might think there weren't many things to remember about a girl you only met twice, and you might think a child wouldn't have any idea what she liked and didn't like. And you'd be dead wrong. I guess the cello was the only thing that put her to sleep."

Alma closed her eyes. It wasn't a cello they were hearing. "Is that the wind?" she asked. She pulled a hat over her head and zipped up her hoodie.

"Whale."

"It sounds sad."

"Could be. Whales do mourn their dead. Mothers will carry a dead calf for days before finally letting it go. Some people think it's all anthropomorphizing. But the scientists who believe that it's true empathy think it's because they've had a chance to bond that it's so hard to let go."

Alma shuddered and rubbed her hands together. "I can tell you think this is fascinating. Doesn't that story make you feel any amount of sorrow or pain or . . . anything?"

"Well, I don't feel *anything* anymore, really. But I never did think death was sad, Alma. It can be beautiful. I do think funerals are unnecessarily sad in that they exist at all. They're not really for the dead. Just everyone left behind."

"Is that from one of your philosophy books?"

"No. It's just something true. There are only a couple hundred North Atlantic right whales left in the world. They were hunted, almost extinct before people finally got their shit together. They still get caught in fishing nets and struck by boats. Even the massive amount of noise we create is horrible for them. They're all going to be gone soon."

"Don't you have any happy stories to tell?"

"Not if I can help it. Just gives me false hope for humanity."

"Does anything give you actual hope in humanity?"

"Just you. Once you realize your magic exists beyond that radio in a flooded basement that doesn't even have proper wiring."

"Growing up," Alma said, squinting at the shoreline where the waves lapped against the side of someone's shed, "my brother René and I used to reach our hands into tide pools and come up with all kinds of things. Periwinkles, urchins, starfish. Crabs that were still pinching, not just shells left behind by seagulls. But now, I go down to the shore and stare into the pools, and I don't see a single living thing. Where did they all go? And is it even possible to get them back?"

"Now who's depressing the conversation?"

Jupiter wandered the stunted trees, emerging with a stick in his mouth. He dropped it and barked. Oren vaulted the stick over his shoulder, and they watched the dog run off into the bushes again. Oren said, "It's almost time, you know."

"What if you see your daughter and decide you don't want to go?" The question came out of nowhere, and she hoped it didn't sound too eager.

"I was sitting on my roof just before I died. I was watching Fey in the trees, and I was thinking about this weight that had been crushing me. I'd started a habit of choosing one thing each day that I was grateful for and recognizing it."

"What are you grateful for today?" she asked.

"History," he said. "There's a time for everything to leave the present and become history. We play our part, and then we step the hell out of the way and let whoever comes next build on whatever artifacts we've left behind."

"What if they ruin it instead?"

"Every once in a while someone will take responsibility for that history, make sure that doesn't happen. I say this speaking directly to the little hope I do have in humanity."

"Monuments," Alma said, her eyes burning.

"I'm not going to stand in the way of you using your magic."

Alma laughed out loud.

"You *are* magic, Alma Hughes. And you're the only one who doesn't believe it."

She almost reached out to hold on to his arm, even though that wouldn't be enough, when the time came, to make him want to stay. Instead, she reached for the stick as Jupiter bounded back, tossing it again. She drew her hood over her hat and pulled her knees into her chest, wrapping her arms tightly around herself. Her back was burning once again with the fire of new stars.

"Don't you dare let them have a funeral for me," he said.

They listened to the whale moaning in the distance, the sound distinct despite the waves and the whipping wind. Alma saw Fey's dark shape lift on a gust, and she tried to recall the genus of these birds—*Corvus*, yes—and something she'd learned as a child. In her memory, there was a woman in a khaki vest, a name tag pinned to her chest, a raven on her outstretched forearm. She'd spoken of the birds' custom of mourning, bringing objects to place around their dead.

"Ravens hold funerals, too, right?" Alma said.

"Don't let Fey have one for me either."

"You know she's not going to listen to me."

"I have another idea for a tattoo," he said. "One more."

There was always a last time.

Oren put his arm around her, and she gave in and tipped toward him. He had told her once that his only real interest in the world was absorbing as much of it as he could without having to travel too far. It was astonishing, he'd said, how vast one's small world turned out to be when you explored every corner of it.

She wasn't done yet. She wasn't even close.

~~~

She had the roots and branches of a tree. She had a galaxy above it. He insisted that she also have the depth of the ocean below. Now, on her thigh: a whale wrapped in swirling waves, vertical, nose reaching up toward the crease of her hip. When the tattoo was healed, she stood in her underwear in front of the mirror, noting the places where her pale skin was giving in to gravity. The empty eye sockets of the mouse skull watched her from the desk as she turned side to side, examining her body.

Behind her, the radio sputtered numbers into the room, but they were meaningless. When they stopped, for a long time, she stood there in silence. She was alone and her bones hurt and she had nowhere to go. Wrapping a blanket around her naked body, she stepped outside onto the cracked sidewalk, the sea dark and shining. The only sounds she heard were the whales in the distance, breaching the surface occasionally, calling to one another, possibly mourning.

~~~

It was October 2036, the leaves crimson and pale yellow. Lille's twentieth birthday came faster than Alma could ever have anticipated, and when it did—when he said *It's time to go*—she felt a mix of fear and sadness and knowingness, as if something she had long been expecting jumped out and took her by surprise.

He told her he wanted his daughter to have one of his father's paintings, but he couldn't decide which one. He needed her help getting the painting to The City, but after that, everything else would stay there in the cottage. *Her* cottage.

"I don't think you should give her one of your father's paintings," Alma said. "You should give her yours. She should know who you are. Or who you were anyway."

Alma was one step closer to helping him move on. One step closer to Jupiter being her last Echo. But, as agreed, she—along with Oren and Jupiter and one very well-wrapped painting of a sea god—boarded Theo's old fishing boat to travel down the eastern coast of Île des Rêves to The City, where Oren assumed Lille was still living.

She'd told Theo she had a friend in The City who'd begged to have the painting delivered once he heard she'd taken on the works of Tadgh Ainsley. And even though she knew that Theo knew perfectly well she didn't have any friends in The City, he agreed because he *did* have a friend there, in addition to some things he wanted to buy for his workshop. He said he'd bring her there and they could part ways for a few hours, and then they'd meet up again and sail back together.

They kept close to the shoreline. On the water, it was clear and sunny, but a spidery mist curled over the beaches they passed. Alma scanned the stretches of sand and the treetops for birds, but saw only one group of cormorants, jagged black silhouettes, that lifted off pyramid-like concrete blocks jutting up from the shallows. They grunted as they rose into the sky and passed over.

Theo was standing behind the wheel, smiling big when she came and stood next to him.

"What are you so happy about?" she asked.

He shook his head, his gray-streaked hair catching the sunlight. He'd been letting it grow long, past his earlobes. His beard had become unruly. "Nothing," Theo said. "I can tell you're up to something, and I don't even want to know what it is. I'm just happy that you're doing it, rather than sitting in that office. You're different when you're on a mission. A little crazy, maybe, but in a good way. Like you're not thinking too hard."

All she could tell him was that she'd had an idea for an article and wanted to make sure she didn't lose it. She wrote furiously, Oren Ainsley invisibly beside her, filling her ears with his history. When he'd told her he wanted to finish his story by the time they reached The City, Alma had protested, but Oren had shouted over the wind, "It has to happen now! It's important that you give it to her."

She'd started to say, "What if . . ." But she already knew the answer and was pulling out her pen and notebook before Oren had time to shake his head.

Though The City was losing people quickly—aside from the flooding, a wildfire had consumed hundreds of acres of forest just a few miles north—it was still shocking to see a place with so many more than were left in Violette. When they arrived, Theo left to find his friend, and Alma—Oren and Jupiter by her side—carried the painting into town, stopping when she reached a brick school with a skateboard ramp in front. There was a tennis court across the street and a church that was three times the size of the one in Violette. They didn't know where Lille lived, but Oren had done some investigating and found out she taught at the middle school.

This was how Oren imagined Lille: she'd have gold hair and green eyes, like Oren's mother. She'd be tall, like Oren, but have a soft voice, like her own mother, Fiona. The only characteristics he could not imagine seeing in his daughter were those of his own father.

He reconsidered everything as they approached the school. "Maybe not," he said. "Maybe we should abandon the whole painting idea. I'll just have a look at her and be gone."

"Nah," Alma said. "This is the right choice. We carried it all this way." She sat on a park bench, resting her arm on the tall painting. Oren paced in circles around the bench, Jupiter following nervously and occasionally looking at Alma as if questioning what he should be doing.

Under an elm tree, a group of kids sat in a circle, a young woman at the center. Oren stopped when he saw her. The long black hair wound into a bun at the base of her neck. She wore a flowered dress. Oren knew it was her immediately, even if she looked the complete opposite of how he'd pictured her.

"Ah, fuck, she looks just like my father," he said, pressing his palm into his forehead. "Of course she does. Her hair was so light the last time I saw her. But that was a lifetime ago."

The kids sitting in a circle around her each had a mortar and pestle in their laps, and they reached out for bowls filled with various items—flowers, nuts, seeds—to mix in and grind. They sang a song together, though Alma couldn't make out the words.

"She was only a kid," Oren said. "But we did that together. She helped me grind up powders to make paint. I can see it so clearly, how her little fingers and cheeks were covered in all those colors."

When class was over, Alma hesitated, realizing she hadn't considered what to say. "I just remembered that I can't mention you," she said. "I mean the actual you, standing here. She's not going to remember."

"Just go," Oren said, turning her around by the shoulders and giving her a gentle push. "Before I have second thoughts again. You'll figure it out."

Alma knelt down beneath the tree and helped pick up the multiple bowls that the kids had left scattered in the grass. Swirls of crushed flower petals and seeds colored the green.

"I liked that," Alma said. "Your lesson."

Lille looked up from beneath long dark lashes. "It's a sneaky kind of lesson. The best kind. They think they're just playing and making a good old mess. But it actually teaches them spatial recognition. It's all about learning about your place in space. How you relate to the atmosphere around you. I have this vague memory of doing it when I was a kid. I had no idea I was learning something so important at the time."

"You don't know me," Alma said, handing a stack of mortars to Lille. "But I have a friend who . . . who knew you and your mother, a long time ago."

"Who's the friend?" Lille asked.

"Just . . . someone. He's an artist. He wanted me to bring this to you, as a gift."

Lille's eyes traveled the painting's perimeter until they fell on the bottom right-hand corner where Oren Ainsley had signed his initials. A brief flicker of recognition flashed in her eyes, but then her face relaxed, and she smiled. "It's beautiful. It's mac Lir, right? And it's a gift for me, not my mother?"

"Is your mother still . . . ," Alma began, then shook her head. "It's very much for you," she said. Leaves began to rain down around them, and Alma looked up into the branches of the maple to find Oren sitting there, gazing down at them. She scowled secretly up at him as Lille brushed a leaf from her shoulder. "This too," Alma said. "It's a story that goes along with the painting, in a way."

Watching Lille hold the notebook in her hands, almost-but-not-quite opening to the first page, Alma had the urge to grab it back and tell her there'd been a mistake. Instead, she bent to pick up a red maple leaf and pressed it between her fingers, wishing Lille all the best before forcing her feet to carry her back to the bench.

"I think she actually remembers you," Alma said.

"No, she doesn't," Oren said. "What was she like?"

"Calm. She seemed like the calmest person I've ever met besides Bea," Alma said. "There was seriously only good energy radiating from her."

"I don't know if I should be proud or disappointed," he said. "That she turned out so well adjusted without me."

"You should be proud," Alma said.

~~~

Somehow the trip back seemed even colder, and Alma wished the first season without Oren wasn't going to be winter, but there they were. They sat on the washboard at the stern of the boat, where the waves were loud enough that Theo couldn't hear her talking. There was no moon, and the ocean stretched vast and sapphire before them. The water that had always been comforting in the past suddenly seemed like the dark, icy abyss that it was.

"Please don't hang on to Jupiter," Oren said. "Promise me you'll let him go and that you'll live a real life."

Alma coughed out a creeping tightness in her throat. "I don't even know how I would do that. I can't send him on. I don't know his story."

"Oh, I think you do." He looked up. Fey soared above them. "No funeral, remember."

"No funeral. At least not the traditional kind."

"Not even the nontraditional kind. I mean it."

"All right, all right."

"Have you heard about sky burials?" He pointed toward Fey as she landed on the roof of the cabin. "Sometimes, I wonder if she's ever been part of any. And if she has, how many."

"I don't think I can do that for you. It seems kind of horrifying, to be honest."

"Well, it's a really spiritual thing in many cultures," Oren said. "But no, if I could choose, I'd do what the whales do—at least the ones that don't end up on a beach somewhere. I think I'd like that feeling—just one long fall into the abyss, drifting down, feeding the sharks and crabs. Then the snails. Worms burrowing into my bones. Transforming along the way into an *actual habitat*, feeding thousands of creatures and eventually just becoming new life."

Alma tried to picture it—other organisms picking apart and devouring his flesh. She trained her eyes on the water. "So, why can't you choose?" she asked.

"I suppose if I knew someone." He put his hand on her back, and beneath his light touch she felt the entire galaxy burn.

"You'd never make it that far," she said. "You're not nearly big enough. You'd be recycled by the time you got a hundred and fifty meters down."

"Well," Oren said. "It's a bet then. I'll go first. A long, slow drift, we'll see how far I get. One day, you make the journey, too, and we can give our reports when we meet again. When I come back a rock crab and you're a moon snail."

As their boat barreled its way through the waves toward Violette, Alma ducked inside the cabin and peered through the window at Oren sitting there. Waves struck the hull hard, and water sprayed up around him, but he leaned steadily into it, hands gripping the gunwales. She'd asked to stay with him, to be there when he left, but he said it was better for both of them if he went alone, and Theo already thought she'd lost her mind.

She imagined Lille back in The City, sitting at home, opening the notebook pages and reading the story of how her father came to not be in her life. Alma felt her stomach tighten with the longing to turn the boat around and try to stop it from happening.

Then another wave crashed high over the back of the boat, and Oren Ainsley was gone.

For the first time, Alma didn't want to go back to Violette. She had no desire to return and find the body of Oren in his garden. Perhaps that had been part of his intent, taking her away before he moved on himself. Showing her there could be something else, somewhere else.

Behind the boat, Theo had hitched a large metal vessel that looked, to Alma, like every spaceship she'd dreamed up as a child. It was a round, rust-orange pod with small circular windows around the top half and a hatch door. Otherwise, it was fully enclosed.

"It's just us now," Alma said, holding on to Jupiter as tightly as she had the first time she'd seen him, wandering toward her in the middle of a vast, sunlit forest.

"What did you say?" Theo said.

Alma stood quickly and pointed to the tethered capsule. "That's your 'workshop stuff'? What is it?" she asked, pulling her hair back into a ponytail to hide the fact that she was wiping tears from her cheeks.

"Hurricane survival pod. It's about time you have a backup place to be when the next big one comes."

"We, right? It's about time we have a backup place?"

The towed vessel bounced on the waves. It looked as if it could withstand anything.

Theo put one muscular arm around her and squeezed. Alma breathed the sea air deeply as the boat pressed into the rough wind. It was too cold, but it felt good. It was too dark to see anything ahead, but that felt good too.

20

Oren Ainsley, penned at sea, 2036

He thought of it more like a rescue than a theft. But whatever it was, rescue or theft, it wasn't what Oren Ainsley was thinking about the night that his daughter was conceived. It wasn't even the possibility of an idea that had glimmered into being yet.

Fiona lay on her side, facing away from him. He looked at her back, a few inches of salty air between them. His hand rested on her hip, and he pressed his nose into the curve of her neck. They were sleeping on a sailboat they'd rented for the weekend, despite Fiona only partially knowing how to sail and Oren not knowing at all. It had taken most of his savings, and it was impulsive, but being impulsive was in his nature.

They were not in love. Or, at least, he knew he was not in love with her. But that didn't matter. He was visiting from Ireland, staying in his father's cottage. She had taken time off work to spend the week with him, before he planned to fly back.

"I think I'm going to stay for a while," he said.

"Why? What would you do here in this tiny town?" she asked. He blew on her bare skin and watched goose bumps rise on her arms.

"Maybe I'll open a tattoo shop," he said. "Why not? I can stay in my father's place if you won't have me."

She giggled and turned around. There was a scar on her temple from a childhood dog bite. He kissed it. "But you've never tattooed anyone. What about school?" she asked.

He'd been enrolled in an art school in Ireland. Something his father had wanted, perhaps to educate the cartoonist out of him. He liked to insult his father by saying things like this, when he knew it wasn't the style of his art that his father didn't like. It was the subject matter.

Tadgh Ainsley wasn't just a realist. He'd had his abstract periods, and they'd been some of his favorites. But he was a political artist at his core, and he never understood Oren's irreverence when it came to responding to current events. Tadgh cared about how art could influence the future, and this is the kind of education he wanted for his son—the kind that embedded a sense of artistic responsibility.

"I'm done with it," Oren said. "It's not for me."

Oren didn't know what was transpiring inside Fiona's body at that moment. He might have imagined it if he hadn't been so captivated by the wisps of hair curling behind her ears.

One moment, he was lying there on a boat, and then, somehow, before he knew it, it was two weeks before her due date and they were lying in exactly the same position on the couch in her living room, a pillow between her legs. She jumped when he sat up behind her and began rubbing her shoulders. She said she wished the whole process would just speed up already, and he traced the black seashell that he'd put on her shoulder.

"It'll happen when it happens," he said, knowing this would only annoy her, yet feeling it was true. She sighed.

The phone rang.

There were two pieces of bad news delivered at that moment. First, Oren's father was dead. Hearing this was shocking enough, but it was the second bit of news that was most disturbing. The aunt who called to report of his father's death took a long, deep breath. Then she told him she'd just found out that for the last ten years, all of Tadgh Ainsley's paintings had been stored in the basement of a library gallery in Dublin. They hadn't been on display, as the family had thought, although nobody'd actually gone to look. This was maybe the saddest part. That they hadn't known because they hadn't been paying any attention, when in fact they should have been his most devoted patrons.

Oren looked at his girlfriend lying on the couch, her ballooning stomach. He knew this was going to be an impossible situation.

Finding out about his father's paintings under a cloth in the basement of a gallery took Oren back to an evening when he was eighteen years old. He'd come home late from his job at the distillery to find his father had opened a bottle of scotch and was sitting at the table. He'd set an empty glass in front of an empty chair, and was pouring before Oren sat down.

Oren smelled like mud and wet grass. His sweatshirt was caked with it, too, from being in the bog. But he sat down and drank.

"Let's see what you've been working on," his father said.

They hadn't been talking about Oren's artwork for some time. It wasn't any mystery that Tadgh didn't appreciate what Oren created in the way a son would hope his father did. He took his sketchbook out of his backpack and passed it across the table. His father opened it and stood up and held the page closer to the dim light above. His rough fingers were flecked with blue and white paint. Tadgh pulled his glasses from the top of his head to rest on his nose. Then he sat down.

"It's good," he said.

Oren took another, larger sip of his drink. The sketchbook lay open on the table between them. It was a watercolor painting of some buildings he'd seen on the road that led out of town. They were crumbling inward, tilting, seemingly taking the telephone wires and poles with them. The buildings were outlines in thick black ink, colored in with washed-out earthy tones—yellow, brown, gray.

"But what is it saying?" Tadgh asked. "What are you trying to tell me?"

Oren folded his arms across his chest. "It doesn't mean anything, and I'm not saying anything," he said. Oren wasn't sure why, when his father questioned him this way, he always insisted this with the same defiance, when the truth was, his art meant a lot to him. It was trying to say a lot. "Things don't always have to mean something." His dirt-caked fingers dug into his ribs as he pulled his arms tighter around himself.

Inside Tadgh, Oren knew, there was a storm rising up, gathering force. It was only a matter of when he would release it. It didn't take long. Tadgh slammed his fist on the table so hard his drinking glass shook and the scotch sloshed out. "You're wrong about that," he said.

Tadgh Ainsley had started his painting career politically, and for him, there was no other way. Most of his work was influenced by violence, and over the years he became a more honest and immediate artist. He threw color at blank white sheets and made it no secret that his paint-splattered canvases represented bloodshed and the debris scattered in bombings.

As he grew as an artist, his ideals were reflected in his personality, and he became more and more a brutally honest, impulsive person as well. "You *have* to say something," he told Oren that night. "Otherwise, what the fuck are you doing it for? Something pretty to look at? The world has enough of that shit."

Oren drank the last of the scotch in his glass, bent down, and slowly pulled off each of his bog boots. Semidry mud dropped to the kitchen tiles. He stood up, took his sketchbook from the table. "If you have such important things to say," he said, "then why don't more people care about your work?" And he walked down the hall to his room.

His father didn't say anything. He didn't get up.

~~~

The problem was that the paintings were in the basement of a library that had recently come under private ownership. The paintings had belonged to the library—Oren's aunt had clarified that Tadgh's will left them all of his work, though she pointed out that he probably expected they'd be hanging on the walls of the gallery—but everything stored there was transferred to the new owner. Oren's aunt had heard that, in the coming months, the new owner planned to auction off most of the paintings they had in storage. Which meant that one person would potentially profit from all of Tadgh Ainsley's work, and no one could ensure that the paintings would be any more valued than they were in the library basement.

Tadgh Ainsley would have been horrified by the idea.

When Oren heard the news of his father's death, and remembered that evening when he told his father that he wasn't as appreciated as he could have been, there seemed only one answer.

"You wouldn't dare," Fiona said.

"The timing is horrible, I know," he said.

"If you go now, I won't be here when you come back. *We*. We won't be here."

He believed her. Her black eyes were determined. She was a lot like his father that way—impulsively honest, firmly convicted. He wished, for the first time, that his father had been able to meet her.

"The paintings will be gone," he said. "This is the only chance."

"We're about to have a child. *This* right here is your only chance. You're going to miss her birth to make up for some stupid things you said in your past."

"It's not just that. I have to."

"And what's your plan?"

He bought a ticket to Dublin the following morning. Fiona didn't say goodbye. She took a walk, thirty-eight weeks pregnant, up the coast, so she wouldn't see his ferry leaving the inlet. Oren boarded his plane, more than once thinking about stepping out of the line, but ultimately getting on and spending most of the flight trying to re-create in his mind the old buildings he used to sketch as he walked down the road in Arden.

His father's old house was damp and moldy, except for his studio, which was the brightest room in the house. He'd put in larger windows and never hung curtains. Oren found the room filled with half-finished paintings, one of which was propped on the easel. It was the image of a woman, one hand covering her face. Her long black hair was the most complete part of the painting, which was otherwise in sketch form.

A wooden stool sat in front of the easel. The floor and walls were splattered with years of paint. Small tables held jars of water and turpentine and brushes. On the door handle hung an apron, not because Tadgh was particularly tidy when he painted, but because the door led to the kitchen, where he was often making a beef and stout pie for himself.

Oren began looking through stacks of books and papers on his father's desk. Tadgh had insisted that having a desk made someone a legitimate businessperson, which one had to be in addition to being an artist, if one wanted to be successful. In the bottom drawer, Oren found his own sketchbooks, every single one he'd used since he was a child. He took a beer from the fridge and stepped out the kitchen window onto the ladder Tadgh used to get to his roof.

It was in Tadgh's rooftop sitting area that Oren finally found the empty bottles of Grá whiskey. He made a point of not drinking the Sólás brand, the distillery where Oren had worked as a teenager. There were trees and ferns growing on the roof, a metal chair and a folding table in the middle. On the table was a chessboard, a match left unfinished. Tadgh had played chess with people through the mail, and this was where he drank. Oren never thought the roof was the best place to be drinking, but Tadgh never drank while he was painting, and he never painted on the roof. Up there was his one escape. It was the one place where he was able to allow the world to stay apart from him, made easier by the alcohol, and by the impersonal notes he received with his opponents' chess moves printed on them.

The cushion Oren sat on was still damp from the rain the night before, but he crossed his legs and opened one of the sketchbooks in his lap. The first was from when he was very young—maybe ten or eleven. It was filled with character drawings from stories he made up. He'd always been able to draw this way, but he gave up on it eventually, a result of his father's constant disapproval. In the next book, he found the buildings he'd been thinking about on the plane. The ones he had drawn the day his father sat across from him and criticized his lazy artistic philosophies. They weren't all that bad, but his father had said they were good, and that it was only his ideals that were wrong. The truth was, Oren felt a strong sense of purpose as an artist, as well as a sense of artistic responsibility. He just hadn't ever admitted that to his father.

What he saw, what he was trying to say when he'd drawn these buildings, had more to do with history and the landscape of home than it did with politics or some ideal future. Maybe his father would have understood that. That, at least, would have been better than the answer he'd given, which was childish and selfish and, frankly, embarrassing to look back upon.

Oren saw the landscape of his country like a deep sadness that embeds itself inside a person's body and dwells there. The land itself had wounds and scars, and it had suffered violence, and Oren had aimed to capture this visually, even if he couldn't put it into words until just then while sitting on his dead father's roof on a damp cushion as it started to rain once more.

In the last sketchbook he opened, he found some drawings he had done when he was twenty years old. They were ogham inscriptions he'd copied and then altered. They were not simple lines, but elaborate and ornate words, some in thick black ink and some accented with a splash of bright watercolor.

These old drawings turned out to be the seed of what would become the mark Oren left on the world when he returned to Violette to an empty house. Perhaps his brightness was his connection—albeit a defiant one—to the past.

Oren's childhood friend, Tommy, had once asked him to steal six cases of whiskey from the distillery. They'd done it together, but it was really Oren whose ass was on the line, since that had been his one and only job from ages fourteen to twenty. Since then, Tommy had broken into a number of other buildings, and had become quite good at it. It was time for Oren to cash in on the favor he'd been promised.

For three days while Oren planned his father's funeral and cleaned his house—all but the painting studio—Tommy studied the alarm system and security plans used by the library. He went to the library and took all the guides and maps he could find.

Oren rented a car and drove, while Tommy ran through the plan one last time.

They parked two streets away and walked in the dark. There was a garden behind the brick building, and the back door was not as well lit as the front. Tommy used a crowbar to pry the door open, and once inside, Oren went to play his part. He left Tommy to disable the alarm while he found the stairs to the basement.

Oren passed through dark rooms with glass cases that housed ancient documents, weathered parchment pieced together and barely resembling what it had been centuries before. There were books with gilded covers behind glass, a tiled pool, the bottom of which was filled with pennies that glittered under the dim lights.

He found the room in the back corner with the elevator and stairs. It was a room not normally used and seemed to be where the library stored supplies and extra exhibit materials. An orange light came in through the tall windows, and there was something uncomfortably familiar about it. Like the light his father had over their kitchen table. He was home here, but home wasn't the same, and it never would be again. He realized he had both missed this place and been happy to leave it.

Before Oren opened the door to reach the stairs, he thought about Fiona and his daughter and wished he had just said *fuck it* to the whole thing. If he could have turned around then and taken it back, he would have.

In the basement of the library, he found multiple boxes, all unlabeled. There were canvases twice as tall as he was, covered with heavy, quilted blankets. Tapestries hung from the walls, cobwebs gathering in their folds. Oren pulled away cloths, trying not to disturb too much but also attempting to find what he'd come for quickly.

He found his father's paintings against the back wall. He didn't know how many he'd expected, but he'd expected more than thirty. Most were three feet tall and two feet wide, and he was able to carry only one or two at a time. He kept them covered as he pulled them up the stairs, where Tommy was waiting to bring them to the car.

Just before he finished, something glinting in another room caught his eye. He ran in quickly and hefted the phonautograph under his arm, carrying it out along with the last of Tadgh Ainsley's paintings.

When they were all loaded into the back of the car, Tommy shook Oren's hand and said, "I'm going to walk. I'll see you at the funeral, my friend." And he turned and disappeared down the dark alley.

As Oren drove back to his father's house, the clouds lifted and the moon came out. He still had a long way to go to be clear of the crime he'd just committed, but there was something calming about it. The feeling that someone was just behind him, chasing him, vanished, and he wished he could call Fiona then and tell her he liked the name Skye.

He left the paintings in the car for the night and slept on the roof. In the morning, he began the long drive to the coast, where he would board a cargo ship back to Canada. That morning, people gathered at the old cemetery and said goodbye to the body of Tadgh Ainsley as it was lowered into the ground. But Oren drifted further and further away. His father's most important works of art in the back of his car. He hadn't told anyone—not Tommy, not his aunt, no one—that he'd never had any intention of attending his father's funeral.

Oren spent most of the cargo ship ride in the small room they gave him, lying on a floor with his back up against his father's paintings. It seemed he'd gotten away with it all and his father was in the ground and his aunt would take over the details of sorting out the rest of the Irish estate. Everything should have felt complete, and yet his previous calm had been replaced by anxiety.

Lying there, he tried to think of the right words, a way to explain to Fiona why he'd needed to do what he did, and how sorry he was. How he'd stood there in the hallway of the darkened library and wished he could just blink and be with her again.

When he reached Newfoundland, and took another, smaller boat to Violette, he found his father's cottage empty. It was his cottage now, he realized, but without Fiona and his daughter, it didn't feel like home anymore. He hauled the paintings into the back room one by one.

He tried to find her, of course, and he succeeded eventually. She was in The City, living in a small apartment with Lille, their daughter. Fiona told him she didn't want anything from him. She'd be angry if he even tried. "You abandoned us," she said, "when we needed you the most. Both of us."

He'd forgotten all the words he'd thought of on the boat, and so he said something untrue. "I never really expected you to be gone," he stuttered.

"Which is exactly why I was. That was your past. We were supposed to be your future. You made a choice. It's harsh, but I had to make one too. I can't be with someone that works that way. Not to mention the crime you committed. What kind of life would we have? Someday, any day, you might just be gone again."

He wanted to say he would never leave again. Lille began to cry. She was lying on the floor beneath a mobile of rainbow leaves. Fiona told him to go, and so he did.

When he returned again to Violette, he sat on his own roof and looked out at the ocean, across which he'd traveled, across which was some life he'd finally said goodbye to for good. He closed his eyes and listened to the moaning of the humpbacks. He looked again at his old sketchbooks.

At age twenty, he'd driven to the west coast of Ireland, where he'd sat in the middle of an ancient cemetery and copied the inscriptions on the old tombstones, written in ogham. When his sketchbook was full, he'd used the pen to write on his own arm, replicating the stone that read *Branwen, Branogeni*. Branwen, Born of the Raven.

Alone yet again, he looked at his arm, where the ink had once been, and just then, a black ball of feathers dropped from the plum tree and into a patch of lupines. A few moments later, the raven chick hopped up a granite boulder and immediately tried again to take flight. This time, she managed to catch the wind and was lifted up. She soared toward the ocean briefly, then turned, came back, and landed on the roof by Oren's feet. She looked like she might step onto his outstretched legs and walk right up them, maybe say something. Instead, she turned her back to him, opened her tiny wings in a stretch, then settled again. They sat there for a long time that way, both looking out in the same direction.

He called her Fey, and she wandered and traveled far, but always returned. Oren opened his tattoo shop soon after. He didn't know much about tattooing, but the idea for a specific kind of place came from his sketchbook of ogham tombstones. Someday he thought he might expand, but for the moment it was simple, and he liked simple. He called the shop Turas Tattoo, from the Gaelic word for "journey."

He didn't think many people would be interested, and he didn't care. He didn't need much to live on, and he'd tattooed himself first, along his forearm, with the ogham translation for the phrase *bí dílis duit féin*, or "be true to yourself," which he vowed at that moment to be, always.

Surprisingly enough, the people of Violette *were* interested, and eventually, more and more, they came to him with something they'd seen in their dreams, or heard coming from the walls. One of his first tattoos was for a woman named Bea, one week after her husband's death. It read: *rien n'est éternel.*

Oren didn't see Fiona and Lille again until nine years later, when they came to visit, just before the big storm and the flash of light. Just before his death. They crushed pigments and mixed paints and made hundreds of sketches, and Oren wondered then if things were going to change.

He wondered about the future.

21

The responsible thing would have been to go right away. To immediately begin walking—running even—up the shoreline path as she had for ten years, to find the body of Oren Ainsley that she knew would be waiting in the garden.

Instead, she helped Theo detach the hurricane pod and drag it to shore. It was too heavy to pull farther up the beach, so they walked to the house to get his ATV, Alma's now-empty notebook under her arm. She'd gone to The City with two ghosts, a painting, and pages filled with one very important story. She'd come back with half of those things, yet somehow the math didn't work out. It seemed she had even less.

When Alma entered the workshop, there was a new canoe propped on blocks in the center of the floor. The wicker seats were lying inside it, waiting to be assembled, but otherwise it looked complete.

"Looks ready to sail out of here any minute," she said, even though it was silly to think he might just paddle away in a canoe.

"Nah," he said, searching a tin box for the keys to the ATV. "Not *any* minute."

There weren't many people left in Violette by then, and she'd been anticipating the day that he finally went too. Still, Alma found that a tumbleweed had lodged itself in her chest and was spinning, rattling up everything else in there. Despite her throat closing, she managed to mumble, "But soon?"

"Yeah," he said, tossing the keys in the air. "Pretty soon."

"You didn't say. You weren't going to ask me to go too?"

"Would you have said yes?"

She looked down at Jupiter, lying on top of her feet. Alma shook her head, squeezing her notebook until her fingertips were pale and bloodless. "You're not actually going to paddle off in that thing, are you?"

The canoe was stained a deep copper, and it reminded her of the one Theo's father, her uncle Hubert, had made for her parents. The one she'd spent so many hours lying in as a child, hiding away from the world, dreaming about Alex.

Theo laughed. "No, no. I mean, it floats, thank you very much. But this is just a labor of love. Something for my father, or for the sake of history maybe. I'll probably leave it behind. That reminds me. I have something for you."

He handed her a knife. She drew it out of the leather sheath, gripping it, turning it slowly. The handle was carved from a marbly, golden piece of birch. She hooked her index finger into the notch near the top. The silver blade was long and thin and curved upward at the tip—made for filleting fish.

"This is incredible. Did you make it?"

He nodded. "You'll probably need it."

Theo had been kind to her after she'd lied to him about Lucie, had brought her supplies and carried out her strange travel requests. Besides a little light teasing, he'd never asked questions when she needed space. And what had she done for him? In some other version of life, she might have been the only friend he had left—and he, hers. Instead, she'd retreated further into her ghost land and allowed him to become lonely.

But not sad. He'd never seemed sad, and she was grateful for at least that.

"You've always been so good to me," Alma said. "And I feel like I haven't done anything for you in return."

"I don't know that I've done all that much," he said. "Besides let you do your thing, strange as your thing is at times. That's not a lot to ask, in my opinion."

She slid the knife back into the sheath. The image of a whale's tail had been burned into the leather. "It's a lot to me," she said. "And it's been too much to ask of most people in my life, before I came here."

Theo sat on a wooden crate and bent forward, tying one of his boots. He continued looking at his feet, wiping sawdust from the leather, and said, "One time, when we were kids and our families got together, I found you sitting on the back porch of one of the cabins, curled into a ball, crying like I'd never seen anyone cry before. Do you remember that?"

Alma shook her head. Too many times when she was younger and had been overwhelmed by noise or a crowd of people, she'd retreat and sob so hard she was dizzy and blacked out. Sometimes, after, she didn't remember anything about it.

"You told me you were crying because you were thinking about people, strangers out there somewhere, who didn't have homes or food or families like we did. You just couldn't understand why the world was so cruel to some, and why we were so lucky. Everyone always told you that you weren't tough, right? But you *are* tough, Alma. It's hard to take in all the shit in this world and feel responsible for it and keep trying to do good."

"I didn't know anyone actually understood any of that," she said.

"Well, maybe I'm smarter than you think."

Alma wrapped her arms around Theo's waist. He rested his chin on the top of her head and patted her on the back.

"Oh, you," he said coolly, backing up and giving her shoulder a squeeze. "Sometimes I feel it, too, the weight of it all. And I always admired you. You don't compromise."

"Thank you," she said. "I'm sorry I wasn't better to you."

"You just keep doing what you're doing. We're good, you and me." Theo smacked his hand hard against the side of the canoe, the hollow boom resounding through the workshop. He winked and smiled his big, bearded, eye-squinting smile, then spun the keys on his finger.

"Want to come back tomorrow and help me finish this?"

Alma nodded.

As they parted ways at the statue of Esmée Taylor, Theo said, "We're all responsible for our own happiness. That includes me. I'd be sorry to leave you behind, generally alone, if I didn't think it would be the thing that made you happy too."

Theo headed down to the beach on the ATV, and Alma turned onto the path to Oren's—*her*—cottage. Jupiter kept in step with her, joyful and unaware that he was the only ghost she had left.

⌒⌒

She delayed once more at the garden gate, looking up to catch Fey on the roof. Since she hadn't been the one to find the other Echoes, she didn't know what to expect, and was surprised to discover that Oren looked exactly the same, as if he hadn't aged at all. As if, perhaps, he wasn't actually *dead* at all.

"Supposedly," she told his body, "even though whales can live for seventy, eighty, ninety years, when they die, it's only the beginning of their story. The 'fall' in a whale fall isn't the actual act of falling either. The 'fall' is what they call the whale's body at the bottom of the ocean, and that new ecosystem that it's become . . . that can go on for another half century. I'm sending you on your way, but you better still be there when it's my turn."

Then she crouched behind his head, hooked her arms beneath his, and dragged Oren Ainsley out of the tomatoes. His neck had broken in the fall, his head twisted at a disturbing angle. It took all her own weight to pull him to the shed, where Tadgh Ainsley's old skiff was waiting in the dark.

Alma stood over him for a while, hands planted on her hips, breathing deeply, before pulling the boat down to the water. She'd said goodbye to him once already, but now, knowing this was the last time she would ever see him, she wondered how long she could make this expedition last. Bending down, she pushed the long hair from his eyes and found that they were bright and focused on the sky.

The ocean was calm, the sun reflecting from its surface in bright-yellow flashes. If any of the dozen people still living in Violette remembered Oren Ainsley, if anyone glanced down at their arm with the sudden revelation of where the ink had come from, Alma would never know. The impact of Oren's remembrance was not something she cared to hear about anymore. Right then, at that moment, stillness was all that mattered.

The boat was tossed rhythmically from side to side as she rowed out past the rock formations that rose from the sea just north of Oren's cottage. It was as far as she could get from town, and she knew there was a chance that he would just wash up on the beach eventually, but she intended to do exactly what she'd told him she would.

She'd weighed him down with stones from the yard, ensuring he would at least fall in the beginning, before the waves took him and the ocean decided where he would rest.

Alma stopped rowing, and the boat settled on the waves, and when she looked up, she saw Fey flying overhead and hoped that what they were doing was not so ceremonious it could be construed as a funeral.

It was nearly impossible to push him over the side without tipping the boat, but Jupiter nudged him from beneath, and together they slid his body into the water. Waves lapped against the sides of the skiff, and just before she let go of his wrist, she had the urge to hang on for longer, maybe travel at least part of the way down with him.

But goodbye had to happen somewhere. He disappeared slowly, sunrays through the water casting flickers of light across his face. She leaned back in the boat, her throat clenching, holding her breath so she wouldn't cry. There's nothing he would have hated more. Jupiter stretched out next to her, and they both squinted into the brightness above to see Fey flying away, shrinking to a fleck of black against downy gray clouds.

The days that would follow Oren's departure were not something Alma had allowed herself to think about, though she knew a line was about to be crossed. There was the side she was on, where she led her almost-real life, with almost-real people and an almost-real dog, but also the realest, truest sense of herself she'd ever known. The side where she could go on pretending she wasn't clinging too hard to the past because she had Oren there to set her straight once in a while.

But then there was the other side, the one she was about to leap into, where all of that was her responsibility. She'd have to make a decision, once she rowed the boat back to shore, whether to keep holding on to Jupiter and continue reaching out for Alex, or to do what Oren had hoped she would—let go.

He was long out of sight when she felt something push against the bottom of the boat. Gripping the gunwales, she peered over the edge to see if he'd floated back up and saw a whale instead, nose cresting the surface of the sea. The whale drifted farther out, keeled over on its side, then pushed the boat again gently, in the direction of the beach, with its mottled gray flipper. A smooth motion.

Alma thrust out a desperate hand, catching only a handful of cold seawater before she watched the giant whale fall.

~~~

We're always having make-believe conversations.

The first time Alex had written to her. For a moment, she could picture him at the Marconi wireless transmission site years ago, when they were both just children. Then she realized it was harder to recall his face, the exact shape of his nose, the clearness of his eyes.

Is all of life, she wondered, simply one long journey narrowing in on those particular people who bring you peace, only to have them taken away?

Alma switched the transceiver on, turning the volume knob as high as it would go. She scanned through the channels, listening for some sign of any of the Echoes. If she could catch a bit of Oren's voice, even one last time before . . .

But she heard nothing. She pulled off the headphones, unplugged them.

She reached for the talk button and began speaking, not considering what might come out of her mouth. "We're always having make-believe conversations in my head. I read that there are now nine hundred star systems out there that we could contact, and reason tells us with a number like that, there has to be other life. And if they're out there, then you have to be too."

The lights on the transceiver began flashing—red, green, yellow—and a series of robotic voices came tumbling out into the room. The sounds in the background of the transmission were like resounding echoes in a large open space. Alma pushed her chair back from the desk, not wanting to touch anything in case she made it all stop.

A man said, *Lost and f*—, and it didn't come from the transceiver but from somewhere behind her in the room. When she turned, there was no one there.

"I'm listening," she said, holding the talk button down again. "I'm here and I'm listening."

Lost and found. One thousand. Times.

She leaned close to the wall, the air vents, the electrical outlets. But the voice was coming from nowhere, or everywhere. It was all around her.

"I'm listening," she said again.

Outside, the sky had darkened, and a bolt of lightning lit the rain-splattered window. Water began streaming beneath the door and down into the room. It was happening more quickly now, the flooding, as soon as it began to rain. Alma went to the window, water swirling around her ankles, and touched her hand to the glass.

When lightning flashed, she could see the lighthouse out on the point in the distance. True, it was going to fall one day, but perhaps not for years yet. No one knew the future. What Alma did know, right then, was that it was the same for floods as it was for radio signals—the higher the better.

The lights on the transceiver stopped blinking. Alma closed her eyes and listened, the transmission fading too. *Lost and found . . . one thousand . . . times.*

22

His last note wasn't signed because he was there, the envelope casually slipped between the forked branches of a balsam fir alongside the trail. Coming up behind him, she reached for it, held it for a moment before lifting the flap, drawing out the card.

A picture of them, standing at the summit of Mount Katahdin—the sign nailed to a tent-shaped wooden structure. Behind it, they leaned into one another. The frame was slightly tilted because they'd used the camera's self-timer, had propped it on a makeshift stand of rocks and backpacks. It was a photo Alma remembered taking but had never actually seen until then. They'd used Alex's camera, and she'd forgotten about it after they'd descended the mountain. Then there it was—a snapshot of their past that she came so close to letting slip away.

When Alma looked up, Alex was standing on a boulder in the middle of a stream, hands on his hips, surveying the treetops like he didn't know who to blame. *Who, me?* his eyes said when they met hers again. She forgot where she was. She forgot everything.

The note was addressed to *La Seule*, which she mistranslated at first, caught up in the moment, assuming it meant "soul." But her mind reached back and remembered from high school French that it meant "the only one," and it was followed by a simple enough phrase: *At the end of the world.*

Alma supposed he meant *the only one* for him, or *the only one* who understood him. Or *the only one* he could "be alone" with. All of those were what the phrase would have meant to her. But she didn't ask him to clarify, and she would regret this later, when he was gone.

The specificity didn't seem all that important at the time, because it could only mean something good. What particular brand of good was just one of those details, the kind you don't think to ask about, but the kind that is vital when you are no longer able to ask. When you have to live the rest of your life wrestling with that one small distinction.

∼∼∼

The trip began with a view of the Big Salmon River, followed by a set of steep stairs that they climbed to a cathedral-like forest of towering pines. The sunlight broke through the canopy, and they were surrounded by brilliant green ferns. They crossed pebbly beaches and grassy meadows, hiked over the hills that rose up around them.

The first night after the proposal, they set up their tent in a clearing and sat by the campfire, talking about what kind of wedding they would have, or if it might be better to simply ask someone to officiate on a trail like the one they were on. No guests. No expenses. No seating-chart drama. *Choose a stump and put your ass on it.* They laughed.

A fog that came in during the night was gone by midmorning. They waded through cold rivers that rushed over their knees. They walked barefoot across gravel beaches while their boots hung drying from their packs.

They'd *almost* lost their way once.

The second night, they walked until it was almost dark. Alma looked up between craggy branches and caught sight of the waning moon against a darkening sky. The plan had been to set up the tent near a sandy beach so they could swim in the morning before starting their last day of hiking. The accidental detour had dragged them behind schedule, but they still wanted to reach the site Alex had pointed to on the trail map. So as the sun set, they continued, pushing until they needed headlamps to see.

"It has to be soon," Alex said, and Alma believed this because she believed they were still on the right path and headed in the right direction. She believed they were on their way to some unparalleled beauty.

"We're going to have to stop," she said after another ten minutes had passed. "It's not worth getting lost again."

"You're going to love it though. It's the best camping spot on this trail, I promise. We'll get there. Any minute these trees are going to open up."

They pressed on, the trees becoming silhouettes of spiny, fingerlike monsters. Crickets replaced the chirping of birds. They came out onto a beach, and she was sure he'd turn around and say this was it. That they'd found the place.

Instead, he told her to stay where she was, that he'd run ahead, and if it wasn't just past that craggy pitch pine, he'd come back and they'd camp right there.

She watched the dark shape of him disappear around the tree, and when she turned back to the sea, Alma thought she saw a blinking white light in the distance and she felt dizzy, the way she sometimes did when others around her were in pain. She felt as if she was falling, though she wasn't, and then there was only darkness—only an empty black hole where her memory should have been.

Alma woke in the morning, alone on the beach, water lapping over her numb feet. She immediately searched for Alex, for the pine tree where she'd last seen him, but nothing looked familiar anymore. She didn't know how long she'd been there. She didn't know which direction she'd come from or in which she should go. Her head hurt, but she couldn't tell if it was from being struck by something or from dehydration or from sleeping on solid rock. There was no blood any-where, but the pain was immense.

She called for Alex, feeling silly at her immediate fear, her impulse to assume the worst, but when he didn't respond, she swallowed hard, assuring herself it was okay. He'd be back from wherever he was in a moment.

She took her water bottle from her backpack and drank slowly, attempting not to panic about being lost and alone. For a long time, she stood in the same spot, trying to decide which direction made the most sense to start walking. She hadn't brought enough food to be in the woods for longer than a few days, and Alex could have been anywhere. If she'd been hurt, he could have been, too, and possibly worse.

Alex's compass told her how to head east, but she knew that infor-mation wasn't good enough, and her common sense told her to stay put, so she waited for a while by the sea, sorting through what was in her backpack to keep her mind busy. Without something to do, she knew she'd begin to panic.

From her pack, she laid out water and food. Her water bottle was two-thirds empty, and Alex had been carrying the filter. She had sun-screen, a towel, one extra change of clothes. She spread the towel on the ground and set down her toothbrush, pocketknife, sunglasses, and headlamp. She had a first aid kit, some rope, a few maps, and a lit-tle book Alex had given her—*99 Survival Skills*—which she'd brought more as a joke than anything, but now that joke seemed distant and stupid. These appeared to be the right things, the exact items one would want to have when lost in the wilderness, but Alma surveyed them dumbly, amazed at how useless they seemed.

The panic began to set in—it rose into her throat, but she pushed it down. She was not going to scream out of fear. If she was going to scream, it would be out of practicality.

"Alex!" she yelled. "Alex!" Only birds and rustling leaves answered. The third time she yelled his name, it was with more terror than she'd ever felt before.

She picked up the survival book, remembering when it had arrived wrapped in brown paper, her arm tucked against her chest in a sling. She'd been so relieved to leave summer camp after her bravely stupid jump, and she'd been dizzied with teenage love when the package arrived with the teasing note from Alex about her lack of basic knowledge of the woods. But out in the woods once more, without him, she kicked herself for not learning a thing or two before leaping from that tree.

Looking at the map of the trail, Alma realized that staying where you were while lost was the right move if you had some general idea of where you'd started, but the truth was, there was a significant gap, if not of distance, then of time—the length of which she didn't know—between where she'd started and where she was now.

She began walking along the water, generally northeast, toward where they'd intended for their hike to end. She pushed through thickets and climbed over downed trees, looking for any kind of trail. A few times she thought she'd found one, but if they were trails, they'd been damaged too badly by windstorms to be of any use. She climbed over the fallen trunks, reorienting herself continually, staying as close to her original direction as possible. She crossed animal tracks she couldn't identify, passed what she thought was a beaver dam as she walked a log bridge over a stream.

After hours of thinking the trail would be just around the next corner, then the next, then the next, and worrying that she'd run out of food and die, or never find Alex, she spotted a cairn. She'd seen no other people, but surely this was a good sign. It seemed the wise thing was to keep to that trail, though it took her farther away from the sea and into forested hills. After she found another pile of rocks and then another, the path stopped abruptly at the edge of a cliff.

There were footprints in the dried mud that disappeared at the edge of a hundred-foot drop into the bay and then disappeared. Once again, Alma shook off assumptions, telling herself there was no way Alex would have come that far without her. Across the open space, the tips of the trees were glowing orange. She'd been walking all day and was just as lost as she'd been that morning.

Attempting to keep the dread at bay, Alma turned back to find a hill, which she thought would provide a better view of the area. When she reached the top, she sat on a rock and removed her shoes. Her feet and ankles bled. Thornbushes had torn her pants and scratched her calves. The wind rushed violently around her, the sound lulling her fatigued brain.

A woodpecker bounced up the trunk of a nearby tree, the thud of its beak fragmenting Alma's thoughts. "Shut up!" she yelled, immediately sorry for it.

She looked again at the survival guide, holding it now not out of necessity but out of longing. It was almost twenty years old. She pressed her fingers into the faded orange cover, flipped through the soft pages. Navigation. Signaling. Shelter. Edible plants. These categories seemed to depend on how long she was going to be out there, and she didn't know the answer to that question.

And because she didn't know the answer, and because she was at the top of a hill that offered her no useful perspective, she began reading a section of the book entitled "Center of Gravity." When descending a slope, the most important thing to do is always maintain control over your center of gravity. The goal is to fall—if you must fall—back into a position in which you can slide, versus forward into one in which you will tumble farther down. The book said, "The proper attitude is one of caution: expect to fall at any moment and be prepared to do so."

Alma had climbed up and down other hills. She'd forged through weak streams as well as raging rivers. She'd found herself at the edge of a cliff that someone else may or may not have fallen from. But she hadn't fallen yet.

Stopping for the night seemed like the only option. She still had enough food to last another two days, and there was a large downed tree that she could crawl under to sleep. The pain in her head had eased, but her body ached and her chest still pounded with an anxious heart. Her thoughts were frantic, bouncing from one distressing scenario to another. Alex might find his way out and then get help to come for her. Or he might be looking for her, walking in the same impractical circles she was. Or *he* might be in trouble, needing her to get herself out and find help to rescue *him*.

She flipped through the maps beneath her headlamp, finding among them one she hadn't seen before, one Alex must have slipped into her bag, that showed the constellations of the northern sky. As she attempted to start a fire with damp wood, Alma wondered when it would be acceptable to use the maps as fuel. With her pocketknife, she stripped away as much of the bark as she could from the smaller pieces, then arranged the larger pieces on top to dry them while the kindling burned. She'd learned this from watching Alex, and she whispered, "Thank you, wherever you are," and then couldn't breathe she was so scared.

Thick smoke rushed up toward the sky, and she hoped that maybe this would have the added benefit of attracting someone's attention. Of course, no one would be looking for her yet. They'd left notes with their families about where they were going to be, and for how long. She still had another day before anyone might even notice that she hadn't returned.

Things would have been so different if she and Alex had been lost together. Whatever had happened, if they hadn't been separated, she knew they could have figured it out. They would have been encouraging each other to move forward, and hugging each other when they began to despair, and they'd both have been a sounding board for good versus bad ideas. Being alone like this seemed infinitely worse.

Her head ached again, and she could no longer focus on the maps, her mind unable to rationalize the best course of action. She folded the map of the trail, opened a protein bar, and used her headlamp to examine the chart of the stars.

When she clicked off the lamp and looked up, it was clear right away that something wasn't right. It was like the universe had shifted somehow. The stars seemed wrong. But of course, her judgment was less than reliable. Alma sat surrounded by the dark silhouettes of trees all pointing up toward this strange, untrustworthy sky. She was sure it was altered, celestially aligned perhaps to where it should be in winter. She hugged herself, head thrown back, scanning the black void above.

It was true that she wasn't very good with the wilderness, but Alma knew her constellations. Cetus, the whale, rested in the southern sea of stars. Monoceros—an impossible creature in an impossible sky— charged northward. The moon was full, yet she was sure it had been only a wedge of silver light the first night they'd camped.

She'd never been so tired and was forced to attribute the disturbing phenomenon to exhaustion. And as she began falling asleep, she thought of something a philosopher had said that Alex often paraphrased: "There's no such thing as the wrong stars, Alma. It's all in how you're looking at them." The words that used to enable her to take the world's difficulties piece by piece now made her feel powerless. These stars *were* wrong. Nothing at all about them or the last two days had been right.

Alma pulled her jacket hood over her head, zipped it up to her chin, and closed her eyes, imagining herself as simply one swell of water in the ocean of stars above. She slept that night on the ground beneath a tree, beneath the wrong stars, and in the morning, she began walking again, this time without the help of a compass or the sky that had betrayed her, but strictly by instinct.

Just before the rain came, she thought she'd found her way. Then within minutes, the steep hills were swept by rapids, rivers rushing down them, washing away any sense of a route and pooling in muddy puddles at the bottom. She slipped and grasped for a tree branch, but missed and slid down the hillside, slamming feetfirst into a tree trunk. Both legs shot through with fire, and she looked down to see the left bleeding and the right bent awkwardly, the bone bulging beneath the skin. The trees spun around her. She focused long enough to flip frantically through the survival book for what to do, felt for a pulse beneath the break in her leg, and finding it, went in search of water to clean her wounds. She hobbled through the mud, staying away from the hills as much as possible, until she found a freshwater stream. The water bottle in her backpack was empty, and though it was ill advised to use the river water, she splashed it over her bleeding leg anyway and even took a few sips.

That night, she pulled pine branches and moss over her body to keep warm, and she nibbled at plantain leaves and berries she'd identified with her guidebook. She forced herself to think only of positive things, only of the moment when she would see Alex again or hear his voice. She pictured them, the relief tangible, the way they would laugh a year from now when they talked about the worst marriage proposal in history.

The rain stopped in the night, and when the sun came up, Alma had a renewed determination. She made herself a walking stick and limped onward. The hallucinations began, but she shook them off each time. She thought she saw houses in the distance. Music and radio broadcasts turned out to be the sound of running water. Trees looked like trail signs. A deer was Alex, appearing at the edge of a stream.

So it wasn't that surprising that she almost walked right past them. Alma stumbled in a daze toward the four figures between the trees, assuming them to be more hallucinations. Just before she reached them, something moved and drew her attention to the right, and she changed direction involuntarily to reach out for it.

Then she collapsed.

As the woman wrapped a blanket around Alma's shoulders, Alma tried to explain that her boyfriend—it killed her to realize later that she'd said *boyfriend* and not *fiancé*—was still out there somewhere and may need rescuing more than she did. Even as she said it, she was hoping someone, anyone, would say, "No, no. He's already been found. He brought us to you." She waited for Alex to emerge from behind two men in orange jackets holding a stretcher.

When no one said any of these things, and when he didn't simply appear, she pulled the postcard from her jacket pocket. It was wet and already worn soft, but the picture of them was still intact. She read the reverse side again—*the only one*—and gripped it tighter as she handed it to the woman.

"That's him," she said. "He's still out there."

The woman looked at the picture and handed it back to her. "You can hang on to that," she said. "We'll find him." Then the woman began cleaning Alma's legs and making a splint for the break. Alma caught sight of her reflection in the window of the van and saw purple bruises beneath both of her eyes. Her head still ached. How could they be so sure that he would be found?

She touched her cheek, and the woman said, "Head injuries. The blood pools under your eyes like that. Can you tell me what happened?" Alma closed her eyes, trying not to scream from the pain in her leg, or cry at the realization that at some point over the last few days, she'd come to accept her situation because she had no other choice. But the fact hit her hard then: she still had no idea how she'd gotten lost, how she and Alex had been separated, but she remembered, clearly, the feeling she'd had before she blacked out—the undeniable sense of someone else's pain.

She tried to stand up.

"You need to sit down," the woman said. "We're going to get you out of here soon. We just have to make sure you're stable."

It hadn't occurred to her that they might actually leave before finding Alex. "No, wait," Alma tried to say, but she was dizzy and so thirsty, and the trees began to spin around her again. She turned her eyes upward, past the treetops, past the clouds. She knew she wouldn't be any better at finding Alex than the rescue crew.

When she looked down again, she saw something real.

There: the shape materializing between the fluttering leaves of the aspens. Then: the certainty even before he approached that, somehow, he belonged with her. She pulled him close, buried his face into her shoulder and her own face and hands into his brown-black fur. She smelled the dampness of the woods on him and breathed it in.

"Is that your dog?" the woman asked.

There was the sudden fear that they might take him away, and so Alma mustered a steady voice through her sobbing and lied: "Yes, yes. He's mine."

PART 4
THE ECHO OF EVERYTHING

2058

23

If we hadn't known better, we'd have thought the place was empty. Alma Hughes was the only one left, and when our boat sailed into the inlet and up to Violette, she was there, watching. I thought she was a siren, clinging to the rocks.

Her red hair, streaked with white, was wet, as if she'd just stepped out of the sea. Her squinting eyes, shielded by a flat hand, followed our boat as it skimmed straight up to a statue—a girl and her dog—that was lying on its side.

It was a fading place before, but despite my expectations, nothing could have prepared me for the wildness there, or the desolation. It was a place adrift.

Passing the lighthouse on our way in, Birk and I watched a mound of rocks at the edge of the bluff tumble into the sea. The waves lapped at the cliff, drawing out its slow promise of death. A timber barricade, already dangling in front of the keeper's house, was pulled down, too, disappearing into the waves. It seemed a miracle the lighthouse was still standing at all.

The town was a mess of wreckage and debris, from flooded buildings to fallen electrical wires to downed trees. It was a vast mudflat, broken by pockets of water, rivulets carved by the streams running through it.

There was one boat left bobbing in the shallows—a copper-stained canoe. Next to it, a shed, dragged from someone's yard, was nearly submerged. I could have reached out to touch its roof as our boat glided past. The homes and buildings that hadn't been swept out to sea were empty, windows broken, water sloshing in and out of their doorways. They'd all taken too much damage to repair, and the former owners hadn't even bothered to board them up before leaving.

When I kept my eyes up, and squinted into the sun, I could almost imagine what the place might have been like before the floods had destroyed it.

Behind the town, the mountain loomed, forested until the top, where the face of it was bare rock. That's where the tower was, one of the two reasons we were there. From the boat, it was only as tall as my thumbnail, but in reality it shot up even higher than I'd expected, ringed by clouds.

By the time I finally met Alma—the other reason—I hadn't spoken a word in all the fifteen years I'd been alive. At least that was how everyone who had ever known me remembered it. But that was simply one way of looking at things. When I was alone, I could speak just fine. I talked to birds and foxes. Once, when Birk and I were in Scotland, I met a seal on the Isle of May, and our conversation lasted nearly an hour. No one believed it—except for Birk, who never doubted me—which I suppose I expected, because I'd never once said a thing out loud in the presence of another human.

Getting to Violette hadn't been an easy feat. We'd exhausted all our resources trying to find someone to sail or fly us there, and eventually had to buy our own boat and make the trip alone. We faced rough seas and long, dark days of rain, but this was not the most danger we'd ever been in.

We traveled, looking for rocks—anything from gems and crystals to fragments of meteorites. Along the way we also collected artifacts, vintage items that we sold to antique dealers. We were interested in reclaiming pieces of the past, whether it was a few years or a few centuries ago.

We weren't scientists. We didn't have geology or archaeology degrees. We were finders. Birk was in it for the money, and I was in it out of insatiable curiosity, and because I had no one else in the world, and because I had a knack for finding tiny things amid a million other tiny things. It was one of the skills I pursued with vigor.

Birk hauled our large chest off the boat. It was really too big to carry around, but we always brought it with us, no matter how uncomfortable it made a trip. Technology had left us behind, but we never claimed to be professionals, despite being terribly good at what we did. The chest was filled with trowels and sieves. Little cases for holding the rocks we found. Brushes and picks that we used for cleaning them. We did the laborious work of traveling to remote places, uncovering specimens, and carrying them back to let someone more qualified analyze them.

I jumped from the boat onto the muddy boardwalk with a backpack that held everything I owned: three changes of clothes, some field guides, a toy Morse code transmitter, a map of Laniakea—the galaxy supercluster—and a digital tablet on which I'd written notes about every expedition Birk and I had ever taken, and on which I scribbled the things I could not get my voice to say.

"There's nothing here anymore," Alma yelled at us. Or she tried to yell. Her voice came scratching through the mist like she hadn't used it in a long time. She hadn't moved from the rock, but she'd sunk into a squat, her elbows resting on her knees. Her right arm was an array of tattoos. A knife in a leather sheath hung from her hip. "You might as well just get back in that boat."

Once, we uncovered a piece of a pallasite, flecked with olivine crystals, that was older than the solar system itself. The oldest material to exist on Earth. There was always something, everywhere.

"You the only one here?" Birk asked.

Alma turned to the large black-brown dog at her side. Then she nodded. "Yep."

"Good," he said. "We're not going to be long. We just want to see the tower."

Alma grasped her hair, squeezing the water out. It was forty degrees and cloudy, the hills covered in a low mist. It was freezing, but even dripping with water, she didn't shiver.

"You can't," she said. "It's all washed out and flooded. There isn't even a trail anymore. Plus, if a storm hits while you're up there, you're a goner."

I remember things. Like the wrinkles in the corners of Birk's eyes then, when they narrowed, and he said, just for me, "Well, we're going, one way or another." He waved a hand toward the houses, the ones that still had all their exterior walls and doors and windows, farther back on the hill. "Can we stay anywhere we like?"

We'd been everywhere. There were many times when we'd gone after a particular rock in a particular place, yet never found it. On those occasions, we packed up and moved on. There was little discussion, and no wavering.

But this time was different. This time, we were here for me. We had no plans to take any souvenirs. We just knew there was something special about the tower—something mysterious, magical—and we weren't going to stop until we were standing close enough to touch it.

Alma hesitated. I could tell she didn't want to appear too welcoming, but also didn't want us to die in her deserted town, so she shrugged and said, "There's a cottage, back on the hill. The turquoise one. You can stay there." And then, somehow, she was gone, like she'd simply slipped into the sea or evaporated into the fog.

Alma's old cottage was small and dark, like most of the places we stayed throughout the years, so it felt just as much like home. There were no curtains, but we'd brought some of our own and hung them up. The sheer red fabric with embroidered stars on it always made any place familiar, comfortable.

She'd left behind cups, plates, utensils; some empty clay pots; a fully made bed. But there were no photos or paintings on the walls, no books on the shelves, no blankets draped over the back of the couch. It was a house that had clearly been *occupied*, but not necessarily *lived* in. The hallway closet was also empty, with the exception of a folded towel and an old phone that I attempted to charge and turn on just for fun. It never connected—the spinning spiral mesmerized me for a few moments before I placed the device back in the closet and closed the door.

The next morning, I explored the abandoned buildings, wading through ankle-deep water to the front door of the library, looking for information about the area. Anything about the town and the strange things it had experienced. A map of the mountain, though I doubted I'd find one, would have been perfect.

The small building had a "Closed" sign in the window, though the door had fallen off its hinges and the entrance was wide open. I went in, searched the dark shelves, even paused in the nonfiction section to carefully scan each of the spines. It occurred to me then that what I was looking for might not have been classified as nonfiction at all, and so I searched under the letter *M* in fiction as well. The books on the bottom shelves had all been steeped for years in water, so they were mostly just covers with pulp in between, and the most recent book I could find that wasn't destroyed was published in 2025. I went down every single dark aisle and walked out with a pamphlet about the animal sanctuary on the north edge of town and a book about electromagnetic radiation. Then I moved on to my next task, which was to check old copies of the newspaper.

The newspaper office was clearly as abandoned as everything else, but I knocked anyway. There was one window intact, plastered from the inside with printed pages, but it was hard to tell if they were there for display or to give the impression that the office had permanently closed. The dates didn't go past 2040 and seemed to mostly be stories about local people.

Before I could open the door, Alma's dog came bounding through the mud toward me. He buried his wet nose into my chest, and I knelt down to pet him. I picked up a stick from a swampy flower bed and threw it. Jupiter—long, damp fur rippling as he jumped—had just gone running after it when the door to the office opened.

"What are you doing?" Alma asked, holding a large square battery with both hands.

Jupiter came back, chewing on the stick, and Alma reached for my arm like she thought I might attack him. "What are you doing?" she said again.

I stood up and watched her eyes grow wide. She pressed her hand over her mouth, then said, "That's my dog." Jupiter pushed his forehead into the palm of my hand.

I could tell he was not quite of our world. I'd known it since we stepped off the boat and Birk didn't acknowledge the jumping, barking, bear-cub-size dog. Dropping my backpack from my shoulder to the crook of my elbow, I took out my tablet and wrote *Kricket*, then pointed to myself with the pen. When she looked confused, I wrote beneath it: *Kristienne*. I pointed at her and then the windows covered with newspaper.

She made some apologetic hand gestures, whispering, "I don't know any sign language," and so I wrote, *I can hear just fine*.

I remember things. How my mother's amethyst pendant rested on her chest, and how she rubbed it with her forefinger and thumb when she was nervous. How my father made exceptional shadow puppets with his hands of moose and wolves and snails. And the way my grandfather, before he died, walked two fingers across his palm to demonstrate the rock crabs he used to find with his sister in the tide pools when they were kids.

And so the image is very clear in my mind: the way Alma's eyes clouded, like a gray veil was drawn over them, when she began to cry. "I'm Alma," she said, trying to stop herself, but the tears didn't stop, even after she began walking away through the drowned street. "You really shouldn't be here, Kricket."

I followed her up the path without asking, and she didn't tell me to leave. It was a longer way than I expected to her house—the cottage that had belonged to Oren Ainsley and his father before him—and it looked like a time capsule from before my birth. The world had changed so much since she'd come to Violette, but she'd gone on living the way she always had, determined to stay in this place, where Jupiter still existed and the radio tower opened doors to all the other worlds she needed. I can't say she was still searching for Alex—she'd lost a lot of hope by then. But she went into and out of those worlds freely and deliberately with something that resembled courage, if not belief.

We sat at her small kitchen table and drank tea, and I took out my tablet again to ask about the mountain and the tower. Alma looked like she'd been caught hiding something, but I couldn't imagine what. Not then anyway. "There's nothing to know," she said quickly.

We need to go up, I wrote.

"Why?" She sat back in her chair and looked out the window at the rain on the thriving garden. "Why do you care so much?"

It's important.

"Don't you need to get back? Isn't your grandfather worried about you right now?"

He's not my grandfather. Will you go with us?

There was a moment of pause in which I felt her almost let something unravel inside her, like a loosening of strings. But she pushed my tablet across the table and sighed, shaking her head and crossing her arms over her chest. "Look, I've been up there many times. It's dangerous. And there's nothing to see that you can't get from being down here."

But you could take us.

"I don't need any projects. I wish you the best. I really do."

I walked around the room. Carved figurines, hanging wire sculptures. Beautiful, enormous paintings. An antique machine in the corner that I knew was one of the first to record sound—the phonautograph. There were so many books on the shelves. Things like this—tangible things, handmade things—were harder to come by in the world we'd traveled from, which is why our business of uncovering the past was so valuable. It's not that books were gone for good. They were just . . . *different.* My parents had a few, but most people's books existed only as sound waves. Our eyes had become too precious.

I touched the soft wood of the shelf, ran my fingers along the books' spines. And then I saw it there, and my chest collapsed—Hayden MacKenna's *Tower of Echoes.*

I didn't have time to sign a word to her—she was already telling me to take it. To take anything at all, as long as I left, and then my hands were holding it. Real pages and binding and that damp paper smell.

Exactly the way I remembered it.

I thumbed through it as I walked back to the cottage in town, finding my favorite page, my favorite line. She had underlined it too.

They had been there before, and they were there again. They would always be there.

～～～

The rain stranded us for almost a week. During the day, I visited Alma at Oren's cottage, where she mostly ignored me and I read books from her shelves about Irish philosophers and the rise of pop art. But at night, when her signal could travel greater distances, I found her at the top of the lighthouse tower, where she'd set up her radio station looking out over the sea. Her equipment was organized on a piece of plywood held up by two cabinets, and on top, she had spread out her monuments like a little silhouetted congregation: a snow globe with a spaceship inside, a recipe card and a stack of papers, various crystals, photographs and cards, a compass. A walkie-talkie that looked like it came from a kid's dress-up set I'd seen once at a vintage store. She was always sitting at the desk in the semidarkness, headphones on, recording the things she heard in a notebook. Sometimes she stated her name, attempting to make contact.

Each time I saw her, I begged for her to come with us up the mountain. And each time I asked, I saw flickers of desire, like she wanted to say yes, and it wasn't until later that I realized why she refused: she wouldn't allow herself another single ounce of real connection.

One evening, I climbed the spiral iron stairs into the lighthouse gallery and sat on the floor with my headlamp, turning the pages of MacKenna's book, remembering reading it on our island, before the virus had come and spread. Before my parents had begged Birk to take me away when they'd learned it was too late for them. For a brief moment, I was back there, the sun shining, an iguana sleeping on the shed roof outside my window.

There was so much brightness.

The silence was broken by a multitude of radio broadcasts. They came from various places in the room—a pair of scissors on the desk, an electric heater that wasn't even plugged in, a coffee maker, a metal chair in the corner. The room was full of chatter. There were deep voices and higher-pitched ones, male and female, all speaking different languages and all speaking over one another, although not the way actual people do. They weren't in competition. They were simply rambling on independently, taking up their own space in the air. No more, no less.

On the fifth day of harsh wind and rain, Birk let me put a dash of his whiskey into my tea. He was examining some of our previous finds at the small kitchen table. The light on his headlamp flickered, and he leaned in close to inspect the dusty fragment of rock.

Static came barking through the bare bulb overhead, and the trill of a woman's voice discussing the impossible task of trying to classify faeries, as they are creatures of the imagination. I stood on a chair, leaning close to the light, listening, wondering how she knew for sure.

Then Birk's little loupe fell to the floor and rolled under the table, and as he crawled down to get it, there was a loud crack and the whole house shook. The roof broke apart and tree branches came tearing through it, followed by the massive trunk, collapsing the round table, trapping Birk beneath it. His arm was pinned, but not crushed. Not yet.

The tree was immovable. I'd never pushed against something quite so heavy—my shoulder scraping against the bark—only to see no result, not even the slightest movement. I pushed even harder, even though there was no point, my knees shaking under me, my mouth opening to scream despite no sound escaping.

Birk and I, we'd been to so many dangerous places, had so many close calls. Confrontations with bears in remote parts of the Arctic. Violent exchanges with greedy humans. Running out of water in the desert. We took care of ourselves. But this, I knew, we couldn't handle alone. There was no getting out of it without her.

"Go," Birk said, trying one last time to pull his arm free and crying out when the tree shifted and the broken table dropped a little more.

I believe in signs from the universe. In that moment, at the same time that I was afraid for Birk's life, I knew we were meant to be there. My mind made several leaps to a future self, Alma by my side. I was running for the door with a marker in my hand, scribbling the word *help* on my wrist as I sped barefoot across the cold rocks.

In the night, the path to the lighthouse was enveloped in a deep-blue fog. My feet made slapping noises on the wet earth. I tripped, fell, tripped and fell again. The third time, the palm of my hand met some sharp stone and tore open. I arrived at Alma's bleeding, shivering, steam leaving my mouth in bursts as I banged on the tower stairs with a stick.

She came barreling down, her hair tied back with a bandanna, the thin knife in her hand. "I told you, you shouldn't be here, Kricket. This isn't a safe place."

Her eyes searched me for answers—what was so important—then she grasped my wrist with both hands, swiftly but gently, like I was a delicate bird she needed to inspect for injury.

But she was stronger than anyone I'd ever seen. That's how I remember Alma Hughes. Sixty-four years old, slicing through the fallen tree trunk with a chainsaw, rain dripping onto her from the open roof. Lifting giant pieces of tree from the kitchen table, releasing Birk's body. Standing there—her muscular arms tattooed up and down with dots and lines, a compass and trees, the night sky—taking a long breath and closing her eyes and tipping her head back, the sleet spattering her cheeks.

I know that was the moment she decided to come with us. Maybe she was just waiting for a good excuse. "I can't have you dying up there," she said. "But then you have to leave. I don't have room for any more ghosts."

～～～

We left as soon as the skies cleared, hiking north along the coast to reach the eastern side of the mountain, stopping first at what had once been the animal sanctuary. Alphie had died years before, and though no one could really replace him or properly care for the animals, occasionally wildlife still came around, like their instincts just told them they would find refuge. Alma visited frequently to check on those creatures, a responsibility that no one had given her but that she seemed to take very seriously.

The sanctuary looked nothing like the pamphlet I'd found in the library. The roof of the barn had collapsed, and there was a pond in the middle field, a swampy depression in the earth.

"It used to be that the seabirds came here to rest," Alma said. She told us it had been a safe place once, but now that was just a history lesson, because when we stepped to the edge of the bluff and looked down to where gannets and guillemots had nested in the crevasses, and puffins had burrowed into hollows, instead we saw the bodies of hundreds of dead birds.

"Seabird wreck," Alma said, her hair blowing wild around her face as she leaned over the cliff edge and examined the scene. "There aren't many birds left, but this still happens all the time now, with cyclones off the coast. They die of starvation, usually, and this probably isn't even close to the real damage. Thousands more birds went into the sea."

We stared at the carcasses. Three years before, in Norway, we'd seen a similar kind of disaster. I noticed then the distinct lack of wingbeats and birdcalls.

Alma told us to wait while she checked on the snowshoe hares that were burrowing nearby. They spooked easily, she said, but they'd grown used to her coming around. She walked silently across the field—her hands tucked into the pockets of a heavy wool coat sewn with multiple patches—toward a stand of low-growing evergreens, getting on her hands and knees to peer under a bush. Then she moved on to other parts of the area around the sanctuary, pausing often to investigate something, though she didn't tell us what she was looking for.

Birk climbed down to the beach to search for crabs, his pants rolled up to his knees, hood pulled over his head, arm bandaged from wrist to elbow. He didn't find anything. There was so much space there and the gray of the sky was so intrusive, so encompassing, it made me dizzy. I sat on the lichen-covered rocks, away from the view of the bird wreck, and sketched a picture of a fish I'd seen skirting through the river that morning, before we'd left Violette.

A tern appeared in the sky—at first it was just a wisp of white against the clouds, and then the black cap on its head and the red-orange tip of its beak became visible. It soared down and landed in a patch of yellow flowers, looking directly at me through black eyes I could barely see. It shifted from one foot to the other, tilting its head, trying to warn me.

Alma returned half an hour later with wild cranberries and some long rounded leaves. When she saw the tern, she sat gently next to me and whispered, "Holy shit."

I opened a pocket guide to birds, showing her the page with a picture of the roseate tern, but she shook her head.

"No, it's a Forster's. He's a little heavier, see? And his tail is shorter."

I wrote on my sketchbook page: *He says there's another storm coming.*

Alma looked at the tern, then back at me. Maybe she was wondering if I'd really been talking to the bird. Or maybe she was just wondering what sort of talking we did. It was never words, never actual language. It was always more like a reading of minds. But she didn't spend much time considering it, whatever it was. Alma scanned the sky, glanced around at the wind-rustling bushes, and said, "Yeah. He's probably right. Put this in your pocket." She handed me a yellow-green sprig of leaves. "That's bog myrtle. It'll help keep away the bugs." Then she dropped some cranberries into my palm. "These you can eat."

I popped the tart berries in my mouth, and they made my temples sting and my eyes water. Alma bent over my drawing, gave an approving *huh*, and said, "They're better cooked. You should have caught that fish."

～～～

When we reached the base of the mountain, she marched ahead of us, a compass clutched in her fist, even though I never saw her use it. Not even once. We crossed a plank bridge over a stream, then began the hike up. Alma paused occasionally, searching for a path only she knew was there, and only from memory, but she never took us in the wrong direction.

"Don't touch that," she said, not turning back, pointing to a patch of jagged leaves. "Nettles." Otherwise, she didn't say much of anything. She seemed to be thinking about something or someone that existed elsewhere.

Birk and I followed behind Jupiter, climbing over downed trees and pushing aside bushes that had grown over the trail. I could hear Birk behind me, out of breath, stopping once in a while to lean against a tree. A little over halfway to the top, the terrain became rockier and we had to do more scrambling. There were rope ladders secured to the boulders and pieces of iron rebar driven into the earth, and I realized that she did climb the mountain often. She'd made her own way up when the one that was there before was destroyed.

At the top, there was no shelter, only scrap pieces of plywood and two-by-fours that had been reassembled into a high-backed bench that faced the view of the inlet. Alma walked directly to the tower and picked up a tree branch, then swung it at the tower's base. The metal rang out like a gong—long and deep, reverberating.

"Is that what you wanted to see?"

But she knew it wasn't.

It was so much windier up there. My ears and nose stung with the cold. Alma pulled a hat over her hair, then reached into her backpack for two more. Birk mumbled thanks as he tugged it down onto his bald head.

"So," Alma said. "What is it you expected then?"

I stepped up to the tower, reaching a hand to touch the cold metal. I crawled inside the base of it, so it was rising up all around me like a massive cage, then sat on the ground and took a chunk of galena from my backpack, chiseled and shiny gray, the size of my palm. Birk and I had found it ourselves in India.

I placed it on the ground beneath the tower and waited.

Alma had retreated again into her own private world. She was staring off at the horizon, watching as charcoal clouds slid across the sky toward us. Every thirty seconds she tossed a stick for Jupiter.

Galena is an ore of lead. It was used to make the first crystal radios, which needed no power other than the radio signal itself. They're obsolete, but I'd seen one of the first crystal sets, built in 1925, when we were in Japan.

I stared at the rock, waiting. My hand reached out, almost touching it, when it began vibrating, moving across the dirt. The voices spoke through the rock.

Cosmic Chronicle X, X, X . . .

Each *X* grew quieter, yet more dramatic.

"Oh my god." Alma laughed and turned to us. "That's the first thing I ever heard up here. I can't believe that's still happening." She looked at her watch, even though I'd caught a glimpse of it earlier while we were sitting at the sanctuary, and it was no longer ticking.

We sat on the cold ground in a circle, listening to the old radio show, originally broadcast more than a hundred years before. Alma's eyes met mine, and I nodded that yes, this was what I'd come for.

I let it wash over me, thinking about Hayden's book again, and the words: *They had been there before, and they were there again. They would always be there.*

As we listened, I drew. I sketched a lynx I'd seen on one of our walks on a neighboring island. The place was abandoned as well, and the lynx was walking through the empty streets at night. It had told me a story about seeing inside the body of a deer before he killed it, and about the secret of the woman who lived on the eastern coast of Île des Rêves, and about what it felt like to be the last of its kind on the island. Just like she was.

I wrote on my tablet to Alma: *He told me about you.*

"Who told you?"

I pointed to the drawing.

Birk leaned over to look and said, "If you see a lynx, it's a sign that things may not be what they seem. Or it's a sign that you're a good listener."

I'd always been a good listener. When you can't speak, what else is there?

It took her a long time to ask, but eventually Alma said, "I don't think I want to know, but what happened out there?"

I watched Birk consider how to answer. Many were as furious as he was about the lack of care for the planet, but not so many lived the way he did—as if he felt personally responsible and owed the planet a great debt that could never be paid. He suffered daily for it.

He told her about the fires, how much of the earth was burning. The global temperature rise surpassed even the bleakest expectations. Whole species of trees had been wiped out for good. Aside from what was lost to the fires, ash and white cedar were nearly gone from insect infestations. New diseases were popping up all the time for humans too. And he told her how quickly the animals were disappearing. Attempts in the Gulf of Saint Lawrence to protect the harp seal had failed—they'd been added to the growing list of extinct species a month before. The last North Atlantic right whale had been recorded a month before that. Seabirds were vanishing at an astonishing rate. The piping plovers we used to see skipping across the wet sand had already gone.

Alma didn't need to hear this. She'd heard about all of it on the radio. She wanted to know what *really* happened.

"They just . . . ," Birk began. "They just lost their way, terribly. It happened slowly, over many years, but now they've forgotten. They've forgotten how it used to be, and how it could have been different. Earth has stories, but nobody remembers them. It can't tell the stories on its own, so it's becoming an echo of itself."

At this, Alma's eyes went wide.

We both still had secrets then. She hadn't told me yet about the Echoes—about their forgotten stories. And I hadn't told her that I had more than one reason for being there. That it wasn't just because of an old book and a metallic, conductive mineral. That not long after she'd moved to Violette, her brother, René, had moved away from home, too, even farther than she had gone, and that he'd had children, and that one of those children had had me.

~~

Wind shook through the trees, the underside of the leaves flashing silver, and it didn't seem like an unusual wind, but Alma's eyes immediately began searching the horizon. "We have to go," she said, grabbing the piece of galena from the ground and pressing it into my palm.

The sky turned a dark greenish gray, and thunder rumbled as we ran. Birk and I slipped in the mud but kept running, trying to keep up with Alma and Jupiter. Halfway to the base, some rocks slid and tumbled down the side of the mountain. We jumped to the side of the trail, watching them crash by. Hail dropped from the sky, beating down on us even through our jackets. We used our backpacks to shield our heads.

We reached the edge of town just as the sea came roaring over the cliffs like a monster there to gulp us down. "Get into the pod!" Alma yelled over the wind. The survival pod was tethered by cables to a giant steel anchor. We climbed inside and I watched through the tiny round window as Alma disappeared into the fog.

Alma joined us a few minutes later, dripping wet, her cheeks red, slamming the circular hatch shut behind her. The hurricane pod rocked inside the storm, and something large and heavy must have blown into it, because there was a loud crack and everything shook. It was dark, and the air was already hard to breathe. Lightning sparked across the windows every few moments.

"Is this going to hold up?" Birk asked, sounding more impatient, less trusting, than I knew he meant to.

"I've only come in here once. Just before my cousin left. But I think it will."

Birk pulled off his headlamp and hung it from a hook on the ceiling. It cast a dull, warm glow. Then he cinched his jacket tighter around his neck and tucked his chin down, going inward. It seemed he'd gotten older without me realizing. It had been five years since he'd taken me in, since the virus had sprung up and wiped out much of our island—my parents included—in the span of nine months.

Alma passed around a bag of nuts and dried seaweed she'd foraged, and nobody said anything for a long time. Birk closed his eyes, and I squinted in the dim light to read the copy of *Tower of Echoes* I'd taken from Alma's shelf. It was a book my father was always reading—and he'd told me it was one of only two copies in the world, given to him by his father's cousin—but I hadn't been able to take it with me because he was quarantined and they couldn't risk me catching what he had. I'd been looking for the other copy ever since.

> Once upon a time you saw a man die. You didn't know what you'd witnessed at the time. You didn't know what it would mean. Across the water there had been a light. Perhaps there was a lighthouse; perhaps not.
>
> Perhaps the celestial bodies had aligned just so.
>
> Your mind played tricks. You saw the man again, and he was standing there, you were sure of it, but he was different. The helicopters whirred overhead while they searched for a body they would not find. Not just yet.
>
> Then you remembered. There had been someone else, a woman holding a letter, reading out loud. After she spoke, the vision of the man was

gone, and they were pulling a body from the sea. His pale skin was tangled with kelp, and when they all saw him, everyone standing on the beach was shaken from their trance.

You've always doubted yourself. You've watched the floods come, each time wondering how you were going to push it back this time. You've held your ground, braced yourself, heavy as the stones they used to fill the retaining walls.

But it wasn't until much later, when you'd survived yet another one, and the swells subsided and the echoes faded, that you learned the walls aren't made to withstand the full force of a storm. You watched as they allowed some of the water to seep through the cracks, dispersing with such grace the energy of even the roughest waves.

Then there was the sound of the earth breaking apart. Alma pressed her nose against the window that faced the violent sea and cried out: "No, shit, no." She tried to wrestle the door open, but Birk held her back, and she fell onto Jupiter. Enclosed in the dark pod, she watched the lighthouse fall, all her monuments inside, swept up like it was nothing.

It was just one more piece of her home—on the outside, no more magnificent or powerful than any other wreckage the storms had taken. I think it was the piece, though, that needed to go, because she lifted her head from Jupiter's fur and that tangled-up rope inside her loosened, finally.

"The dog," Birk said. "What's his story?" Though he couldn't see Jupiter, he believed me when I said he was there. He knew that I saw and heard things that others couldn't.

Alma hugged Jupiter like she thought he might spontaneously vanish and said, "I don't know where he came from. I don't know his side of the story—I only know my own."

I showed her the drawing of the lynx again, then pointed to my ear.

Alma sighed. "I thought *I* was a good listener until I met you. You and the animals, how do you do it?"

I drew large circles in the air with my index finger—*always*—and it seemed like she understood that it was just a part of my life from the beginning. But there was more to it than that, and I needed her to know. Some lightheartedness took over, and I wrote the word *magic* and shrugged.

Alma leaned over, biting down on her bottom lip when she read it. "Someone told me once that I had a kind of magic," she said, pulling back again. "I thought he was right for a while, but I never learned how to use it. You should use yours."

I handed her my tablet and watched her read the words: *I do. I can tell you his story.*

Alma's eyes searched for a way to flee. She wrapped her body around Jupiter's again, as if shielding him from some great violence, but then she looked back over her shoulder, out the window to where the lighthouse used to stand, and nodded.

She knew what it would mean, even if I didn't yet, and she said it anyway.

"Okay, Kricket. Tell me about Jupiter."

24

Jupiter, felt, translated, and recorded on a tablet in the dark of a survival pod, 2058

The first light he saw was the sun filtering through the cracks in the walls. He opened his eyes for the very first time and was bathed in sunlight. His mother was beside him, warm and soft. His three siblings fighting for milk, wiggling their way into position as he squinted for a long moment into the brightness.

Even though the beauty of his birth was a lie, he had this. Sun, warmth, brightness. Very quickly, things went from radiant to dark and ugly.

Only days later, his mother was gone and he heard talking outside. Their agitated voices. Someone wanted something. Maybe him? Maybe one of his brothers or his sister? He didn't know, but in the dirty kennel, the one he had never left, he listened and he knew. Whatever they'd offered, it wasn't enough. So they went away.

No one else came.

He wondered what might have happened if things had gone differently. If someone had decided he or the others were worth the enormous price the voice was asking for.

After that, there was silence. A long, quiet, hungry silence except for the sound of the wind howling. For weeks they laid and rolled around in darkness. And then, finally, when it was too cold and one of them—his sister—died, he knew they couldn't stay any longer.

He scratched at the kennel door, the thin plywood giving with only the slight pressure of puppy paws. He pushed and the wood panel fell away and he was blinded. He toppled into the snow—a thick tangle of black and light-brown fur, all clumsy bones underneath.

He bounded happily until he remembered. Until he looked back and saw only the two puppies behind him. There were no people.

He began walking then, his two brothers following with slow, unsteady steps. They traveled a long dirt road and crossed a bridge and found endless possibilities for which direction to choose.

They walked with the ocean beside them for days, until they entered a dense forest, where one brother slipped into an icy river and was swept away, and the other was carried off by a bobcat.

After that, he slept each night alone, expecting some darkness to consume him, but each morning he woke, and the illumination of the sun from behind his closed eyelids made him rise and begin running with a sense of pure joy.

Following the long line of a wood fence, passing post after post, he found himself at the entrance to a farm. When the owner saw him, he wrapped him in a thick flannel blanket and brought him inside.

The heat of a wood fire, the smell of cooking potatoes. He rested, though he knew, somehow, that this was not the end. Even when he was settled in, with no hint of change, and all time seemed to slow down.

He was on that remote farm for two years. It was dark and biting cold in the winter, but he'd grown strong, and his coat was more than enough to keep him protected. It was bright and warm in the summer, and the world tasted of lupines. After his second summer, he knew it was time to walk again. He knew that despite this pause in this comfortable place, it was not where he was meant to be. He knew that he was needed somewhere, even if the where or why was not yet clear, and so when the farmer fell one morning and didn't rise again, he waited as long as he could without being found, and then left for the woods.

The sky began to play tricks. Though he attempted to head toward the salty smell of the ocean, he kept finding himself in deep forest. At night, when he realigned himself by the great bear above, the constellation moved. The arrangement of the stars changed constantly, so that each time he corrected his direction to go east, again he was sent south.

The stars seemed to be sending him there.

He crossed through woods and streams, day after day, not sure exactly where he was going but finally trusting the stars to guide him.

When he came to a trail, he decided to follow it. His paws bled and his fur had been matted by rain and wind. He'd been going for so long, the memories of his mother and sister and brothers fading. He could almost recall the vegetable soups the farmer made. His eyesight began to blur, and somehow all that was left was the image of that light from his birth.

On a long rocky beach, he fell down and slept, though he couldn't have said for how long. A great blue heron grazed the sky above him as he picked himself back up and stood with his paws at the water's edge. Gentle waves rolled over them.

He saw the heron again, swooping low back and forth over one spot down the shore, and he walked the beach until he saw the pile of fish she had left there. Switching from one long leg to the other, she stood in the reeds and watched him eat.

The trail came and went, but he continued. Sometimes he felt the presence of someone close by. In the wind he thought he heard humming, singing, crying, shouting. Every time he followed the sound, he was brought right back to where he'd started. The same trail, the same direction.

When the trees all began to look the same, and he became dizzy from trying to distinguish the path between them, he saw her. There was a truck, and busy people in hats and brightly colored vests. They spoke into radios and walked in circles. A helicopter whirred overhead.

But she was still, silent, broken like he was.

On four tired, clumsy paws, he stumbled over to her. She was sitting in the back of the truck—shivering, bleeding, gripping a photograph. Her red-brown hair was as matted as his own fur. When she reached for him, he collapsed into her shoulder, closing his eyes to the words: "Yes, yes. He's mine."

25

By the time the hurricane passed—somewhere between my writing Jupiter's story beneath the light of Birk's headlamp and all of us falling asleep—he had left us.

I could see the wound in her when she woke and found him gone. This gaping hole that she'd always had and that she'd tried to fill with fragile, impermanent things. Things that moved in and out with the tides. That void was still there, but she opened the pod's hatch a resolved being. The void had always been her home, but there was something else out there.

Birk ran down to the shore to see if our boat had survived, and Alma and I walked through the debris—piles of broken planks, the remnants of the final homes that had been torn to shreds—to the edge of the cliff. She stared hard at the water below like it was the only thing she could see, like someone she loved was in there, sloshing around with the cold, rough waves. Not with them, not inside them, but a part of them.

Come with us, I wrote.

"I've always been better alone. And you don't need me. You have Birk."

We're family.

"We hardly know each other." She knelt in the mud, taking a heavy breath. "There used to be magic, you know, right here, in this place."

Clouds were lifting off the water. I gasped when I saw a right whale breach the surface of the sea—the last one was long gone, we'd been told—but Alma didn't seem surprised.

There still is.

"I used to feel things," Alma said. She pressed her palms against her temples. "I heard them and saw them, but then they were all gone, and the feeling went, too, so far away that it seemed impossible to find it again."

That's when she told me about the Echoes. About Hayden, and his desire to name everything and get all the details right. About Lucie, who recited recipes to calm herself and spied on the ones she loved. About Oren's casual but timely accounts of the things he'd read, his ineffable belief in her.

About how she'd told their stories because she was the only one who could and because it was the only way to help them move on.

And about Alex, too—all the years she spent searching for the echo of him somewhere on the radio waves, only to be left drifting and directionless. Her hands curled into tight fists, then dropped, open, by her sides. I grasped one of them with mine.

So, what happened?

"I guess I forgot where I started," she said, looking around as if she expected someone else to be there. "I've been alone a long time."

I was about to start writing that she didn't have to be anymore. Instead, I waited while she reached into her jacket pocket and unfolded a letter and a photograph. The paper was worn soft, the picture, taken a century and a half ago, of the Marconi National Historic Site. Next to four wooden towers, interconnected with cables, the building Marconi had broadcast from seemed minuscule in comparison. The date was printed in the top left corner of the letter: 2004. The handwriting was difficult to read after so many years of wear, but I could tell it was written by someone young.

I'm writing a letter because this place reminded me of you, and we're always having make-believe conversations in my head. Like I'm sending you signals. Signal back if you want.
   Alex L.
   PS: Do you know Morse code? You should.

The words shot through me, my fingers tingling. Birk had taught me Morse code, had made me memorize it, because he said it was the most reliable form of communication, and in this unpredictable world, we never knew when we'd need it again. I dropped my backpack to the ground and dug out the object I'd been carrying around for so long, never knowing who it had really belonged to, but loving it wholly because it was old and made for children and I liked the way it felt in my hands.

The plastic toy transmitter I'd found when I visited my grandfather's hometown was one of my favorite things. It was olive green with a big light in the middle, and I held it in my palm, pointing out the letters etched into its side: *A+A.*

She hesitated to take it. And she looked at me for a moment, with a mix of fear and disbelief, before reaching out. "No," she said. "That's not . . . where did you get that?"

My grandfather.

"I thought he wasn't your grandfather."

Not Birk. René . . . René Hughes.

I underlined the last name, and the clouds in her eyes cleared, the color of new ferns shining through. She touched the green box like it might turn to dust beneath her fingertips and inspected the carving in the plastic like she didn't believe it was real.

"He lost it. We were just kids. I told him he was an astonishingly idiotic excuse for a human being. I disowned him as a brother . . . for two months."

Alma sat cross-legged at the edge of the jagged rock, the transmitter in her lap, and rolled up her flannel shirtsleeves, revealing Oren's intricate linework once more. Her hair twisted around her face, and the sun broke through the dark clouds. The world came alive again.

I wished I could say something to her, reassure her in some way that what she'd done had meant a lot. That her life had meant a lot. That people leave in the middle of a path sometimes, and we have to keep walking. That small things done with great love become great things.

I wanted to. But silence was my skill.

She pressed the transmitter button, the long and short beats, sending her signal out into the air: *Where did you go?*

We listened and there were creases around her smiling eyes, as if she was no longer expecting any kind of response, but simply reveling in the joy she found in the broadcast. For a long time, we sat in utter silence. The world whooshed on around us, but the various noises didn't register.

And then I heard it. Life, against the odds.

A bird pecking at a shell. A crab walking, scratching its claws on a rock. A tree branch behind us, up on the hill, smacking against another. The repetitive flutter of wings. The whale we'd been watching, striking its fin against the water's surface. Eventually, the sounds took on a consistent pattern. They blended together and became an answer.

Do you hear it?

She closed her eyes to listen better, but it wasn't until she took her boots off and touched her bare feet to the ground—a cursive tattoo running along the edge of her foot read *lost and found a thousand times*. It wasn't until she put her palms on the rock beneath her and closed her eyes that the wild land she'd once been so afraid of really spoke to her. It kept repeating, roaring above the thundering of waves, like a reverberation of Earth's very voice.

From all around us the response came: *I'm here.*

Epilogue

We heard it, and we felt it, the pulse of a dying planet that had stories it could no longer tell on its own. It was beautiful and comforting, that rhythm—suffused with pieces of everyone and everything we had loved—but it was also broken.

We asked Alma again to come with us, and for a little while, she resisted. I sensed it was purely out of habit. But people still needed stories, and she knew she was made to tell them. Maybe in a different form, maybe despite the world's hardened resistance to remembering what things were like before.

Violette was not a forgotten place. The man-made structures—walls, roofs, foundations—these all had to be left behind. But the land itself—and all the lands we traveled to after—those were the stories we told. The birds, the seaweeds, the glaciers. They all had an echo.

We kept looking for fragments of history because that was a necessary part of the process. We never forgot, but we always moved forward.

Sometimes people listened.

The earth was deeply scarred, and the damage could not be reversed, but perhaps the wild places could be mended, reshaped, honored. The best we could do was listen to them, speak for them, remind people of all the wonder and of all they had lost.

I remember things. Like the dried mud that fell from Alma's boots when she stepped steadfast onto the boat. Like the sun in her narrowed eyes when she finally peeled away from that place, like a leaf from the branch, and floated. Boundless and light, shaded on one side as the brightest things tend to be.

ACKNOWLEDGMENTS

I have many people to thank for the creation of this book and for the writer I've become. The first is my father, whose echo is everywhere, and who spent the second half of his life being my best friend and ensuring I valued nature and words and the combination of the two. Many thanks also to David Nikki Crouse, for being a much-needed friend and mentor from day one, and for helping put my feet on this path despite my first awkward attempts at story writing. I cannot thank enough my agent, James McGowan, for having faith in my earliest publishing endeavors and for being my voice of reason, humor, and optimism (*Onward!*). Thank you to Alicia Clancy for editing more hope into this book—a thing we can all use and that is not, as it turns out, at odds with heartbreak. And thank you to everyone else at Lake Union who brought this book into being. Much gratitude to early readers, Fiona Otsu and Will Frey, for your honest and insightful comments that helped immensely. For all the support and encouragement along the way, thank you to my mother, Donna Bryant Winston; and also to Joshua Bryant, Bethany Adelman, David Winston, my Klagmann family, Christopher Myott, Ann Blodgett, and Kate Keenan. Thank you to Jazmine Torres and Susan Klagmann for the precious gift of writing time. Thank you to all the Bryants and Comeaus from Nova Scotia, New Hampshire, Maine, and everywhere else we have scattered to. Particularly heartfelt thanks to my grandmother, Joan Bryant, for so persistently pulling together our family for so many years, and for keeping such meticulous historical records. Special thanks to Ken Bryant for the lively stories and Karen Leonard for the photos, both of which shook things up right when they needed shaking. Merci beaucoup to Amanda Saunders for answering all my random radio questions with such enthusiasm. A huge, bear-size thanks to Elke and River, the wildest, most imaginative kids I know, who have brought so much necessary chaos and joy into my life. And the biggest thank-you of all to Jamison, my first reader always and my partner in all things creative and otherwise, who started dreaming with me at forty below zero and hasn't stopped since.

AUTHOR'S NOTE

Although this is a work of fiction, ideas often come from real places, and a few should be acknowledged here. The setting of this book is very loosely inspired by a town in New Brunswick, where broadcasts from abandoned shortwave radio towers were once heard crackling through the appliances in people's homes. The character of Esmée Taylor was also rooted in the true story of Ann Harvey of Newfoundland. Finally, because I owe so much to the influence of music on my writing, and on this book in particular, I would like to extend my greatest respect and appreciation to the eternally bright Gordon Downie and The Tragically Hip.

ABOUT THE AUTHOR

Jessica Bryant Klagmann studied writing in Fairbanks, Alaska. Every good idea she's ever had came while she was running, so she tries to stay within sight of a mountain or canyon trail at all times. She and her family live in northern New Mexico, but they also spend time in Maine, where they're restoring a hundred-acre forest. Her work has been published in environmental journals like *Whitefish Review* and *Terrain.org*. This is her debut novel.